Books by John Patrick

Non-Fiction
A Charmed Life: Vince Cobretti
Lowe Down: Tim Lowe
The Best of the Superstars 1990
The Best of the Superstars 1991
The Best of the Superstars 1992
The Best of the Superstars 1993
The Best of the Superstars 1994
The Best of the Superstars 1995
The Best of the Superstars 1996
The Best of the Superstars 1997
The Best of the Superstars 1998
The Best of the Superstars 1999
The Best of the Superstars 2000
The Best of the Superstars 2001
The Best of the Superstars 2002
What Went Wrong?
When Boys Are Bad
& Sex Goes Wrong
Legends: The World's Sexiest
Men, Vols. 1 & 2
Legends (Third Edition)
Tarnished Angels (Ed.)

Fiction
Billy & David: A Deadly Minuet
The Bigger They Are...
The Younger They Are...
The Harder They Are...
Angel: The Complete Trilogy
Angel II: Stacy's Story
Angel: The Complete Quintet
A Natural Beauty (Editor)
The Kid (with Joe Leslie)
HUGE (Editor)
Strip: He Danced Alone
The Boys of Spring
Big Boys/Little Lies (Editor)
Boy Toy
Seduced (Editor)
Insatiable/Unforgettable (Editor)

Heartthrobs
Runaways/Kid Stuff (Editor)
Dangerous Boys/Rent Boys (Editor)
Barely Legal (Editor)
Country Boys/City Boys (Editor)
My Three Boys (Editor)
Mad About the Boys (Editor)
Lover Boys (Editor)
In the BOY ZONE (Editor)
Boys of the Night (Editor)
Secret Passions (Editor)
Beautiful Boys (Editor)
Juniors (Editor)
Come Again (Editor)
Smooth 'N' Sassy (Editor)
Intimate Strangers (Editor)
Naughty By Nature (Editor)
Dreamboys (Editor)
Raw Recruits (Editor)
Play Hard, Score Big (Editor)
Sweet Temptations (Editor)
Pleasures of the Flesh (Editor)
Juniors 2 (Editor)
Fresh 'N' Frisky (Editor)
Taboo! (Editor)
Heatwave (Editor)
Boys on the Prowl (Editor)
Huge 2 (Editor)
Fever! (Editor)
Any Boy Can (Editor)
Virgins No More (Editor)
Seduced 2 (Co-Editor)
Wild 'N' Willing (Co-Editor)

Worldwide Praise for the Erotica of John Patrick and STARbooks!

"John Patrick is a modern master of the genre! ...This writing is what being brave is all about. It brings up the kinds of things that are usually kept so private that you think you're the only one who experiences them."
– Gay Times, London

"Barely Legal' is a great potpourri ... and the cover boy is gorgeous!"
– Ian Young, Torso magazine

"Collections of stories have become increasingly popular in the past couple of years: leading the way is the prolific and consistently entertaining John Patrick who, under the STARbooks imprint, has edited fifteen or more collections of erotica written another dozen books himself and published several handfuls more by other authors. ... Burly (500-plus pages) anthologies of erotic writing, the perfect bedside companions..."
– Richard Labonte, Q Magazine

"A huge collection of highly erotic, short and steamy one-handed tales. Perfect bedtime reading, though you probably won't get much sleep! Prepare to be shocked! Highly recommended!"
– Vulcan magazine

"Tantalizing tales of porn stars, hustlers, and other lost boys...John Patrick set the pace with 'Angel!'"
– The Weekly News, Miami

"...Some readers may find some of the scenes too explicit; others will enjoy the sudden, graphic sensations each page brings. Each of these romans clef is written with sustained intensity. 'Angel' offers a strange, often poetic vision of sexual obsession. I recommend it to you."
– Nouveau Midwest

"Angel' is mouthwatering and enticing..."
– Rouge Magazine, London

"Superstars' is a fast read...if you'd like a nice round of fireworks before the Fourth, read this aloud at your next church picnic..."
– Welcomat, Philadelphia

"Yes, it's another of those bumper collections of steamy tales from STARbooks. The rate at which John Patrick turns out these compilations you'd be forgiven for thinking it's not exactly quality prose. Wrong. These stories are well-crafted, but not over-written, and have a profound effect in the pants department."
– Vulcan magazine, London

ISBN 13: 978-1-934187-92-0

Many thanks to graphic artist John Nail for the cover design. Mr. Nail may be reached at: tojonail@bellsouth.net.

ISBN 13: 978-1-934187-92-0

Herndon, VA

Virgins No More

Volume 1

Edited By
JOHN PATRICK

Herndon, VA

Editor's Note Most of the stories appearing in this book take place prior to the years of The Plague; the editor and each of the authors represented herein advocate the practice of safe sex at all times. And, because these stories trespass the boundaries of fiction and non-fiction, to respect the privacy of those involved, we've changed all of the names and other identifying details.

CONTENTS

INTRODUCTION: VIRGINS NO MORE
John Patrick

Playwright Arthur Laurents, in his delightful new autobiography *Original Story By*, recalls that he lost his virginity at fourteen a kid his age. This youth, he discovered, went from house to house like the Avon lady, blowing everyone available and acquiescent on the block. "Age of consent was no obstacle and daytime was safe because nobody thought sex occurred in daylight," Arthur recalled. "He grew up to be a respected professor at home and at the Sorbonne. Until recently, he taught in both places and was still on his knees, though less frequently.

"His blowjobs continued to be given sporadically until we went away to different colleges. Our relationship was both distant and intimate: no mutual friends except a girl who lived next door to him who had a crush on me I wished she hadn't, no mutual interests except the movies and blow jobs. Even though we were aware we each read a great deal, we never discussed a book. We never mentioned blow jobs either, but the title of a movie we saw as teenagers at Loew's Kings on Hatbush Avenue supplied a verbal signal we used to announce readiness for The Act'. Why that title, how there could be such a prescient coincidence (this was in the early Thirties, you know), but the movie was called "Let Us Be Gay. ""

At sixteen, Laurents said he was "at once too sophisticated and too naive. I overcompensated by learning to smoke, drink, and gamble. I also wore bow ties and joined a second-rate fraternity against my father's wishes but I listened to no one. Because they wanted me, I insisted on joining. My fraternity brothers believed if you were a virgin, you weren't a man, and it was their upperclassmen's responsibility to make a man of me...." The boys take Laurents to a whorehouse, with predictable results: "The whorehouse was a walk-up which smelled of failure. My whore's room was shabby and bare except for a thin bed, a chair, and a rickety dresser and cold linoleum floor. Naked except for her shoes, she was skinny with pancake-like breasts. Embarrassed and terrified that I wouldn't be able to get it up, I undressed as ordered, put my clothes on the chair, careful not to disturb her kimono draped across the back. With old soapy water, she washed my penis. Her touch didn't

1

help. If anything, the reverse: my homosexual prick tried to crawl back in. She struggled to find it in order to put a condom on it but failed. Shaking her head (she foresaw our future), she played with it lackadaisically. Foolish optimism.'"

"You a virgin?' she asked.

"I nodded, not looking at her."

"Hey, I got a cherry!' she shouted.

"Me too! Me too!" came from the other rooms. Misery didn't get company. From those other rooms soon came shouts of pleasure; not from mine."

"You have to pay anyway, " she said.

"...Back in the car, my tale of triumph wasn't as long as the others...."

In Fred Kaplan's biography of Gore Vidal, Vidal's longtime companion, Howard Auster, said that at about ten he discovered that he liked sex, especially with boys and men, the secretive, transgressive element a great thrill, partly connected in his mind to his mother's having hit him when she found him masturbating: "I did it once, I think, with the super's son – that was enjoyment. I did get blown in the park, I must have been eleven, by a twenty- or twenty-one-year-old guy. But I really did the seducing. ...I was really very aggressive about it as a child. Far more then than I would ever dream of being now. And that kind of sex was so exciting. I continued that in high school."

Rick Sanford, in his novel The Boys Across the Street, talks about telling Levi, one of the students from the school across from where he lives, about losing his virginity: "Levi just looked at me for a moment. I felt he was trying to use my answers to reach some preconceived notion he had, but I wasn't sure what it was.

"I suddenly thought of something else. "Oh, and that boy? That boy I was in love with? Well, he was raised Catholic, but he was adopted and I think he was really Jewish. He had curly brown hair and a big nose, and it's because of him that I've always been attracted to Jewish boys. You know: big noses, big cocks. I could sense a war going on within Levi. He was being tom, by his contempt, on the one hand, and his curiosity, on the other. I was just about to ask him if he had a big cock when he suddenly spoke up. "So you think of us as sex objects?' "'Some of you. There's a boy named Mendel who I think is cute, and there's a beautiful boy named Mordecai....'"

"What do you find attractive about men?'"

"Basically, I think the most beautiful thing there is in the world, the most amazing thing, is an erect penis ejaculating, and every time I've been around one I've felt honored. I've felt that was dose.' And I paused to think what I was saying. "I had felt that I was God, so to speak."

"Somehow that wasn't quite right."

"When was the first time you had sex with a man?' Levi asked."

"When I was sixteen, when I was visiting my grandmother in Phoenix. I was sitting out by the pool at her apartment building, and I was getting red, and this guy asked me if I had some lotion for my skin and I said no, and so we went up to his apartment and he said...what? – oh, I remember, he said, "I'll give you a blow job if you give me one."

"And you liked that?"

"Well, I had never had sex before. ...Later when I went home, I thought about it and suddenly everything I knew and had heard about sex all came together with my experience and then I wanted to have sex again, over and over.

"Levi glanced over his shoulder, back toward the school, as if he was afraid someone might see us talking together or overhear us. "When was the next time you had sex?"

"I thought for a moment. "The next time I had sex was, let's see, the next summer when I ran away from home and went to Hawaii. I stayed at the YMCA and had sex with some guys there. And then the next year I came to Hollywood and that's when I really started having sex a lot. It's just a rough guess, but I think I've had sex with more than two thousand men.'" In Neal Drinnan's hilarious novel Pussy's Bow, Murray, a youth from the country in Australia has to go to the big city to lose his virginity: "Murray looked down at his trainers, his trusty Levi's and the ugly parachute-silk jacket his mum had bought him

3

"because it rains all the time in Melbourne.' He overtook a group of conspicuous and up-themselves queens who snickered as he went past. He felt his heart sink. Was this the sort of tribe he wanted to join? He moseyed on to the Exchange. People in there didn't seem quite so full of attitude.

"A big, handsome guy of about thirty emerged from the smoky haze and started chatting him up. Shell-suit aside, Murray was pretty gorgeous. He was no good at making first moves, but once someone started talking to him, well, he opened right up."

"Yeah, mate, I'd love another beer.' He eyed the guy through the gloom."

Turned out the bloke was staying in a hotel too, only his was in the city. They went back there and Murray noticed he was wearing a wedding ring. Damn, he thought, he could have it off with a wedding ring back in Albury. The other guys in the park used to laugh about them. "You think they'll be all fuckin' butch and wanna top you, but they're always the ones who want to be fucked up the proverbial wedding ring."

"But this guy wasn't like that at all. He was a salesman from Perth, and more aggressive than Murray bargained for."

"You like getting fucked?'"

"Oh no, I've never really got into it.'"

"You should!"

"Murray kept sucking his cock; it would keep his mind off the other thing, he thought. The engorged dick was too big and not the sort of thing he wanted to be shafted by for the first time."

The guy was squeezing Intensive Care lotion all over his hand and rubbing it into the valley between Murray's buttock cheeks. His middle finger took a savage lunge into Murray's shy rear passage. It contracted violently, but as the lotion ran round to his balls and the guy started taking long greasy strokes of his hardening cock, Murray found the finger less of an imposition. "Unngghh,' he exhaled from somewhere inside, closing his muscles on the invading finger pushing as if to expel it like shit. But the finger had plans; it pushed and worked its way

4

further in. Another finger joined it and he felt the hot terror of too much intrusion.

"Suddenly he stopped, the burning fingers shot themselves free. For a minute Murray thought it was over. Then big arms turned him over; the salesman clearly had invasions of a larger scale in mind."

"No!' cried Murray as the man plunged into the tiny, glistening fret of flesh. It was pure white pain. "It fucking hurts. ""

"You love it, all that cock up your greasy arse, " the salesman grunted.

"The white pain fragmented into hundreds of colors. Murray meditated on it for a time. The searing, raw tearing of flesh suggested the possibility of internal damage. He felt cut inside. The guy was pumping harder like he was getting dose. Murray moaned painfully, rhythmically. Whether they were sounds of pain or pleasure made no difference to his assailant. He was fixed on his goal. Spurts of white into crimson chambers.

"As the guy topped the crest of his thrusting, Murray twisted free and the glistening cock burst from Murray's seared viscera and waved about, showering the bed with a beaded rain of pearly sperm. Murray's asshole spasmed and burned. Tears escaped his eyes, absconding shamefully down his cheeks."

"Shit, you made me pull out too soon,' gasped the salesman."

"Too fucking right. I didn't even want you in there.'"

"I thought you were into it. ""

"Yeah, right. What part of no don't you understand? Haven't you heard of condoms? Fucking AIDS?'"

"Don't sweat, I hardly ever do guys and I'm nobody's bottom, if you know what I mean." Murray was putting on his clothes, eager to get out."

The salesman asked, "I'm in town for a couple of days, you want to get together tomorrow?"

Later, Murray was alone, recovering, and "he pulled his shirt off, his body skinny and tight in the mirror's shadowy reflection. He dropped his trousers and kicked the shoes off his feet, running his fingers over

5

the muscular ridges of his tummy. Then he shed his boxer shorts. His hands ran up his chest, pausing for a moment at the meaty red nipples. Bold and chunky, they shocked people a little on first sighting. Even girls had grabbed them excitedly on intimate occasions. He surveyed his body and felt happy. He was happy with his cock, a decent size even on the droop. He liked the way its pendulous softness contrasted with his tight skinniness. He felt his arse to see if it still stung to the touch. It seemed to have recovered from the savage intrusion of a few days ago. ...There must be more to getting fucked than he'd experienced. Doc was full on into it, moaning the way chicks did. "Fuck me, fuck me....' Murray's woozy mind shifted to Claudette. There was something wise and seductive about her. His hand reached for his erection and as he surfed through the porno channels of his imagination he began to feel magic build up in his cock. He changed his tack, pushing now like he was trying to take a piss. He breathed deep – in and out – feeling the blood rush to his face, intensifying the heat in his cheeks. He arched his back, holding his breath until he almost passed out. Then came the searing rush, filled with flashing memories and images, all impossible to trace. He heaved his bum up further from the bed and felt the warm spatter of cum on his chest. He let the dizzying breath out with a long, noisy sigh...."

In Playguy magazine, a cute young model named Mike Disanti said that he lost his virginity to a, surprise, Playguy editor, who got him to pose for Polaroids in his hotel room, then gave him his first rim job, which really excited the lad and which led to a full-out fuck in the shower. "He said I was ready and then he put himself in me and took my virginity. He did me very hard and it hurt, and he didn't stop until he was finished even though I was making sounds like it hurt because it really did ... I mean, no I didn't tell him to stop but I thought if he really liked me he would stop."

After that, Disanti says that he went to Playguy to have his pictures taken and there he saw copies of the magazine and in one was an interview where this editor was quoted as saying how he got many guys this way. Disanti felt "used" by this man who "took away my innocence in my ass and he didn't even like me, just my ass. And he never called me again." Wasn't it P.T. Barnum who said there was one born every minute?

Even straight boys are getting in on this virginity act! Village Voice columnist Tristan Taormino recently told straight boy readers that there was something they must try "at least once ...You've got something to pick up from your gay brothers. And it's not just those fashion and decorating tips you marvel about on "Will and Grace.' Something your wives and girlfriends can be taught by their lesbian sisters? No, it's not a crash course in expert muff diving. There is a craze sweeping the nation, and you oughta know about it. It's ass fucking – with you on the receiving end!

"...It's as undeniable and obvious as tense sphincter muscles: anal sex has become one of the hot sex acts of the new millennium. And this time, it's not just for butt pirates. While they are getting their share of the booty, gay men have not cornered the anal market. It's a falsehood that all gay men have anal sex, and it's equally mythic that gay men have more anal sex than straight people or lesbians. In. fact, that oh-so-traditional pairing of man plus woman may just surpass the man-on-man statistics in this particular area.

"....Every single day that I worked at the woman-owned sex-toy store Toys in Babeland, at least one heterosexual couple bought a dildo and harness for her to fuck him. Remember My First Pony, a sweet toy for little girls? Well, for these adventurous women and their partners, I recommended what I called "My first strap-on for the ride of his (and her) life.' It's a slim silicone dildo named Mistress, which I consider to be the best for virgin voyagers, and a simple functional harness. And, of course, I recommended lots and lots of lube.

"The growing popularity of boys bending over was equally apparent on the West Coast at the sex store Good Vibrations. The video "Bend Over, Boyfriend' was on the Good Vibrations best-seller list for 12 consecutive months and named the best- selling video of all time, until "Bend Over, Boyfriend 2' knocked it off the list. ...The video's got dirty talk, cross-dressing, role playing, s/m, shoe licking, real couples who love anal sex, a butt plug with a horse tail on the end of it, and lots of other sex toys.

"Since anal pleasure is still taboo in American culture, anyone who admits to being a backdoor betty is on the front lines of sexual liberation. As women, since we are already positioned as the receptive, penetrated partner, we need only reorient ourselves to focus on the other orifice. Men, on the other hand, are the penetrator, the active partner, the pencil to her sharpener. Straight men are coming out of their own doset (who knew they had such a fabulous one?), proudly saying, "I want to get fucked in the ass!' and "I love getting fucked in the ass!' ...These guys have gotten over their shame and fear and embraced all the ass has to offer, those nerve endings, that sensitive tissue, and the pleasures of prostate gland stimulation. A few inches inside the rectum and toward his navel, the "male G-spot' and a new world of ecstasy awaits."

"When I fall in love," Austin Bunn, a writer for Village Voice, admitted, "I fall upward. I swoon over bow ties, bald spots, second acts, and salt-and-pepper. I catch my breath at daguerreotypes of Walt Whitman. I'm sweet on reading glasses and on survivor's grace. I am attracted to age.

"I realized it for the first time on an afternoon excursion to New York when I was 15. On the second floor of the Museum of Modem Art, I stood, transfixed, in front of a single photograph, titled "Side Torso Bent With Large Upper Arm.' Taken from the side, the shot showed an older man's naked body from the neck to the knees. It was a brutally honest portrait, frank and quiet.

"The photographer who creates these giant self-portraits, John Coplans, will turn 80 this year. Coplans makes no attempt to mask his age or the loose folds and failures of his skin. The results, incredibly intimate and revealing, are sometimes hard to look at. When I first saw that self-portrait, I was scared by how sexy it was, so raw and radical. I didn't have the language to make sense of how it spoke to me, or how my body spoke back.

"In college, I tried to talk about this attraction with my roommate, a man who was charming and fluent in his love affairs with men. He laughed in disbelief. As a young guy I know explains, "It's like you have to come out twice – once because you're gay and once because you're attracted to older men.' Other gay students would approach me, and I'd tell them the shy truth – that I had been with men my age but didn't feel the same rush that I felt around some of my middle-aged professors. The boys insisted I was just "going through a phase,' a statement that burned and confused me until I recognized that perhaps they had once been diminished in the same way. Surely one of the cruelest ways to attack someone's sexuality is to call it temporary, transitional.

"I had my first relationship with an older man when I was 23. Daniel, a 65-year-old composer, was married and had three kids my age. We were a pair of firsts; I was the first man he had ever been with (or so he said); he was the first man that I had ever loved blindly. The only first we never managed was spending the night together, for our relationship was an absolute secret. I never saw his apartment or ate a meal in his company. After a few months, he offered to shatter his settled, married life. Even though I loved him, I couldn't bear the responsibility for that sacrifice."

And speaking of sacrifices, Kho, a 20-year-old, closeted college student says he lost his virginity to long-dicked New Jersey escort, author, and video maker Aaron Lawrence: "I wanted my first time to be a great experience that I could learn from, and my wish was granted. Aaron is a kind, smart, funny, caring person and a great teacher. Upon arriving at his home, he immediately began to make me feel comfortable with the situation and myself. He taught me a wide variety of sexual skills, but his most important lesson was that sex has no rules and should only be fun. I had a wonderful experience with Aaron that I will cherish for my entire life." Kho says that he "thinks" he is bi-sexual and before Aaron's fuck, he had only limited encounters with women and nothing with men. "I had my first homoerotic encounter occurred when I was six, developed an affinity for white men as an adolescent, and realized it wasn't just a phase when I was 18."

Another young man revealed that he wanted nothing but the best for his first time. He picked veteran porn star Ted Matthews, who advertises regularly in the L.A./N.Y. markets. Studly Ted made the young john feel comfortable and was "all he claimed to be: Hot bodied, and hung very nicely. He was also a hot kisser. He sucked me, let me rim him, and then he fucked me. He was very concerned that he might hurt me because it was my first time, so he was very gentle at first. Ted knows what he's doing."

Another porn star who knows what he is doing is Miguel Leon, featured in such Kristen Bjorn videos as "Thick As Thieves." Miguel says he lost his virginity one day when he was especially horny: "I got into a bus just to get away from my home for a while (this was in

Venezuela). This guy got on the bus, very cute, looked like a model, and he walked to the back of the bus where I was sitting. Then he began looking at me and touching himself. So I moved over to where he was sitting and began touching him and he was touching me. We got off the bus and went into this very old, failing down building and had sex. It was very exciting!"

"My first night in a gay bar," Christopher Scott, featured in Falcon's "Red Alert," says, "a man came up to me and he was quite attractive to me, at the time. And he started deep French- kissing me. I had my dick out and I was hard; he was hard, at the bar. He said, "Do you want to come to a party?' I had a little apprehension. And then I thought, "Well, okay. I'll go to the party and whatever.' I didn't know it was a sex party. There were six guys and me. I had never been fucked before, nor had I even thought about it. They were all the bartenders from the bar. They had rooms upstairs. We went up there and right away, he's like sticking his finger in my butt. "What are you doing?' I said, "I've never been fucked before,' and of course, that was just like, "Yes! A virgin.' They got the lube and started. It really did not feel good. Then they gave me a bottle of poppers, and I said, "What are these?" He said, "That'll make you relax.' That was it. Then they were starting to put toys in me-those anal balls. I didn't really know what they were doing. They were really preoccupying me with these guys saying, "Suck my dick, suck my dick....'-so I was kind of learning that, and then they were stuffing these balls in. All of a sudden, I'm like, "What are you doing? What are you doing?' They said, "Well, we got four of them in. We've got one more.' The other one wouldn't go in, maybe "cause I was conscious of it or whatever. So, I really got initiated. I loved it! I was hooked. I became the boy toy for the bar. Everybody wanted my ass, and that's just the way it was."

And speaking of initiations, consider one of the incidents porn star/stripper Sean ("Man Academy") Storm so vividly recalls of his high school days: "Most guys spend four years of their lives enduring one embarrassment after another while trying to survive these years, but if I had to choose that one most embarrassing moment in my adolescent life, I would have to reach back just a couple years earlier to 7th grade ... it was the time when I realized what a boner was.

"The year was 1988, and up until then I had seldom masturbated. I was definitely a late bloomer, and didn't even have my first orgasm until I was 16 (unless you want to count a few wet dreams, one of which involved John Tesh from "Entertainment Tonight,' which is perhaps my second most embarrassing moment). In 7th grade I didn't have a lot of male friends, except for a few geeky band fags I knew. But the point I am trying to make is that I never had anyone to tell me what a hard-on was, or what caused them to occur. My erections just usually happened without giving much thought to them. During this time in my life I was also dealing with why I was more attracted to David Andrews instead of Monique Hollandsworth.

"Still, whatever same-sex thoughts I was having, I knew enough to at least keep them to myself. No one in junior high knew I was gay, including myself. However, during the last month of 7th grade, I was about to discover what it all meant...the "hard' way.

"I loved going to my physical education class each day. Our teachers required us to strip down and take showers, sometimes even joining us. Already I knew I liked watching boys and men. In junior high half the class was in the process of reaching puberty, so some of my classmates were getting hair development under their armpits and in their groins.

"I also loved watching the mature Coach Trammell get naked in his office and join us boys in the shower. He was probably in his early thirties, and had a deliciously hairy body, as did a couple of early developers like Matt McCarthy and Justin Campbell. I have vivid memories of Matt bending over in front of me and removing his underwear. Even in seventh grade he had a nice trail of hair growing up his ass crack. Mixing that vision with the aroma of the sweat in the locker room obviously turned me on. Right there, in front of all my classmates, my 12-year-old penis turned into this rock-hard cock. And there lies the brilliance behind this entire experience! I had actually become turned on by watching these other guys-without even realizing that I had been turned on. Clueless Sean...walking to the shower room with a woody, soaping up my body with my soaped-up woody, toweling off my woody, and then getting dressed. If I had known why I had gotten the erection in the first place, I doubt I would have walked around with it poking straight up. The thing is, I was oblivious to it even being hard. Up until then no one had told me that you get a boner by being sexually aroused. That is, no one told me until the next day.

"The next morning, I took the bus to school, just like normal. Kids were in front of the school waiting for the doors to open. A nice bright, normal sun warmed us all up, and everyone was in good spirits knowing that summer was fast approaching. I remember walking over to Matt McCarthy (Mister Hairy Ass) and saying hello to him. So far, so good. But then, within a few minutes, storm clouds were brewing.

"A guy named Darby Underwood (an appropriate name now that I think about it) walked up to us and proceeded to tell Matt how my dick was sticking straight up in the shower room the previous day. Matt started laughing, then just walked off. Darby, laughing himself, then headed over to another small group of people and began to engage in conversation. Soon, the whole group was laughing along with him. I wondered if they were talking about me. In fact, I thought everybody was talking about me. The rest of the day was really hard ... er, rather, difficult ... to get through. I wasn't all that popular I didn't think, so when people started noticing me, smiling at me, I feared the worst. For the first time, I didn't want to go to PE class. I put two and two together and concluded that it was inappropriate to have a hard dick in front of other guys. If I continued showing a boner, then my same-sex thoughts I'd been having might give me away as being abnormal. But wait, that had to mean there was something inside me different from the other guys, like maybe I was gay...?

"As it happened, my fears were unfounded; my woody in the shower was never mentioned again, not even by Matt or Darby. Furthermore, not once was I ever called a faggot or queer in junior high, high school, or even college.

"I can laugh about my locker room boner experience today, but at the time it happened I was in pure turmoil, constantly feeling like an oddball. Today, though, I am no longer an oddball. All I have to do is visit Gold's Gym in West Hollywood, hit the showers with my boner, and I fit right in. And I say amen to that!"

Another porn star, the legendary Al Parker, recalled getting a boner for the first time with other guys around to see it. According to Roger Edmonson in his biography of the late Al Parker, when the future porn legend was 17 he attended the infamous Woodstock concert. Parker sensed an incredibly strong sexual aura surrounding the event. He passed irrigation ponds where throngs of young people were congregating, trying to cool off. "Lots of them had their clothes off," Parker remembered, "and I was aware that most of the guys swimming nude had really big cocks. It was the first time I had ever been in a situation to observe a lot of nude strangers." Edmonson reports that Parker soon noticed that he was watching the guys rather than the girls and found himself wondering what that meant." ...For a long time, he hadn't quite allowed himself to believe he was gay. Maybe it was just a phase or something. Whatever the case, he couldn't keep his eyes off the guys. "...I was aware that I had a raging hard-on, but I didn't care who saw it. As a matter of fact, I was hoping that everyone could see. All I wanted to do was find a gorgeous guy and jump his bones. Woodstock was a sex fiend's wet dream."

And speaking of wet dreams, a guy who calls himself Kenny Gallagher was once one of the East Coast's leading Internet hustlers-until the police caught up with him. His arrest made headlines in the small Pennsylvania town he once lived in, and he was forced to flee to the more liberal environment of New York City. He told Mandate he started when he was just out of high school and the idea of going straight to college didn't appeal to him. Kenny says, "I had a friend take a nude photo of me and I posted it on this website that had a free bulletin board for escorts. I advertised as a young guy with a virgin ass (and I was). I got tons of e-mails from all these guys asking if they could be the first to pop my hole. I charged $150 per session for blowjobs and touching and stuff, and $200 if you wanted to actually fuck me or shove a dildo or anything else up my ass, I made like $3,000 in the first week. I couldn't believe it! I began to build up quite a client list. My secret was that I would take anything up my ass – and I mean anything. Bottles, dildos, beads, you name it. I had guys flying me all over the Northeast. They all wanted to hire the guy whose ass could swallow a soda bottle.

"One of my clients was actually married. He lived in the same town that I did. His wife found out that he had hired a male prostitute and she fuckin' flipped and called the cops. They looked up the Web site and saw my ad, and they had an undercover cop call me and set up an appointment. The newspaper in my hometown put the whole story on the front page, and my parents flipped and haven't spoken to me since then. I just got a big fine from the judge because it was my first offense, but that was enough for me. I packed up and moved to New York, and

I'm still hustling, but I don't advertise online. It's too risky. I have enough regular clients here that I don't need to advertise much. And when I'm short on cash, I go to this great hustler bar in Times Square. There's always lots of business there." We'll bet – even for a kid who's a virgin no more!

Kenny Gallagher, photographed for Mandate magazine by Body Prod, was a virgin when he started advertising his charms on the Internet (see story on the preceding page).

THE WATCHERS
John Patrick

The apprentice gardener clutched at his loose trousers as he watched the Marquis enter the ass of Dario, the comely young stable boy. Dario lay there on the hay, struggling valiantly as the huge cock entered him. The Marquis pushed against Dario's body inexorably, his massive thickness disappearing gradually into the boy's ass. The apprentice could see sweat on the boy's brow as finally the Marquis was fully in him and began moving. At one point, the Marquis drew his prick out so that the apprentice could see the head, and then thrust himself home again with a massive grunt. Dario raised his long legs over the Marquis's massive back, and the Marquis thrust his tongue into the stable boy's mouth as the stable boy began moaning, whether with pain or with pleasure, the watcher could not tell. The Marquis's rhythm increased, and the stable boy raised his body to meet his. The hay shifted under the pounding pressure, and Dario's moans increased in intensity and number as the tempo of the fuck went on. The Marquis changed the speed of his thrusts. They became slower but deeper, almost brutal. His belly slapped down onto the boy's, and finally he had the boy crying out, begging, "Please, please," asking him to stop or continue, the watcher could still not tell.

The Marquis raised his head from Dario's and his face became flushed. "Oh ... oh!" he cried as he slammed into the boy's ass and the boy raised his head in ecstasy as the Marquis's body jerked violently with the power of his orgasm.

The Marquis lay on Dario as if he were dead. At last, impatiently, the boy twitched his leg, and the Marquis grunted and rolled off of the boy. He was a giant of a man, and the boy appeared even younger than he was next to the Marquis. The boy now stretched voluptuously, then lay his hand on the limp, filthy prick beside him. The Marquis grinned, said something in a low voice the young watcher could not hear. Then the Marquis stood up, and after adjusting his clothing, he walked out of the bam. He said nothing more to Dario, who lay there, his cute face calm, his eyes almost closed.

The apprentice gardener stared at the sexy sight below him.

He shivered as he stuck his still-hard cock back into his trousers. Just then, Dario rose up onto his elbows, and looked up to the loft where the apprentice thought he had adequately hidden himself. "Well, Leonardo," Dario yelled, "did you enjoy that?" Leonardo tried to swallow, but found his throat dry. Dario ordered, "Come down here." Leonardo could only nod. He rushed to the stable boy, who had by now stroked his own cock back to full rigidity. "Do you like my cock?" Leonardo stared at it. He nodded.

"The master doesn't. He only uses me as he would any whore. He thinks my ass is just another pussy. He never touches my cock." Leonardo stepped closer.

"Here, feel my cock." Leonardo bent down, stroked the cock. It was big, nowhere near as big as the Marquis's, but substantial; far more substantial than Leonardo's.

"Let me see yours," Dario said, reaching up, stroking the bulge in Leonardo's pants. Leonardo complied, opening his trousers. His uncut prick sprang out. Pre-cum oozed from the head of it. "That's too small for me," Dario laughed.

"After the Marquis, I only like big ones." Still his hand did not leave the cock. He squeezed it, not enough to really hurt, but Leonardo reached down to push the offending hand away. Leonardo, confused both by his lust and his inexperience, mumbled,

"I want you. I want to make love to you."

"I can see that," Dario said, his hand leaving the prick. "Maybe when you grow older, Leonardo." But Leonardo was not to be deterred. He reached back down and took the stable boy's erection in his hand.

"We are the same, you and I. The same size, shape. Look...."

"Yes, it is true," Dario said as he drew Leonardo next to him on the hay and allowed the boy to take both cocks in his trembling hand and play with them. "You keep that up, I will come."

"Do you want to do me the way the master did you?" The stable boy stroked Leonardo's ass. "Perhaps. It is such a

pretty ass. Has the Marquis requested you yet?"

"No. He doesn't know I exist."

16

John Patrick

"Ha! He knows everything. I will ask him. God knows, if you do it, I'll get some rest."

"Does he call on you often?"

"Almost every day, for something. He loves me to suck it, too, so if I'm not spreading my legs, I'm opening my mouth." He laughed, and at that moment, he started to come. Leonardo was shocked by this and stared at the prick shooting gob after gob on his hand. He came too, and the cum melded together and ran down his hand and arm.

Dario kissed Leonardo on the cheek. "Now, go. They must not catch us together. I have a room over there...." He pointed to a walled-in area of the bam.

"I know. When can I come to see you?"

"Tonight, if you can sneak away."

"I will." Leonardo knew the old gardener, Joseph, with whom the apprentice shared the hut on the edge of the vast estate, would fall asleep early and not notice the lad had left his bed.

That night, Leonardo offered up his ass to the stable boy. He breathed harshly and arched his back as he sat on Dario's prick. Dario had said it was the easiest way for the virgin to take a cock. He was able to control how much he took of the cock and at what speed. When it was finally fully in him, Leonardo could jump up and down on the prick, and jerk himself as he did. He rode Dario in such a way that Dario was never able to reach the orgasm he craved. He rolled Leonardo over onto his back and got between his thighs and began ramming his cock into Leonardo, leaning forward to kiss the lad as he fucked him. This was perfection – he exploded wildly, filling Leonardo with a torrent of cum.

For his part, Leonardo was filled with disappointment as he felt Dario's cock shrink inside him as soon as he had finished.

But Dario was not entirely finished. He took Leonardo's hard-on between his lips and brought his new lover to orgasm, swallowing the seed.

They lay in each other's arms for a time before Dario insisted that Leonardo go back to his lodgings. "You must. They cannot find us together," Dario said. Reluctantly, Leonardo agreed.

17

Still unsteady from the fuck, he began walking towards the shade of the trees that hid the hut from the main house. As he approached, he stepped on a dry branch, which broke under his feet. A human figure popped up suddenly from behind a bush. Leonardo gave a short surprised yelp, and then paused. It was the Marquis, who licked his lips slowly as he reached out a hand and said, "Don't be afraid."

"I have been waiting for you...."

"You...?"

"Yes. I was watching, through the window. Dario let me. Here, feel what you have done to me."

The Marquis pushed Leonardo's hand to his crotch. At Leonardo's touch, the huge prick rose and knocked against the Marquis's exposed belly. The Marquis loosened the ties of his trousers, and his full erection swung free. Leonardo was frightened and tried to push him away, and his hand slipped, and he touched the swaying member, unintentionally. Leonardo gasped with surprise. The prick was almost the thickness of his wrist. Now Leonardo stared at it in the moonlight with a mixture of dread and anticipation. Now that he held it in his hand, he wondered how Dario could have taken such a thing up his ass.

Seeing the eager gleam in the Marquis's eyes, Leonardo knew what lay in store for him. His head was shoved down toward the prick and the wide, dark tip of the prick seemed to stare at him blindly from one eye. He shrieked and pulled his hand away from it. The Marquis held the boy down and he was grinning. Leonardo struggled and squirmed to extricate himself, but the Marquis's knees forced the lad's legs apart. He wedged himself between the boy's thighs as he struggled desperately to escape. They fell to the ground. The Marquis pulled the boy's pants from his body with one hand while he held him down with the other. Then he forced Leonardo's legs apart and he pushed. His prick missed its target and it slid up the lad's tummy. Excited by the boy's reluctance, he tried again. He pinned him to the ground with his body and stuck his fingers into the soppy opening of the ass. Leonardo groaned.

"Dario opened you up well, young Leonardo," the Marquis sighed. "Ah, yes...." He kept on moving his hand while pinning the lad down with his body. Releasing the lad's hands, which began to beat on his shoulders without much effect, the Marquis pushed the lad's thighs farther apart. Leonardo screamed.

Spread beneath the Marquis, the boy's asshole, which had been virginal only minutes before, presented an irresistible target. The Marquis slammed his body forward from his position on all fours, and his prick hit the mark. Leonardo screamed again, louder this time, as the Marquis's cock slid into the just-fucked asshole and surged upward and inward. The Marquis rotated his loins in delight as the lad lay moaning beneath him.

His prick began the pumping motion that had so awed the boy earlier in the day when he had watched from his lofty perch. The Marquis's huge cock appeared to be almost too excited for him to control, as if it had a mind of its own. He drew it out almost to the tip, then thrust home once more. Again and again he repeated his action, as the lad's pained stare began to change into a look of not wholly unpleasant surprise. Before he could explore this sensation further or begin to understand it, the Marquis came deep inside him. He bored into the boy, uncaring, his eyes open and staring as if in a fit, his hands seizing and crushing the mounds of the lad's ass until Leonardo cried again in pain.

When it was over, he lay, panting, on Leonardo's belly. Leonardo whimpered and moved slightly beneath him. Obligingly, the Marquis finally rolled off the lad and smiled happily. His hand roved over the lad's erection and down to the heavy balls. "Your cock is lovely, Leonardo." He then delved again into the sopping ass, spreading it, shoving a finger in. Leonardo tried to move away from his touch. "Let me do this while you pleasure yourself."

"But Master...."

"You know you want to...."

And so Leonardo jerked his "lovely" cock and quickly came again that night while being fingered by the Marquis.

"Tomorrow I'll do it again, and you will enjoy it even more. Each time it will be easier."

He rose up a bit and Leonardo stared in fascinated horror as the glistening length of his prick began to swell again.

"Oh my, watching you pleasure yourself has got me hard again. Hmmm, you do excite me, little one," the Marquis cooed.

And then he spread the lad's thighs brutally once more. He delighted in his power.

"Oh, no, Master, please, not again."

But the Marquis was drunk with the smell of sex that reeked from both of their bodies, and he boldly entered Leonardo once again. Now the lad's gasps became a heady mix of pain, fear, and a newfound delight as the Marquis shoved his rampant prick into the tom hole. Unfamiliar waves rose from his ass to his spine and head. The pleasure became unbearable as the Marquis slammed into him. He wrapped his legs around the Marquis' body to force more of him into his ass. The pain of having such a huge cock within him did not disappear, but added to his joy. Eventually, the Marquis collapsed on the lad and he dosed his eyes, allowing his prick to slide out and cum to trickle gradually out of his ass and down the crack.

"Oh, that was grand, my son."

"Yes, Master."

"I have an idea, Leonardo. You will join Dario tomorrow and we will all enjoy each other."

"Yes," Leonardo gasped. "Yes, oh yes, Master."

The next afternoon, the Marquis was winking salaciously at Leonardo as if they were sharing a secret. "You fuck Dario. He likes to be treated like a whore."

Leonardo swallowed. He looked from the Marquis to Dario, who was grinning inanely at him. Leonardo felt small and weak, and angry that they made him feel like that. He had been excited about the prospect of sex with Dario again but now the way the Marquis was looking at him, he had changed his mind. "What?" he said quietly.

"Come now, I bet you'd like to try it. I bet you'd like to pay Dario back for taking your virginity."

"No," Leonardo mumbled. This was too bizarre. For the first time since he'd been in the master's service, he thought of Joseph, working alone in the hot sun while he was here, and the thought gave him the strength to turn and head for the door. "Joseph is waiting for me. I really have to go."

"I told Joseph you were to be with me this afternoon. And be with me you will...."

Leonardo tried to open the door to Dario's room but it wouldn't budge. He spun round to find the Marquis ready on the bed and manhandling Dario. Dario knelt up obediently and the Marquis kissed him full on the mouth. They did this for several moments, kissing each other with such passion that Leonardo's fear was soon subsiding and being replaced by something far more terrifying. He should have been looking for the door keys, letting himself out, running away – doing anything but edging his way slowly back to the bed. But he was, at heart, a watcher. He loved to feast his eyes upon a man and a maid having sex, or, now, a man with a boy. Shuffling inch by inch across the floor, he watched intrigued, bemused, exhilarated as the Marquis unbuttoned his fly and brought out his monstrous cock. He watched as Dario wriggled and moved his head from side to side to try and not have it forced down his throat. But Leonardo could see it was a game for them, that the more Dario fought, the more aroused the Marquis became. He watched as Dario submitted and his head was held still. The Marquis's fingers pulled at the lad's hair and kept him where he wanted him while his hips began to thrust.

"See, Leonardo? See how Dario loves my prick?"

The apprentice was now beginning to see things inside himself he really didn't want to see. He felt his prick getting hard again and he was ashamed. But his shame didn't stop him from watching. No, he was compelled to get closer and closer to them. He could see what appeared to him to be insanity in the Marquis's eyes. Dario gagged a bit but the assault kept on.

Leonardo stood by the side of the bed and watched that massive cock sliding in and out of Dario's tiny lips. Leonardo was overwhelmed when he thought the cock was being slammed far too hard against the back of Dario's throat The sinews in his neck were taut with fear and the strain of trying to get away from the Marquis's especially brutal assault. Leonardo loved it. He wanted to make Dario feel like that; he wanted to hurt Dario for the hateful things he had said about his prick, a prick that was just as fine as Dario's, if not finer.

Dario coughed and spluttered obscenities as the Marquis pulled out and stood there waving his cock. "See how he did that? Now, you shove it in his mouth. Let's see him enjoy it for a change."

"No," Dario pleaded, but the Marquis pulled his head up by the hair. Dario looked exhausted and excited and edgy, like an addict. "Oh, all right, I want him. I want him," he whispered hoarsely.

"Hear that, Leonardo?" The Marquis raised one eyebrow. "He wants your prick. He wants you to hurt him with that young prick of yours. That sweet young prick."

"I will not hurt him," Leonardo said.

"No, he will love that prick. It is the image of his own. It will be like sucking on himself. Go to him."

The Marquis stood like the devil at Leonardo's shoulder, "Oh, yes, fill his mouth with your sweet young prick."

The tension in his gut gave way to pleasure as Dario swallowed his prick and began sucking.

"Yes, he wants this. Look at him go at it!"

After a few moments of sucking, the Marquis impatiently pushed Leonardo off Dario's face and shoved Dario back on the small bed. Then he pushed Leonardo towards the bed. "Fuck him now, Leonardo. I want to watch you fucking him. I want to put my face down there as you fuck him. You will fuck him hard, until he begs for mercy."

Smiling, Leonardo climbed on to the bed and knelt up in front of Dario.

Dario's eyes were full of the madness of the addicted. Tears fell down his cheeks. "Fuck me," he whispered, his voice shivering like his body. "I'm yours now, Leonardo."

Leonardo ran his fingers through Dario's tears, over his throbbing erection and back to the asshole. He bent slightly to bring his penis to the asslips. Then, holding on to Dario's hips, he slid his cock inside Dario.

He fucked Dario hard. He fucked him the way he'd wanted to that first time he'd seen the two of them together. He pumped into Dario fast and hard. The Marquis got down on the bed and, his head propped up by his elbow, he watched the cock slamming in and out of Dario. Leonardo waited to hear Dario begging for him to stop and he increased his thrust. At last he had Dario where he wanted him, and he felt Dario surrendering to him. Dario brought his arms around Leonardo and drew him down so that they could kiss as Leonardo came inside Dario.

But then the Marquis carried on where Leonardo had left off. The air became sticky as the Marquis got into position and began. Leonardo lay next to Dario as he submitted to the master once more. Leonardo held Dario's hand; he could sense that Dario was numb to the huge prick and he felt the desperation in his fingers as they clutched on to his.

He heard Dario's breath being pulled into his lungs and could tell by the bunched muscles in his shoulders that he was gripped by the agony.

The Marquis was lost in a world of his own, fucking this stable boy. He pushed his cock in and out. Leonardo's passion had turned into anger. He was disgusted with Dario, letting himself be treated in this manner, and having an erection while it was being done. Dario's cock looked painfully hard and while one hand clutched Leonardo's, the other hand was busy with the cock until spasms took hold of him. Dario lost control. The cock was pushing in a rhythm that synchronized with Dario's screams as he came. The Marquis fucked him too hard, wanting to hurt the lad. He fucked him until his whole body shook, ravaged. Then the Marquis came and time stopped here in this little room in the stable, while each enjoyed his own perversions.

Pulling the huge cock out of Dario's asshole, the Marquis moved up on the bed and knelt at Dario's head, cradling him in his lap and holding on to his wild arms, keeping him still. "Again, lad. Do it now, fuck that ass. Fuck it after me."

That was exactly what Leonardo was going to do. He pushed Dario's legs apart. Drained by the force of the Marquis's fuck, his knees flopped open. Leonardo was happy now. He would have Dario again. He was going to fuck Dario again and again, until the stable boy couldn't take it any more – then he was going to do it again.

And he knew that the Marquis would join them, but he had no idea of the things that the Marquis would do with the two of them. That he

23

would fuck him while he fucked Dario, that he would go from asshole to asshole while they sucked each other, and on and on. The combinations, if he had imagined them, would have excited him. But that was to come. One thing he did know at this point, nothing was ever going to be the same again.

FAMILY BUSINESS: A CHIP OFF THE OLD BLOCK A CONVERSATION OVERHEARD
John Butler

Man, what a great fuck! I knew when I saw that monster cock of yours I was in for a treat, but god damn, it's the way you use that beautiful tool! Jesus, I haven't been fucked like that in a long time. I've had a few porn stars inside me with even more meat than you've got – well hell, we watched one of "em fuckin' me while you were plowin' my ass tonight – but I've never had a client with a dick like yours, and damned few who could just flat out fuck butt like you do! Jesus, Richard, you are a complete fuckin' stud!

Yeah, I wish you didn't hafta wear a rubber, too. It woulda been great to feel your cream shootin' inside me. If it was anything like the load you blew on my face when we sucked each other off, it woulda fuckin' filled me up!

Sure, I wanna see it. Tell you what: pull out, and I'll roll over on my back and put a rubber on. You can pour the cum outa your rubber to lube up my cock and your butt. Then you can sit down on my dick and ride me while I give you the fuck of your life! It'll take a while – you know how big a load I gave you when you sucked me off – but I'm ready to start on the next one; if you hadn't stopped me jackin' off while you fucked me, I probably woulda blown another load then.

Hell no, there's no hurry – we've got all night and tomorrow morning. You're payin' a lot for it, and I want you to get your money's worth. Just keep fuckin' me nice and slow like that for a while, though. Christ, your dick feels as big as it did before you shot your wad.

No, you're not too heavy. I love to feel you lyin' over my back ... and Jesus, your pretty little ass feels great while it's humpin' me like that! Slow and deep and sexy – God, I love it! I guess I've been fucked doggie-style thousands of times, but it isn't often the guy fuckin' me is such a stud he hammers me down onto my belly the way you did. And I think I'm gonna have a helluva hickey where you were bitin' my neck when you shot your load. I'm scheduled to take Jeff Skyler's ass-cherry on camera day after tomorrow, but I guess makeup'll hide it.

Oh yeah. We're supposed to do a flip-flop, and he's probably gonna fuck me senseless. I've been wanting to get that monster of his inside me since I first saw one of his videos, and I made sure I was finally gonna get it when I signed the contract. But I'da taken the gig anyway – imagine being the first guy to fuck Jeff Skyler! Well, I don't mean the first one to fuck him, of course – from what my ... from what I hear, he adores getting screwed. But the first one to tap that hot ass of his on camera – man, that's quite an honor! Mmmmmnnnn ... wiggle that ass and keep givin' me that dick – it really feels good!

I still think it wasn't very safe for you to take my load in your mouth while we were suckin' each other off, but I gotta admit, I'm glad you did. Nothin' quite like blowin' a load while some hot stud is actually suckin' it outa you. And Jesus, baby, you really are a hot stud! And then when you kissed me, and we passed all that hot come back and forth ... Jesus! I sorta wish you had swallowed it, but you were right – it was safer for me to. At least we didn't let it go to waste, right?

No, none of yours really got in my mouth when you shot the first time – just all over my lips – and you licked up every bit of that. I gotta admit, though, your tongue really tasted good after you swallowed.

Oh man, I hate for you to take that hot dick outta my ass – I wish you could stay in there forever. Here – let me get a rubber on. Jesus, look how much is in yours! Yeah, now empty some of your come on my dick. Don't forget to save some to lube up that sweet ass of yours. Man, what a load – that oughta do the trick! Here – pour the rest on my hand, and I'll get your butt ready.

You like that, huh? Oh God, what a hot ass! I can hardly wait to get my dick in this tight hole. My finger feel good? Oooh, yeah! Your finger feels good in me, too. Not as good as your dick, of course.

Sure. There are some dildoes in my bag. Get one and fuck me with it while you ride my dick – that would be hot!

Yeah, that one's fine. No, it's not too big, it'll feel great. Grease it up and get over here and shove it in. Oh yeahl Oooooh ... shit, that feels fabulous! Now get up there and get ready to ride! Can you take all of it? Don't laugh, a lotta the guys I fuck say they don't think they can take all of it, but most of "em are beggin' for every last inch by the time I'm really into it. I've heard a lotta studs go from "Oh, that's too much

– it hurts!" to "God, I love it, fuck me as deep and hard as you can!" And I always oblige!

Jesus, I can tell! Man your ass is amazing – it's hard to believe it could be this tight, and you could sit all the way down on it that hard. You really wanted it, huh? Oh yeah, it wants you! Ride it, baby!

God, that was fantastic! I can't believe you blew another load so soon – and you weren't even touching it when you shot! I'da dosed my eyes if I'd known you were gonna shoot that far – but that's all right, it doesn't sting anymore, and besides, I wouldn't have wanted to miss seein' your big cock flopping up and down and shootin' everywhere like that!

Yeah, okay, go ahead. I hate for you to dismount, but if you gotta pee, you gotta pee. No, leave the dildo in for a while – it still feels great, even if you did damned near wear me out with it while you were ridin' me.

Jesus – sounds like a horse pissin' in there! Hey, no wonder it sounded like a horse pissin' – your cock looks like it belongs on a horse! Jesus, it looks so good, bobbin' around when you walk. My God, even half-hard like that, it's major meat!

Thanks! Nobody's ever told me I didn't have a big enough cock either, half soft or not. And when I've got something in my ass, even if it's just a dildo, like now, I stay hard. You wanna put a dildo up your butt too, and we can snuggle here for a while that way? Yeah – that's a good one – that's the Jeff Skyler model. I've been fucked with that hundreds of times, and I'm lookin' forward to getting the real thing this week – it's gonna be even better! Here, lie down here and let me put it in you. There – how's that? Yeah, great isn't it? C'mere and kiss me ... damn, I swear you're as good a kisser as you are a cocksucker! I couldn't believe you swallowed my entire dick – almost no one does that.

Well sure, I swallowed all of yours, and it's really huge, but, hell, that's what I do for a living – I'm a professional.

Oh, I've been selling my ass since I was seventeen, but I didn't make my first porn flick until I was nineteen – two years ago. It was right after that I learned that my ... are you sure you wanna hear all this? Okay, I'll tell you, and maybe you'll see why I lost my hard-on

27

and asked you to switch to a different tape when that Chip Day video came on.

Jiggle that dildo a little, like I'm doin' to yours. Oh yeah! That feel's great, doesn't it? First guy I ever took up my ass had a cock just about the size of that Jeff Stryker model you've got inside you. It was a helluva way to start my career – no training wheels at all!

No, that was before I started sellin' it. It was Drake, my best friend in high school in Atlanta. He'd been hinting he wanted to fuck with me for a long time, but he'd never come right out and say anything. God, if he'da asked earlier, I'da jumped at the chance; he was the only one of my buddies who had a cock as big as mine, but his was even bigger – it was the biggest one I'd ever seen up until then. And he was cute as hell, and built like that proverbial brick shithouse.

I knew by then I was queer, for sure – and I sure as hell wasn't a virgin by then. It was the summer after our sophomore year, and I'd already sucked off almost as many guys as had blown me. I'd even sucked Drake off one night when I was stayin' overnight with him, but he was asleep – or pretended to be – even while he fucked my mouth like a demon, and blew a huge load down my throat. I could hardly talk the next day, my lips were so stretched! But he wouldn't let me talk about what had happened, anyway; he pretended nothing had happened.

But about a week later, Drake began to loosen up, and make a lotta sexy remarks to me. And then one night when he was sleepin' over at my house, we'd no sooner got in bed than he grabbed me in his arms and laid a big ol' kiss on me, and begged me to do what I'd done before. I was more than willing, but before I could tell him so, he'd gone down on me, and was suckin' my dick like there was no tomorrow. We swapped ends, and finished each other off, and then spent the whole night kissing and cuddling, and suckin' each other's cocks.

We still never talked about it, even when we were alone together. And even though we started having sex regularly, and we were both swallowing each other's come every time, he still continued to date the girls who flocked around him all the time. Drake had started fingerin' my ass every time he sucked me off, and pretty soon after that he was fuckin' me with his finger – sometimes two – and fuckin' me deep, and really hard! He wouldn't let me put a finger up his ass, but he loved it when I would shove my tongue as far in there as it would go. He started rimming me back, and that's when he started hinting he wanted to fuck me for real. He didn't have to hint long, because by then, I was hungry to get fucked – his fingers and his tongue felt so good in me, and I loved him so much, I woulda done anything to please him.

The first time he put that dick in me he was gentle but I still thought he was going to split me in two. Once he was all the way in, though, I knew I'd gone to heaven, and Drake fucked me like a pile-driver. And he screwed me twice that night before he ever took it out.

The next morning, I was so sore I could hardly stand it-but he fucked me again, and I loved it. My butt went from virgin to veteran in one night!

A couple of months later, I learned that even though he was having sex regularly with me, Drake was also fuckin' a half- dozen other guys in our school, including one of his football coaches. I guess I was heartbroken, or something, and I told him it was all over. He was shocked, and to keep me from cutting him off, he even let me start fuckin' his ass – which he absolutely loved, by the way – but pretty soon I learned he'd been takin' it up the ass for quite a while, from both the coach and one of the seniors.

As much as I loved Drake, I was mad enough that I broke off with him, but by then I was addicted to ass and cock. I'd stopped havin' sex with the guys I'd been exchangin' blowjobs with before Drake and I got together, but I went back to them, and pretty soon I was exchangin' buttfucks with "em as well.

The summer before my senior year I started cruisin' outside the gay bars around Atlanta, and I never had trouble pickin' up most of the really cute guys I zeroed in on. I turned down a lot of guys who I didn't think were attractive, but one night an older guy hit on me, and when I told him I wasn't interested, he offered me a hundred bucks if I would fuck him or let him give me a blowjob. It sounded fair enough to me, and within an hour or so he'd given me the best blowjob I'd ever had until then, and I had fucked him, too. And I had a hundred-dollar bill in my pocket, and a new part-time job!

The guy was so satisfied with what I gave him, that he became a regular customer, and referred a lot of his friends to me. Pretty soon I had a whole lot of regular customers, and I didn't hafta hustle on the street any more – I made appointments, and serviced clients. I'd become an escort, no less – but they're called models in the magazine Hotlanta 2Nite, where the escorts in Atlanta advertise.

It turned out I was able to perform with older guys, and with some I didn't find terribly attractive, almost as well as I did with the hot young studs I had been fuckin' for free. In fact, I found that I enjoyed myself more with the more mature guys most of the time – they were more interesting, they were a lot more appreciative, and they were usually better sex partners. And I was makin' a helluva lot of money enjoyin' myself.

My dad thought I was still workin' at this huge parking facility in Northeast Atlanta where I'd worked since I was sixteen, and since I wasn't doing much with all the money I was makin', except for savin' it, he never suspected anything. He worked as an insurance adjuster, I thought, and had to travel all over the country, especially to L.A., where his Home Office was supposed to be. And he was out of the house at night a lot of the time when he was in town, so I was on my own a lot. He never realized I was doin' overnights with tricks most of the nights he was away.

My mom left us when I was about twelve. She didn't say why, and my dad kinda beat around the bush about why she did, but I'd always been so dose to him that ... oh hell, that's got nothin' to do with anything anymore.

I was just gettin' to that. One of the tricks I fucked knew a guy who was with Eagle Video, and he thought I would be great in porn. He took pictures of me with his Camcorder, and sent them to Eagle. They flew me out to San Francisco for an audition, and I guess they liked what they saw, "cause before I flew back to Atlanta I had already starred in my first fuck film. I didn't even know then that Eagle was the biggest porn company. I had hardly seen any porn, and almost no gay porn at that time. They decided I would be a top in their films – well, hell, I guess you know that – but pretty soon I was gettin' fucked off camera by some of the biggest and the best cocks in porn. I was fuckin' a lot of other exclusive tops off-camera, too. I started having a helluva time. And I had my new name: Cody Dean. They named me after two of the biggest-dicked guys in porn, Cody James and Kevin Dean – said my dick was every bit as big as theirs. I don't think it really is, but it's dose. Like I said, nobody's complained that it wasn't big enough – but quite a few have told me I was too big!

Dad never knew I had flown out to the Coast, and when I went back out to make my second video, I told him I was goin' out to look over San Francisco State University. I was gonna graduate soon, and Dad was willing to send me to whatever school I wanted to go to. He never asked why I wanted to go to San Francisco State, but he had been in San Francisco a lot, and agreed it was a great place to live.

The guy who directed my second video knew someone in the Admissions Office at State, and he didn't have any trouble gettin' me cleared to go there as soon as I graduated. I probably coulda got in anyway – I always kept my grades up, even when I was turning tricks four or five nights a week. Before I came home that time, I had also turned a couple o' tricks in San Francisco, and since I was now a porn star, I was gettin' four times the money I had in Atlanta.

Anyway, I graduated and moved to San Francisco in 1998, and I was goin' to school, and makin' videos, and fuckin' my brains out for fun and profit. And I still hadn't watched much gay porn, if you can believe it – mostly just what tricks had playin' on their VCR's while I had sex with "em.

Then one day, out of the blue, my Dad shows up on my doorstep. He'd never visited me in San Francisco, and he's lookin' as serious as a heart attack. Before I could even say hello he says something like, "We've gotta have a long talk, Steve. Or should I call you Cody?"

Yeah, that's right It's really Steve – Steve Owen. You can call me Steve if you want; I'm only Cody Dean when I'm working. Well, hell – guess I'm working now, though.

You're right But I'll go back to work in a little while, and you can call me Cody again when we replace these dildoes with our dicks. So – for now it's Steve, okay?

Right, my Dad shows up, and I'm thinkin', Jeez, if he'd walked in here an hour earlier, he'da found me with about eleven inches of Race Rivera's cock up my butt, and my come all over his chest. I was supposed to shoot a scene with Gundo the next day – that's Race Rivera's real name – and we were havin' a helluva good time gettin' to know each other. But what really blew my mind was, how in hell did my Dad find out I was Cody Dean? There wasn't any point in playin' dumb, so I just started to spill my guts, but before I could really get going, he hands me two videotapes and tells me to watch them, and he'll be back in about three hours to have that long talk. Then he turns around and goes out, and I'm standin' there with my mouth open and two rented videotapes in my hand, both of "em in clear plastic cases – no boxes or pictures to show what's on "em, just the names: Day in and Day Out and All in a Day's Work.

Right – Chip Day movies. But I had never seen a Chip Day video. I'm not even sure I'd heard the name.

Anyway, I put one of the videos in the VCR, and started watching. I damned near fell out of my chair. The first scene showed a guy sittin' in an airport, waitin' to board a plane, and ... well guess who the guy was?

Well, yeah. It was Chip Day, sure, but guess who Chip Day turned out to be? My father, that's who! He was a lot younger, but no mistaking who it was. My father! And in the next two and a half hours I sat there and watched him kissing with unbelievably hot men, suckin' cock and fuckin' butt, and gettin' blown and gettin' fucked – once even gettin' fucked by two of the biggest cocks I've ever seen, and both of them fuckin' him at the same time! I couldn't believe I was seeing what I was seeing! I knew my Dad was beautiful and really well-built, and I knew he had a big dick – even though I'd never really got a good look at it hard. But Jesus! I'd never really thought about him havin' sex with anyone but my Mom ... and I sure hadn't thought about that very much!

Day in and Day Out was a bunch of scenes from different Chip Day movies, and a lot of them were made around the time I was born, 1979. Dad was around nineteen or twenty, and safe sex hadn't been thought of yet, I guess. He was blowin' his load in guys' mouths, and eatin' their come. Nobody wore a rubber, and there were a couple of times when he was gettin' fucked by somebody who'd pull his cock out to show he was startin' to come, and then shove it back in Dad's ass to finish blowin' his load inside. In one of the videos Dad lays on his back on a desk and gets fucked by five or six different guys who're taking turns at his ass, and they all look like they're blowin' their loads inside him – and it doesn't look like they're acting, either. And Dad is practically screaming for them to fuck him harder all the time. And there's a close-up of the last guy pullin' out, and when he does all this come just starts pouring out of Dad's asshole – and that's followed right away by another dose-up of Dad's face, and he's obviously in heaven!

By the time Dad came back to my apartment – right on schedule – I was in a state of shock, could hardly think what to say. He had a bottle of bourbon with him, and he just said, "Get us a couple of glasses, and I'll tell you all about it." So we sat down in the living room, and he tells me all about his career as Chip Day.

He started out pretty much the way I did – hustling tricks around Atlanta after he found he could make money sellin' his ass. And finally he learned enough to start escorting, and a guy with a movie camera shot a couple rolls of film – this was before they had video recorders, I guess – and some guys out in L.A. brought him out there to make movies. He made his first video in 1978, when he was only eighteen years old, just about the time he got my Mom pregnant, and married her. I always knew my folks got married only six months or so before I was born, so that was no shock. He said growin' up he'd always thought of himself as straight, but he always knew he loved sex with guys, too – took a dick up his ass the first time he let his best friend talk him into it, and he loved it! He had sex with a couple of girls before he met my Mom, but when they got married, he said he never had sex with another woman, except in a couple of bisexual movies he made. Of course he told me he didn't really want to have sex with any other women – by then he'd decided he really only wanted dick!

He'd been makin' a lot of money as an escort, but he never told Mom about that. He did tell her about the movies – he'd made three or four of "em before I was born – and she didn't freak out or anything. Dad said it turned her on, and they used to watch his movies together, and she even flew out with him to California a few times and sat in on the filming of some of his movies! But she made him promise not to have sex with any guys except for in the movies. He'd pretty much stopped his escorting in Atlanta anyway, so that was no big deal, and he still had his best friend – who's my Godfather, by the way – to go to bed with when he really needed to fuck butt or get some dick. The problem was that the movies didn't pay much – even though pretty soon he was makin' twelve or fifteen of them a year. What really did pay was sellin' his ass to high rollers out in California, who wanted to fuck the famous Chip Day, or to get fucked by him, and were willin' to pay plenty for the opportunity. So any time he went out to the Coast to shoot a movie, his agent scheduled five or six overnights for him, at a thousand or fifteen hundred bucks a crack.

My mother never found out about the escorting, Dad said, but somethin' went sour for her, because when I was about twelve she just left us. I never really got an explanation for why she was leaving, and she moved away, and I never saw her again. Dad offered all kinds of lame excuses, but it was always a mystery to me. I think Mom found out about Dad and my Godfather – I learned they'd never stopped gettin' together for sex.

After she left, Dad started doin' tricks around Atlanta again, and all over the country – usually overnights with guys who were willin' to pony up plenty of cash for a night with a famous porn star. And Chip Day was one of the hottest porn stars in the business for fifteen full years. He made his last video about seven years ago – and he doesn't even know how many he made all together, but he thinks it's something like a hundred and fifty of "em! He retired from the porn biz, but he kept escorting, and still gets big money – Chip Day is still a big star, even if he isn't makin' videos any more. He's about forty years old, and he could easily pass for thirty – and his body and dick look about as good as they did when he started doin' porn.

Anyway, a while after I moved to San Francisco, one of the guys in the front office at Eagle figured out the relationship between me and Chip Day – mostly from income tax stuff, I guess – and he called Dad and told him what was goin' on. He had known Dad for years, since he made a bunch of videos for Eagle in the 1980's, and he thought Dad would want to know. Dad hadn't been watchin' porn for a while so he had never stumbled across any of my movies. He rounded up every one that'd been released, and watched "em, and then booked a flight out to San Francisco to talk things out with me. He wasn't mad at all, and he didn't think there was anything wrong with what I was doin' – hell, after all, I was doin' pretty much exactly what he'd done, so how could he? He was totally cool about it. But he did want to warn me about some of the pitfalls of doin' porn, and about escorting, and he wanted to be sure I was bein' safe, and all that. He just naturally assumed I was escorting, by the way.

We had a great visit, and I think we're closer now than we've ever been. And you know how I feel about Chip Day the porn star? I've managed to round up almost eighty of his videos, and I've watched every one of them several times, and I'm proud as hell to be his son! He's an absolutely beautiful man, hot as anyone I've ever seen, and he's as talented at fucking and sucking as I can imagine. His dick and his ass and his mouth oughta be declared national treasures. It's no wonder he's a legend! But as much as I admire him, in all those ways, I am totally not turned on when I watch him having sex! There is absolutely no way I could ever have sex with him, even if we are both porn stars. He's as beautiful and as hot as any of the guys I get to fuck with on camera, but he's my Dad, for Chris sake! I love him and admire him, and I love and admire his work as Chip Day, but like you saw a while ago, I lose my hard-on as soon as he comes into the picture.

At first it really weirded me out when I realized I had fucked and sucked guys Dad had fucked and sucked, and had dicks up my ass and down my throat that had been in him. It took me a long time to get ready for sex the next time I filmed a sex scene with one of Chip Day's old co-stars – and there are plenty of them still around – but I realized it didn't make any difference, it wasn't even like having sex with him indirectly.

We've kept it a secret about us bein' father and son, but every once in a while one of his old tricks or co-stars will tell me I remind him of Chip Day, and they always go on and rave about what a beautiful man and hot piece of ass he was. It doesn't bother me at all – in fact, it makes me feel really proud of my Dad and I'll give "em an extra good fuck, kinda like "a block off the old Chip'! If they only knew!

The reason I didn't mind tellin' you all about my Dad is because Eagle is gettin' ready to make a video where Chip Day does a one-shot return to porn, playin' my father in the story – strictly non-sexual when we're together, of course. In fact, Dad said he doesn't want to be around when they film my sex scenes – but you know, I may hang around where he can't see me, and watch them filming his! When they have it ready, they're going to announce that Chip Day is Cody Dean's father in real life.

Well, that's the story about me, and about why I lost my hard-on when Chip Day appeared on your tape. I wouldn't even care if you were one of the guys who hired him as an escort, I ...

You did? Well, good, I hope he was great!

Wow, three times! That good, huh? Thinkin' about that what got your dick so big and hard again? Mine got big and hard lookin' at yours, and thinkin' about how good it's gonna feel up my ass again. C'mon, I'm ready to go! Pull that dildo outa me and give me the real thing.

Ooooohh! Yeah ... that's fantastic!

THE KITCHEN BOY
An Erotic Tale in Two Parts Bamabus Saul

"Torquil's lovely prick was standing ready for action and soon was bobbing eagerly against his belly."

I. He Shared His Charms

The kitchens were vast; it was like a whole city in there. The cavernous interior was divided into countless zones each dedicated to some aspect of food preparation. Throughout the whole day came blasts of steam and heat from the large boilers and ovens that dwarfed the army of kitchen boys who scurried to and fro at the behest of the Fat Chef. Young, virginal Torquil had crawled into his favorite "hidey hole," a niche at the back of the bread ovens where nobody ever went and where he could be confident of snoozing undiscovered until the shift changed. His white kitchen boy uniform was grubby and tom, he would not have passed a health and safety inspection, but then there wasn't a health and safety inspector in the entire principality who dared enter kitchens ruled by the Fat Chef.

Young Torquil was tired from long hours of scrubbing floors and washing dishes. He was on the lowest rung of the kitchen hierarchy and it appeared to him that he might well be staying there forever. He curled his knees dose to his chest and allowed his shoulder-length hair to drape itself across his face. Luxuriously his eyelids drooped and he fell into a light, floating semi-slumber. The only effort in his entire body was concentrated in one finger which tickled, with the tiniest and most delicate movement imaginable against the tip of his semi-rigid prick, gently moving his leaden consciousness through galleries of warm erotic images. Time stood still for Torquil as a succession of hard naked athletes posed and performed in the recesses of his imagination. A knight of the most dashing good looks, on a gleaming white steed, rode with the power of an express train across country to rescue him from these grimy kitchens and take him off to a distant castle high in the mountains. The horse neared the cladel and took off in a death-defying leap to smash through the vast cathedral window which was the only source of light in the whole kitchen complex.

As the glass smashed, time, with a sudden searing shock and in the shape of the Fat Chef, resumed possession of the youth. To be precise, the Fat Chef had taken advantage of a tear in Torquil's kitchen breeches to seize the boy's ample plums as they lay low-slung in their relaxed hammock and yank him out of his cubbyhole. Torquil let out a bellow which was ten cups terror at being caught by the Fat Chef and fifteen cups pain. But loud as it was, his yells were lost in the general din of the kitchen bustle.

Torquil lay helpless on his back like an upturned beetle, his face a mask of terror, his balls damped between the blubbery digits of the Fat Chef's fat hand. "Sleeping on the job my pretty it is it?" fumed the fat chef using his handhold to slide Torquil several feet further along the passageway. "Aaaaargh" agreed Torquil. "Perhaps my pretty is tired of his job and yearns for the cold streets and the gutter?"

"No no, please, Lord Chef! I'll work harder."

The Fat Chef gasped with exertion as he used his handhold to heave Torquil's body from side to side making a polishing cloth out of the seat of the boy's breeches. "Or perhaps my lovely would like to see these served in a dainty dish to the Archduke's dogs?"

"Oh please, Lord Chef, please,"

The Fat Chef paused a moment to collect his breath, much depleted from the exertion of talking, gripping and polishing at the same time. He allowed Torquil to get up on his feet while retaining hold of his delicate organs and wheezing from the effort of raising himself upright.

The Fat Chef was considerably shorter than Torquil and used his grip on the youth's nuts to force him to bend his knees and bring their heads level.

"Such a silly boy to abuse the privileges of the kitchen," mused the Fat Chef and he dragged a wet, outsize tongue across Torquil's lips.

"No ... no, please, Lord chef," Torquil cried, trying not to wince at the stench of the Fat Chef's sulfurous breath. He felt his erection abandon ship leaving no more than a tiny pimple resting on the Fat Chef's dumpy fist. The Fat Chef licked

Torquil's cheek and chin very slowly, rather in the way he often licked the dishes in which had been prepared the rich food intended for better men.

"I could have you thrown on the streets where you belong," the Fat Chef's tongue silenced any further begging from Torquil by clamping itself tight across his mouth. "Such a pity to lose such a promising youth," he continued, licking towards Torquil's neck and sucking luxuriously on his ear lobe.

Torquil could feel the Fat Chef's other hand kneading his backside with the practiced firmness achieved through making a million loaves of bread. "Such a pity to lose such a pretty youth," wheezed the Fat Chef continuing to slobber over Torquil's flesh.

Suddenly from the distant din of the kitchen came an extra loud crash, and cries of "Chef, Chef, come quickly!"

The Fat Chef snarled in annoyance, "I'll deal with you later. Meantime you can do an extra shift for the Starters Chef. We are short staffed today."

Torquil nodded frantically, grateful to escape so lightly. For a moment they stood looking at each other expectantly. "Well?" bellowed the Fat Chef.

"Shall I go now, sir?"

"Of course now you stupid youth, what are you waiting for?"

"Please, you're still holding on to my balls, sir!"

Reluctantly the Fat Chef let go Torquil's balls and the boy scampered, limping a little, towards the section where starters were prepared.

The boys who worked in the Starters Section were accorded very high status among the kitchen workers, the equivalent of Grade Three waiter, and out of bounds to the 14 lower grades of waiter. Torquil reported to the head of section and was put to work cleaning the Starter Boys' private lounge.

The Starter Boys had gathered together in their steam room. They were all naked as you would expect in a steam room, except that they all wore plastic briefs, which Torquil had never seen before and thought extremely ugly and unbecoming. They sat around laughing and joking, and none of them acknowledged Torquil as he scrubbed and cleaned around them, until he accidentally splashed one of the youths. This was a surly, pouting boy with thick lips, a stocky athletic build and an unruly forelock of curly black hair, whom gentlemen customers doubtlessly found infinitely cute and desirable, but toward whom Torquil took an instant dislike.

"Watch it you fuck," bellowed the surly youth, giving Torquil a good kick on the shoulder.

Torquil went tumbling off the raised platform, much to the amusement of the whole group. Torquil picked himself up angrily but remembered his place just in time to stop himself from attacking the youth. Instead, he apologized for his clumsiness and continued with his scrubbing work.

Then the Starter Chef arrived, all bustle and self-importance and took command of the situation as though it were some military operation. He ordered Torquil to a bowl of strong soap and clapped his hands for the first of the Starter Boys to approach. He produced large magnifying glass and began to scrutinize him minutely for unwelcome blemishes or stray hairs. Then he ordered the boy to remove his pants, which he did, lobbing them straight at Torquil to wash in the sink.

This caught Torquil by surprise as the garment smacked him full in the face causing all the other lads to laugh heartily and Torquil to gasp at the sudden overpowering odors of concentrated boy-crotch which had accumulated there. He began to scrub at the stains and crusts inside the sweaty jarring briefs as he watched the Starter Chef fit the youth with a metal contraption of warm gold that encircled the root of his tool causing it to stiffen in a rush and point eagerly at the ceiling. It also had the effect of pulling his scrotum into prominent view beneath, and proudly displaying the coat of arms of the Principality just at the junction where the tightly packed eggs met the root of the shaft.

The Starter Chef took a coarse hairbrush and teased the boy's bush out around this arrangement, finished the preparation by taking a pair of sharp scissors and snipping away a few untidy ends that threatened the design.

One by one, all the Starter Boys were prepared in this way until they were all ready and were ushered through a door where Torquil was not allowed to follow. He finished scrubbing the last of the pants and hung them on the line. Then he sank down, grateful at long last to be able to rest his weary body. He had been working since four in the morning, with only a short rest apart from his stolen sleep and no more than a couple of crusts and a bowl of gruel, aside from some burned pie crust he had stolen to eat.

But, suddenly, and before he was even halfway drifted into slumber, he was shouted awake again, by a senior waiter. "Hey you, there has been a spillage at table four, you'll have to go, we're short staffed tonight."

Torquil found himself bustled, clutching a small bowl of cleaning fluid and sponges, through the serving doors into the luxurious dining salon. His kitchen rags contrasted bleakly with the gold and crimson brightness and the glittering chandeliers. He barely had a chance to take in the scene around him; all he was aware of was how extravagantly ornate everyone and everything was, and hoped that everyone was so grand that they could not possibly notice so humble a servant as himself. The spillage was seeping deep into the carpet. Torquil first sponged the shoes of a diner, then he set about the bigger task of the carpet. The diner, presumably the one who had caused the spillage, took out a coin. Torquil felt the hand seeking out the pocket of his own tom kitchen trousers and placing the coin there, whereupon, discovering the tattered state of Torquil's kitchen clothing, the hand found itself able to explore Torquil's undercarriage and stayed to enjoy the soft warmth there. It rolled Torquil's rod from side to side as a connoisseur contemplates the pleasure of a costly cigar. Another hand from another diner followed and having deposited its coin, headed off in the opposite direction to discover the warm crevice between the kneeling buns. Torquil concentrated hard on his cleaning job as a finger searched out his most intimate orifice, tried it once, then twice, and gained entrance. The cigar-rolling hand in turn became more and more appreciative of the excitement that this maneuver caused and Torquil began to fear that, far from cleaning a spillage he was likely to create a second far worse than the first.

At the next table the maître d' was fluttering around new arrivals: a very distinguished party of four. They had been consulting the menu and the maître d' invited them to choose their lobsters from the huge tank against the far wall. He noted their preferences and expressed utter amazement at the superior taste displayed by each one.

"And will your honors take something to commence?" he asked, indicating the enclosure dose to the service door where the Starter Boys waited to be called. Proudly, arrogantly, they stood or leaned against the wall, each concerned to display his athletic torso, his elegant bearing and most of all, his vertical organ to their best advantage. No youth was allowed to join this elite corps whose manhood achieved less than 90 degrees from the horizontal, and the assistance rendered by the golden ornaments made each youth a prodigious sight to behold. The diners made their choice and the maître d' snapped his fingers to a waiter to lead them across.

Torquil busied himself with the stain on the carpet trying not to be seen watching as each Starter Boy presented himself to his appointed diner. Standing by the table each Starter's erect genital was conveniently at nose height for the diners to sniff delicately at the pubic area, and appraise every detail of the quality of the meat before him. For this was truly meat to be savored, being both well hung and allowed to stand. They pursed their lips and strained their eyebrows aloft in an extravagant display of connoisseurship. Then with a special golden implement, not unlike a common teaspoon, each testicle was lifted and appreciatively weighed. After which the diners buried their noses deeply a second time into the wiry bouquets. At length each commented on the pleasing ripeness and heady promise of his choice.

One by one, as each diner nodded assent, the maître d' indicated to each Starter Boy to take his place. Each youth climbed with practiced skill onto the table before his diner so that he was seated on the place mat with his feet on the arms on the diner's chair and his erection perfectly placed. The maître d' snapped his fingers to summon an individual known as "the Gentlemen Rollwright of the Foreskin", whose sole and hereditary task it was, for a small additional fee which appeared on the bill as "knobbage," to slide back the foreskin of Starter Boys thus blessed, which he did with consummate skill, lodging each foreskin behind a bulging helmet and receiving with unctuous grace, murmurs of approval and light applause from the diners. The diners pursed their mouths in the approved manner, summoning a small quantity of saliva, and applied lips and tongues to the meat on the bone before them, it being considered inexcusably vulgar and contrary to all rules of etiquette for a diner to take the whole helmet into the mouth at once. Conversation disappeared from the table, to be replaced by a symphony of slurping and sucking sounds.

Just then the maître d' noticed Torquil still lingering over the stain on the carpet and hustled him to his feet, apologizing profusely to the two diners with whose hands Torquil's genitals had been interfering. "Get along with you, get back inside."

Torquil returned to the serving area and sank exhausted onto a bench. But just as he did so the sound of a commotion out in the dining salon caught his attention and he peeped through a crack in the door to see what was happening.

He could see the maître d' fluttering around one of the center tables, the one near where Torquil had been cleaning. It soon became obvious that one of the diners had called him back to complain. It was almost unheard of! Imagine the scandal!

Torquil pressed his eye close to the peephole in hopes of seeing the maître d' humiliated. The diner was speaking extra loudly while the poor little maître d' was almost making little shushing noises.

"I say this one's off, look it's gone soft," the diner was flicking in his hand dismissively between the Starter Boy's legs. The maître d' was all apologies and grovels and he took it out on the poor unfortunate youth who had unaccountably lost his peak of rigidity. Torquil was doubly gratified to note that this was the very same youth who had kicked him off the platform; maybe there was justice in the world after all. Torquil allowed himself a brief private grin.

The maître d' had seized the boy, whose name Torquil learned from the whispers around him, was Karel, by the ear and was pulling him up from his seat astride the diner. "You fool, you dolt, you worthless idiot. I do apologize, your honor. I can't think what can have happened, the boy will be flogged I promise your honor, what a terrible insult. I pray you will forgive our humble establishment. May I fetch your honor a replacement immediately? Take that you stupid youth," delivering a box to the ears and a kick to the hind quarters of the cringing boy as he scampered for the safety of the service area, his hands desperately attempting to hide the shame between his legs from the eyes of the other diners.

The serving doors burst open and Karel was propelled through by a further kick to his backside, landing in a heap against the wall opposite Torquil.

Torquil pursed his lips and shook his head in mock sympathy for the youth's manifest inadequacies. The boy blushed, then scowled.

Meanwhile, within the kitchen all was panic and high drama. The maître d' summoned the Starters Chef and began complaining loudly. The Starters Chef wrenched the golden ornament from the dick of the boy, causing him to yelp, and gave him a further box on the ears. In truth the youth's prick had not declined from the vertical by more than perhaps 20 degrees, but standards in that restaurant were insufferably high. The Starters Chef summoned the Hygiene Chef who set the youth to scrubbing floors.

Meanwhile, the maître d' was busily calling for replacement Starters. Yet in all the vast kitchens there were none to be found. The kitchen's entire complement of Starter Boys had been exhausted in one way or another. Either they had gone home or gone limp. The maître d's eye lit upon Torquil. In despair he ordered him out of his kitchen rags, and fortunately Torquil was able, with little provocation, to pass the test of verticality. The maître d' with a despairing moan and much fluttering of hands and wincing at the lack of culture about the boy, called an under waiter to perform a quick shaping of his bush and to deposit his kitchen uniform in the cloakroom.

With a practiced nose he gave the area an epicurean sniff, "I suppose it's ripe enough," he muttered, "it will have to do. But the boy still looks like a street urchin to me."

Torquil's prick was standing ready for action and bobbing eagerly against his belly. The Starter Chef took up one of the gleaming golden garnishes and clamped it around his rig, easing the firm, elastic meat into its coils with practiced fingers. Torquil was given a quick sponge-down and his whole body was gently wiped with oils. Then he was hustled by the maître d' back into the glamorous restaurant.

The other diners were almost at the end of their Starter by this time. Indeed as they arrived, two of the boys were reaching the last of their

44

gaspings and strainings and their diners were preparing to savor their juices. The maître d' resumed his cringing pose and his effusive apologies as he presented Torquil for the remaining diner's approval

The disgruntled diner sniffed Torquil in the approved manner of the connoisseur as taught on all the best blue ribbon "Appreciation of Youths' Genitals" courses. The golden spoon was produced and Torquil's balls were lifted and weighed and graciously confirmed to be of a satisfactory standard. The diner solemnly nodded his approval.

The maître d', unable to keep just a whisper of relief out of his voice, purred, "A most excellent choice if I may venture to be so bold, your honor. May I assure you, you will not be disappointed. This is one of our most choice youths, fed on only the choicest of proteins, who is rarely...."

"Shut up and piss off," said the diner, eager to test the promise of this delicacy.

The maître d' bowed and smirked and after hurriedly seating Torquil on the diner's placemat, withdrew backwards. Torquil sat on the table with his feet on the arms of the diner's chair so that his knees were drawn up and his prick was presented at the most advantageous angle for the diner to gain access. Torquil was keen to do well in what he already dimly perceived as a possible career move; at any rate he wanted to escape the fate of Karel. His hard-on had curled back and was gently nuzzling at his left nipple, which certainly did not disappoint the diner, who summoned the Gentleman Rollwright of the Foreskin to fully expose Torquil's high gloss acorn and then to hold the shaft in place with a special pair of tongs, which were not often needed.

The diner pursed his lips, swishing saliva noisily through his teeth, and applied his mouth delicately to the purple dome before him.

Tired though he was, Torquil did himself proud. Within a very short time his abdomen was in spasm, pumping his rod and balls like a jockey riding a prize mount. With a gasp (for anything more was considered intolerably vulgar) he delivered a copious portion of creamy hors d'oeuvre that delighted his diner and overflowed to drizzle down his shaft and plums. The diner finished off with a few lip-smacking licks that were not strictly within the etiquette code for such activities and sat back drawing air over his teeth in the manner of the experienced connoisseur who savors a great delicacy to the last. He nodded and beamed his appreciation. As the maître d' reappeared and began to shuffle Torquil off the table, he slid a large- denomination banknote behind the metalwork of Torquil's golden prick ornament.

The maître d' escorted Torquil to the serving door. As Torquil entered he made a sudden grab for the banknote, but Torquil was too lithe for him and writhed his muscular feline waist out of the way. The maître d' snarled, but another table had called for cigars so he had no time to pursue the matter.

Torquil watched him as he self-importantly clapped his hands to assemble the Smoker Boys, each in a wispy silken tunic that ended just at the crease where hairless creamy little buttocks met creamy hairless young thighs. The maître d' shepherded them to the table where they presented their cigars, lit them and turned to touch their toes so that their diners might mingle the taste of a fine smoke with the warm, earthy scents of an adolescent crack.

Torquil's shift was long over for the day. He had done three hours overtime, for which he was unlikely to be paid, and in nine hours he was due back for the next shift. He wanted nothing more than to hurry home to the attic where he lived and get some sleep.

He made his way to the Starters' section to return the golden ornament. As he entered a yell from the side room caught his attention and he put his head round the door to investigate. Another yell followed and another, all in rapid succession. Karel had evidently finished his floor-scrubbing duties for he was now to be found suspended by his wrists from a pair of giant meat hooks. Behind him the Starters Chef was berating him loudly over his performance at the diners's table. He had brought shame and disgrace upon the Starter Boys, and upon the Starters Chef. Each new object of shame was announced with a fierce blow to the unhappy youth's buttocks, now with a fish slice, now with an omelet pan, each blow bringing a louder cry of pain and regret. Thus does one flaccid willy diminish the whole of mankind.

Torquil slowly unwound the golden ornament from his barely diminished erection. His lip curled into a self-satisfied smirk as he swayed his hips and caused his rigid organ to dance provocatively in full view of the whipping boy. He, in reply, let out an extra groan at the presence of an audience, and a mere kitchen boy at that, which increased tenfold the humiliation and pain of his punishment. Torquil nodded his head at Karel's rod, which had diminished to a thumb-sized peg almost lost in his bush.

"You need a starter, boy?" smirked Torquil, offering his rod with a series of little dancing thrusts.

"Yowww!" bellowed Karel as a tin tray landed across both buttocks together. "Fuck off."

That the Starter Chef mis-heard as addressed to himself and which brought him to an even greater peak of wrath so that he began all over again the list of worthies and innocents upon whom Karel's spongy knob had brought disgrace and turpitude.

Torquil watched a while longer, savoring his victory just as the diner had savored his spunk. Then he headed to the cloakroom to collect his kitchen rags and go home. The area was deserted, for most staff had gone and those who were staying would be there until morning. His hand went to the pocket to check whether the coins he had been given were still there. They were, and the amount surprised him. Added to the banknote he was holding almost three months' pay. One of the diners had included his card along with his tip, which Torquil was about to throw away when for some reason he thought better of it and wrapped it with his money.

Torquil began to pull on his ragged trousers when a sudden thought occurred to him. On another rack at the far end of the cloakroom were the pegs belonging to the Starter Boys. Karel's clothes were the only ones left. They were fine clothes, for Starter Boys get many tips and collect many generous admirers. Torquil was overcome with a sudden urge to try on those fine garments. He inspected the well-cut suede trousers, and ran his hand over Karel's waistcoat with its intricate and colorful embroidery, a garment that showed off so well his biceps and abdomen.

Torquil knew that he could be flayed within an inch of his life if he were caught, but the temptation was too much. He slipped on the trousers, feeling the supple leather skim the length of his long lean thighs and settling his tail where Karel's tail had recently been. They fastened at the front with a leather lace, more like a shoe than any trousers Torquil had ever seen. He tied them at the waist with an extravagant bow just below his navel. His dick and balls were clearly outlined under the suede, for this intimacy with Karel, not unlike being between his sheets, had given him back the full strength of his boner. He had never in all his life worn anything so elegant and so comfortable. He pulled on Karel's knee-length boots which fitted him perfectly, and slipped on the embroidered waistcoat, adjusting it to display either his nipples or his armpits. Torquil was carried away with the novelty of such gorgeous clothes, and strode the length of the cloakroom, pausing to pose in the little broken mirror like some Grand Chevalier.

Torquil now knew it was time to get out of this borrowed finery and go home. Instead he dumped his own kitchen rags on Karel's peg and strode from the kitchens as though he were the very ruler of the Principality himself.

The next morning, young Torquil awoke at his usual time and was frantically searching for his kitchen rags before it came back to him that he was no longer a kitchen boy. He sat on his bed and fingered the fine craftsmanship of the waistcoat he had stolen the previous night. The rent was well overdue and his entire worldly wealth amounted to these garments and the schillings he had received for having his arse groped and his rod sucked. Which reminded him that his assets, to wit, item: spunk-production organs, one pair of prodigious capacity, item: ramrod, one, of unparalleled virility, extendibility, rigidity and vertically, item: buns, one pair of breathtaking elegance, pertness, tightness, elasticity and beauty. These assets far outweighed any debts he might be temporarily saddled with. Torquil rolled his legs over his head so that his feet hit the wall at the head of his bed.

From there, he was able to walk down the wall, curling himself into a ball sufficiently tight that he was able to greet the tip of his yard with his tongue and lips.

"So, my beauty," he told it, giving it lingering kisses and tickling it affectionately with the tip of his tongue so that it bobbed and smiled affectionately back, "no more kitchen work. In future my treasures shall be my fortune, and I shall seek to serve any man who wishes to take pleasure in me. At the right price, of course. What do you say my gorgeous, gorgeous lovely?"

And his lovely agreed in the only way it knew how, by delivering him a handsome protein breakfast of what it prepared best. Torquil lay back on the bed and gasped with pleasure. What he had not swallowed dribbled thickly across his cheeks or dung to his hair.

"What then is poverty?" he asked himself. "Why, if there is no money then I shall feed myself. You will always feed me won't you, my beauty?" He stroked the length of the still swollen dick. "My goodness but they will be lucky men who get to share in your charms! Lucky and rich, of course. I hope they appreciate you as much as I do my lover."

II. His Pleasure With His Prick

Torquil lay back on his bed luxuriating in the early morning and in the strange knowledge that he no longer had to report to the smelly old kitchen. He shared his pleasure with his prick which, as always, had awoken early and bobbed at his belly demanding attention. Torquil tickled it gently with one finger of each hand, an affectionate gesture to which it responded eagerly prompting Torquil to take it firmly in one fist and cuddle it warmly. A long, creaking noise emanating from Torquil's stomach reminded him that he was hungry and that now he had left his job in the kitchen there would be no more breakfasts provided for him.

Torquil recalled the events of the previous night when he had found favor in the eyes and hands, not to mention one of the mouths, of some of the wealthy and distinguished gentlemen, who had given him more than enough money to go and buy breakfast at any of the finest eateries in town. "Well my love," he said to his dick as it looked lovingly at him with its one eye, "it's you and me from now on. We're a team. From now on we shall feed ourselves on our wits and our talent. And I have a strong suspicion that since you're the most talented member of this partnership, that it will be you doing most of the work. But you won't mind that, will you my beauty?" The prick nodded gently so that Torquil was convinced it understood every word. When he was young he had owned a small dog that knew most of what it was told, so why should a part of his own body not be blessed with perfect comprehension? Torquil threw his legs over his head and walked down the wall so that he could plant a warm, wet kiss on the purple dome. "And from now on," he purred, "I shall call you Kaxel, after the boy whose clothes I stole, and in whose trousers you rest so warm and comfortable. For he is a fine-looking boy and wouldn't it be grand if one day the two of you could meet on intimate terms and you could burrow deep inside him? How do you like that my beautiful Karel, a name all of your own!"

Just at that moment there was a hammering on the street door. "That will be Rejak," said Torquil, "will you excuse me for a moment, Karel my love? I must answer the door and tell him that I won't be going to work with him anymore. Perhaps he will come in for a quick snog." Torquil jumped off the bed and scampered naked down the three flights of stairs, Karel bouncing happily from thigh to thigh to belly as he ran. The door was on a security chain, but he opened it anyway to greet his friend Rejak before releasing it. And it was just as well he did, because it was not Rejak who stood on the doorstep but a most unsavory character who growled "Rent."

Torquil and Karel stood motionless for a moment, their three eyes staring in astonishment at this unexpected intrusion. "Rent," repeated the visitor, looking from Torquil to Karel and back. Torquil slammed the door, but the rent collector's foot was in the way and it would not shut. He was able to push his head in far enough to watch Torquil's alternately squeezing buns charging for all they were worth back up the stairs.

In his room Torquil cast quickly about over his possessions. There were precious few of them; there were rags he wore to go to work, and a few old books which he could easily replace, and the fine clothes he had stolen the previous day from Karel at the kitchens. These last he seized as he heard the chain on the door downstairs give way and heavy footsteps pounding the stairs. He threw open the window and clambered out onto the roof, leaping across the sloping tiles like an acrobat and only pausing when he gained the safety of a chimney stack. From the direction of the attic room he had left he heard a snarled curse and the window being slammed shut.

Torquil nestled beside the warm brickwork to restore his breath. It had been quite a shock to be ejected from his home quite so suddenly, and Karel thought so too, for he had retreated and softened to make himself more manageable in the flight, and pulled his hood over his head. Torquil put a hand underneath him and weighed him gently.

"There there my lovely fellah. Were you frightened?" he stroked along his length with one finger of the other hand. "You must never be frightened, for I'll take care of you and you'll always be my best lover. You and I will be together always." And Karel smiled confidently from within his warm hood of skin, and snuggled up small and soft.

"So then Karel my love," said Torquil after they had rested a while, "we must find a way down from this place." Gingerly he stood up and, still holding the bundle of clothes, picked his way carefully to the edge of the roof. By careful climbing down drainpipes and leaping across the small gaps between the slum houses, Torquil managed to descend to below first floor level in safety, until he lost his footing at a vital point and tumbled the last few feet, landing with a yell in the road where he was instantly surrounded by a crowd of gentlemen curious to know by what agency this prime specimen of elegant youth had suddenly descended like Icarus from the heavens. Torquil lay on his back and groaned, but he was not hurt so much as overtaken by shock. The circle of men gaped down upon him.

"Are you all right?" ventured one.

"I'm as all right as any poor boy who has tumbled bollock naked out of the skies on an empty stomach," Torquil snapped back. "Now which of you good gentlemen will be so good as to spare me the price of a breakfast?"

The little crowd pulled back slightly at the mention of a price for their entertainment. Torquil tried again, "Very well then. You've all had a good look at the quality of the meats I carry between my legs and the general composure of my torso. Would you say I was a desirable boy, sir? Look at the smoothness of that chest sir, and the definition of my pecs, and the lithe muscularity of my tight belly muscles. Bend down and touch my belly, sir. Wouldn't you agree there isn't an ounce of fat on me, sir, not least because I'm starving for want of breakfast? Now look at my legs, aren't they an athlete's legs, sir? Can't you imagine your head clamped between those muscled thighs, sir? And now will you look at that cock draped, (soft, mind soft, just think of what I'm not showing you yet sir) draped across my thigh sir, and imagine the weight of those two bulging eggs he carries in his knapsack. I'm a good-looking boy wouldn't you say sir?" One or two of the audience nodded or muttered agreement. "So which of you gentlemen would be willing to part with the price of a poor boy's breakfast in exchange for a suck of my cock and a lick of my balls?" This time hands were already reaching into pockets in order to check loose change. Torquil continued his sales pitch: "And I'll even throw in a finger up my arse to the first five takers." Torquil raised his knees briefly to his chest displaying for the first time his backside and the jewel hidden in the deft between.

Now hands reached for wallets and Torquil found himself overwhelmed by the crowd of men thrusting notes in his direction. He got up from the ground and found a convenient doorway where he could keep an eye on the bundle of his clothes and receive his admirers who formed a queue along the pathway.

One by one, they eagerly paid over their banknotes, which Torquil slid carefully into the pocket of the trousers which he had secured to his ankle, and knelt to enjoy their feast. He timed each customer carefully by the dock tower across the way, two dicks of the minute hand to suck Karel and another two for licking the balls. Then he roughly pulled himself away, touched his toes and allowed a finger to penetrate him for what he judged to be thirty seconds. Each punter left him begging for more and swearing undying adoration and devotion to him. When he pulled away from the sixth customer the man stood waiting expectantly."

That's it, what more do you want?" demanded Torquil. The man gazed up at him with plaintive, pleading eyes and extended one finger. "Be off with you," snarled Torquil, "you weren't in the first five. Don't think you're giving your finger a treat at my expense if you can't show sufficient eagerness to be first in the queue."

But the man persisted. "Oh please kind sir, you are so beautiful and I have been hovering on the very portals of bliss while licking and sucking your beautiful genitals, please take pity on a poor worshiper and allow...."

"Be off with you," snarled Torquil, "can't you see I have a queue to satisfy?"

"Fifty zlottis," gasped the man, "a hundred. A hundred and fifty, oh please, please beautiful sir. See, two hundred zlottis," he opened his wallet, "it's all I have to last the month, I shall starve for three weeks.

Take it, lordling, I pray you, only allow me thirty seconds of ecstasy and I will starve happy."

Torquil's upper lip curled. He snatched the wallet from the man's hand and bent over. For twenty seconds he allowed the finger to explore inside him while the man delivered rapturous kisses to the surrounding flesh. Then he stood up and pushed the man aside. "Now be off with you, you dirty old bastard. Next."

And he found the next and subsequent customers more than willing to meet the increased price, so that by the time all had gone away in a state of intoxicated dissatisfaction, all yearning for more, Torquil's breeches were bulging with more cash than he had ever seen before in his life.

"Well, my love," he said to Karel as he tucked him gently into the leather trousers, "we have done well, we make a wonderful partnership do we not? And you two," he added, easing his balls into a comfortable resting place, "you did well too. I must set about finding some names for you, I cannot go on thinking of you as Port and Starboard after an impressive performance like that. And while we're giving awards," he added, "who would have thought my little pucker would prove such an attraction?" He slid his hand down the back of the trousers and gave it a gentle pat of congratulations, "Well done lovely toy, you too shall have a name when I can think of one. But in the meantime look at this," he held the wallet aloft, now stuffed tight with notes and coins, "look at this for a substitute scrotum. And all without the loss of a single dribble of my juice. Come along lovely lads, it's breakfast time."

And with that he tugged the knee-length boots onto his legs, slid into the embroidered waistcoat and swaggered down the road towards the smell of cooking.

Heads turned as Torquil entered the little eatery. He sat opposite a man who looked like a salesman, who nodded politely and asked if he might have the honor of buying a meal for so elegant a breakfast companion. Torquil felt a hand sliding up his thigh and agreed to the bargain. The youth who came to take his order was a cute boy so Torquil tried a little exploration of his own, sliding a hand under the apron and in through a rip in the over-trousers. Inside he encountered a set of surprisingly plump nuts constrained in a sac of velvet smoothness.

The lad shifted his position slightly to allow Torquil easier access as he wrote down his requirements, just as Torquil adjusted his own position to prevent the salesman from opening his trousers. "Could you show me where the washroom is?" Torquil asked the boy, and grinned knowingly at the salesman as he followed him towards the back of the shop. The boy called out the orders as they passed the kitchen and led Torquil to a door marked Washroom. As he made to return, Torquil held him by the arm. "Could you do something for me?"

The boy lifted an eyebrow.

"Fact is, I'm a virgin. And I'd be very grateful if you could help me out."

"Sure thing mate," returned the waiting boy and led the way into the washroom. Hurriedly they both stripped. Torquil's trousers hit his ankles and his waistcoat was hooked over a door. The boy's apron joined it, his under-shirt landed on the floor and his work trousers fell to the floor. The boy's dick was not impressive, a mere peg poking rigidly from a nest of curls, but it was eager and his balls were very large indeed, and Torquil ran appreciative fingers over them once again. The boy was gaping in amazement at Karel who had stood up eagerly to inspect the prize that he had heard promised to him. "Hurry up," muttered the boy, "I'll have to serve your breakfast in a minute." He turned and bent over, presenting Torquil with a pair of bright golden moons between which Karel eagerly sniffed and plunged. Torquil took firm hold of the youth's hips as his pelvis pumped energetically, his balls swinging between his legs, slapping against the waiter's until in a sudden rush that screamed though his entire muscular system he reached his climax. He flopped forward across the boy's back and nuzzled gently at his ear. "Are your balls naturally smooth?" he asked.

"I get "em shaved, I think boys should." said the youth.

"You must tell me where," said Torquil, standing and gently withdrawing.

The waiter showed Torquil back to his seat, just in time to pick up his plate on the way. Torquil winked knowingly at the salesman, who resumed stroking the inside of Torquil's trouser leg while he ate. When Torquil had finished he snapped his fingers for the bill, stood up and said, "He's a good lad, when you pay for this don't forget to include a big tip." And he leaned forward as the salesman produced his wallet and extracted two extra-large banknotes, gave them to the boy and sauntered out onto the street. The salesman's face gaped a little at this, especially since he had been disappointed in his expectations of entering Torquil's trousers. "Could you show me where the washroom is?" he asked.

"It's out back," snapped the boy and set off with Torquil's dirty dishes.

"So it's true what they say, Karel darling," muttered Torquil as they strode along, "the rich pay for nothing and the poor pay always. Well if we have cracked this secret of the world, let us go forth and enjoy."

Some distance along the road, Torquil came to the barbershop which the waiter boy had recommended. He watched at the window while a naked youth on a high bench received expert attention between his legs from the barber wielding a fearsomely sharp looking razor. Inside he settled onto a chair and studied the pictures around the wall while he waited his turn. The pictures bore the names of current fashions and showed this season's bush designs. Balls were being worn bald this year, though there was the option of leaving a lengthy wisp from the side of each, or a tail from the lowest extremity. Torquil opted for the smooth all over. He was undecided whether to have his groin shaped to a clipped rectangle with a T incised in it, or whether to go for the whole shaped into a T, and he spent an enjoyable quarter hour debating the merits of each with the barber's apprentice, Qatano, who proudly displayed his own initial, intricately decorated and tended to almost hourly.

Torquil left the shop feeling fresh and smooth, with an incised T hidden beneath his fly flap. When he had put his hand into his pocket to pay he had discovered among the notes there, the card of an individual of infinitely grand status and connections. He recalled that it must have been given to him the previous night and had slipped his memory. He held a quick business meeting with his partner. "Well Karel, old chap, what do you think? We have nothing in the appointment book for the rest of the day and nothing to detain us. What do you say we pay a courtesy call upon this fine gentleman? For who knows but that it might do us a bit of good and we shall see a profit from the encounter?" Karel was playing the role of sleeping partner at this point, a little bemused by the strange feel of his recent and rather severe haircut, and barely stirred beyond granting tacit consent.

The address on the card was not hard to find. Torquil hailed a sedan chair and ignored the operative's quizzical look as he gave his instructions. Outside the palace he was challenged by a guard who would have turned him away but for Torquil's possession of the visiting card. His eminence was contacted and agreed to spare Torquil a minute of his time. Torquil was escorted through long and opulent corridors, past paintings and displays of unimaginable pomp and elegance to a pair of doors fully twelve feet high and guarded by two swordsmen in gilt and brocade. One of the doors opened a fraction, and a face peeped suspiciously out. Torquil had not seen the face of the gentleman who had enjoyed him the previous night in the restaurant, but this could well have been him, as it could as well have been anyone else. If he were rich and powerful Torquil was willing to accept his bona fides.

"Mmmm?" said the aristocrat. The aristocracy rarely employ facial expressions while speaking and this is known somewhat to inhibit their syllabic range.

"If you please your honor, you gave me your card."

"Yerr?"

"I've come for the position you promised me." Torquil knew this was a bit of a wild try, but he knew he was losing his advantage.

"Bgrrr." commented the aristocrat with a dismissive flutter of the hand which the accompanying guards knew very well as the announcement that the interview was terminated. They began to escort Torquil back whence he had come. It looked as if Torquil had missed his big chance, when Karel suddenly reminded him of his major asset.

"But just a moment if you please your honor," spluttered Torquil, placing his hand to his crotch, "your honor surely cannot have forgotten the pleasures of barely twelve hours past."

The aristocrat raised a contemplative eyebrow, and motioned the guards to return Torquil to the doorway. Torquil shrugged his shoulders vigorously so that the waistcoat fell from his back and the full warmth of his athletic body reached the aristocrat. Torquil relaxed again as he noticed that the aristocrat's mouth was agape and seemingly no longer under his control, and his breathing was not regular. He mechanically put out a hand and brushed the marble contours of Torquil's chest, running one finger absently along the pathways until it ended on the flat plain in the inch or so between Torquil's navel and the top of his trousers.

Torquil stood with his hips thrust forward confidently like a model. "Go ahead, my lord, you cannot even guess at the wonders that await the discerning aristocrat inside there," he said.

The aristocrat's hand pulled tentatively at the lace which held Torquil's trousers dosed. The bow dissolved and the cross strings loosened, until, with a little more easing of the suede material, a sudden push from within parted the flaps and Karel stood throbbing to attention. Karel allowed the trousers to fall to Torquil's knees and held the aristocrat's gaze as they stared eye to eye at each other, wondering who would blink first. "Go on, stroke him," encouraged Torquil, "he won't bite." And the aristocrat carefully did so with one finger. "Do you know what that is?" continued Torquil. The aristocrat, still incapable of speech, shook his head. "That sir, is no mere penis. That sir, is the hook on which you shall hang all of your fantasies. It is the spike on which you may spear all your desire. Is he not perfect? Is he not beautiful? Only take me into your employ and he shall serve you well, that I promise. And with only the most minimal of conditions. He must always be referred to in the third person (unless by yourself or nude princes of the blood royal) as "Sir' or "His Worship' or "His Honor'; he must always be saluted by your soldiery and bowed to by members of your household, council and servants. Observe the proper protocol and you shall suck and lick until your tongue is worn away." (The aristocrat moaned softly.) "At weekends you shall dress me as a rough country youth and I shall whip you until your buttocks run with blood." (The aristocrat groaned.) "And on the feasts of Saint Oral and Saint Orifice you shall worship the whole day at my holy hole. How much will you pay me?"

The aristocrat stuttered a price, rapidly agreed to a figure treble the original proposition, and Torquil swaggered into the apartments kicking his boots and trousers aside.

Some weeks later, out of boredom, Torquil asked his friend Rejak how he had fared. The reply was interesting: "I have a new job, at the palace. No I'm not a cook any more. If you could only see me draped right now across a red velvet chaise longue, I tell you I'm living in perfect luxury. I have soldiers to salute me, and sweetmeats at the snap of my fingers, and there are musicians to entertain me. I have the barber's apprentice call twice a day to trim my bush and I can have my way with any youth in the palace any time I please. Yes, of course the master knows; as a matter of fact, he's here now sucking on my dick, as he always seems to be. I give thanks that it's not made of sugar for it would have been clean licked away by now. I will send you some money, look out for it."

Torquil now ordered: "Have a hundred zlottis put into an envelope and mark it "Rejak."" But none of the soldiers or servants stationed around the room moved.

Angrily, he pulled Karel out of the mouth of the aristocrat who was kneeling by the chaise longue. "Did you hear what I said?" he snapped.

The aristocrat nodded to a footman who bowed and set off on his errand. "You know what I think?" mused Torquil, "I think I ought to have a servant boy all of my own, I'm tired of having to get your say-so every time I want something."

The aristocrat shook his head and went to return to his meal, but Torquil pulled Karel out of reach. The aristocrat nodded.

They arrived at the restaurant and ordered the carriage to wait. The best table was already occupied by a party of Earls, Admirals and their retinues, so it was cleared to make way. The maître d' appeared and fluttered obsequiously, evidently failing to recognize Torquil as a kitchen boy who had been the butt of his abuse until so recently. Torquil took the envelope marked Rejak from his back pocket and held it out to the maître d', asking him to be so kind as to see that it reached the person named. The maître d' bowed and grinned broadly, barely able to believe his good luck as he tucked the package into the pocket of his tails.

The two diners scanned the menu and made their choices. Torquil beckoned the maître d' dose and whispered confidentially, "Be so good as to check the contents of that envelope carefully. I shall be contacting that boy tomorrow, and if he tells me it contains a centizlot less than three hundred zlottis I shall have your bollocks cut off." The maître d' swallowed hard and bowed to indicate his understanding.

"And will you partake of a starter?" asked the maître d', anxious to change the subject. Torquil peered in the direction of the Starters on offer.

"That's the one I want, I want him. That one, that one there." demanded Torquil pointing firmly in the direction of Karel. Karel was pacing arrogantly back and forth among the other Starter Boys, all proudly drawing attention to the curvaceous swan-like necks that rose haughtily from the roots of their bellies.

"A most excellent choice if I may venture an opinion in the presence of so accomplished an epicure," fluttered the maître d' and oozed across the deep pile carpet to secure Torquil's prize.

Two Starter Boys were accompanied to the table and positioned to the side of each diner in readiness for when conversation should lag and the diners deign to notice their presence. Karel's genitals were positioned at head height awaiting Torquil's appreciation. He surveyed with the savoir faire of a practiced connoisseur the way the gold support secured a fully perpendicular erection and pulled the balls forward, slightly separating them. He looked up along the gleaming contours of Karel's oiled torso. The boy was staring straight ahead, as was required of Starter Boys in the inspection phase and Torquil had detected no glimmer of recognition. He called for the scale, a small gold implement with an indentation in one end which was used for the purpose of lifting and weighing the testicles. He set it under the left ball and applied slight pressure, unsettling the organ slightly in its sac. "You have impressive balls, boy," he said, "I hope you produce as much spunk as they promise."

Karel remained silent, as it was proper for Starter Boys not to speak in the presence of their betters, but Torquil could tell that he glowed just a little from the compliment. He lifted the other ball and let it fall and nodded his head appreciatively.

Torquil set the scale aside and prepared to savor the youth's odors. He placed his face dose to the scrotum, until he could feel the tip of his nose tickled by one or two random hairs and took three quick sniffs in quick succession. A puzzled look crossed his face and he repeated the action.

"Strange," he muttered, unable to see the expression on Karel's face, but more than aware of the impression that his actions must be making. He took the scale from the table and used the other end to separate the scrotum from the inner thigh where it was pressed and took another sniff, his nose pressed dose to the crevice thus opened.

"No, no, no!" he muttered, aware that Karel's heart was

beating faster and sweat was beginning to break out. Karel had once before disappointed his diner, and a second disgrace would be the end of him.

"Maybe," Torquil muttered in a conciliatory tone, sniffing along the height of the rigid organ and admiring his reflection in the glossy bulb. He felt Karel relax just a little. He sniffed back down the length of the rod and used the scale to probe between the other ball and thigh. Karel was breathing easier now, so that when Torquil suddenly cried "Maître" a shock went suddenly through his whole system.

The maître d' arrived fluttering. "Sniff this," commanded Torquil. The maître d' pressed his nose to the area and sniffed. "Your honor?"

"It's ripe," said Torquil. "but it's not as ripe as it could be. It hasn't been prepared properly."

"Certainly, your honor," groveled the maître d'. "Allow me to take it away and bring you another."

"You will do no such thing," Torquil barked, restraining him, "this is the one I want and this is the one I shall have. Take him away and give him a sound flogging. That will concentrate his odors I don't doubt, and then bring him back to me."

"Of course, your honor. It shall be done at once, your honor. A thousand apologies, your honor," muttered the maître d' and began to usher Karel away from the table.

But before they left Torquil managed to catch Karel's eye and give him a wink, at which point recognition settled upon Karel. For a moment his jaw dropped and his eyes widened as he took in the face of Torquil the kitchen boy he had once kicked aside, and the beautiful trousers and boots and waistcoat that had once been his.

There followed an instant when Karel's rage might well have boiled over and he would have hurled himself upon his persecutor and tom him limb from limb. Instead the volcano was capped and he was led away scowling with resentment, his lower jaw jutting and his breath deep and measured, to endure his whipping.

Ten minutes later, the maître d' returned to Torquil's table escorting Karel, who was limping a little. Torquil turned him around and examined his buttocks. They had taken on a bright ruddy complexion, and radiated a warmth that could be felt by the bare hand at an inch or so's distance. Half a dozen neatly parallel red lines of deeper hue crossed the deft between the firm alabaster bubbles and there were also patches of dark color as though from a fish slice or some similar implement.

Torquil returned to the youth's crotch, took a further sniff and pronounced himself satisfied. "There, you see how firm treatment improves the odors," he explained to the maître d', who agreed absolutely, and sought permission to withdraw. "But just one further matter," Torquil said. The maître d' returned his attention. "Do you not feel the organ itself," Torquil indicated the elegant and bobbing swan's neck with one finger, "is a trifle, as it were, a touch, on the small side?"

The maître d's eyebrows danced on his forehead.

"Small, sir?"

"For a Starter Boy, I mean."

"Oh for a Starter Boy, sir?"

The maître d' winced.

"Would sir have the starter removed?"

"No," said Torquil in conciliatory mode, "but I think I should like an apology."

"I do indeed apologize, sir," said the maître d', who was indeed well practiced in the art and easily slid into apologetic mode, "may I say sir that on behalf of.."

"From the boy," interrupted Torquil.

They looked up at the youth's face: beneath an unruly lock of curly black hair there was a thunderstorm of fury. He was apparently

61

resentful from an undeserved beating and the fiery pain that still remained in his buttocks. He was scowling with rage at being forced to serve a scummy kitchen boy who had thieved his beautiful clothes, and he was now scarlet from embarrassment. Added to his naturally pouting lips and his pretty little boyish turned-up nose, Torquil thought he had never seen a youth looking so adorable.

Karel mumbled a few words deep in his throat.

"I didn't hear that," said Torquil.

Karel repeated the words more dearly so that several surrounding tables paused to listen. But the message had yet to reach Torquil's ear, who required yet dear enunciation.

"I apologize for my undersized penis, sir," bellowed Karel, which was followed by much amusement among the diners and a spontaneous round of applause. Torquil joined in the laughter and good-naturedly gestured for Karel to climb up onto the table.

It was much to Karel's credit that his humiliations did not in the slightest diminish the strength of his organ or his ability to perform, for to do so would have been the end of his career. He sat on the place mat before Torquil and placed his feet on the arms of the chair. Torquil leaned forward and kissed the tip of Karel's tool as it pointed directly towards him. He summoned saliva to his mouth and flushed it rapidly back and forth through his teeth, then placed his lips delicately to the dome of Karel's shaft. For a while he worked gently, teasingly at the shaft, using his teeth and tongue with all the expertise that he had many times practiced upon himself. Karel began to moan slightly, gently, and his rig began to throb with a life of its own, shortly delivering into Torquil's mouth a tasty hors d'oeuvre of deliciously salty yet sweet spunk. Torquil smacked his lips and wiped them with a napkin. He took a small banknote and tucked it behind Karel's cock support. "Your temper improves your taste lovely boy," he grinned.

The maître d' arrived to shepherd Karel back to the kitchen, but Torquil placed a restraining hand on the tight elastic of Karel's still heated left buttock. He leaned across the table and said to the aristocrat. "You remember what I said about needing a boy of my own? Well, he's the one I want. Yes, I want him! Buy him for me tonight, buy him now, call the manager and buy him for me to take home tonight."

The aristocrat nodded obediently and sent the maître d' away in search of the manager.

That night, after the aristocrat had retired, Torquil lay back on his down mattress and smiled a satisfied smile. It had been arranged for his new servant boy, Karel, to sleep in a box at the foot of his bed where he would be constantly in attendance on his new master. The warm distant sensation of Karel gently sucking his toes gave him a heady, floating feeling.

"Do you resent what I did to you in the restaurant tonight, boy?" asked Torquil, "you deserved it. I bet you don't even remember when you kicked me that evening."

"I don't resent it, master," said Karel, sliding Torquil's second toe from his lips and wiggling an eager tongue between it and the third. "I hope to be happier serving you than I was working in the kitchen."

Torquil looked down at the curly black hair and upturned blue eyes of his new servant. "Do you want your clothes back?" he asked.

"No, master, they look better on you."

"Well, we shall share them, but I shall have some new ones made especially for you. I think you will go about largely in body paint, with big silver mirror stars stuck on your bottom. Would you like that, my boy?"

"Oh, whatever pleases my new master," agreed Karel, and he returned to teasing his toes with his tongue.

After a while, Torquil said, "Come along in here now, there's someone I want you to meet." Karel slid under the single sheet alongside Torquil. "Karel, meet Karel," grinned Torquil, introducing the body of the one into the hand of the other.

And shortly afterward, he introduced the body of the one into the body of the other, much to the delight of both.

COERCION: TEACHING THE TEACHER
Thomas C. Humphrey

Lawrence Hoffman sat stiffly on the edge of the vinyl-covered chair in the cheap motel room and nervously twirled his drink between his fingers. Sexual tension and promise filled the room, so strong he could almost smell it. From time to time, he slyly leered at one or the other of the two boys whose mere presence caused him to go empty in the pit of his stomach. Yet he sat frozen in indecisiveness and fretted that he had made a major mistake letting them coerce – he could almost say extort – an invitation for a drink. In the more than twenty-five years he had taught high school in Wilkinson, his one cardinal rule had been never to get involved sexually with a student or ex-student. A second rule had been never to have sex with two youngsters together. But here he was, alone in a Macon motel room with two ex-students, barely eighteen and too young to be drinking. Despite his self-recrimination, though, his groin tingled with rapidly growing lust every time he stole a glance at one of them, although neither was particularly good-looking, in any conventional sense.

Tony Stamas sprawled on one of the beds, sneaker-dad feet on the faded spread. He lethargically played with his obvious erection as he stared loose-jawed at TV, completely immersed in an early-morning infomercial, breaking his gaze occasionally to gulp from a glass of scotch and water. Hoffman knew very little about Tony, who had dropped out of school early in his freshman year, when his failing grades made him ineligible for football. Tony was dark-haired and dark-complexioned, with vacant brown eyes. Hoffman had heard that the kid had a cruel streak and had reveled in football because it gave him a socially-sanctioned means of inflicting pain on others. This knowledge and Tony's compactly-muscled body frightened Hoffman, but simultaneously created a nearly overpowering desire for him.

It was Ray duBignon, though, who Hoffman knew was fully in control of the situation in the tawdry motel room. Ray had been in Hoffman's ninth-and-tenth grade English classes, a gangling kid with a shock of straight dirty blond hair, a prominent nose, and full, rosy lips. Time had not changed him; he was still a gangling kid, even down to a couple of acne pimples on his long, thin neck. Hoffman knew from experience that the youngster possessed a keen intelligence, coupled with a quirkiness of behavior that school counselors had attributed to a horrendous home life. No one had been really shocked when Ray gave up on school during tenth grade, despite his superior intelligence. Watching Ray pace the room like some caged animal, Hoffman wondered if he was anything other than super-straight and feared that he could be dangerously unpredictable in the face of any unwelcome sexual overture.

Sex was exactly what Ray had in mind, and he was rapidly losing patience with Hoffman's timidity. Making a sudden decision, he moved beside his old teacher and stood dose, his leg shoved against the older man's thigh.

"You don't seem to be having a good time," he said. He pressed his leg tighter and began openly massaging his crotch. In no time, the fabric of his baggy jeans bulged, hinting at a possibly formidable erection building beneath his clothes.

Hoffman swallowed with an audible gulp and squirmed in his seat, breaking contact with Ray's leg. Ray moved closer, reestablishing contact. "C'mon, you little shit, make a move for it," he thought, a contemptuous sneer forming on his lips. He almost despised little mousy, effeminate men who panted and pined over him but lacked the balls to act on it. Hoffman was so indecisive Ray was certain he would never make a move.

Ray bunched his jeans, showing off just what kind of hard he was packing. "I'm sure you remember," he said, pointing his boner toward Hoffman, "duBignon is spelled with a B-I-G. That's what it is, is big. You can find out easy, but you'd have to lay some green on us."

"Wha ... What do you mean?" Hoffman stammered, eyes bulging at Ray's display.

"Green. Bread. Money, Mr. Hoffman. We'd need a little money for gas back to Wilkinson and things." After all, that's why they had come to Macon. It wasn't that important to Tony, who'd stick his dick through a Greyhound glory hole if he was horny enough, but Ray damned sure wasn't giving it away; he'd wait and jack off later before Hoffman would get it for free.

"You mean you sell yourselves for money?" Hoffman, who was accustomed to the sex-for-money exchange, said with exaggerated outrage. "I ... I ... I'm certainly not interested in that kind of sex. You're completely mistaken if you think I am that way. Maybe you'd better go."

"We can't go before we come, Mr. Hoffman. Remember that poem you taught us? Something about women coming and going? They had to come before they could go, just like us."

"Prufrock? You remember that?" Hoffman said with genuine surprise. "I thought it went right over everybody's head the one time I tried teaching it to tenth graders."

"Naw, I liked it. It was about this skinny old dude who wants to ball this chick, only he hasn't got the hair to put a move on her."

"Ah, yes, I suppose you could put it like that. I'm pleased that you even remember it."

"Something else I remember: The dude wished he was a crab or something and could just reach out and grab what he wanted." Ray again bunched his crotch, displaying what he was certain Hoffman wanted.

When Hoffman did not react, except to lick his lips, Ray continued, "Sometimes I think you're just like that dude in the poem, Mr. Hoffman, afraid to go after what you want. But you don't have to be afraid with Tony and me." He reached down and took Hoffman's drink from his fingers and set it on the table.

"What're you doing?" Hoffman asked with a hint of panic in his voice.

"I know all about you, Mr. Hoffman. Even when I started ninth grade, you couldn't get enough of sniffing after my dick, could you? I used to tease you right in the middle of a lesson by spreading my legs and giving it a rub or two, showing you a bone-on. Your eyes would zero in, and you'd start stammering and stuttering and completely forget what you were talking about." Ray broke into a naughty-boy snicker, remembering.

"I never...." Hoffman began a denial and then cut it off, knowing that he had fully exposed himself to this youngster when he walked out of Macon's only gay bar and almost collided with Ray on the sidewalk, knowing also that Ray had made a veiled threat to carry word back to Wilkinson unless he went along with their wishes, but knowing most of all that he

did want their cocks, desperately wanted them.

"You gotta reach out and grab what you want." Ray took Hoffman's hand, decisively lifted it to his crotch, and closed Hoffman's trembling fingers around his cock. "What did you find?" he teased.

The teacher squeezed and sculpted Ray's rigid dick through his jeans. "Your penis is fully erect," he forced out through tightly constricted throat muscles.

"Aw, Mr. Hoffman," Ray said with feigned disappointment, as if he had lost patience with a child. "You taught us that language has to fit the situation, right? Well, in this situation, you're not examining my penis, you're playing with my dick. And I don't have an erection, I have a roaring hard-on that needs some relief. You can give me that relief and get your pleasure, too, for just a little bit of money."

"But with Tony here..."

"Tell you what, Mr. Hoffman. Since we know you, and since I'd like to see you some more back in Wilkinson, how about a two-for-one special for tonight only? Me and Tony both for twenty-five bucks. How about it?"

Not trusting his voice, Hoffman nodded his head.

"Tony, c'mere," Ray called.

Tony rolled off the bed and slouched over in front of Hoffman. "What you want?" he asked.

"Why don't you strip down and show Mr. Hoffman what you got?"

Without a word, Tony peeled off his tee shirt and flung it onto the bed. He preened and posed like a body builder, showing off his broad, tanned chest with a dark fuzz in the cleft between his well-developed pecs and around his large chocolate nipples. He flexed his abdomen, which knotted up like successive layers of precision-fitted steel covered in velvet. He pried off his sneakers and kicked them aside and, massaging his chest with one hand, unsnapped his jeans and unzipped the fly with the other. Gyrating his pelvis, he shimmied his jeans off his hips, down his thighs, and onto the floor, where he stepped completely out of them. He moved in between Hoffman's legs. He locked his fingers behind his neck and stood flexing his cock, which danced inside his worn briefs.

"Why don't you find out what I really got?" he said. He moved even closer, forcing Hoffman's legs apart, and pressed his knee into Hoffman's groin.

Hoffman turned Ray's dick loose and reached toward Tony. Thinking a cock already in the hand had to count for something, he changed his mind and quickly grabbed Ray again. He groped at Tony with one hand. As he rubbed and pulled and tugged, Tony's prick popped out of the loose leg hole of his briefs and reared up across his thigh.

"My God," Hoffman practically whispered in awe, "I've heard of beer can dicks, but my God!"

He tugged Tony's briefs down past a thick forest of kinky dark hair and on down to expose his full cock and heavy balls. He grabbed Tony's shaft and discovered that his fingers would barely dose around it. Relinquishing his hold on Ray's prong, he stacked his hands up Tony's thick rod. Both palms barely covered its full length.

"Try it out for size," Tony said. He grabbed his ex-teacher's thinning hair with both hands and roughly jerked Hoffman's head down and smashed his lips against the broad engorged head of his cock.

Hoffman stretched his mouth open until he was afraid his jaws would become unhinged before the cavity was wide enough for Tony to slip his pole inside. Immediately, Tony set up a staccato pumping, brutally fucking the older man's mouth, driving his knob to the back of Hoffman's throat on every thrust. Hoffman's eyes filled with tears, and he tried to back off and give the massive tool some tongue action, but Tony tugged at his hair painfully and kept him trapped on the huge meat.

"Let me try him out," Ray said.

Hoffman had been too busy handling Tony's massive shaft without choking on it to pay attention to Ray. When Tony popped his dick out of his mouth and stepped back, Hoffman looked up at Ray advancing toward him, naked and fingering his hard-on. Hoffman's eyes slid from his smooth, thin chest with flat pecs and tiny pink nipples on down to his rounded, boyish hips and locked in on his pale uncut cock jutting straight out from a mass of tightly curled blond hair. Not as thick as Tony's, it was at least three inches longer and perfectly formed, the foreskin evenly pulled back just enough to reveal the tiny piss slit. It was the most beautiful thing Hoffman had seen in recent memory, and he eagerly opened his mouth to take it when Ray crowded in and jabbed it in his face.

Unlike Tony, Ray did not try to choke him with his cock. He stood virtually still, gently running his fingers through Hoffman's hair, and let the older man enjoy the big prick at his leisure, occasionally gyrating his pelvis and sighing with pleasure. Hoffman squeezed Ray's thin, flat buttocks with both hands and used every technique he knew to build the kid to the highest excitement, occasionally tugging forward on his buttocks and swallowing the long shaft until his lips crushed against Ray's pubes. Every time Hoffman deep-throated him, Ray involuntarily groaned with animal delight and tightened his grip on the teacher's head, holding him on his sensitive cock until Hoffman struggled to back off.

"Hey, let me in on the fun, too," Tony complained, tugging at Ray's shoulder.

Ray stepped back and dragged Hoffman to his feet. "Get your clothes off," he ordered.

Hoffman would have preferred turning out the lights, but he didn't dare suggest it to the boys. He removed his shirt and carefully hung it across the chair. He slipped off his shoes and demurely turned away to slide down his pants and underwear. He meticulously started to straighten the crease in his trousers, and Tony impatiently snatched them out of his hands and tossed them into the chair.

"Hurry the fuck up!" he muttered. "My balls is aching!" He twirled Hoffman around and shoved him toward the bed.

Ray had already stretched on his back, his head about midway on the bed, legs splayed. He watched with mixed amusement and revulsion as Hoffman stumbled toward him, his flesh fish-belly white, tits and stomach sagging with age, his thin arms wrinkled and untoned.

"One more English lesson, Mr. Hoffman," he said, folding a pillow beneath his head. "Active and passive. I know which you are. Well, old Stamas there is active Greek. He's gonna fuck you bowlegged. And old duBignon here – I'm hyperactive French. You can give me head till sunrise. You can milk me till all I've got left is a promise of more when my balls chum it up. Come on down here between my legs and suck my dick."

Hoffman knelt between Ray's legs, weight on elbows and knees, and wrapped one hand around the base of Ray's long pole. Tony grabbed Hoffman's thin hips and tugged him toward the foot of the bed until the teacher's knees were balanced precariously on the end of the mattress, his flat buttocks thrust up on spindly thighs, open and vulnerable. Ray shifted down and readjusted his pillow.

Hoffman craned his neck and watched uneasily as Tony advanced on him, his cock streaming great threads of precum which he rubbed around on the fist-sized knob of his thick prong. Tony grabbed Hoffman's bony hips and spread his cheeks with his thumbs. He probed around for a second and then leaned forward. With one quick jab, his huge cockhead penetrated Hoffman and burrowed more than halfway up his chute. Just as the teacher began a scream of protest, Ray snatched his head down and crammed his rod down Hoffman's throat. Hoffman knelt gagging on Ray's cock as Tony's giant pole seared his insides like a thick firebrand.

Ray eased off to let Hoffman breathe, but, unmindful of his pain, Tony began pounding the older man's ass like a jackhammer, pulling out until the teacher's puckered hole closed around the tip of his cock and then driving all the way to his pubes on every brutal thrust.

Hoffman forced himself to relax and accept Tony's thick timber, which he hungered for, despite the pain. Within minutes of Tony's initial penetration, Hoffman was straining backward to meet Tony's pile-driving thrusts, encouraging the kid to sink his dick into him until his balls smashed against Hoffman's bony cheeks. At the same time, he was ecstatically gobbling up Ray's prick, licking and sucking and drooling over it like a kid with an all-day sucker. Ray lay with thighs flexed, eyes closed, and head crushed into the pillow, sighing and moaning at the keen pleasure of Hoffman's mouth.

"Ah, man!" he said. "You're the best cocksucker I know! But slow down. I don't want to cum too quick!"

"You're a damn good fuck, too," Tony growled, "and I do want to cum. Now! I'm gonna flood your ass till it runs out your mouth, motherfucker!"

He made several quick, brutal lunges, driving his cock to the hilt. Hoffman felt the pistoning rod balloon deep inside him, felt jet after jet of hot jizz wash over his inner walls and seep out around the base of Tony's ramrod, which by then was still, except for the pulsing tube which continued to spurt cum out of the broad cockhead.

Ray grabbed Hoffman by the ears and brought his attention back to him. "Give my dick a rest," he said. "Suck on my balls awhile."

Hoffman let Ray's long rod slide up his cheek as he burrowed down and took first one, then both balls in his mouth, practically swallowing the tight, hairless nutsac. Ray squirmed and moaned and pawed at the older man's bony shoulders until the sensation on his nuts became too intense. Shoving Hoffman's head even lower, he raised his splayed legs and smashed the teacher's face into his spread ass cheeks. Hoffman greedily licked and lapped until he found Ray's tight pucker. He rimmed it, swirling his tongue round and round the opening.

"That's it! Eat my ass! Tongue-fuck that hole! Ah, yeah, that feels great!" Ray babbled, almost incoherent with passion.

Tony, who had stood as still as a statue, his rigid cock buried completely in the teacher's ass, started up his deep, pounding jabs again. At the same time, Ray grabbed Hoffman by the ears and guided his mouth back to the huge pulsing dick above him.

"Now, cocksucker, do it like you mean it. Suck that dick right off my body. Show me how much you want it," Ray said, lifting off the mattress until his cockhead slid down Hoffman's throat.

Ray hunched and thrust and shoved the older man's lips down to his pubic hair time after time, much rougher than he had been before. Matching him stroke for stroke, Tony began slapping Hoffman's thin buttocks with both hands, causing Hoffman to flinch away in pain and clench his ass around the huge pounding rod splitting him apart with each deep jab. Reveling in the double-pronged abuse the boys were inflicting, Hoffman knew that he would carry bruised imprints of Tony's thick palms for days as a reminder of this night that would really need no tangible reminders.

In no time, Ray started moaning almost as if he were in pain and set the bed to rocking with his lunges off the mattress in an attempt to drive his whole body down Hoffman's throat. As abruptly as it started, it ended with Ray's arched body frozen in midair, not a muscle moving, except for the great pulsing and twitching of his big cock between Hoffman's lips as he exploded, sending blast after blast of cum to the back of Hoffman's mouth, faster than Hoffman could swallow it.

As if waiting for a signal from Ray, Tony made a couple of short, quick jabs up Hoffman's ass, then one final long shove as deep as he could go. Hoffman nearly fainted from the ecstatic thrill of receiving both boys' offerings at the same time. He greedily milked Ray's long cock with his fingers, making sure he left nothing untasted, and flexed his ass ring around Tony's rod, hoping to squeeze out every drop of his manhood.

Ray collapsed, limp as a dishrag, and Tony followed, crashing down on Hoffman's back with all his weight until Hoffman lay prone on Ray's chest, his hair tickling Ray's chin. There the three of them rested, each anticipating the next round.

Early the next morning, bleary eyed from a sleepless, exhausting night, Hoffman drove the two kids to Ray's beat-up old car. His ass was too tender for him to sit comfortably, and his throat muscles were so sore he could hardly swallow, but he had a peculiar glint in his eyes, and a curious little smile curled the comers of his lips.

"You fellows split this," he said, handing Ray a bill as the kids got out of his car. Ray saw that it was a fifty.

"Yee-haw!" Ray shouted after he unlocked his car, punching at the early morning sky with a clenched fist. He thought: I hope the little fucker's got a big bank account. Now that we've got him hooked, I plan to drain him of everything he's got. And toe don't even have to drive to Macon any more. Then he shouted again: "Yee-haw!"

THE IMPOSSIBLE MIRACLE
Peter Rice

"You really like being fucked, then? "

"Very much. The rougher the better, actually Eddie's sister was beautiful. He had to admit as much. She attracted boys as a honey pot attracts bees. She reveled in her power to attract. She flaunted her charms and in her wake lay the epitaphs to discarded lovers.

Any one of them would have been snapped up by Eddie, given the chance. How he would have liked to comfort them after they had been cast adrift. But he knew that could never happen. He knew that he was not the only boy in the world, even in his village if the statistics were true, who fancied other boys, but it sure as hell seemed like it. Any one of his sister's cast-offs would have done.

She was okay – as a sister – he conceded, but when she took up with the boy from the library, jealousy began to gnaw at his soul.

From the day that boy had started to work at the library two years before, Eddie had been in love – hopelessly, painfully and ever-to-be unrequitedly, in love. Eddie was just a teen, and the library boy a bit older, and totally beyond Eddie's reach.

Eddie began to visit the library more and more frequently to change his books. Few had been opened, let alone read, despite his love of reading. He always made sure that the boy was at the desk to take his books and to check them out. Inevitably the boy took note of such a regular customer and formed greetings gradually gave way to conversation. The small branch library was never very busy, and talk developed into a limited friendship that served only to emphasize just how unattainable the boy was.

His blond center-parted hair framed a conventionally handsome face – perhaps too handsome, but Eddie's heart would lurch whenever he saw him. He was quite tall, but possibly Eddie would outgrow him and have a more powerful build. The boy's finest feature, for Eddie, was his deep tortoiseshell-colored eyes. They seemed to shoulder like a cat's eyes, Eddie imagined, when they focused on him as they talked together. There was more to Owen than books. He was a fine swimmer and diver. Modesty had prevented his telling Eddy how good he was, but then Eddie and Sarah had caught sight of him training, on a casual visit to the baths. Eddie liked to dream of their chat taking a personal turn: "I want to tell you something."

"Yes?"

"About me, I mean "Go on, I'm listening" 'Well, the thing is, I'm gay, you know, and I fancy you like crazy." "I'm glad you told me ... I'd never have guessed. You see, I'm gay, too."

"Really?"

"Yes - how soon can we get together, then? " If only.

The usual running time for one of Sarah's boyfriends was three weeks, give or take a few days. This was week three for the library hunk. It wasn't surprising, in a way, that she should tire of him. For a librarian, suited to organizing things, he was strangely inept at remembering times of arrangements. "Where the hell has he got to, now?" exploded Sarah on the Monday evening. "He's only ten minutes late," commented Eddie, who still sat at the table, finishing a portion of apple pie and custard. Sarah stood looking at her wrist watch, her lovely face marred by a scowl. "And you needn't jump to his defense either. It's not as though it's the first time, and he couldn't even be bothered to watch me do the gym competition last Saturday!" Eddie leaned back on his chair and smiled sweetly. "There was the little matter of his diving competition on Saturday, as well." Sarah had missed it. "My event was very important for me, and he should have been there!"

"Don't you think you might be being just a tad unreasonable?"

"Of course not. He is supposed to be my boyfriend."

"You don't know when you're lucky." Eddie stood to take his dessert dish to the kitchen. "Well, I'm going. I'll catch the bus," she decided. "He can find me at the Blue Moon. Trida and Joanne are going there tonight." At that moment their mother came through from the kitchen. Sarah was putting on an outdoor jacket. "Aren't you waiting for Owen, then? I'm sure he won't be long."

"He'll have to learn that I'm not going to be kept waiting by anyone. Ta-ta, then. I'll be late I expect." Their mother looked worried. "You will take care, dear, won't you? Get a taxi home, if you're alone. I'll pay for it." Sarah's manner softened. "Don't worry, Mummy, I won't do anything stupid. Don't wait up." She picked up her purse, and was quickly out of the house. Mother and son looked at each other. "She's mad," observed Eddie. "I'm afraid you've both been spoilt."

"Spoilt – moi?" Eddie's mother smiled. "Oui – tu aussi, " said his mother. Eddie took the dish he was holding to the kitchen and put it in the sink with the rest of the washing-up. When he came back into the dining-room his mother had gone into the sitting-room and switched on the TV. He still had to get down to his English homework. He was just about to switch off the dining-room light when he saw a piece of white card under the sideboard. He picked it up and turned it over. "Wow!" he exclaimed. It was a five-by-four photo of Owen in his swim trunks, sitting on the ladder to the diving board, and looking as sexy as hell. Sarah must have dropped it. Eddie was soon up in his room. Flopped down on his bed, he quickly unzipped his jeans and pulled out his cock and balls. His cock sprang to attention and he slowly massaged the foreskin back and forth, relishing both those sensations and those stimulated by the boy wonder's photograph. He delayed the orgasm twice and was reaching the inevitable when the doorbell rang. Owen! He stuffed his equipment back inside his jeans and dashed downstairs to open the front door. His mother was unlikely to have heard the bell, what with the TV and being a bit deaf as well. Jumping down the last five stairs he yanked open the door. There was a bedraggled Owen standing in the pouring rain, albeit wearing a waterproof jacket. "Hey, come on in mate. You're too late, though, she's gone," said Eddie. "Gone? I'm not that late, am I?"

"Too late for our Sarah. She's gone to the Blue Moon. She's meeting Tricia and Joanne there."

"Oh, god, not those two!" Owen looked disgusted. "She says she'll see you there."

"No, she bloody won't. I hate that club, and her two pals are no better." Eddie looked at him, wondering if there would be any point in trying to seduce him. Owen really didn't seem all that worried that Sarah had gone without him. This was the fourth time now that he had missed a date with Sarah. Yet he was here. He must have meant to go out with her. "I could do with some company while I do my homework, if the idea doesn't seem too boring." Owen grinned a white smile. "Well, now, that's the best offer I've had tonight," he said. "The only, I expect," Eddie retorted. "That may be true," he countered, "but I don't mind keeping your nose to the grindstone." That's not where I'd like my nose to be. "Okay, come on up to my room, then."

"I'd better say hello to your Mum, first."

"No need, she's watching "Coronation Street.' It'll disturb her. We can come down later."

"Okay, then. Lead on." Eddie was very conscious that, as they climbed the staircase, Owen's eyes were on a level with his backside. He was also aware that his ass was very attractive – at least it was such as he would have admired on someone else. If only Owen might feel like that, might plant his hands firmly on each bubble-shaped buttock. Nothing happened. He hadn't really expected it to. In Eddie's bedroom, Owen perched himself on the side of the bed as Eddie sat at his small writing desk. "What homework are you doing?" enquired Owen. "English Literature," Eddie replied, glad that it was something he felt pretty sure Owen would have an interest in. "Oh, what in particular?" Eddie turned in his office swing chair, and held out two books. "It's "Paradise Lost – Part One,' and "Hyperion,'" he said. "We've to compare the passages where I've put markers." He turned back and started writing. Owen read through the pages from the markers as Eddie wrote his essay. Having read a few pages from those points, he turned to the beginning of the Milton poem. Before he had read through half of it Eddie finished and put the A4 pages together. "That'll do," he sighed. "Finished?"

"It's enough," replied Eddie. "Do you like these poems?" Owen asked. "I quite like the Keats. "Paradise Lost' - well, that's harder going."

"I had that to read. I found it a bit dry at the time. I like it now, though. You have to get used to the style of writing. It's very stylized; classical, I suppose you might call it." A discussion ensued, far more searching than Eddie's essay. It progressed naturally to other literature, and on to some of the latest novels to come into the library, and then to sport. "I'm already in Sarah's bad books for missing her last gym competition."

"You missed seeing me at the same time."

"Really? She's never mentioned that you were competing as well."

"Typical of our Sarah. No one else exists."

"You must have a nice build, then, if you do gym that seriously?" A chance – a very remote chance – but let's try it. "Not bad, I suppose. Do you want to see?"

Eddie was already peeling off his clothes, without waiting for an answer. He didn't wait for Owen to say, "It doesn't matter," or whatever. He was about to slip off his briefs when the front door was opened and slammed to. "Mummy!" called Sarah from the foot of the stairs. They heard a muffled response from the sitting-room. Owen glanced at his watch. "Hey, d'you know what time it is? Eleven o'clock!"

"I think you'd better go down. I'll follow in a minute," said Eddie. Owen grinned broadly. "Yeah. Nice strip show." He winked. "See you downstairs." Eddie swore to himself. Trust his sister to get in the way at a critical moment. He was sure that Owen had been interested, at least in a lighthearted way. Before he followed Owen, he heard Sarah's voice raised in anger. She was having a go at him. "...And then I bloody find you here. I told Eddie where I was going. He didn't tell you, did he?" Owen raised his eyebrows. "Calm down. Have you any idea what you look like when you go off like this?"

"When I what?"

"Lose your temper. As a matter of fact Eddie did tell me. You know what I think of that stinking place. I told you before that I would never go there again. On top of that, when I knew you were meeting those two zombies I decided I would be better for a chat with Eddie." During this, Sarah's face was gradually suffused with crimson. "All right, if you prefer Eddie's company to mine you can fucking have it!"

"Sarah!" Mrs. Daykyn's voice, although softly spoken, cut through the tirade like a knife.. "There is no need to behave like a harridan. There might be faults on both sides, but you will solve nothing like this." Sarah seemed instantly subdued, but Eddie's knowing eye could see that she was far from composed. "Sorry, Mummy," she said. Her lips were frozen in a tight line.

"I think perhaps I'd better go," said Owen. "I think that might be best, Owen," agreed Mrs. Daykyn, "for tonight. It is bedtime anyway, for Eddie. He has to be at school in the morning." Sarah took a proprietorial hold on Owen's right hand and led him out of the room. "I'll get ready for bed, then, Mum," said Eddie, who had arrived on the scene. "I didn't know Owen was here." His mother's words were not quite a criticism, but they demanded explanation. "You were watching telly when he got here. I invited him up to my room. I was doing my homework."

"That would have been very stimulating for him, I'm sure." If anyone else had said that, he would have said it was sarcasm. It was sarcasm. "We had a long talk about poetry and books, and stuff," explained Eddie, "as soon as I'd finished my homework. The time just went." His mother gave him a smile, in which there was still a hint of rebuke. "I'm glad you finished it, dear. I'll bring you a hot drink when you're in bed." Eddie was glad Owen didn't hear his mother say that. She was still inclined to treat him as a child. "Okay, thanks Mum," he said. "I won't be long." As he went into the hallway and up the stairs he could hear Sarah and Owen talking – Sarah mostly. She was over her tantrum, but she seemed to be laying the law down. Poor Owen, he thought.

Eddie was sure Owen's relationship with Sarah couldn't last much longer. He loved greeting him at the door, having him in the house. His heart always flipped over when he saw Owen's ready smile. The conspiratorial wink and smile he had given Eddie since their evening in his room seemed to Eddie to bind them ever closer together. It seemed to be reserved for him alone. Owen's face contained a wealth of quiet humor, and a depth of emotion lay behind his eyes, he was sure, and he was convinced in his heart that he was the one to release it. It was wrong that Owen was being used as Sarah's passing fancy. Owen had started to bring books for Eddie to read. They were always to Eddie's taste. It was as though he could read Eddie as easily as the books. When he was together with Owen and Sarah, the conversation between the two of them would become animated, leaving Sarah sidelined, to her great annoyance. "Anyone would think you came to see Eddie, not me," she exclaimed petulantly on one occasion. Then he had given

Eddie that conspiratorial wink and smile that seemed to be linked together. Sarah and Eddie's next gym competition was some forty miles from home. Their dub was one of four in contention. Owen had no commitments of his own, except his Saturday morning training session. He had promised to be there as soon afterwards as possible. When the day arrived, cold and foggy, Sarah was worked up as always. "I can't possibly eat any breakfast, Mummy. I'll be sick."

"I'll have hers if she doesn't want it," Eddie said, imagining bacon and eggs being thrown in the bin. "That's just as bad as Sarah having nothing," their mother reproved. "But I'm still hungry. Mummy," he pleaded, little-boy-like. "All right then, be it on your own head." She handed him Sarah's plate. "You had better take a snack with you, in that case," she persisted, turning back to her daughter. "There's no need, Mummy. There's a refreshment bar at the Leisure Center."

"Don't bother about her, Mummy," Eddie interrupted. "Let her starve if she wants to." Sarah turned on him. "I don't need you sticking your oar in either. You have no idea how I feel before an event. My nerves are in shreds. You have no temperament at all." She was almost in tears, and Eddie felt a bit guilty. "You'll be fine, you know, Sis, you always are."

"It's all very well for you, you don't know what it's like to have butterflies in your stomach."

Eddie thought he'd better be careful what he said. He'd got to travel with her and she could be ... well... difficult. He was really very fond of his sister, and admired her gym work greatly, but she was a challenge to be with. He had always found the best thing was to make light of her fears and bolster her confidence.

"No, but I never perform as well as you either."

That mollified her a little.

"Even that isn't true, and you know it," she said, but her tone was gentler.

Their mother took in their little scene with some amusement. It was always much like this before a competition.

"You'd better put a move on anyway, now, or the minibus will be here," she said.

After a fraught journey in the foggy conditions, dad in their gym kit, track-suited, they waited anxiously for the first disciplines of the morning. Sarah started on the beam, and Eddie on parallel bars at the opposite end of the vast gymnasium. They both performed particularly well on those and other apparatus, and the morning flew by. The lunch interval passed and there was no sign of Owen. Sarah was particularly edgy.

"He's not going to turn up. It'll be just like last time, only he's got no excuse now."

Eddie was disappointed, too, that Owen had not arrived. The time came for the competition to resume. Sarah's disappointment turned to anger. Her floor exercise was her best event, and it was due. She looked around for any sign of him before she went on, but he was not there. Her ill temper affected her precision and control and instead of an expected 9+ points she scored 8.2. It was very competent, but well below her best.

The afternoon wore on and as the last change-over was about to take place, Owen arrived, obviously harassed and feeling upset. There was only one discipline to go, Sarah's asymmetric bars and ironically, Eddie's floor exercise, which was far from his favorite. Sarah took a moment to go over to Owen, her face like a thundercloud.

"Where the hell have you been?" she hissed at him. "You promised you'd be here. Now it's all over." The last sentence seemed to encompass more than the gymnastics.

Owen tried to explain.

"There was a serious road accident. I was a witness. I had to talk to the police," he said, but before he had finished she slapped his face and turned away from him to walk haughtily back to the bench to sit with her teammates. There were some amused smiles from the spectators. Many knew Sarah and her long line of boyfriends, and knew that it was time for the next.

"Oh, hell!" Owen said. Eddie went over to him, loosening his chalk-coated hand guards, having just completed his work on the high bar.

"Sis didn't seem very happy," he observed inconsequentially.

"You have a nice turn of phrase," Owen responded with a wry smile. "I think I've blown it ... I've missed her big moment."

Eddie cocked his head on one side and said, smiling cheekily, "You can watch me instead, then. I'm on floor in a few minutes."

Owen couldn't resist Eddie's perky self-assurance. Eddie was rewarded with the trademark wink and smile.

"Right," he said, "I'll enjoy that."

Where Sarah's routine had been accompanied by music, Eddie's was in complete silence. It was almost perfect. As far as it was possible Eddie expressed his secret feelings for Owen through the movements he executed. They were crisp, vital and secure, as always, but this time there was a sinuous elegance to them that had been lacking before. Everything seemed to go right: somersaults, back flips, suppleness and strength movements. To Owen's eyes nothing seemed flawed. The slower movements had a sensuousness that was beyond his experience, though the poise and balance of them he could equate with his own diving skills. The interplay of muscles fascinated him, and some of the somersaults at the apex of their movement seemed even to defy gravity. This was a unique performance from Eddie. None he had ever produced before had been in this class

Those who had been watching the floor exercise had gradually been gripped by its special quality, and by its end were full of that bursting excitement that produces at the end a precarious stillness. How many seconds it lasted was impossible to judge, but as Eddie held his final posture, he felt obliged to maintain it until the silence was broken. It was broken by Sarah, who, watching her brother, instead of another girl in her own event, had been thrilled, and then overjoyed at his inspirational effort. She gave a screamed whoop of delight that echoed into the roof and broke the tension. The hall then erupted with wild, tumultuous, applause.

Owen looked, for a moment, for Sarah then. He hadn't realized that it was her scream that had shattered the silence. When he saw her she was already gazing up at a hunk from one of the other clubs. He wasn't bothered. He had known she would turn her attention to another boy pretty soon anyway. In fact he had counted on it. He was not proud to have used Sarah, knowing her reputation as a man-eater, in order to get to know Eddie, but that was the long and the short of it.

What he did not know, and what no longer mattered, was the fact that, had he not let her down, she might well have really fallen for him. He would never deliberately have hurt her, but, for more than two years, he had noticed her brother coming into the library and wondered how he could ever get to know this attractive boy. Now, he was not sure of his ground, but he guessed he had at least half a chance.

The next day, Sarah announced at breakfast that she and Terry, the hunk of the day before, were an item.

"He's a wonderful gymnast," she gushed, "and really, really nice. He says he likes me too."

"He doesn't know you like we do," commented Eddie, through a mouthful of cereal.

"Pig," responded Sarah, with good humor; nothing, it seemed, could quench her good humor.

"I suppose Owen's off the scene, then, is he?"

"Owen! Don't talk to me about him. There's no comparison between him and Terry."

"I think Owen's brilliant."

"Okay, he's all yours," she said, picking up her cereal bowl and looking at him intently. "That's what you wanted all along wasn't it?"

Eddie began to blush. "What do you mean?" he said.

"Nothing ... but if the cap fits you can wear it."

She went through to the kitchen.

Eddie was stunned. Had his sister guessed how he felt! Oh, well, so what? She was right, after all. It would be a bit of a relief to have someone dose who knew, but not Mummy yet. Definitely not Mummy.

Eddie was preoccupied with the thought all that Sunday morning. Terry had called for Sarah early that afternoon and they had gone off in his car. In the evening, about six-thirty, the doorbell rang and Eddie went to the door. Owen stood there. The smile and the wink were almost routine now, but this evening they seemed even warmer than before.

"Sorry," said Eddie. "Sarah's gone out.""

That's all right," Owen said easily. "It's you I came to see, anyway. D'you fancy seeing the new Matt Damon film at the Metro?"

"Me?" Eddie stood open-mouthed, eyes sparkling and wide. "Wouldn't I just?"

He rushed to tell his mother where he was going. She was pleased, though she raised her eyebrows in surprise. She did feel that Owen was a nice responsible young man to go out with her young son, but it was a bit curious. As he dosed the sitting room door, Eddie stood still a moment and put his palms together in an attitude of prayer.

"Oh dear God," he muttered. "Please say miracles can happen."

He was ready in less than a minute.

Eddie felt sure that Owen would turn out not to be Owen at all, and that he would find himself in a nightmare where nothing was as it seemed. Only when he was comfortably seated in the cinema at Owen's side did the sense of unreality begin to fade. He was finally able to relax and watch the film.

How long Owen's knee had been pressing against his he had no idea.

Was it deliberate?

The pressure didn't decrease.

Could it really be? ...

Perhaps it could."

Oh, please! Oh dear God, please! "

His heart began to thump as his attention was completely diverted from the screen. He tried a little experimental pressure of his own. There was a return knee pressure from Owen. Then he felt Owen reach over under the cover of darkness and take his hand, holding it companionably. No more, only that: but just for the moment it was, to use Eddie's own expression, brilliant. Nothing explicit had been said, or needed to be said, between them.

Over the next week, both of them were very busy. Owen was being coached intensively for a diving contest at the weekend. Eddie had a heavy load of homework, his two regular gym evenings and soccer practice after school.

The following Saturday morning, Eddie caught the bus to the local Leisure Center, the venue for the diving. He bought a spectator's ticket and was soon in his seat. He was early, so there were few spectators or competitors there. After a while, when time was passing ever more slowly, he heard the squeak of trainers coming down the stone steps behind him. He turned. It was Owen, clad in blue shell-suit.

"Hi, Eddie."

The smile and the wink were his exclusively, he knew that now. He grinned broadly in return. Owen dropped down into the seat beside him, dumping his sports bag on the floor.

"I'm glad you're here," he said with simple sincerity.

"I wouldn't have missed watching you for anything," said Eddie.

"Not even a gym contest?" he asked, grinning.

"Well ... maybe," Eddie reflected.

"I'll have to go and change," Owen said, putting a hand on Eddie's knee and squeezing it.

"Okay ... good luck!"

The day passed swiftly for Eddie. Owen was good, really good, obviously in his element. He loved the grace of the divers and their fine bodies, but it was the sheer beauty of Owen's physique in flight that took his breath away. He was forced to admit that a number of other competitors had good style as well, but for him there was only one contender. Owen did have a couple of faulty dives but even those were wonderful in Eddie's eyes. At the end of the day's events Owen had won the teenagers' and the men's individual competitions. The team as a whole had second place.

When Owen stood on the Center block to receive his awards Eddie felt a pride far greater than for himself on the previous Saturday. Later that evening they went to Owen's flat. "Just make yourself comfortable. I'll get some coffee, then cook us a meal," he said as he closed the door behind them. After sitting for a moment Eddie got up and followed Owen into the small kitchen. Owen had his back to him as he dried two mugs. Quietly Eddie slipped his arms around Owen's waist, and, resting his head against Owen's back, pressed his body dose to his friend, feeling his warmth. "I want you," he said. "Bed first?" sighed Owen, the tension in his voice betraying his emotion. He turned and looked down into Eddie's eyes He kissed him firmly on his lips, then long and deeply. Eddie's first real kiss. "Bed first," Eddie agreed.

Owen led Eddie by the hand into the small but tidy bedroom. "Welcome to my parlor," he said. "Said the spider," added Eddie. "I intend to have my wicked way with you."

"Make it very wicked."

"Oooh, me lovely, I intend to," Owen said, in his most menacing piratical tone. He turned, and pulled Eddie gently into his arms. Eddie's response was far from gentle. He put both hands behind Owen's head and brought their lips urgently together, eager to repeat the experience of a minute or so before. He had always assumed the practice of kissing to be overrated, but now he had rapidly revised his opinion. Owen's mouth was a marvel to him. The delicious intimacy of his tongue playing with Owen's was a sheer delight that he could happily indulge for a long time. It was so new an experience. His cock had quickly assumed its maximum proportions and was feeling very uncomfortable. He put a hand down to his crotch to rearrange things and was surprised when Owen seized it. "That dick is for me to deal with now," he said softly, breaking off the kiss and licking into Eddie's ear. "This one's yours," he added, placing the hand firmly on his own crotch.

Eddie was thrilled. The idea that his own body was being claimed as Owen's territory, and at the same time Owen's was being freely given to him to do with as he wanted, was tin amazing concept, and one that he found both moving and arousing.

Owen was stunned that this boy whom he had secretly hoped for, and coveted for so long, was actually here with him and obviously felt as he did. He squatted down, forcing Eddie to release his new-found property, and drew Eddie's denim- dad crotch into his face. He felt the erect prick beneath and took it between his teeth, gnawing the shaft through the fabric.

Eddie so wanted to lift his cock from the restricted position it had assumed, yet he reveled in the sensations being ministered to him. He ruffled Owen's silky hair and then pressed his groin hard against his lover's face. Owen's hands were attempting to release Eddie's belt buckle.

At last he succeeded, and unzipped the fly, wrenching Eddies jeans to his ankles. Eddie was wearing only the briefest of cotton underwear, but it held his sex firmly imprisoned.

Owen continued to gnaw at the stiffness, driving Eddie into a lustful frenzy in which the boy attempted vainly to force his cock down Owen's throat. Owen maintained this torment impossibly long and to his amazement Eddie's body stiffened and his orgasm exploded in spasm after spasm of violent eruptions, wetting the front of the thin white doth. Owen, judging rightly that he was Eddie's first true sexual partner, sucked into his mouth as much of the semen through the fabric as he could. This was Eddie's first offering to a lover and it tasted simultaneously sweet and bitter.

As Owen sucked in Eddie's cum, the lad looked on amazed.

"Oh god oh god oh god," he murmured in gratitude for the gift bestowed on him. It didn't seem profane. Everything he and Owen were doing together was a miracle, the impossible miracle he'd prayed for, sometimes flippantly, sometimes with deep earnestness.

Owen heard the murmured words and looked up. Eddie's eyes were dosed. Owen grasped what this first moment meant to Eddie. He stood, kissed him on the forehead, and then sat on the bed, taking Eddie down with him. They stretched out and Owen slowly undressed the boy beside him. Eddie was, for the moment, relaxed as Owen raised the rugby-style shirt from his waist. The gym kit had never allowed a sight of Eddie's torso, although the leotard top had been dose-fitting enough. A recollection of Eddie in his blue leotard and white gym shorts flitted across his mind. His still-aching cock twitched at the memory. The body beneath had obviously been firm and well-muscled for his age. Since that day he had dreamed of having Eddie's powerful young thighs wrapped around his waist as he fucked deeply into his buttocks.

Now that the moment might be drawing near, how would Eddie react? He was a virgin and vulnerable. While Owen had no intention of betraying Eddie's love in the future, he worried that Eddie might not want to go that far.

Thrusting his doubts away, he pushed the shirt hem up to Eddie's armpits and left it there. He ran the palms of his hands over the taut belly. He almost worshiped him in what he did. Eddie's body was even firmer, more aggressively defined than his own. He was proud of his own musculature, but here was hardly any hint of fat at all. Eddie's lat muscles, too, were well developed and the pecs were outstanding.

Owen had expected to see tiny little nipples surmounting Eddie's pectoral edge, but they were surprisingly large in diameter, the nub in the centers rigid and pronounced. He gripped each between a thumb and forefinger and rolled them back and forth. Eddie moaned, his eyes dosing, and his mouth a round "O.' As Owen explored Eddie, the lad felt himself almost drifting on a sensual sea. His penis stiffened again, flipping up and over to lie on his abdomen, occasionally moving as though with a nervous tic. The foreskin was ample, due to the frequent massage Eddie had been in the habit of giving it.

Owen was like a child in a sweet shop. He did not know what to sample first. Every part of Eddie, every tiny discovery, made his spirit soar and his cock thrill. He lavished his kisses on every part of him. Yet he also felt protective of his young partner. He knew he would enjoy rough sex with Eddie, but for the present he really wanted to fondle, caress and savor every glorious inch of him. He arrived at the teen's ample bush, crowning and surrounding a cock and balls of which no-one would need to be ashamed. He licked upwards from the base of Eddie's rigid penis.

Eddie had long fostered a secret desire to have another boy's cock in his mouth, but, apart from betraying his sexuality, the act would have totally destroyed his masculine credibility. Rightly or wrongly, he did not see the two issues as the same thing. When he realized what Owen was going to do, he was overwhelmed that a young man, so obviously masculine, even if he were gay, would do this for him. He did not, for the moment, consider that Owen's desires might be similar to his own. He felt Owen's tongue paint the sides of his cock with saliva, giving them coat after coat. Then Owen pulled back the foreskin, tickling the exposed and sensitive lining with his inquisitive tongue. Its tip advanced to the rim of the glans and circled it with fluttering strokes,

Eddie writhing with pleasure. He thought that nothing in his life so far had been so marvelous. Still pulling back the foreskin tightly, Owen tongued a slow line from the base of Eddie's cock along the urethral line through its most sensitive area to the very tip, where he probed the piss-slit.

Eddie was nearly beside himself with the exquisite torment and he beat on the bed with his fists, at the same time as he surrendered himself to more and more of the same. Owen suddenly took in the desired object, impaling his mouth and throat on it in one movement. Eddie could feel Owen's lips down at the very base of his dick striving to press it ever deeper into his throat. Owen repeated this a number of times and then abandoned it, licking the balls and taking them into his mouth. He swirled them around and then, holding them firmly behind his teeth, began to draw his head away.

Owen heard Eddie's protests, but he maintained the tension and slapped the cock in front of his nose with the flat of a hand.

"Ow ... oh, oh ... I'm coming again, it's – "

Owen pulled back even harder, hauling the beating prick into an upright position, and the second creamy offering jetted into the air before spattering over Owen's face and hair.

When all was still, Owen released the imprisoned spheres and the still-erect cock sprang back to slap against the flat belly. Eddie raised his head and saw Owen's bespattered face. Owen grinned, and massaged the cream on his hair into his scalp like hair cream, and then into his face, finally putting cum-coated fingers between his lips and sucking them dean.

"Now lick my face dean," he ordered.

Eddie hesitated. "Come on," insisted Owen, "it's your spunk all over my face, clean it off." Tentatively Eddie did as he'd been told, and found the taste not unpleasant. "Anything to oblige," he said when he had made a thorough job of it. He found what he had done, for some reason, had kept him hard throughout. He was astonished at himself. Owen was well pleased at the result. "There's enough stored away in there," he said, cupping Eddie's balls in his right hand, "to last all night." Eddie glanced at the watch on his wrist. "Damn!" he said. "It's gone ten o'clock already. I'll have to go. Owen looked at him, thinking for a moment.

"Do you want to go, yet?" Eddie's face showed his incredulity at the question. "Of course not!" he protested. "Ring your mum and tell her the diving finished late, and you haven't eaten yet. Say I'm getting a meal ready, and ask if you can sleep over, here. You could ask if you might spend tomorrow with me too. We could go to Cheddar Gorge or somewhere." He grabbed his crotch and rubbed it lasciviously. "I'm sure we can find something to do!" Eddie grinned. "You're so devious," he accused. "You're leading me astray!"

"Yep," agreed Owen, "that's about the truth of it."

"All right, I will ... if you'll take that bloody gear off. Only you've got to do a strip routine for me, now." There was a moment's silence. "You don't want much, do you?"

"You said your body was mine...." Owen pulled off Eddie's trainers, followed by the jeans and briefs from about his ankles, with a flourish. "You're not going to need these for a while," he said flinging them across the room. "Now, get that shirt off, and phone your mum while I prepare something to eat. Then I'll show you a strip." Eddie was surprised how quickly his mother agreed to his staying out. He knew that, at sixteen, she couldn't actually prevent him. Nevertheless, he wouldn't have gone against her wishes over something like this. "Hi, Mum? "

"You "re a bit late aren't you?"

"Sorry, Mum, I'm at Owen's "OH, good. How soon will you be in?
"

"Well, I was wondering ...the competition finished a bit late and Owen's only just started to get something to eat "OH?"

"Well, would you mind if 1 have a "sleep over' here at Owen's?"

"A "sleep over. " Well, what does Oxoen say about that? Eh? What did you say? Oh, yes, I'll tell him. Sorry dear, that was Sarah. She wants a word. She's going up to her room to take over the call. "Now, dear, I don't mind at all your staying over with Owen. Just don't make a nuisance of yourself "I won't, Mum. See you tomorrow evening "Evening? " Click. The phone in Sarah's room had been picked up. "Is that okay? Owen says, if you "re all right with it we might go to Cheddar Gorge in his car "OH, I see. Well... what I've already said ... don't be a nuisance"

"I promise, Mum "See you tomorrow night, then, Yeah. Goodnight, God bless "God bless you, love. " Click. "Cheddar Gorge? Owen never drove me anywhere, except round the bend "Where you've stayed ever since. You just didn't know how to treat him "I'm sure you do! "

"And what's that supposed to mean, Sis? "

"You know "The hell I do!'' "Come on, Shrimp - we both know. A "sleep over, " huh? "

"Yeah, so?"

"Not much sleep I'll bet. You "re two of a kind, Shrimp. Enjoy your "sleep over. " 1 mean that. Good night, Shrimp" "Night, Sis. Hey, I'm glad you know."

"Enjoy. Goodnight Click Eddie was simply dumbfounded. His sister really did know. She had said earlier, "If the cap fits." She needed no telling about Owen, either. It must have been deduction on her part. She'd been great about it, too. He went through to the kitchen where Owen was making omelets over the gas cooker, and microchips were cooking in the microwave. "How'd it go?"

"No problem, but I'm not to make a nuisance of myself."

"You do, I'll put you across my knee." Eddie came and pressed himself against Owen's back, grabbing Owen's crotch with both hands and grinding himself into Owen's arse. "Is that a promise?" Owen half turned and kissed Eddie's brow, then he turned his attention back to cooking "Not much of a meal, I'm afraid," Owen said. "It's fine. I'm not that hungry, anyway."

"Sit over there on that stool. I want to look at you." Eddie skipped over to the high stool and sat on it. He spread his legs wide, wearing only a broad grin. His cock was already firmly at attention, and his balls hanging pendulously beneath. "Boy," said Owen, "but you are beautiful."

"When do I get my strip show?"

"After we've eaten."

"You haven't washed your face, have you?" Eddie accused. "No need. You did." Eddie giggled. Owen lifted the huge folded omelet from the king-sized pan and put it on to one of two plates warming on the grid over the cooker. He sliced it into halves and slipped half onto the other plate. Once garnished with chips he put both plates on the breakfast bar. "Eat up, you're going to need the energy," Owen advised. "You "re the old man in this partnership," rejoined Eddie. "You'll regret that."

"Do you keep these promises?"

"You'll see." Eddie opened his eyes wide in mock horror, then; "I can't wait," he said, stuffing his mouth with chips. Eating occupied them for a while.

When they had finished and had had a cold milk drink, Eddie was shooed to the bedroom.

"I'll wash the pots in the morning. You go and get on the bed and wait. I'll only be a jiffy."

Eddie did as he was bidden. He played with his dick and wondered just how many times he could come successively. Perhaps he was due to find out.

Then he heard the strains of some classic big-band music with a powerful beat coming from the speakers in the next room. He watched the open doorway expectantly. First a leather-covered hand appeared, followed by a strong muscular arm, and the strip was in progress. In the brief interval, Owen had changed into a leather outfit of cap, briefs, jacket and boots.

Does Owen ever go out dressed like that?

It was a professional performance and Eddie had to let go of his cock or he would have come prematurely. Owen was sensational. When the music ended and he was naked he walked over to the bed and put two fingers in Eddie's mouth.

Eddie sucked those two fingers. They were part of Owen; his Owen. Owen had given his body to him, had given himself to him. It was beyond his grasp that anyone would want to do that for him. I'm his too. Yes, completely. He continued to enjoy the fingers, even when they probed deeper and he gagged a little. His compliance encouraged

Owen who pressed his stiff cock down to Eddie's lips. Owen wasn't aware that this was Eddie's dream made real.

Eddie saw his lover's penis approach his lips, the foreskin almost totally peeled back, so powerful was the erection. His tongue stretched forward to lick the slit which was slightly open. He plunged the tip of his tongue into it as far as he could. Owen gasped and his body shuddered, but he kept his cock where it was. Eddie repeated the action to the accompaniment of a moan from Owen. Then he could resist his impulses no longer and he moved his head forward to take the shiny head into his mouth. He wrapped his tongue around it, lapped at it and tickled his tongue under it, to an accompaniment of noises and trembling from Owen. He began to realize the power given to him. He found what actions brought corresponding reactions, although they were never exactly the same. He found he could lick and suck further and further down the long shaft. He discovered for himself that by using a swallowing action he could take it beyond the soft palette into his throat without gagging too much. He didn't, at first, succeed in taking every last inch, but he could leave that a while.

One should have goals in life.

He chuckled around his mouthful and began to cough as a result. Owen, anxious for a moment, reluctantly withdrew.

"No, no," Eddie almost cried, "I want it. It's mine!"

"Of course it is," Owen soothed, feeding it back to him. "Of course it is."

Without taking it from him again, Owen carefully lay in the 69 position at Eddie's side and took Eddie's straining prick in his mouth.

Now Owen was glad that it had been nearly two years since he had last had sex with a partner. He was also glad that, two HIV tests later, he was certain that he was dear, for Eddie. He took Eddie's prick straight down his throat.

Eddie, striving manfully as well, found it much easier in this position and he found he was able to press his lips into Owen's wiry blond bush. He was immensely proud of himself. His success went directly to his groin. This was Owen's cock down his throat, the boy he had yearned for such a long time. He had his hands on the back of Owen's thighs, stroking their smoothness.

Owen had not had an orgasm for twenty-four hours. He was reaching that point now. He disengaged his mouth momentarily.

"I'm so dose. Just wank me, or you'll get my load in your mouth."

He was a little surprised, but immensely pleased, that instead of taking the hint, Eddie quickened the movements of his head. At once he returned to Eddie's succulent shaft and worked all his skill on it, coupling the action with thrusts of his pelvis, driving his cock into Eddie's throat. And he came, with a violence born of an overwhelming desire, such he had never felt for any other person. Wave after wave flooded from him into Eddie's mouth as the lad strove to swallow every last drop. Even a more experienced partner would have had problems. Eddie found it oozing from the comers of his mouth and over his bottom lip to drip down his chin. He mentally compared the

remembered taste of his own with Owen's. Owen's was sharper, he decided, less sweet, but he loved its underlying muskiness. He chuckled again around his meaty mouthful, that his thoughts ran like those of a wine connoisseur. The taste got to him, and he felt his own balls tighten, his body stiffening in its own climax. Eddie had less difficulty than Owen. It was, after all, Eddie's third time in a short period, and Owen was not a novice. Both satisfied, for the moment, Owen swung round and stretched himself out beside Eddie. He kissed him deeply, with a gratitude and respect that is only to be found in love. Both had nurtured this love and lust for two years and its realization did not disappoint. They kissed, fondled, examined, explored, both finding joy and awe in one another. Before long both were homily poised for further journeys into their unknown. "I want you to fuck me," Eddie whispered into Owen's ear, while he licked its convolutions. Owen's cock leapt, but his head stayed cool. "It'll hurt you, you know?"

"So I've heard. But that's only the first time, isn't it?"

"Well, it gets less painful as you get used to it, but I've heard that a few people never do."

"So, are there any pluses?"

"There are for me, doing it."

"That's enough reason, then." Owen kissed the tip of his nose. "7 get a great thrill out of being fucked."

"You do?!"

"Why so surprised?"

"I just thought ... well, you know ... that you'd be a top man."

"My body's yours and yours is mine, remember?" Eddie hugged Owen hard. "I'm glad we got together at last"

"Ditto."

"You really like being fucked, then?"

"Very much. The rougher the better, actually."

"Wow! If you like it, then I know I will ... eventually, anyway."

"Do you want to try now?"

"Please!"

A few minutes later there was a stifled squeal, as the end of Owen's cock opened wide Eddie's tight little rosebud. "Fuckin' hell!" Eddie lay on his back with his legs slung over Owen's broad shoulders, his eyes staring widely up into Owen's. "It does bloody hurt! But, yeah, there's something else as well. Oh, oh damn, I'm coming again!" His cock discharged its fourth load over them both. "Do you think I'm going to be a natural at this?" he asked Owen, displaying his cheekiest smile. "I'd say you're a sexual gymnast, in the making,"

"Okay, get that big thing swimming up my channel then, Aquachamp" Owen thrust in deeply, evoking another howl, but Eddie's cock still stood proud. Owen gripped and squeezed it. "You're insatiable."

"Do "you think you can keep pace with me, big boy?"

"Well, that, Edward, you are about to find out!"

ONE STICKY SUMMER
Nathan Foster

"...Then he went back to my cock, shiny now with his saliva and twitching madly under the ministrations of his hot mouth and tongue. We had known each other at school but our orbits didn't coincide very much. He was two years younger than I and as if that weren't a big enough boundary, he was the freak and I was the fag. The fact that I was a fag was common knowledge in the school before I had fully realized myself that it was true. There were occasional taunts along those lines but in our liberal suburb, frankly, not many of the kids were bothered. The freak had a slightly harder time of it.

His name was Chris and he was bald. Not just on his head but everywhere. There had been some kind of accident – knocked over by a motorbike or something. Nothing broken, nothing damaged, he was simply knocked out. Two hours later and he was waking up in hospital with the first few clumps of the hair on his head already falling out. This happened when he was seven years old. The doctors told him it was some kind of shock reaction and for the first few weeks they tried to maintain that it would not be permanent. You might guess from my intimate knowledge of the affair that Chris and I did not remain total strangers!

Even though the accident happened when he was so young, the hair on his head never grew back and (I knew this from the malicious talk of his peers) it never began to grow anywhere else when the right time came. It was the talk of the school for the couple of years during which Chris and his classmates were going through puberty. I listened with a fascinated interest to the younger kids' speculations about him and slowly became completely intrigued by this young, smooth boy. By the time I was sixteen, I had a fully developed fantasy life featuring Chris as the main attraction and by the time I left school at eighteen, I knew with a sinking, gut-emptying feeling that they would remain forever fantasies. I had tried. Throughout school I had made little movements in words and position towards Chris, I had made myself available to be talked to, I had even followed him home one night, but it didn't work. For whatever reasons Chris wasn't picking up on it and there was no way, in the middle of my own insecurities about growing up gay, that I was going to push any harder than that.

It wasn't until I got to college that I came out properly. I mean not just came out, but came out of myself. I discovered that I could dance and took myself clubbing at every opportunity. I discovered that if you were eighteen, a good dancer and had half a body, the men would be pawing you all night at most of the fast-paced London dubs that I was frequenting. Life exploded around me. My cock saw action in earnest for the first time that year. Certainly it saw more action than my brain.

By the time I was nineteen and starting my second year at college, bad grades and terminal exhaustion forced me to slow down a little to take stock. I still went out, but I was less likely to annoy my house-mates by interrupting their breakfasts introducing them to the latest fuck-buddy who they and I would never see again. More often than not I would come home from a dub at two in the morning rather than five, and in those lonely moments before dawn, with the buzz of heavy-duty techno still throbbing inside me I would bring myself off to those old fantasies of the boy with no hair.

In my head, we were still at school. He knelt before me in the showers after football and engulfed my cock with his mouth. He sat beside me in class and reached over, took my hand and placed it on his crotch and through his thin school trousers I would bring him off to a suppressed and hidden orgasm. I followed him home a thousand times in my dreams and watched him through his bedroom window as he undressed and then unknowingly gave me a show as he jerked off in front of the mirror and fingered his own ass. In my dreams! It was good, I figured, to have a person like that in the past, someone whose image would never tarnish with time and who would always be able to produce a hard cock in my hand.

You'll have guessed that we did meet again. It happened towards the end of my second year at college, London was heating up ready for a sticky summer and term was winding down. It was a gay dub, the steam had been rising off the dance floor all night, the club was packed with "boyz' naked from the waist up, shining in the oppressive heat. I was on the main floor, dancing on stage in fact with a group of friends, Chris was in the chilling lounge upstairs, but there was a window in that bar which looked down on us and there he was. We both did a double take. There was no doubting it though and I jumped off the stage and ran, or rather pushed quickly, through the dance floor and found the stairs. By the time I reached the doorway of the upstairs lounge he was standing up on his toes at the far end of the room trying to see over heads to the door. When he saw me I stopped, and he walked directly to me in the doorway, looked me straight in the face and said, without missing a beat, "I was in love with you at school." It seemed disingenuous to repeat his words back to him but I could have done.

The slightly weedy boy that I had known was grown up. He was not much taller but his body was now chicken-muscled and hard. His bearing was more upright and spoke of a confidence that he hadn't had at school. He had added a single silver hoop to one ear. His features, which had always been narrow and sharp, slightly elfin, were the same but somehow broader, deeper and richer. His eyes were the same, hazel with flecks of gold, leaf-shaped and with the blackest pupils. And his skin, still that alabaster smooth patina, not a hair in sight on his cheek, his arms, his lip or his head. I sucked in this revitalized image of my dream lover.

"Hazel with flecks of gold." I said. Until then we had been staring at each other intensely but my odd remark, born out of shock more than thought, brought the lopsided smile to this face it seemed I had always loved.

"What?" he asked, and the amused question hung on his face.

"Your eyes, sorry your eyes, hazel with flecks of gold." I might as well have said, "I was in love with you too at school, and afterwards and still now."

"You remembered the color of my eyes...?" He was astonished and obviously shocked. "...I remembered that you had the nicest hair in the school," he said, and as he remarked on it, almost involuntarily, he raised his hand as if to touch me. I caught it halfway and placed his long thin fingers in my hair. We fell at each other in seeming slow motion, our mouths opened and we kissed a long, passionate, wet kiss.

We were hungry now but it seemed that both of us had been starving for years. His tongue in my mouth was the most erotic sensation I had ever felt. But there was one more to come. I cupped his face in my hand, pulling his head further towards mine, and for the first time I felt that gorgeous skin. His cheek was smooth, but not smooth like after a good shave, his face had the smoothness of skin that had never known hair. His jaw was smooth like a boy's or like one of the few places on the body of anyone else were hair never grows, where the skin has never been ruptured by follicles and never tickled by even the softest, downy hair. Touching his clear, dean skin was, and remains, the most erotic thing I have ever felt.

We were shaken out of our dream kiss by other dubbers trying to get into the chilling lounge and we had to move; both of us were grinning inanely, like schoolboys I suppose. We moved to where Chris had been sitting when we spotted each other. We sat on the soft couch overlooking the main dance floor and through the soundproof glass we watched the heat of summer take hold of the revelers beneath us and basked in a heat of our own. We talked of school, of course, we talked of the people we had known. I discovered from him that several people I knew had come out since leaving school and home behind them.

One of the many stored-up fantasies that Chris' image had provided over the years since school was fulfilled right there in the dub. Amongst our kisses and our conversation he took hold of my wrist and guided my hand to his groin. I squeezed and massaged what seemed to be a nice-sized handful of cock through well-worn denim. It was furtive and took a long time since we were both aware of the crowd pressing in around us. I even had to wave to my friends on the podium below at one point, who had noticed us through the window, but eventually his head fell back against my shoulder and his whole fragile frame shuddered. With people all around us I slipped my hand under the waistband of his jeans, not far enough to confirm the school rumors, I wanted to save that for later. I delved just far enough to scoop some of his cum off his belly with my thumb and lift it to his lips and then to mine.

It became dear on the way home that he had lost none of his impish charm and good humor. He was full of jokes and turned out to be quite a giggler, which I love. Under his trademark baseball cap which went on as soon as we left the dub, his face had a heart-rending way of crinkling up with mock hurt whenever a joke was made at his expense and he looked like a puppy who had just had his paws trodden on. I had never felt so in love as I did on the top deck of the night bus home that night, the lights of London flashing past outside, a laughing, happy-go-lucky, (and did I mention sexy as fuck) old-new friend beside me.

We couldn't stop laughing and talking and I swear our good humor must have woken the neighbors and had them curse the student drunks next door. As soon as we stumbled up the stairs of my shared house to the top floor room, where I had so often fantasized this moment, the smiles on both our faces faded into the significance of what we were going to do. For the first time in my over-sexed and over-indulgent life, I swear I thought about saying "we don't have to do it if you don't want to.' That was how significant it felt.

On the bed, his slender form lying on top of me, his arms crossed on my chest, we stared at each other for the longest time; there was a lot to take in. Our thoughts obviously began to coincide though as I felt the hardness of his cock beginning to strain down to meet mine pressing up. The faintest of movements turned into a slow grinding and eventually we were gripping each other firmly at the waist and ass, locking our hips together and drilling furiously at the other's crotch while we licked, bit and sucked on each other's faces. My clothes came off in a hurry.

Chris ripped the seam on my T-shirt as he yanked it free of my head and then bowed to suckle on my nipple. His thin shoulders and firm back felt like cream under my fingers. He moved swiftly down my body, running his tongue over the ridges of my stomach and lapping my navel. He needed just the least of help with the stiff button of my jeans before tugging them off and casting them aside, underwear followed. He fell to his knees by the side of the bed, parted my knees and settled in between, his mouth engulfed my dick.

Another fantasy check box was ticked as I finally allowed my hands to venture onto his head and hold his mouth in place. His scalp was smooth as, I don't know, glass, silk, satin... Really I find it impossible to describe. Every sinew in his neck, the pulse at his temple, the veins on his head, all of it was there to be touched and explored as his mouth wrapped itself around my engorged cock and slobbered and sucked on it. He seemed inexperienced and I found I was glad about that. I guided his face every now and then, away from my cock and down between my legs to the hard ridge below my balls, then I would really pull his head hard towards me, squashing his perfect lips and nose into my most tender and intimate place. Then back to my cock, shiny now with his saliva and twitching madly under the ministrations of his hot mouth and tongue.

When eventually I had to push him aside for fear of coming without him he stood up and just looked at me. He was still fully clothed and simply stood there looking at my naked body. I had never felt comfortable being looked at naked until then. Chris began to undress. His top, already tight enough to reveal every contour underneath, came off first and as he crossed his arms above his head I saw the first of what I wanted to see. His nipples were small and a bit boyish but his maturity was belied by their dark brown coloring. The small dark ovals stood out against and accentuated the plane of his chest and stomach, but it was still the absence of hair that was most startling and most erotic. I realized then how few men actually have no hair at all on their chests, if only a faint downy covering that softens lines and muscles. How many men do not have even the faintest trace of a line of hair to the navel, often tantalizing when seen on a bare-chested man because it seems to beckon to what is hidden beneath the belt where it disappears from view; its absence was more of a tum-on still.

I began stroking the head of my cock gently as Chris began to unbutton those jeans. When eventually he stood naked, I could do nothing but stare, kindly I hope, for he had clearly lost a little of the confidence I had seen earlier. How dreadful I realized it must be to have to worry each time he undressed for a man if they would be turned off, or even laugh, at his nudity. And nude he was. I have never seen anyone look so vulnerable and raw. His lack of hair gave new meaning to the words naked and nude. Armpits, groin, chest and legs – everywhere where there should have been something, even a slight protective fuzz, there was nothing. I have seen a shaved cock and balls before but always there had been a slight shadow or a roughness to the skin where it had been scraped by a razor. On Chris there was nothing – just glorious, fabulous skin.

I beckoned him to me and he sank into my arms; he felt small and delicate as we held each other naked for the first time, our cocks pressed hard against each other, his smooth form melting into mine. We rolled over and with him on his back I began to lick him, allowing my tongue to savor the uninterrupted glide over his flawless body. His nipples rose to points when I sucked them; his arms stretched back when I ran the broad flat of my tongue along his armpits; his back arched up from the bed as I ran my tongue from his stomach down over his exposed pubic mound and began licking and sucking at the base of his cock and on the loose flesh of his ball sac.

I pushed his legs up, towards his chest and plunged my tongue along the crack of his upturned ass. He squealed with delight, but also I realized, with surprise. This was the first time someone had done this to him and he, like me the first time, hadn't realized it was ever done let alone enjoyed. He gasped as my tongue pushed past his outer ring and squirmed just a little way inside him. He liked it. He began pawing at his ass cheeks and pulling them further apart so I could go deeper and deeper, poking my tongue far past the hairless pucker of his ass.

He was wriggling on the bed now like a little boy being tickled, agonized by the excitement my mouth was rendering in his backside. I had to stop, my jaw ached, but I replaced my tongue with a finger and slowly drilled it up inside him. He began panting and was almost uncontrollable when I seized his cock with the other hand and began to squeeze it and rub it. His cock was perfect, not too long, nicely rounded and with a head the color and shape of a ripe plum.

When he came, he screamed – an enormous whole-hearted yell of release. It probably woke the whole house but I didn't care. His body heaved once, tense for three seconds as cum pumped out of his cock and his ass muscles contracted and pulsed around my finger. When he flopped back to the bed I moved on top of him, wanning his wet cock with my ass, and I jerked off until I came over his chest. The last thing I remember before we both lapsed into unconsciousness was helping him to smear his cum and mine over that smooth, perfect, edible torso.

By the time we woke up it was late in the morning and I could tell by the blanket of silence over the house that all my house-mates were already out at college. Chris and I showered maintaining the silence. We simply held each other, his smooth head resting on my neck, the water splashing down over us and making a small lake where our chests and arms met. I ran my hands over his body, feeling again, as if to make sure, that this was the same Chris whose body I had lusted over for so many years. The nude skin and smoothly covered muscle reassured me that it was. We kissed, allowing the hot water to fall in and out of our open mouths.

We didn't get as far as breakfast. We came down the stairs naked, confident in the knowledge of everyone else's schedules. I walked down the stairs behind my new lover watching the skin, the beautiful skin, flickering and glowing in front of me. In the kitchen I started to make coffee but he was on his knees again, sucking on my rising cock, his upturned face gazing intently into mine while the width of my dick stretched his lips thin and taught. I grabbed the work surface for support and allowed him to swallow his way up and down my shaft.

The idea struck me out of nowhere, or perhaps I had fantasized it years ago and it was waking in me again now. With my cock still plugged into his mouth, I reached into one of the cabinet behind me and took out a green bottle, unstopped it and began pouring it from some height over Chris as he knelt on the floor. A stream of Extra Virgin Olive Oil, spilled like gold out of the bottle and cascaded over his head, ran over his face and then onto my cock, it trickled over his shoulders and neck and ran in sheets downwards across his chest and into his groin. Every inch of his body was covered, he shone like a saint, anointed and holy.

As the last few drops dribbled onto his head I slid down his body until we were face to face, pressed him backwards and ended up full length on top of him on the hard kitchen floor. I slid my body over his, allowing my cock to ride up as far as his nipples, wiping the sheen of oil around his body with my rigid dick.

The sensation was beyond words and I was soon lifting his legs high over my shoulders, taking a good aim and slowly but in one long movement entering him to the hilt. His open mouth gaped soundlessly as the oil smoothed my entry into his ass, his arms flailed at his side and his hips pressed up to meet my crotch. I felt his ass give and finally I was buried deep in his bowels, connected forever. I took his virginity that morning on the kitchen floor and, as I shafted his slick, hairless ass and twisted his cock with my oily fist, the look on his face was a wordless commitment that we have maintained for the seven years since.

LESSONS IN LUST
Daniel Miller

From the minute I saw him, I could tell that the new guy in my boarding house had come to San Francisco to get laid. Not that he was any different than three-quarters of the men moving into the city that summer of 1977. I'd left my own small-town closet only the year before and plunged into an all- male world of bars, beds, and bathhouses. It looked like Craig, as he'd introduced himself the day he'd moved in, was on a similar journey of sexual self-discovery.

For about a week I watched him come and go from the room next to mine. Every night he went out wearing tight new bell- bottoms, soft silk shirts open to the waist, and gold neck chains that glittered against his mat of dusky chest hair. I figured he'd do okay, with his tall, toned body, chiseled face, and longish dark hair. Hell, the men downtown would probably be lining up to get a shot at that tight, narrow ass.

But something seemed to be wrong. Though he stayed out at least three or four hours every night, he always came home alone, locked his door, and played disco records until a little before midnight. After that his light would go out. No matter how hard I listened through the thin wall we shared, I couldn't even hear him jacking off.

I wasn't sure what to think. Either Craig preferred to get his horn blown in the park and spend the evening alone, or he was striking out big time. It seemed hard to believe, but it had also taken me a while to get into the swing of things, so to speak. Maybe Craig needed someone to show him around – someone who knew how the game really worked. Luckily, I knew the perfect guy for the job.

The next night, I waited around while he went through his usual ritual of showering and dressing up. This time, though, I didn't plan to just let him walk past my room. I cracked my door open, crawled up on the bed wearing only a T-shirt, and spread my legs wide open. The minute I heard him step into the hall, I curled my fingers around my cock. A few practiced tugs and it sprang up hard and ready. I began to slide my fist up and down its rigid length, feeling the plump veins pulse with a familiar, growing need.

Craig's footfalls grew louder as he approached my room. I stepped up the pressure on my shaft, squeezing and kneading my horny flesh. As I'd expected, he stopped walking and sucked in a breath the minute he passed my open door.

For a long time he just stood there with his mouth hanging open, his wide eyes riveted to my cock. When I raised my eyes to meet his, he blushed and stepped hastily backward. "Oh, sorry," he stammered. "Your door must've popped open." Slowing my hand-strokes, I looked up at him and grinned. "No, it's OK," I said. "You can leave it open. Or if you want, you can come on in and close it behind you."

Though I did it for his benefit, Craig looked a little disappointed when I shifted my hips and flicked a sheet over myself.

"Come on, man, don't be shy," I prompted. "Remember, you're in San Francisco now."

Despite his obvious nervousness, he walked into my room and kicked the door shut with his heel. Though he tried to hide it with his hands, I saw the swelling mound in the front of his tight pants.

"I guess I did forget for a minute," he said. "The truth is, sometimes I don't really feel like this is the same place I've heard so much about."

"Taking you a while to settle in?" I asked.

"I guess so," he said. "I mean, I go and try to meet people...but I don't know, for some reason they just seem to ignore me."

I sat up in bed, arranging my cock so it could rub against the mattress, keeping it hard and ready. Then I took on a thoughtful expression and nodded slowly. "I think I know what your problem might be, Craig. You're still a virgin, aren't you – with other guys, I mean?"

His cheeks flooded with red, and I could imagine a similar blush spreading over the rest of his body. Under the blanket, hungry tremors rippled through my overheated nuts. "Well...yeah," he finally confessed.

"See? That's your problem. Guys around here can sense when you don't know what you're doing. Turns "em right off. You need to get yourself some real experience, then go back out there. Trust me, they'll be flocking around you."

"You think so?" He brightened.

I flicked the sheet aside to expose the palpitating cylinder between my thighs. I grinned. "Try it and see."

I'd figured that after a long dry spell in the middle of an oasis, Craig wouldn't need an engraved invitation to slurp up my shaft. But I had no idea he'd go as hog-wild as he did. In two seconds flat, he was naked and crouching on my bed, his lips wrapped around my fat cockhead. He wasn't graceful, but what he lacked in technique he made up for in enthusiasm. He hauled me down until my dilated piss-slit collided with his tonsils. To my surprise, he didn't even gag.

"Smooth and steady, Craig," I gasped, sliding my hands through his hair and steadying his head against my crotch. "Just take your time."

"Mmm, yeah," Craig murmured, his mouth stretched so wide around my shaft that I felt, rather than heard his voice as it vibrated against my body. Slowly, he began to respond to the guiding movements of my hands. His savage lunges mellowed into even strokes, and soon he learned to curl his lips around his teeth to avoid shredding my sensitive cockflesh. Before long he also began to alternate shallow sucks with deeper ones that stirred the cores of my balls. Every now and then, his tongue would twist around my shaft and circle my corona, the pointed tip prying the tiny folds of my piss-slit.

"Ungh, yeah, that's the way," I grunted, kneading his scalp with my fingers. Sweat was pouring down my body and filling the crack of my ass as my orgasm built steadily inside me. I was totally focused on what Craig was doing to my prong. I could feel the stark ridges on the roof of his mouth massage my tender length, while the faint stubble on his chin scraped at my balls. My cock shivered in his mouth as it puffed out to what seemed like triple its original size.

Slippery and wet as an eel, his tongue darted over and around the base of my shaft, then slithered back up to the tip. Hot jizz bubbled up in my groin, and this time I pushed his head down harder. My hips pumped up and down, my balls clenched up like twin fists, and I fucked his mouth wildly until I detonated from within.

For a moment, it seemed like another one of those famous earthquakes had hit the Bay. My hips thrust and twitched involuntarily, my ass muscled spasmed, and my juicy fuck-blast doused his throat with liquid heat. There was so much jizz that it boiled out between his parted lips, slopping down his hairy chest and pooling on my sheets. I could see his red cheeks puffing out as my balls surged and I came.

After I'd shot off the last round, I slumped back on my pillow, satisfied and totally burned out. Craig's wet face broke into a proud grin. There was no hiding how much pleasure he'd given me.

"Think I've got the hang of it now?" he asked eagerly.

I patted his cheek. "Buddy, you just graduated Magna Cum Loudly from the University of Cocksucking," I joked. "I'd say you have a bright future ahead of you."

"I hope you're right," he said. "But you know, I'm not sure I'm ready to face the competition just yet. There's still a big part of me that...um...you know, hasn't been tried out yet."

His voice was so innocent that my drained cock stirred on my cum-drenched thigh.

"Is that so? Well, then, I guess you'd better turn over. Can't send my prize pupil out into the world only half-cocked."

Craig scooted around so that his bare rear end was sticking up at me. He tried to help me out by gripping his ass-cheeks in both hands and pulling them open as far as he could. I covered his hands with my palms, forcing him farther apart, baring the raw, pink meat to my lecherous gaze.

I tongued him for a moment, trying to relax him, and he shivered with wonder and pleasure. He whimpered out something about never knowing anything could feel so good. I felt a little sorry, knowing that what I was going to do next wouldn't feel quite so wonderful – not at first, anyway. But we both knew he had to start somewhere.

After I'd licked him nice and wet, I slipped my thick fingers into him one at a time, until the first three were wedged up his ass and the pinky was stretching his tender rim. He was pretty tight down there, but when he twitched and moaned pitifully, I knew he was ready.

"You want it bad, don't you?" I murmured in his ear, my voice as smooth as the silky hair that cushioned his nuts and hole. I knew, because by then I was reaching between his legs and feeling up his growing hard-on and low-hanging sac. Every now and then, I shook my

108

bulbous cockhead against the outside curve of his ass-cheeks. I could feel my pre-cum slippery and thick, paint the quivering flesh there.

"Oh, yeah," Craig whispered, sliding his rear end up and down against the up thrust tip of my rod. "Really bad, man."

My pre-cum acted as a natural lubricant as 1 positioned my prong against his raw hole, then slid about half my cock inside him. It slithered down without a hitch, his ass-canal fitting me as snugly as a foreskin. He was still whining as I started a slow, cautious rhythm in and out of his hole, but he quickly seemed to melt around my cock's spreading heat.

As he opened for me, I stabbed his butt harder. Craig was a quick learner, quickly learning to do with his ass-muscles exactly what he'd done with his throat. He wrung and rubbed me, shaking his hips faster and then slower, chewing my pole with his hole until my balls were two seething pockets of lava.

Release came rapidly, engulfing me. Stars flashed inside my eyelids as I squeezed them shut and let my hot, sticky fluid shower the depths of his bowels. At the same time, I started yanking his cock in my fist, siphoning a precious load of virgin spunk that spattered my wrist and my already soaked bed sheets.

All too soon, it was over. We lay in silence. I opened my eyes to find Craig stretched out beside me with his lips caressing my left tit. A series of post-orgasmic thrills tickled my spine as we started licking each other all over again. Craig cleaned the excited perspiration from every niche of my body, and I slurped cooling cum from his face, chest, and ass-cheeks.

"Think I'm ready for the real world now?" he asked, beaming.

"Not a chance," I said. "I've got a lot more to teach you, and it's gonna take a lot longer than just a couple of hours."

"That's okay," he said, nodding. "I've been out every night this week, and to tell you the truth, I'm a little sick of it. There's a lot to be said for spending a quiet evening at home now and then, don't you think?"

Craig stifled a groan when I took his cock in my fingers, then rubbed it playfully across my upper lip. I was looking forward to showing him how great it felt to blow your load down another man's face, or up his ass. Maybe for our next lesson, I'd take him down to the baths....

"I try not to think," I said, lowering my head to his crotch and tugging at his tight dark coils with my teeth. "I just do."

BLACK GOLD
William Cozad

I was visiting San Francisco and got lost wandering around looking at the "sights." At one point, I found myself in a seedy part of town and was, frankly, a bit scared. I decided to duck into a fairly decent-looking "coffee shop" connected to a Ramada Inn and try to relax and get my bearings.

I sat down on a stool at the counter near the entrance and ordered a cup of coffee and a slice of apple pie.

As I sipped the hot coffee, I looked over at the four boys in the front section. They were black youths, wearing bright, baggy clothes. Three of them were seated and facing the window. The other was standing up and leaning backward against a stool.

I pretended to watch the customers coming and going, but I confess I was really checking out the black boy who was facing my way. Although he wore low-hanging jeans, he showed a big crotch bulge. He was medium height and muscular. His short black hair was shaved up high on the sides. He had soulful brown eyes, a big nose and thick, sensuous lips.

I couldn't even remember the last time I had had sex with a black guy. I'd always admired their naturally muscular bodies and how they were blessed with big dicks, at least the few I'd had.

My balls rumbled when I thought about how I'd like to slide down those baggy jeans and get my mouth on what was obviously a big black dick. But I dismissed the idea, with his buddies around.

I listened to him talk about, how when he lived in Chicago, it was so cold and windy, and how his mother made him pull his jacket up over his head to keep warm. He demonstrated and one of the other guys slapped him on the head. They all laughed.

After they finished their food, three of them left. The one I'd been eyeballing stayed behind and sipped his soda. I stared at his basket and then made eye contact with him.

"What happened to your friends?" I asked.

"My homies? They split for a concert."

"Why aren't you going?"

"Ha! I don't got the twenty bucks for the ticket." I motioned to him and he came closer. I decided to take a chance. "Maybe you could earn the money for the ticket," I said. "How's that?"

"Do you like getting head?" I whispered. "Hell, yeah! Who don't?" He grinned. "Well, I am staying at the St. Francis and I'd love to have you come over with me."

"Really? But...."

"Look, if you let me blow you, I'll spring for the ticket." He studied me for a moment. "Okay. I really wanna go to the concert." He left the restaurant with me and directed me to the hotel. It wasn't that far, but far enough. He was amused that I had gotten lost. "You embarass' to be walkin' with me?"

"Hell, no," I said. "Are you?" He just chuckled at this. "I mean, you're taken me into the St. Frands?"

"Sure, why not? I always act as if it was the most natural thing in the world," I answered, although I did know how to get to the elevators without passing the front desk. Once in the room, I wasted no time. "Go ahead, lay down on the bed," I said. He sprawled out on the bed. I sat down by his legs. I rubbed his crotch and felt his dick. It didn't feel as big as I hoped. Unbuckling his belt and unzipping his fly, I tugged down his jeans. He wore white cotton briefs. His chocolate skin was totally smooth. I sniffed his shorts. I nibbled his dick through the cotton fabric and felt it stiffen. While I peeled down his briefs, his dick was getting harder. Jesus, it was bigger than I thought earlier. It was definitely a grower. Plus, he had plump balls and fuzzy black pubes. I grasped his dick. The shaft was chocolate, but the crown was pink. I swabbed up the clear, sweet pre-cum with my tongue. Slowly stroking his throbbing shaft, I lapped at his balls. I stuffed them into my mouth. His cock swelled to at least nine inches. Looking up at him, I saw him watching me. "Whatchu think?"

"I think this is one nice dick." Still clasping his dick, I wrapped my lips around the crown. I bobbed my head up and down on it while I jacked his shaft, "Oh yeah, that feels good," he sighed. Letting go of his shaft, I deep-throated his dick. It tickled my tonsils, but I managed to take it all the way down to the base. He held my head and guided me in the rhythm that he wanted. His dick got real stiff, despite its size. The few humongous cocks I'd had before were rubbery. Not this one, it was totally hard. He thrust upwards and battered my tonsils. "Oh yeah, you gonna get me off, honky cocksucker. Keep sucking my big black dick." I fondled and squeezed those hefty black balls and drooled spit down his shaft, slobbering onto his pubes. "Oh shit, I'm gonna shoot!" He tried to pull his prick out of my mouth, but my lips were sealed tightly around the shaft. His dick just gushed, squirting gobs and gobs of hot cum down my throat. I saw fireworks, I swear.

"Hey dude, you ain't gonna swallow that stuff, are you?" I answered by showing him. I drank every drop of his sweet ball-juice. Coming up for air, I let go of his dick. It stayed stiff and throbbed. "That's some kind of dick you got," I said. "Ain't never done nothing like this before. Only been with one bitch, and she wouldn't suck it, just beat it off. She wouldn't let me stick it in because she didn't wanna get knocked up, you know." While looking at the size and stiffness of his dick, I felt my asshole twitch.

"Well, you can stick it in me if you want." I had never had a black one up my hole; I was a virgin as far as that was concerned. "No shit? You take it up the ass? Don't look like no sissy."

"It's not every day you see big meat like yours. Yeah, I wanna feel that big thing up my butt."

"I dunno."

"Oh, c'mon."

"Well, maybe if you gave me some more money so I can party after the concert with my homies?"

"Got a deal."

I was so horny and anxious to feel that big black dick up my hole that I'd have promised him almost anything.

I used to tease straight guys that after they went with a man they'd never go back to women. Now I got the feeling that after getting fucked by this black monster I'd never go back to white worms.

"Let's get totally naked and you can fuck me like a bitch," I said.

"Okay," he said.

I got real excited when I undressed him. I took off his windbreaker and tee. I pulled off his sneakers and socks, tugged off his jeans and briefs together. Naked, he was, to put it simply, awesome. Not a feather on him, except for the pits and pubes. There was nary a blemish on his smooth, chocolate skin.

Shedding my clothes, I felt his eyes on me. I was in decent shape because I worked out a bit recently.

As anxious as I was to feel him inside me, I wanted to taste that body of his.

Crawling on the bed, I straddled his body. I licked his skin, which tasted bittersweet. He watched me sniff and lick his fuzzy pits. I swabbed his chest. He had small pointy nipples which I pinched and sucked on, switching back and forth. He squirmed on the bed. I bathed him in spit, even his outie belly button.

Spreading his legs, I licked his muscular inner thighs. I nuzzled under his ballsac. I lapped the cord of flesh that led to his fuzzy crack. I swiped his asscrack with my tongue and I even darted it up his tangy butthole.

His big black dick was throbbing like mad with pre-cum oozing out of his piss-hole. His fat nuts heaved in their sac.

I plopped down on my back on the bed beside him.

I pulled him over and he climbed on top of me. His dick was like a big black snake and I wondered how I could take it.

I got a gob of spit in my crack. Holding my thighs up underneath, I showed him my hole.

For some reason, I wanted to look at him while he fucked me in the missionary position.

Instinctively, he knew what to do. He scooted forward and rubbed his oozing dick into my crack, smearing it with precum. "Do it. Shove that big dick in me." He punched his bloated crown into my hole. "Whoa! Stay still a minute." When my ass-ring expanded, I scissor my legs around his hips. He leaned forward and threaded his dick up my chute. "Okay, now fuck me with that big thing," I said. He probed slowly at first. "Oh yeah. Give it to me. Gimme that big dick." I watched his face contort. His forehead was beaded with sweat as he humped my ass. He was breathing heavy. "Lemme have it, man." He responded by ramming his big dick all the way in, pulling nearly out, then ramming it home again. "Oh yeah, that's it." After that, he really battered my asshole. I just hung on for the ride.

"Just keep fucking me, stud." He was a natural, this kid. I'd had some good fucks in the past, but never with the enthusiasm of this young buck. Oh yeah, fuck me deeper. Harder! Really let me have it," I wailed. He was not selfish, this kid: it seemed as if he meant to please while he was out to get his rocks off big time. He pulled out all the stops and really tore up my hole. His balls slapped wildly against my ass cheeks. I'd never been screwed so hard and fast and for such a long time in my life. His dick got rock-hard, and was ready to squirt I was sure, when he slowed down his pace. He unscissored my legs. Sitting back on his heels, he looked down at his big black dick as it slipped in and out of my white ass. I watched, too. He bored into my asshole. I moved my ass around and humped back. That's when he really let me have it. He spread my legs like a wishbone. His sweat dripped down onto my body. He gasped for air. I moaned and shivered. "Keep fuckin' me, man. Don't stop. Oh shit, your dick's the biggest, the hardest I ever had. Oh god, it's gonna shoot."

"Got that right. Gonna cream your queer fuckin' ass. Oh shit, here it fuckin' comes, man!" My own dick was hard from his heavy-duty fucking. He'd massaged my prostate beyond the point of no return. He'd reamed my asshole deeper than anyone ever had before. Whether it was coincidence or not, I don't know. All I know is that the instant I felt the hot spray of his cum up my ass, I felt my own balls erupt and squirt cum all over my belly. Exhausted from his big climax, he collapsed on top of me. I held him tight. I felt my cum squish around between us and bond us together. I felt both of our hearts beating rapidly. His ragged breathing returned to normal. I felt his massive dick soften and slide out of my well-fucked asshole. "You were terrific," I said. "You should rent that thing out." He laughed at that and rolled off me, laying peacefully on his back. I leaned over and licked my own salty cum off his belly. I swabbed the cum off his dick and savored the delicious taste in my mouth. He hopped up off the bed and got his homeboy drag back on. "So, whatchu think?"

"I think it was worth every penny." I fished into my wallet and gave him double the amount of the concert ticket. "Hey, thanks, dude," he said, and he hurried out of the room. I was his first john, but I was sure I would not be his last, and I was sorry I didn't live in San Francisco so that I could sample it again.

THE FIRST OF THE MONTH
J. Phillip Elwes

"...He was a beautiful boy when he slept curled beside me at night, snoring softly, sometimes whimpering fitfully at the occasional demon marauding through his dreams...Jason Morgan meant more to me than all of the autographed photos, shiny boxing statues. Global Middleweight Championship belts, and stacks upon stacks of other memorabilia that crammed the dusty shelves of my trophy cabinet, its warped glass doors shimmering across one wall of the back-front room I seldom entered except to entertain exuberant, reminiscing relatives and former trainers. He was a beautiful boy when he slept curled beside me at night, snoring softly, sometimes whimpering fitfully at the occasional demon marauding through his dreams. His hand always slipped around my waist or shoulder, his hairy chest wriggling against mine, whenever I awoke just before dawn and, irresistibly, my hand crept across his pillow and lightly scratched his thick, short-cropped hair. He was unmistakably a man not to rouse recklessly, his face flushed and the sinews in his neck writhing, when he was caught up in a heated argument with another bicycle messenger or, more likely, was earnestly negotiating a truce between rival bike services about to come to blows in the broad public square at Sansome and Sutter streets, its long, curving parapet the turf of dozens of handsomely disheveled, thick-calved messengers swaggering and lounging between dispatches.

Still asleep this morning, he lay naked on his belly in front of me, his muscular, hairy legs slightly spread, the sheet jumbled around his feet in the stifling heat rare even in late summer for San Francisco. Peeling down my sweat-soaked gym shorts and jockstrap, I marveled at his massive calves and thighs. As I straightened and flicked the dirty clothes toward the overflowing hamper in one corner, his astonishingly pale ass drew my attention, its powerful, twin globes covered by a dense forest of curly, brown hair that also climbed up his lower back in a fading triangle spreading out from his spine.

Taking my balls in one hand and gently pulling them out from between my muscular thighs, I swallowed dryly, enjoying the sensation of stretching my sweaty scrotum confined that morning in the tight pouch of my jock, and recalled with growing excitement the night before when I'd carefully turned him over on the bed, my rigid cock sheathed in the velvety, tight warmth of his ass, and we'd finished fucking on our knees.

Grunting and careful to move as little as possible inside him, I was kneading his narrow, brown waist for some time, desperate not to ejaculate first, when he groaned loudly, rearing up to clutch the headboard with one hand, and began slamming his hips back into mine.

Like most serious bike riders' torsos, his upper body wasn't nearly as developed as his legs: his back was lean and sinewy, with wide, square shoulders surprisingly strong from daily pulling at handlebars made grueling by the City's steep hills. When he suddenly bellowed at the headboard and I felt the walls of his ass clenching around my hard-on, I knew he was coming. I flung my broad, hairy chest across his back and grabbed his pumping fist and erection in one hand, his pungent semen spurting like buckshot over his hairy belly and chest, our fists, and the pillows and headboard in front of us. I came listening to the heavy splattering of his load, excitedly extending my chin over his neck to bite his earlobe, as my stomach muscles contracted hard and held my hips firmly against his creamy white ass, the rippling ferocity of my orgasm nearly overwhelming me. I became convinced, as my nuts unloaded round after round for several seconds, that I'd later discover the finger-like tip of my condom bulging to the bursting point with my pearly wad when I withdrew to peel off the translucent latex.

After a while, both of us satiated and exhausted, Jason noisily catching his breath and gripping the headboard with both hands, I remained inside him, comfortably euphoric, and ran my hands up and down his muscular arms, delighted by their wiriness, which differed completely from the bulging biceps and thick forearms of the overdeveloped young men I saw every day pummeling punching bags and each other at the North Beach gym I'd helped my favorite former trainer open years ago.

Now, this morning, my circumcised penis trapped between my thumb and the thatch of glossy, black hairs climbing up my lower groin, I tugged on my balls and watched my member rapidly swell, the wide, pink crown plumping out, as the pale shaft thickened, then dramatically lengthened and curved to the right.

I eyed the impressive network of veins crisscrossing Jason's arms, massaging my testicles more vigorously; and soon my hard-on was throbbing with my pulse, as it waved jauntily against my midriff.

Swallowing dryly, I felt my gaze drawn back to his pale asscheeks and the luxuriant line of hair running between them. His plump, wrinkly scrotum was squashed against the mattress, his large, egg-shaped testicles plainly visible and making my mouth water. Whenever we 69-ed, I liked to devote a good amount of time to washing these, popping each in turn into my mouth and twirling my tongue over the silky surface of his pliant sac, while at the same time vigorously squeezing his rigid cock in one fist or rubbing his salty pre-cum over his impressively large, pink cockhead, until he was wildly bucking his hips and, finally spitting out my cock, begged me to stop.

I released my scrotum and raised a knee onto the bed, glancing down my hairy chest and midriff at my erection jutting out from my hips. I drew my shin over the mattress like a rake to push one of his legs gently aside, then carefully descended onto my knees between them. Leaning forward, with the bed creaking and my heart beating faster now that I drew near my quarry, I sank my fists into the mattress to either side of his muscular, white ass.

"You asleep?" I whispered, ducking my head to lap at the tiny, tangy beads of sweat glimmering along the small of his back.

I was breathing noisily through my mouth, as my tongue danced across the nearly straight line separating his bronzed torso from the pale mounds of his ass. I twirled down the fragrant cleft separating his cool, firm cheeks, slicking over the tufts of coarse hair there with my spit, and probed urgently for the delicate bud of his asshole.

Though my tongue ached with the strain and I was nearly suffocated by the hairs curling in my nostrils, I was soon flicking quick spirals over the deliciously soft ring of his anus.

My erection now throbbing to my racing pulse, I could imagine nothing more exciting at the moment than rimming Jason, my tongue pushing past his relaxing sphincter to dart hungrily inside him.

Moaning, he stirred and twisted his head on his pillow to look back at me. He grinned, sliding his hands across the mattress to clutch my fists and, with his back muscles rippling along his spine, pushed his ass up into my face, encouraging me to plunge deeper into him.

Even more turned on by the obvious pleasure I was giving him, I gazed into his wide-set, blue eyes, not for the first time dazzled by their unusual narrowness under his bushy, blond brows.

Reluctantly, I finally had to jerk my head up, gasping for air, and ogled his wet, bright pink bunghole winking expectantly at me. Then, hardly giving myself a chance to catch my breath, I once more eagerly drove my tongue into him.

"Ah, Tony," he moaned contentedly, bucking his hairy ass up into my face to smother me. "Don't stop....Don't stop, Tony."

Only now becoming aware of his fingers clawing into my fists with his growing excitement, I opened my hands and slid his wrists over the mattress to clamp them against his slender hips. His elbows seesawed violently in the air above his back, as he grunted and tried to struggle free. But, a moment later, his entire body relaxed, and he let out a prolonged, guttural cry, when I wedged my chin down between his cheeks far enough to nudge his testicles and noisily dug my tongue into him the deepest yet.

"I'm going to – I'm going to come," he groaned, grinding his hips into the bed.

Gulping dryly, wanting to be up his ass when he came, I rose up onto my knees, my throbbing erection jouncing crazily before my hips.

"Wait. Wait," I pleaded, the words thick and slurred in my mouth sore from rimming him. "I wanna fuck you."

"Ah, yeah," he moaned, awkwardly pushing up onto his hands and knees.

His creamy, hairy ass even with my bobbing cock, I shuffled closer, mesmerized by his twitching sphincter shiny with my spit and only inches away from my bright red, flared cockhead. I eagerly reached between his powerful thighs, running a hand over his egg-shaped testicles, and pulled his boner straight down under his butt cheeks to get a better look at it, the crown very slick in my hand with pre-cum. I squeezed the rigid shaft a couple times and watched his pink cockhead swell hugely.

"Don't – Don't, Tony," he begged, looking back at me. "I'll come if you keep – doing that."

"All right," I breathed, releasing his erection, and dismounted the bed on unsteady legs. "Come on. I wanna be in the front room."

He rolled across the mattress, one foot landing on the hardwood floor, and took the hand I held out to him to stand before me. His rigid cock was shorter than mine, but much thicker and only slightly bent to one side, with a wide, pink crown, whose shiny, silky surface I never tired of fondling and licking. Always flush with his hairy midriff, his member now jutted straight up, jerking a little from side to side with each step he took toward me. I noticed his plump scrotum was tightly drawn up against his body, his right testicle tucked into his groin like I knew it only did when he was very aroused.

"You come on," he said, making a fist around my pulsating hard-on, compelling me to follow him as he walked first to the bureau to grab a box of condoms and a bullet-shaped bottle of lube with his other hand, then into the adjoining front room.

Marveling at his magnificent torso, massive, hairy legs, and thick erection standing up over his testicles, I realized he was like a modern-day, urban satyr, confidently guiding me by the cock across the sunny apartment to the couch, where he pushed me down and, grinning devilishly, straddled my hips while retaining a firm grip around my member.

"You wanna fuck me?" he asked huskily, hunching his shoulders down to press his lips lightly against mine, his hard- on and hairy belly brushing over my muscular midriff as he softly kissed me.

"Yes," I exhaled, swallowing dryly. He straightened and jerked his head away when I tried to dart my tongue into his mouth. With a rush of excitement, I suddenly recalled the first time I'd been inside him. "Very much."

"Right here. Right here," he murmured, the lid to the lube dicking open behind his back a moment before the cool liquid gushed over my swollen glans. I grimaced, my entire body tensing up at the sharp pleasure, as he vigorously stroked my cock. "I remember the first time. Do you, Tony? It was right here."

I nodded, gently rocking against him, delighted we'd simultaneously recalled that particular morning. Trying to catch my breath, I watched him put the lube down beside us, shake a condom from the box, toss aside the box, then expertly tear the wrapper open with his teeth.

"Let me do it," I said, reaching between us to take the condom. I wrapped my arms around his narrow waist, then violently bucked my hips up in surprise, hissing through clenched teeth, when he stroked my member one last time. Releasing me with a tight squeeze, he next massaged my testicles enthusiastically, as I slipped the rubber on. "You ready?"

Grasping one of my shoulders for support, he leaned over to scoop up the lube bottle and squeezed it until a glob spilled out into his hand. Then, rising up onto his knees, he stroked my throbbing cock several more times before pressing it against his anus.

My eyes wide with excitement, I stayed perfectly still, my hands frozen in the air above his hips, while he slowly sat down on me. Grunting softly, I felt my cockhead slip past the relaxing ring of his sphincter.

He tightly clasped both of my shoulders and began to whimper, his thick cock twitching against his belly, as he settled down on the rest of my rigid penis, gasping and jerking up a few times, until I was once again sheathed inside him, my heart pounding hard and his pale ass trembling on my lap.

"Is this okay?" I asked hoarsely, pushing myself into the couch so I could thrust slowly up into him.

He nodded, the sinews in his neck writhing and an almost comical look of surprise illuminating his face, when I next thrust more vigorously, taking hold of his hips to steady him. His chest heaved and I noticed a trickle of sweat running down his forehead, as he moaned softly and lowered his head to dart his tongue over mine.

With each new thrust, I became more oblivious to everything but the intense pleasure of my cockhead welding with his tight, warm ass, his soft gasps punctuating each time I strained my hips up against him to bury my cock as deeply as possible within him.

"Oh, man," he moaned against my mouth, gyrating his hips against mine and sliding his hands across my shoulders and hairy pecs to tweak my erected nipples.

"Yeah, Jason, that feels great – great," I breathed, feeling my load rising. My balls always pull dose to my groin just before I ejaculate. "That – feels great."

I gripped him tightly, my upward thrusts becoming frantic, as I struggled between wanting to feel myself sliding as rapidly as possible inside him and desperately hoping to delay my orgasm long enough for him to shoot first.

"Come on, Tony," he cried, pressing his sweaty forehead against my shoulder, as he pinched my nipples and, his entire body trembling now, rode me hard. "You first. You first, Tony. I know you're dose. I – can feel it."

I suddenly came, groaning, and wrenched us both off the couch, as my massive leg muscles locked. I grabbed at him to keep him from falling to the floor, stunned by the powerful contractions rippling through my cock. I squeezed my eyes shut, firing my load inside him, and was only dimly aware that I was crying out his name.

"Ah, Tony!" I heard him exclaim, as he damped his thighs around my hips and hooked an arm around my neck, hurriedly stroking himself off until his pungent splooge exploded over my belly and chest and peppered my chin and face for several seconds.

We were both laughing, when I finally collapsed onto the couch, my orgasm ebbing, and looked down at Jason still jerking himself off, his rigid cock spurting ribbons of milky semen against the matted hairs covering his belly.

"You're crazy," he said between gasps, quickly repositioning himself on me. "Do you know that? You'd better – know that." I grinned, damping a hand around his fist and cock to pump him the last few times until he was dry.

"Only because you make me that way," I whispered, using my shoulder to wipe away a trickle of sperm running down my cheek, and leaned forward to press my mouth against his.

"Ah, man," he said softly, running a hand over my muscular arm to still my hand stroking his cock. "That was crazy! What a way to wake up. It's still freakin' early, Tony."

"I know," I said, grinning, and leaned back to study him. "I just got back from the gym. I couldn't resist. You were sleeping naked."

"That's because the weather thinks we're living in Oakland."

"Or L. A." I ran a hand over his chest and around his neck to clasp the back of his head, then playfully pulled him toward me while he struggled to keep his head up. "Can I stay inside you?"

One of the definite advantages of reaching my age was maintaining an erection long after I came. It felt nice being dose to him with my cock still hard inside him.

"Yeah," he chuckled, enthusiastically rolling his head about, as I next vigorously scratched his scalp. "But I have to go soon, or that new dispatcher'll be cussing me out on the radio again."

After Jason had pedaled off to battle ornery dispatchers, quarrelsome messengers, demented drivers, a seething, ebbing sea of sleepwalking pedestrians, and an entire cabal of lobby guards and beaming receptionists secretly bent on stalling him with inane queries and cumbersome sign-in procedures, I showered and dressed for my monthly meeting with my attorneys downtown.

I'd become the Middleweight Champion of the Globe in the age of flamboyant promoters, enormously powerful hotel and casino interests, and Pay-for-View cable. Though no ugly duckling, if I do say so myself, I was never described in the press as having boyishly good looks or charm, both of which easily translate into huge product endorsements. Nor had I cashed in on the animalistic antics most boxing fans seemed to have craved from their pugilistic heroes during much of my reign. Instead, I'd risen steadily to the top after nearly twenty years of hard work and sweat, my uncles and trainers, sometimes one and the same, helping me to stay focused on my dream when I was a nobody on our small comer of West Philly and, later, when the trappings of celebrity loomed over us ominously, at the gym I'd bought in Los Angeles.

I retired after losing my title for the fourth time. By then, I had a nice little nest egg and, more importantly, the open admiration and respect of many of the men I had grown up idolizing. My money situation improved when I sold off the expensive toys I'd accumulated over the years, then shed most of my entourage. AI Sazzini, the trainer I'd grown up with since junior high and more like a father to me than my real father, moved with me to San Francisco. Though he never directly discussed with anyone my being gay, he did pull me aside once and say in his gruff way that here at last was a city in which celebrities disappeared when they chose, and where I could meet the sort of men I liked most.

A few years ago, after an extensive search, I bought an unassuming apartment building on Noe Hill near the Liberty Street steps, converted the two top-floor apartments into a soothingly symmetrical unit with two front doors, and settled into the comfortable, relatively reclusive life I now have.

With the scent of Jason's musk and spunk still strong in my nostrils this morning, I eyed myself pulling on a pair of shorts over a dean jock in the mirrored doors of my doset. Since I no longer competed, I lifted more iron during my daily workouts than I'd previously been permitted, the result being mammoth thighs and legs and an upper torso so thickly developed that I was easily now in the Heavyweight class, though I'm sure I wouldn't have fought well at all with the added bulk.

The serrated muscles of my massive, freckled shoulders and arms danced, as I pulled out a tee shirt from a bureau drawer and slipped it over my head. Tugging it down my bulging pecs and abdomen, I absently watched the hard muscles of my hairy midriff contract impressively with my next breath.

"Not now," I said aloud to myself, grinning, when I suddenly recalled the first time Jason had stood naked and aroused with me before these doors, his erection shiny from a steady stream of pre-cum. He'd silently ogled me open-mouthed, telling me later he'd anxiously waited for me to reach out and stroke his cock before he'd been brave enough to grab mine and jack me off to a quick orgasm.

I stepped into tennis shoes and pulled on my backpack stuffed with paperwork I'd signed for the attorneys. I was locking both front doors, when my cock began stiffening uncomfortably in my jock. For a moment, my hand resting on a doorknob, I debated whether it'd be wiser to turn back and whack off in my room before heading to the meeting.

Then, smirking, I turned and jogged down the staircase coiling through the center of the building, having decided to shoot my wad like some punk in one of the law firm's black marble bathrooms before proceeding to my appointment. I opened the building door and stepped onto Noe Street, unconcerned my loose tee shirt poorly concealed my growing erection poking out of my shorts.

Noe Hill was treacherous down to Eighteenth and Market streets. I was sweating profusely by the time I caught a streetcar clamoring downtown and found a seat in the back. Putting my backpack on my lap, I sported a hard-on for most of the ride, soon finding myself reviewing the last several months I'd spent with Jason.

I first discovered him last fall bundled up in several coats and asleep in a tight ball on my fire escape. Raising the heavy bedroom dormer, I startled him awake and, after assuring him I wasn't mad or going to call the cops, talked him into sleeping inside my apartment. Stepping through the window, he groggily explained he lived a few floors down in a studio apartment with what I took to be an entire tribe of bicycle messengers, but had climbed up to my window that night to get away from a noisy party.

I was heading into the front room to make up the sofa bed, when he stumbled over to my bed and began undressing. I'd seduced plenty of younger men over the years, some fans, some fellow athletes, others members of my entourage or even fight physicians. As I grew older, however, I realized the younger the man, the more trouble he generally turned out to be. Though I had little interest in him at the moment, I stopped to watch Jason peel off his sweater and undershirt to reveal his beautiful, lithe upper body. He then modestly turned his back to me to unsnap his blue jeans and clumsily pulled them off. When I stepped over to the opposite side of the bed to draw back the covers, he carefully faced away from me, too sleepy to realize I could look into the closet mirrors and see his full piss- on jutting out the front of his white briefs. As he struggled under the covers, I watched him absently flick out the elastic band from his narrow waist to reposition his rigid member.

Later that night, curious about the handsome stranger sleeping in my bed, I quietly stripped in the dark and slept naked beside him.

At least once a week the first few months, he'd tap at my bedroom window late in the evening, and I'd dutifully let him in. Almost immediately, hardly saying more than thanks, he stripped to his briefs and got into bed. I usually stayed up later, writing in my journal or reading in the library next to the formal back-front room lined with my trophy cabinet, then undressed and slid into bed beside him.

One cold afternoon, the shadows already long and darkening on the street below, I watched him patiently, expertly bunny hop his bike all the way down the Liberty Street steps. When he finally rocked from wheel to wheel before hopping the last step down to Noe Street, I realized I'd been anxiously clutching the windowsill. He was suddenly met up by another bicycle messenger, who gestured extravagantly up the steps and was visibly disappointed when Jason shook his head, smiling, and rode off.

Things changed the night he came to my window well after midnight. I'd already been asleep for some time. Cranky, I crossed the room with a raging piss-on, and shoved open the window to squint up at him in the street light.

He started to say something, but froze when he saw my hard-on.

"You woke me up," I simply said, about to return to bed, when I spotted the ugly strawberry running down one of his cheeks. "What happened?"

"Sorry I woke you," he slurred, and I knew he was very drunk. "I biffed on Ellis. Some guy opened – opened his car door, and I had to – jerk out of the way. I rolled across the street – and my bike – it smashed into a mailbox."

"You okay?" I asked, helping him through the window.

He nodded, his gaze returning to my erection, as I pulled the window shut and he thought I wasn't looking.

"Bike's – Bike's not, though."

When he told me he'd gone out drinking with his housemates, instead of to the hospital for a checkup, I insisted he follow me into the bathroom so I could at least clean his wound with antiseptic. I pulled on tom sweatpants and tied the drawstring, while he stood obediently beside me in the bright bathroom lights.

"You don't have to," he murmured, as I soaked cotton balls with the red solution, then applied them to his cheek. "I had my helmet on. I'm just cut up – that's all."

"You can get infections, if you don't get cleaned up," I said, dabbing the long wound a second time. "I should know. You

cut anywhere else?"

He nodded, then clumsily peeled his shirt over this head to reveal several more scrapes on his arms and down one side.

"And my legs," he slurred, working off his jeans, which became entangled around his shoes, baffling him for so long I finally lifted him by the armpits and set him on the bathroom counter. "Thanks. Thanks for helping me."

"No problem," I mumbled, freeing him of his shoes and jeans.

I used up an entire package of cotton balls, then started in on the toilet paper, before I'd cleaned his wounds, the worst being the one on his cheek. I was checking it again, when I glanced down his hairy chest and belly, and spotted another strawberry on his hip just past the flimsy elastic of his briefs.

"You got one here," I said, pulling back the loose elastic to dab the wound. I could see the pale shaft of his penis half buried in the thatch of hair rising up his lower groin. "There. You're all done."

"Thanks. Thanks," he whispered, watching me discard the cotton balls and toilet paper scattered beside him on the counter. When I checked his cheek one last time, he suddenly grabbed my hand, holding it close to his face, and smiled radiantly. "I appreci – appreciate – this a lot."

"No problem," I said again, my heart skipping a beat when he turned his head and softly kissed my palm.

He threw an instant, full erection that easily sprang free of his briefs, the wide, pink cockhead bobbing with his rapid pulse against his hairy belly.

"I keep saying, "no problem,"" I breathed, swallowing convulsively, and kissed his forehead. I then playfully tugged his head toward me a few times. "Now, come on. You need to sleep. Look at you: you're falling out of your underwear. You're acting like you've never played doctor before."

"Sorry," he mumbled, obviously confused, as I helped him off the counter and walked with him back into the bedroom. He pulled the elastic over his erection, which made the back slump, so that I saw his very hairy, pale ass for the first time.

I drew back the covers and helped him into bed, pulling them over him as he settled in. I then slowly undressed in the dark, my own cock rigid by the time I slipped under the blankets beside him and contentedly listened to his steady, deep breathing.

After that night, he tapped at my window more often, and lingered later in the mornings, usually waiting until I got up first and headed for the bathroom to piss or shower, often as not sporting a full piss-on I didn't bother to hide from him. Since I now sometimes made fun of his tattered briefs, he asked from time to time if he could wear one of my jocks. He always put them on in the bathroom, occasionally stripped down to one in front of me, once threw an erection while we wrestled in nothing else, and never wore them to bed. He also started jerking off on the dirty ones I flung into the hamper, leaving enormous, pungent stains, a predilection I never called him on, since I knew it was only a matter of time before he screwed up enough courage to seduce me properly.

That happened – sort of – the last night of January.

"Tony, you awake? I'm freezing," he whispered into my ear, his fingers grazing my shoulder, twitching, before lightly traveling across my ribs to my bare hip.

"Turn onto your side," I murmured, and his hand scurried away.

I opened my eyes to find him blinking expectantly at me from his pillow, his slow, steady breath washing over my cheek and neck.

He gulped noisily, and his shoulder reared up under the covers.

"The other way, I mean."

Sighing, he slowly flipped onto his other side.

With a swelling erection, I wriggled over to press myself firmly against his back and ass. I drew a massive thigh and calf over his smaller legs and hooked an arm around his shoulder and hairy chest. I could feel his heart beating wildly against my forearm as distinctly as I felt my own rapid pulse coursing through my member crushed against the soft fabric of his underwear.

"You all right?" I asked some time later, concerned when he'd remained so still I could barely detect his breathing.

"Yeah," he whispered, tentatively clasping my arm with both hands.

We stayed like that for most of the night. I kept waiting for him to make the next move, but managed to fall asleep around dawn when his breathing became slow and rhythmic.

"You stay warm?" I asked him late the next morning, as he stirred under the covers.

"Yeah." He turned his head to look at me, adding after a long pause: "But don't tell my buds we were cuddling, okay?"

"What? Why would I? Why do you care what they think about us, anyway?" I laughed, and he looked away. "I mean, you don't care they joke about the movies you write – all good stories you've shown me. Why do you care if they know we were holding each other last night?"

"Ah, Tony, I – I don't...." he stammered, swallowing noisily, and trained his thick-lashed, blue eyes on me. "I – I guess I feel weird – I'm naked. My underwear came off when you let go of me.

"So, that's what this is about. How long have you been coming over, Jason? Four months? I always sleep naked. You know that. But don't worry," I said coolly, though my heart was beating faster and my cock was growing hard. I knew he was making his move: this was the first time he'd fully undressed with me. "I'm not gonna run downstairs and tell 'em we've been rolling around naked in bed together."

"Yeah, I know. Sorry." His eyes kept darting from my mouth to the wall behind me. "I just – don't do this with other guys – that's all."

After another long pause, during which he stared at the ceiling, I asked, "Don't you need to go to work?".

"Yeah," he murmured, blushing. "But I can't....1 – I got – a problem."

"What kinda problem?" I asked, wanting to kiss him right then for looking so adorably discombobulated.

"You know," he almost whined, unconvinced I wasn't catching his drift, and met my gaze for a moment. "I'd – You know, I'd embarrass myself. I – "

"You mean, you got a piss-on?" I interrupted, finally cracking a smile. "Jeez, Jason, you've seen me with one enough times." I flung back the covers and rose out of bed. My heart was pounding fast and my legs were surprisingly unsteady, as I walked around his side of the bed toward the bathroom. He tracked my progress with his eyes, my hard-on jerking wildly in front of my hips, then pushed backed the covers and slid himself around to sit on the edge of the bed.

"Tony," he said hoarsely. "Can I – Can we – "

I stopped and turned to look at him. He was indeed naked, his muscular, pale thighs spread wide to give me a nice view of his nads and thick erection jutting straight up against his belly.

"What d'you want?" I asked as evenly as I could muster, when he simply sat there staring at my hard-on. "Do you wanna take a shower? We'll have to do it together. I got a meeting this morning."

"Do you mind?" he asked, slowly rising and walking toward me.

"You got a belly boner," I said, smiling, when he stood in front of me.

"Wha – What?" he stammered, looking down at my erection bobbing at him.

"Your hard-on stays against your stomach when you stand up."

"I know." He grinned, meeting my gaze. "It's hell trying to hide it, but, at least, it's not bent – like yours."

I laughed. "Well, I've never got any complaints. You didn't seem to mind last night."

He blushed again and looked away.

"You've felt mine," I said huskily, "so I should be able to feel yours."

He nodded, watching me reach out to grip his member in my fist. It took only a few quick strokes to make him come. Thick ribbons of his semen sprayed against my chin and pecs and splashed over his hairy midriff, as he wildly bucked his hips, ogled my pumping fist, and grabbed my cock to whack me off to an equally quick orgasm.

Then, knowing I could reschedule the meeting, I kissed him on the mouth for the first time, waiting until he was hard again before leading him into the front room so we could fuck on the couch.

To my dismay, I was whisked into a large, dark-paneled conference room the moment I stepped off the elevator. A blushing receptionist presented us with mineral water, and my team of lawyers then proceeded to bury me under a flurry of documents to review, sign, and forward to accountants, property managers, and still other attorneys.

A good-looking, stylishly long-haired tax lawyer whom I'd never before met sat beside me at the darkly polished table. He cast his eyes at my crotch so many times, I finally spread my legs to give him a better view. With my bare knee pressed against his thigh for the rest of the meeting, I soon had an erection jutting up the front of my shorts and enjoyed the younger man's obvious discomfiture, as he calmly discussed my various tax options on certain projects and pretended not to be aware of my boner or his own good-sized hard-on thrusting out one pant leg.

"Mr. Marcellino," began one of the partners across the table, habitually formal, "you're certain you want to set up this limited partnership with Mr. Morgan? You say you've known him for almost a year now?"

I nodded, somewhat annoyed as the elderly men insisted on treating me paternally no matter how old I got. "His screenplays are excellent. My studio friends in L. A. think so, too. When his bike was wrecked in a hit-and-run accident, he worked twice as hard to buy a new one and still managed to buy a used laptop from one of his friends. I know a latcher-on when I meet one. He's only seen my trophies once – He found me in there reading a screenplay he'd given me – and still thinks they're my brother's or somebody like that, because I said they belonged to someone I knew a long time ago."

Everyone chuckled, and the meeting dissolved into hearty handshakes, my backpack once again concealing my boner, as everyone filed past me until only the tax attorney and I remained in the room.

I was turning toward him, admiring his pale green eyes, when I was surprised to see Jason step off one of the elevators. He looked hesitantly at the receptionist, then burst into a wide grin when he saw me rushing across the lobby toward him.

"You delivering a package?" I asked, lightly smacking his bike helmet.

"No," he answered, winking at the receptionist before suddenly pulling a punch at my midriff and nimbly dancing away from my counter jab. "I knew you'd be here – Ha! You missed! You're always here the first of the month."

"Come on. I have a surprise," I said, leading him into the conference room, where the attorney had been watching us. "First, this is...?"

"Oliver White," the taller man answered, shaking Jason's hand. "You must be Jason Morgan. Pleasure to meet you. If I'm not mistaken, Tony has something for you. It's still here on the table."

"Nice to meet you," Jason answered, as I shut and locked the heavy door.

"Oliver," I said, stepping behind Jason to hug him around the abdomen, my fingers sliding under the heavy waistband of his black, spandex shorts, "have you ever done a circle jerk at work?"

Jason chortled and the lawyer swallowed, blinking uncertainly at us. I bunched Jason's shorts up in my fists, then pulled them down his powerful thighs to his knees. I found his silky scrotum surprisingly cool and very sweaty, as I tugged on his large, egg-shaped testicles. His cock became hard when I humped his hairy, muscular ass, my own member rigid in my jockstrap.

"There's another meeting scheduled in here in a few minutes," Oliver breathed, stepping toward us to stroke Jason's erection.

I moved to stand beside them, so that we were now shoulder to shoulder. Even while he gazed up into the attorney's green eyes, Jason easily dug a hand under my shorts to grab my cock. He stroked me off, as I pushed my shorts and jockstrap down my thighs. The attorney was quick to take me by the balls, grinning at me while eagerly massaging them.

"We'd better hurry, then," I said hoarsely, loosening Oliver's belt. The hook to his slacks released with a quick jerk of my wrist. I unzipped his fly to reveal blue boxers beneath, his slacks falling lightly past his calves. He had long, nearly hairless legs. "Let's see your cock."

"This is nuts," the attorney murmured, nodding, and pulled his boxers down with one hand to release his erection.

Freed, it bounced up, thick like Jason's, with loose foreskin bunched up around the fat, almost purple crown. Jason stroked it with his free hand while still beating me off. I pulled at the taller man's round nads in his soft, hairless scrotum, which was mostly hidden under the tails of his dress shirt.

Grunting, the attorney came first, leaning forward and shooting his load in several directions at once. Almost squeezing my testicles too hard, he somehow managed to keep beating off Jason, who whimpered noisily for a few moments, then shot his wad in thick ribbons straight over our heads, some of it pelting the attorney's face and streaking across his shirt.

"Go, Tony. Yeah, Tony," Jason breathed, as I next stumbled forward, still gripping both men by the balls, and unloaded my wad onto the plush carpet at our feet.

When we'd finished coming, I twirled my tongue in Jason's mouth, sliding my hands over his hairy ass cheeks to prod his butthole with one finger. He kissed me back, laughing, but wriggled away as best he could with the tight bike shorts around his knees.

"We had better leave," Oliver said, pulling up his slacks.

"Yeah, I know." I released Jason, and we hurriedly dressed. As I reached into my jock to carefully position my balls, I turned to Jason: "That was fun, huh?"

"Hell, yeah!" He grinned at me and Oliver. "Was that my surprise?"

"Well, no, I wasn't talking about a circle jerk." The tax attorney was grinning now, too. "But I bet that could be the first of many for us, if Oliver's up for more."

"We could do other stuff in my office," Oliver said, nodding and gulping noisily. "Even right now, if you want."

"Good," I said, then clamped Jason firmly by the shoulders. "But, first, I got something for you to sign, if you want." I kissed his forehead, both of his bushy, blond brows, his thick- lashed, fluttering eyelids, and finally his lips.

"Jason, I need to tell you a secret, too. You've never watched boxing, right?"

A PROMISING STUDENT
R.J. Masters

"...The head of his cock brushed lightly against my virgin ass. My muscles tensed. I was so afraid...I strutted down the hallway, still clutching the paper that had been handed back in history class. Scrawled in red ink on the first page was a note: "See me." There was no grade, no further explanation, so I had no choice but to comply.

I hesitated outside Professor Lawrence's office. He was a rugged, dark-haired man of perhaps thirty-five, with a deep, booming voice and intimidating air. I finally gathered my courage and knocked lightly on the door. When he called for me to come in, I wasn't sure I wanted to obey, but slowly pushed open the door and stepped into his darkened office.

"You wanted to see me," I stammered.

"Yes. C'mon in."

He approached me, letting his hand brush lightly against the front of my faded jeans. I shuddered, as my cock hardened involuntarily at his touch. Part of me wanted to pull away, to run from his office, from his knowing gaze. But the rest of me wanted him to continue, hungered for what he could teach me.

I was just a teenager, naive and very inexperienced. I had been with a girl once, but it hadn't been good. Since then I hadn't gotten dose to anyone, and I had been very lonely.

I closed my eyes, steadying myself against the wall as his hand squeezed and stroked my throbbing cock. I humped upward, grinding my aching erection against his hand. "You're a very promising student. But you really must learn to apply yourself," he said, his voice hoarse with excitement.

My knees trembled as his arm slithered around my waist and our bodies were crushed together. His lips sought out mine and his tongue demanded entrance to my moist, warm mouth. It wiggled and squirmed, probing deep into the center of my very being. I answered him back with an urgency – a desperate need I barely recognized. I melted against him, my body completely surrendering to his will. His lips traced a path down my neck, his hot breath

igniting tiny fires as they moved. My head was spinning with delight as I experienced each new sensation. Then his hand crept beneath my shirt, caressing my bare skin so that I shivered. His fingers rubbed my hard nipples, rolling them, then pulling and twisting them until I thought they would be torn from my body. I had never realized that my nipples were so sensitive, that manipulating them would send waves of pleasure directly to my groin.

I groaned and moved against him, feeling his hard mass of cockmeat straining against his tan Dockers. I let my hand rest on his shoulder while he tugged at my button-fly. I could barely wait for the moment when his hand would slip inside my shorts and make contact with my fiery flesh.

His thumbs inched under the waistbands of my jeans and shorts and he pushed them downward until they fell around my ankles in a crumpled heap. My cock bounced upward, slapping against my smooth, hairless abdomen.

I opened my eyes as his fingers curled around my horny shaft. He began to stroke slowly along my length, from the pale blond bush to the wet, sticky cockhead. I was more than a little afraid, but at the same time, I was incredibly turned on. I watched the bright red tip poke seductively from his clenched fist, then retreat.

When his thumb lightly caressed the rim, jolts of pleasure swept through me. My balls churned, aching with their long pent-up load. I humped his hand, coming closer and closer to eruption of the captive wad.

He moved away from me for just an instant, leaving me feeling abandoned. He reached into his pocket and retrieved a shiny foil wrapper. I didn't know what he expected of me, so I stood quietly waiting. I was shocked when he quickly cloaked my cock in the latex sheath and dropped to his knees in front of me. It was like a fantasy come true. No one had ever sucked my cock before.

He looked up at me and licked his lips, then slowly inched closer to my throbbing boner. I waited impatiently for the moment when his lips would touch my horny cock for the first time. When I could wait no longer, I placed my hand on the back of his head and drew his face into my groin. He nuzzled against my aching meat, then let his lips kiss along the pulsating vein.

"Oh yeah," I moaned. "That feels so good."

He continued to tease me, letting his tongue flick against the sensitive head and sending erotic shock waves through my body. I shuddered, not quite sure how much more of his teasing I could take before I shot off.

He kissed the tip, letting his tongue burrow into the covered piss-slit. I groaned and humped against his face, trying to drive my cock into his mouth. But he would not allow it. He insisted on setting the pace.

Finally he opened his mouth and allowed my horny meat to slide onto his tongue. I gasped as he closed his lips around the quivering monster. He sucked and slurped on my horny cock driving me crazy with excitement. No one had ever done such wonderful things to me and I never wanted it to end.

He drew my cock deeper into his throat, then swallowed. The sensations were becoming more than I could bear. My knees trembled and I found myself leaning on him for support. I was not prepared when every muscle in my body tensed, then I shook uncontrollably. My huge wad coursed through my shaft and blasted into the tip of the condom.

He kept his lips locked on my twitching shaft, while a second and third smaller wad erupted into the latex protection. When I had finished coming, he let my cock slide from his mouth and looked up into my eyes. I smiled, fully satisfied for the first time in my life, while he removed the used condom and wiped me clean.

He got to his feet and pressed his lips to mine once again. He unfastened his belt and unzipped his pants, letting them fall casually to the floor. I watched as he stepped out of them and his boxers, revealing a huge slab of monster meat.

I wanted to touch it, to stroke his length the way he had done for me. But I had never held another man's cock and I was afraid. Then he took my hand and guided it to his cock. He held my hand and yanked on his long, thick cock. Gobs of pre-cum oozed from the gaping piss-slit.

"I want you," he whispered. "I've wanted you since the first night I laid eyes on you."

I didn't know how to respond, so I remained silent. I couldn't imagine what it would be like to suck on that monster cock, but I expected I would soon find out.

He handed me a condom and waited patiently for me to apply it to his throbbing meat. My hand was shaking as I stretched the latex to fit his oversized cock. He placed his hands on my shoulders and pushed me down onto the floor.

My eyes widened as the huge slab approached my lips. I kissed it softly, then licked along his length. I could feel the heat of his arousal through the thin latex and it excited me. I eagerly opened my mouth and let his cock slide inside. I swirled my tongue over and around the rim, wishing all the time that I could feel his naked cock in my mouth, that I could taste his sweet cream. At that moment I wished I had come of age before the era of AIDS.

But still, I savored the feel of his smooth hardness sliding over my tongue and into my throat. I hesitated for a moment when I felt his hand come to rest on the back of my head. He was guiding my head into his groin, so that his cock could dive even deeper into my throat.

I gagged and gasped when the monster blocked my airway. But he pulled back quickly allowing me to recover. Then he began to slam into me like a man possessed, his desperate, primitive need taking control.

The huge organ repeatedly banged against the back of my throat, then retreated. I was anxious for the sudden blast of cum into the latex sheath, but it didn't come. As quickly as he had invaded my mouth, he slipped away.

He looked down at me, his eyes hungry with desire. He knelt down in front of me and pressed his body to mine. My cock hardened once again and slithered alongside his monstrous meat.

"I am going to pluck your cherry," he whispered. "You're going to feel things you've never felt before and you'll never want me to stop...."

I heard his words, but they didn't make any sense to me. My head was spinning. I was so overwhelmed with these new sensations that I couldn't think.

We embraced for what seemed like hours, our bodies nearly merging into one. Then he pushed me backward onto the floor and moved between my thighs. My heart pounded in my chest as the reality of what he intended to do to me sank in.

The spongy, latex-covered head of his cock brushed lightly against my virgin ass. My muscles tensed. I was so afraid, I just couldn't relax. He didn't waste any time either. He pushed the thick intruder against the unyielding muscle-ring. Slowly, inch by inch the oversized invader made his way into the heat of my body.

1 squirmed and moaned as the first waves of pleasure overtook me. I had never fantasized about having a big, hard cock up my ass. But it felt so good, 1 couldn't imagine not having it. There was an incredible feeling of fullness as the thick monster forced its way inside me. Then it began to move, rubbing against my sensitive inner walls and massaging the previously untouched nerve-endings.

I thrashed with excitement, as the invader banged against my vulnerable prostate. My cock bobbed against my belly, hard and horny, ready to launch another load of hot, white cream. He moved slowly, deliberately teasing me closer and closer to explosion.

His eyes were squeezed shut, as his own excitement reached the boiling point. The thick monster poked deeper and deeper into my belly with each stroke. Finally I could hold off no longer. My cock jumped and my creamy goo spattered his chest, sticking to the dark, curly hairs before reaching his skin.

As my ass muscles contracted, the intruder began to jerk and twitch inside my tight chamber. Every muscle in his body tensed. His biceps bulged and he tossed his head back in surrender. I could feel the wad of cum explode into the tip of the condom, causing it to swell in my belly.

He collapsed on top of me, his hot breath caressing my bare shoulder. He lay quietly for a while, resting his head. Then he raised himself up on one elbow and looked into my eyes. I still couldn't believe this had really happened – that my history professor had taught me a lesson I would never forget. But there he was, his body still sprawled on top of mine, his half-hard cock buried in my deflowered boypussy.

"I think we've had enough for tonight," he said, smiling at me. "Why don't you come and see me every night after class. That way I can help you with any problems that might have popped up since our last session."

I smiled back at him, feeling better than I had ever felt before. But there was one thing I wanted that I had not received from my teacher.

"Next time, maybe I could give you a little something," I offered.

He winked and nodded as he rolled off me, his cock leaving my stretched asshole feeling empty and abandoned.

"Perhaps. When you show me you're really, really ready," he replied, pulling on his boxers and trousers.

I wondered how I'd know I was ready, as I hauled on my Levi's. Would he tell me, or would I just know? Maybe I'd just have to leave it to him, but my cock certainly thought I was ready right then. Still I left his office, eagerly awaiting our next appointment and my next opportunity.

TO FUCK ARMANDO
Jason Carpenter

I hurried to the window when I heard Armando's delivery truck squeal to a stop in front of my two-story Tudor home. The truck was a deep chocolate brown and complemented his burnished bronze skin. Of medium height, his firm physique resembled an advertisement for the local gym. He was such a tasty morsel, I drooled as I peeped through the blinds. For months I dreamed of fucking him. With his coal-black, slicked-back hair and flashing dark eyes, Armando might as well have had "fuck me," rather than his name, embroidered on the breast pocket of his starched uniform. I touched my cock, watching him wrestle the gargantuan package from the rear of the truck. Every muscle in his upper body was delineated and bulging as he loaded my parcel to a hand-truck for front door delivery. Armando wheeled the box up the walk to the porch and tickled the doorbell. I hurried to the door, wrapping the belt around my thick, white terry robe on the way. "Looks like you been at it again, Michael – home shopping club on TV, right?" Armando gasped, clearly out of breath. "I just get so lonely at night, lying in my bed alone. I have nothing to do except watch TV ... and then I end up buying things I really don't need."

"Do me a favor and don't return this one. I'm gonna get a hernia if I have to move this again-and I'm in good shape. I don't know what you would have done if Fred had been delivering today," Armando said with a beaming smile. "How about a cappuccino to make up for the trouble I've caused you this morning?" I asked slyly. Armando looked at his watch and deliberated. "OK, sounds great. I'm ten minutes ahead of schedule." I helped him hoist the package into my foyer, parking his hand-truck outside the door. "One favor ... please take off your shoes. I have white carpet and it's so hard to clean," I ventured weakly, hoping he wouldn't be offended. "No problem," Armando replied, surprising me with his lack

of hesitation. "Some place you have here. I always wondered what it looked like inside," he added, eyeing my collection of erotic male statues.

"Come sit here while I whip up some fresh cappuccino. Whipped cream?" I asked, guiding him to the pearl-white sofa.

"Whipped cream sounds yummy."

A shiver radiated from my balls up with that comment. After months of trying to lure him inside I suddenly had him in my living room with his shoes off. Now, if I could just get him out of those starched pants!

I placed the two steaming cappuccinos on a tray and set them down on the table to his left, forcing me to reach across him. He didn't flinch when 1 "accidentally" dropped a frothy dollop of cream from my cup into his lap. The cream landed precisely where I had aimed: on top of the bulge in his pants.

"Oh no!" I exclaimed. "Let me get that off before it sets!" I grabbed a linen napkin from the tray and rubbed gently at the damp spot, just right of his fly. His cock sprang to attention like an obedient soldier! So he was curious to taste my life-style. He didn't object when I stripped off his pants.

Pre-cum oozed from his cock-slit like white honey. I snatched a condom from my robe pocket, enveloped his flushed, pink cock, then fisted his rigid hose and stuffed it down my wet throat all the way to my tonsils. I wanted to devour every inch of him!

His cock was so big I had to suck hard through my nostrils to keep from passing out. His lustful panting escalated and he ran his fingers through my hair. I blew him fast and hard until he spewed so much hot cum into the reservoir tip I nearly gagged.

"Shit, man, that was unreal. I've always wondered what it would be like with a guy, but didn't know how to approach the subject," Armando gulped.

"You'll never want one of those tacky females again when I get through with you," I promised, removing the spent condom so I could milk every last drop of sweet, creamy jizz from his love rod. With greedy hands, I stroked and fondled his gorgeous cock and hairy, throbbing balls.

With Armando's confession still hanging in the air, I wasted no time easing him over and positioning him so I'd have a clear shot at his virgin asshole. Reaching under the sofa, I quickly gathered my supplies-Magnum condoms and lubricant. I lubed him up good, using my index finger to coat his rosy orifice with jelly.

With each caress of my inquisitive finger Armando moaned softly. I fully submerged my middle finger up his tender, virgin hole and finger-fucked him languidly, adding two additional fingers to sate his appetite for more.

Lowering myself behind him, I slid my wet tongue over his balls and drew his hot jewels into my talented mouth. I sucked his balls gently, repetitively rolling them around in my mouth, dizzy with the man-smell of him and the wiry tickle of his nuts against my tongue.

He squirmed, ready for more. I slipped the condom over my throbbing ten inches of hard cock and, with one fluid stroke, plunged deeply up his velvet cavity. He squealed as I took his cherry, heightening the intensity I felt in scoring pure, fresh ass-meat.

I rammed him steadily, pulling almost all the way out each time, reaming him good, until his asshole sucked for more, and opened fully to me. "Like it?" I whispered in his ear.

"Yeah, mem, yeah. Don't stop!" he said needlessly.

I screwed him at a leisurely pace, prodding and burrowing to prolong our sweet pleasure until I felt the electric surge radiate from my balls and shoot up my cock. A huge wad of burning cum spurted from my dick up his clenching anus. Sated, I collapsed against his taut buttocks in exhausted completion.

Armando convulsed beneath me. Every muscle in his athletic body twitched with excitement as he, too, erupted in a fragrant, copious spray of cum, staining my sofa – leaving me a pungent memento of our ardor.

I eased out of him, fell back on the sofa, removed the condom and stowed it in my robe pocket.

Armando turned to sit beside me and I kissed his full lips. "Well?"

His dark eyes and broad smile answered for him.

Suddenly, he looked at his watch. "Oh my, God, look at the time!" he yelped, jumping up from the sofa and grabbing his pants from the floor.

When I stood, he pulled me close and thrust his rigid tongue into my mouth. My tongue met his, hungry for more of his youth and inexperience. "Thanks for the coffee break, but I

have to get back to work now." I fondled his rod. "Why don't you take your lunch break now?" I asked. "I haven't shown you around upstairs yet."

"Michael, I got to work for a living."

"Oh, come on, Armando, what difference will thirty minutes make?" I persisted. "Shit! Show me the way," he exclaimed, extending his hand towards me. I took his hand and led him upstairs to my bedroom. "Damn," he breathed as he took in the mirrored ceiling, mock-chinchilla-covered bed and the cozy whirlpool tub sending up wavy clouds of steam at the foot of my bed. An assortment of dildos in various sizes and colors lined the rim of the tub, ready to fulfill his fantasies. Armando's cock rose in anticipation. I unbuttoned his shirt and took him to the side of the tub. "Undress me," I told him, placing his hand on the belt of my robe. He unwrapped me as hurriedly as a child unwraps a Christmas package. Naked, we entered the tub together, locked in a heated embrace. Armando caressed my pulsing tool; its thick, throbbing veins stood out like a relief map of the Rocky Mountain ridges. He lowered his head to take me in his mouth. "Wait, Armando," I begged, taking a rubber from the open box nearby and hurriedly rolling it over my cock, eager to feel his sweet mouth around my stiff cock-meat. He guided my cock to his voracious mouth and swallowed me steadily until he gagged. He dropped to his knees in the warm water and looked up at me. "God, it's enormous!" he declared, but didn't hesitate to encircle it again with his hot mouth. His hand rose up to cup my balls and he massaged them with a careful, rhythmic rolling motion. I could tell he liked to suck cock. I pressed my hand to the back of his head and fed him every inch of me. After a couple minutes, he got up and sat on the submerged love seat. He selected one of my dildos, a foot-long, black model and said, "Lay over my lap." Flushed with expectation, I draped myself over his knees. "Like this?"

Armando asked, rubbing the big, rubber dick-head against my ass-ring, screwing it slowly up my ass. "Mmm ... just like that."

He inched the black monster deep up my guts, then withdrew it halfway, pausing for a heartbeat before ramming it home again, faster and faster with each thrust, manipulating the soft rubber toy in a dockwise screwing motion, reaming out my love hole. Ecstatic tears filled my eyes as he labored lovingly.

The warm water bubbled and flowed around my balls, bringing me to the edge of orgasm, then beyond, as the dildo prodded my prostate and sent a heavy stream of fuckjuice spewing from my swollen cock into the condom covering me.

Armando slow-fucked me with the dildo until I was empty. "You learn fast," I muttered, breathing heavily.

"Thanks. Is it my turn again?" he asked hopefully.

"Indeed," I said, lathering him from head to toe in fragrantly scented bath foam, working it into his pores tenderly with both hands. He smiled at me as my nimble fingers caressed his willing flesh. I sponged his meaty cock and balls, handling them gingerly, teasing him without mercy. His dick stood straight up out of the water like a submarine's periscope.

"Suck me off again," he said.

I took my time shimmying the condom over his rod, then I licked at the sensitive underside and all around his perfectly cut dick-head, feeling his crown pulse with blood. I nipped gently at the fringe around his crown and tongue and teased his dick-slit until he humped upward. Opening wide, I swallowed his cock deep down the back of my throat. He face-fucked me more and more rapidly before erupting in a thrusting, churning eruption of cum. His geyser filled my ravenous mouth.

"Aw, man, cock is great," Armando praised as we rested. I want to eat it and have it up my ass from now on."

"You know where to come," I said, kissing him hard on the mouth.

"Sure do," he said, kissing my neck and working his way down to my rigid nipples. He twirled the right one between his fingers then took it in his mouth to suckle.

147

To my astonishment, my cock became erect again! But we were beginning to prune. "C'mon," I said with a nod.

We exited the tub, dried with thick towels, and fell upon the furry bed. Belly to belly, we fondled each other's glistening shaft, jerking each other off, unhurriedly, ending our lunch sex sticky with our combined cum.

We dressed silently and went downstairs. "Some lunch, Michael!" Armando enthused, standing at the door. I laughed. "Is that all you can say, when you've been so royally and properly sucked and butt-fucked?"

"But you sure got a big surprise package you weren't counting on ... delivered right to your door."

"Well, if I can count on this from now on, the Home Shopping channel is going to get rich!" I watched as he wheeled his dolly down the walk, and heard him whistling happily.

ALL FELL SILENT
Peter Gilbert

"Pertacus, Perfidus, Campester, Lucilianus, Campanus. All fell silent.... " – Inscription scratched on a tile found at Suchester, England: the site of the Roman town of Calleva Atrebatum.

"You could invite them here one afternoon. It could be rather fun. That tall dark one is very attractive."

In any other circumstances I would have laughed. I wasn't actually in pain but it was uncomfortable. Marcus always stopped when the head of his cock had gotten into me. The aim was two-fold. It stopped him from coming too quickly and it enabled my muscles to relax sufficiently to take the rest of him.

"Why don't you ask them?" he whispered.

"No ... no chance. Go on. I'm ready."

After that, of course, there was no more conversation unless you count groans and grunts as "conversation'. I clutched the side of the couch as his cock slid into me. Not even the expensive oil he used made it any easier. Once it was in, it wasn't too bad. In fact it was nice but I could hardly tell the others that.

One of the nicest things about sex with Marcus was being able to let myself go. His slaves lived in an out-building some way from the villa and there was nobody else in the building at all. Just us. It was very different when Perfidus used to come to our house or when I went to his. One of us would hear a sound that the other hadn't heard. Tunics were slipped on hurriedly and one of us would grab something to make us look as if we were doing something "more constructive' than manipulating each other's rampant cocks. Invariably it was a false alarm but we had to be careful, especially in the last few seconds when we had to stifle our gasps and sighs

In Marcus' bedroom I could make as much noise as I wanted and I had a lot to shout about. I was the close (very close) personal friend of one of the most important men in Britain; a man with a superb cock and a man that knew how to use it. On that particular afternoon we were probably both even

noisier than usual. Marcus had just come back from one of his mysterious trips to the north. Our groans, grunts and gasps echoed down from the high ceiling. All too soon, it was over. I lay there feeling his cock subsiding inside me.

"All fell silent," I said.

"What?"

"A quotation from Virgil. "All fell silent""

Later that afternoon, when we were enjoying a bath in his luxurious bath suite, he brought up the matter of the others again.

"Perfidus might. As for the others, forget it," I said. "Anyway, what's wrong with me?" He put his hand under the water and felt for my cock. He squeezed it. "Nothing at all," he said. "It's just that in Rome I'm used to having more than one boy. This place is like the end of the world."

He was right there. I don't know if you've ever been to Britannia. I hope for your sake that you haven't. It is the coldest, wettest outpost of the Roman empire. We lived in the town of Calleva Atrebatum in south Britannia. Dad was the tax collector there. He spent the whole of the time moaning about having been posted there from Hispania where the weather was warm and I spent the whole time moaning about having nothing to do. I'd finished my education and the chances of getting a job in Calleva were nil. I might have stood a chance if we'd lived in Londinium, the capital. That's not a bad place but Calleva? Forget it.

So, my little gang and I hung around the main gate to see who was arriving and who was leaving, sympathizing with the former and envying the latter. Such was life.

It was while waiting at the gate one day that I met Marcus. He'd been living in Calleva for about three years then. The villa that was being built for him was outside the town wall so we didn't see a lot of him in the town. Needless to say, there was the usual Calleva gossip. We knew he was a Legate; commander of a Legion. Some people said he had a wife in Rome. Another theory held that he had a concubine somewhere in the north of Britannia. He'd been seen taking the north road out of town once or twice. The one undisputed fact was that the villa was spectacular: It had its own private bath suite. Craftsmen had come from Rome to lay the mosaic floors. It was obviously going to be last word in luxury when it was finished.

Anyway, where was I? Oh yes. I won't bore you now with the names of my friends. They were all about my age. Somebody said "Here comes that Legate." I looked down the road. There was no mistaking his horse. It was enormous. The sentries on the gate saluted and in he came. He stopped and looked down at us and at that moment – don't ask me how -1 knew my life was about to change. "One of you hold the horse for me," said Marcus. "I need to speak to the guards for a moment."

"I will, excellency," I said. For months afterwards those three words haunted me. Whenever I joined the others, someone would say "I will, excellency," and call me a vulgar name. Not that I minded by then. Their chances of employment were still nil. I had become the personal friend of a Legate – rather more than just a friend. Holding the horse led to an invitation back to his villa; a glass of the best wine – and an invitation to use his bath suite any time I wanted. That alone was worth doing anything for. The public baths were disgusting. The water was a dull green color and enough to make anyone sick. Several people became sick there, and it was never cleaned up till the following day.

I knew what he wanted of course. That became clear on my second visit. He showed me the bath, sat and watched as I undressed and then, starting with my head, praised every part of me with especial reference to the bits not usually on display. Then he decided he might as well take a bath as well, solicitously supporting me as I climbed down into the pool. The support continued when we were up to our necks in the water. His hand went on my behind first, then round my waist. I tried not to show surprise when it found my cock.

"You really are a big lad!" he said, squeezing it softly.

If you're after what I was after, namely a high-powered government job somewhere warm, you have to show willingness so I did the same to his. I said I'd heard Roman soldiers had the best weapons. He never even gave me time to get my hair wet. We were out of the pool in minutes and I was lying on my front and he was oiling me all over – and I really mean "all over'.

Two hours later I'd come in his mouth; he'd shot his load all over me and we'd had another bath. I strolled home happily enough. The muscles in my ass ached slightly from having had a finger in there but he had promised to do all he could to help me get a good job.

I told the others just as much as I needed to tell them. I had to tell them about the bath privilege or they would have shunned me for not taking a regular bath.

"And does he bathe with you?" said one of my friends. "I'll bet he does. He's after your ass, Pertacus. You want to watch him. My dad says there's a lot of that sort of thing going on in Rome these days."

The others rounded on him. Legates weren't like that and, as for stories of goings-on in the capital, everybody knew how those got twisted and exaggerated on their way from Rome to Britannia. So we continued to loaf around the main gate and visit the monthly slave market. It was there that Marcus met the others properly for the first time. I had drifted away from them, heading in my usual direction because Julia Tammonius was at the male stall and one could be sure of a good laugh when she was there. She had a leasing arrangement for her houseboy. Julia's ideas of a house boy's duties deviated considerably from established custom and she changed them regularly.

"You won't find a better-built one this side of the channel, madam," said the trader. The young man on display was a Brit of about twenty-two or three. He stood on the podium in his tiny leather shorts looking down with a puzzled expression. The trader was right about his build. He was quite something.

"I should hope so," said Julia. That last one was very disappointing. I hope he's got a nice straight...." She turned round, noticed me and said, "stick. For the time when the floods come," she added, in deference to my youth and "innocence'. "It's so useful to know just how deep the water is."

"Straight and strong too. You won't be disappointed and there would be no need to send this one to the market to get a basket of fruit. He's got his own. Like a couple of peaches, they are." He swung the slave round so that she (and I) could admire his back view.

As it happened, that was one young man that wasn't destined to appear again on the podium later in the year with rings round his eyes.

There was a slight commotion at the entrance and Marcus strode in. I was surprised because he'd been away for some weeks. I'd had to endure the public baths and miss out on what I had come to enjoy. Looking at that slave hadn't helped.

I'd intended to wait till my cock subsided before again joining the others.

Needless to say, the trader stopped talking to Julia at once. Marcus meant real money, not a leasing fee.

"That one looks just right for what I have in mind," said Marcus. "How much?"

The price the man quoted would have kept a family of four fed for a month. Marcus took out his purse and paid on the nail.

"And dare I ask what purpose you have in mind?" I asked.

"Oh! It's Pertacus, isn't it?"

I grinned. He'd seen me the moment he came into the market. He was obviously being careful. One or two of the shoppers smiled patronizingly at the thought of a kind Legate speaking to a mere teenager.

The trader produced a collar and leash. I was given the job of leading the slave off. I hoped people might think I was rich enough to have bought him. Out of hearing of anyone else, I repeated my question.

"Not what you think. I want him for making tiles for the new wing," said Marcus. "Aren't those your friends over there?"

"Yes. Stupid lot. They only come to leer."

"By the look of that lump in the front of your tunic, you're not one to talk. As soon as we've got this one home, I'll be glad to deal with that for you. But we'll have a word with your friends first. It would be rude not to."

It was all very polite. He asked their names and what their fathers did and they beat me in the vulgarity stakes. They were practically bowing to him. I stood there, holding the slave's leash, feeling more and more angry. Jealousy I guess. Eventually, after much handshaking and Legatorial hands on shoulders, he tore himself away. He'd come on horseback so I led the slave back to the villa. It was quite a distance and he couldn't speak a word of Latin – which is probably just as well in view of the comments that had been made in his hearing.

Marcus was propped up on his couch reading a sheaf of documents; official stuff. One look at the leather satchel on the floor was enough to tell me that. He greeted me warmly enough and that made me feel better. I was beginning to wonder if I was being cast aside.

"If you'd be good enough to hand the slave over to the slave master, Pertacus," he said. "I shan't be long but this is important. It came when I was away."

The slave master got me to help washing the slave down so I was more than happy to oblige. Everything the trader had said was true. His "stick' would have been useful in flood water of up to about nine inches and his balls really were the size of peaches. It's funny. The slave master was completely unmoved. I got the job of scrubbing the slave's back and by the time I'd reached his backside I was panting like a long distance runner. I had to put a hand down inside my tunic for the short walk back to the villa.

Marcus was still reading. I swept the pieces of sealing wax onto the floor and sat next to him. "How are things in Rome?" I asked.

"Much the same as ever," he said. "Jove! By the look of that lump in your tunic, I'd better read the rest later!"

There is nothing, absolutely nothing like being fucked after spending a month as a virgin. Maybe you've found that out for yourself. I hope so. It took time for the longed-for guest to get past the threshold but Marcus had a technique for that. I knelt on the couch and he licked the entrance. A great shudder went through me every time. My cock swelled and my balls ached and I would have shot several times if he hadn't stopped periodically.

"Have you ever met the Emperor?" I asked during one of these pauses and after I'd got my breath back.

"The Divine Hadrian? Yes, several times."

"What's he like?"

"Tall. He's got a beard of course."

"What? Like a barbarian? I shouldn't fancy that!"

"Why not?"

"Well, it would tickle when he did what you've been doing. Do it again."

"I shall have to ask Antinous," he said. His hands parted the cheeks of my ass and there was no more talking for some time. "There!" he said at length. "Let's try again. Just relax now." That time it went in easily. I didn't even have to think what to do. It felt like a hard-boiled egg lodged in me. Once again, he paused and stroked my back.

"Who's ... Antin ... ous?" I asked.

"Oh, the Emperor's boyfriend. He comes from somewhere in Asia Minor. The Empress got slung out some time back."

"And is he beautiful?"

"Yes, but not as beautiful as you. The gods alone know how much I've been looking forward to this moment."

"Does the Emperor...? Aaaah! Oh! That's so good."

It was too. I remember thinking as it went into me what a jealous idiot I had been over the gang. If anyone had behaved badly, it was I. I was the one that got worked up over a British slave when, all the time, a Legate was yearning to fuck me. All Marcus had done was talk to them.

Rational thought was very soon impossible. I soon knew that he, like me, hadn't had it for a long time. His hands gripped my nipples so hard that it was painful and his cock thrust into me like a battering ram. Finally with a triumphant cry from him and a long, drawn-out sigh from me, we both came. I felt his semen shooting up into me. Mine jetted forward, soaking me and the couch.

All fell silent – for a few minutes anyway.

"I wonder if the Emperor fucks Antinous," I said.

"Probably. You can ask him yourself soon."

"How?"

"I shouldn't have said that. Forget it."

I wasn't having that! True friends didn't have secrets. Bit by bit – and with a bit of encouragement from my hand, the story came out. There had been a lot of trouble with the savage tribes in the North. Marcus's strange trips up there had been to reconnoiter the situation. There was nothing else for it, in his view, but to build a wall right across Britannia to keep them confined and the Emperor was even then on his way to discuss it and to see for himself.

"Is he bringing Antinous with him?" I asked.

"Not as far as I know. This colony is a bit too conservative. Anyway, keep it to yourself. This is definitely a case of falling silent."

Naturally enough, I did. I told the others about the beard though. I didn't think that could do any harm. As it was, they wouldn't believe it. The mark of a Roman man was a smooth- shaven face. The thought of the Emperor with a beard was almost sacrilegious to them. The Emperor, after all, was both god and man. If they hadn't been so disbelieving I might have told them about Antinous as well. They decided that I was either making up the story or that Marcus had played a practical

joke in very poor taste. So I left it at that.

Then, for the first time in history, the gods came to my aid. Two marble statues arrived for the forum. We actually saw them before anyone else. We were at the gate when the ox cart arrived. A few days later when they'd been unveiled we went to have a look. There he was: the divine Hadrian himself, complete with beard.

"I wonder who the young guy is," said Campanus. "It just says "Beloved of the Gods' on the plinth. Campanus was half British and never really mastered Latin grammar.

"God ... not "Gods'. Can't you recognize a simple plural?" I said.

"Oh yeah. Must mean Mars. He's the God of War and this guy's got the build of a soldier."

"If you must know, his name is Antinous and he's the emperor's boyfriend," I said.

If I hadn't been right about the beard I'd have been beaten up pretty badly. As it was, they found it difficult to believe and difficult to understand. All except Perfidus.

"He's got the right idea," he said. "He looks to be about the same age as we are and where is he now? In a palace in Rome, being waited on. And what do we do all day? Hang around the town gate. That's what."

The others laughed. "You never know. The Emperor may come through the gate one day and spot you. You never know your luck," somebody said.

A strange shiver ran through me. That was where Marcus and I had met. Perfidus' remarks were encouraging and he'd been cooperative enough with me when we were younger. There was no need for him to wait at the gate for the Emperor. A Legate of my acquaintance would be only too happy. Perfidus wasn't the best-looking young man in the gang but at least Marcus had a chance with him and not, I was sure, with any of the others.

Getting him to the villa was easy enough. Some three days later I told Perfidus that Marcus had a high opinion of him. Two days after that I passed on Marcus' (genuine) invitation for him to come to the villa and use the bath there. On the following day, he was up to his neck in warm water with Marcus by his side. I sat on the edge and watched them. Sure enough, an embarrassed sort of grin flashed across Perfidus' face and I knew immediately where Marcus' hand had landed. They stood like that for some minutes, apparently stock-still and with their shoulders touching. Perfidus' face went slightly red – not, I was sure, because of the temperature of the water! Finally, Marcus clambered out, with his cock seeming to point the way. I stood up. It was time to make myself scarce.

"Don't go," he said.

"You don't want me around," I said. I didn't feel in the least jealous, which might strike you as odd.

"I do," he said. "I need a witness. I don't want him telling the townsfolk. I've got a reputation to uphold. Give me enough time and come in then.""

Enough time for what?' That was the question. I can't say that the idea appalled me. My cock took an immediate interest in the prospect. On the other hand I didn't think Perfidus would approve.

In fact by the time it was all happening, Perfidus was in no state to object. He came out of the pool, still half hard. "It's the warm water. It always does that to me," he explained. By the time he'd climbed down from the couch after one of Marcus' famous rub-downs with oil it was as hard as iron. He grinned shamefacedly as they both went into the main reception room. I put the various bottles away on the shelf, tidied up generally and, holding my sandals so that I shouldn't be heard, I padded along the corridor. That was probably sensible but I need not have worried about being seen. Marcus' entire field of vision must have comprised an extreme dose up of the area under Perfidus' navel. Perfidus had his back to me – his backside I should say for that's what attracted all my attention. It had grown considerably more attractive in the years since our furtive sessions. It was like looking at two plump silk cushions, with the added attraction of being very much alive. It tightened, forming deep dimples and then relaxed before tightening again in time with what he was trying to say.

"Never done... Oh yeah! Yeah! That's it! Oh ... do that again! Oh yeah!"

I sat on the little X-shaped chair in the corner to enjoy the performance. I watched Marcus fingers move slowly across my friend's buttocks until they touched. The big ruby ring he always wore reflected the sunlight over towards me and I had to shift my head slightly to avoid the rays. One fingertip disappeared into the deft. Perfidus gasped loudly but the rhythmic buttock movements continued. It was a clever technique that Marcus had used on me on our first afternoon. It's not that the finger pushes into you. You impale yourself. You can't help it. Sure enough, it happened to Perfidus. How Marcus could manage to stay so long with a cock in his mouth I could never understand, but he did. Pefidus' movements became more and more frantic. He became noisier and noisier. They weren't words any more – just wild, animalistic noises. Suddenly he let out a sort of gasp and stopped moving. I knew and certainly Marcus knew, that his questing digit had gone in. That expensive oil Marcus used was worth its weight in gold.

At last, Marcus disengaged himself. He wiped his lips with the back of his hand and stood up. His toga fell from his shoulders. He caught sight of me and grinned.

"What...?" Perfidus asked. He turned slightly, fortunately not in my direction but I caught a glimpse of his saliva-soaked cock. Marcus threw the cushions from the couch onto the mosaic floor.

"I don't think...." said Perfidus. He might as well have been talking to the walls. I didn't actually see what Marcus did. It must have been a trick he'd learned in the Legion. Perfidus was suddenly sprawled out face down on the cushions. He wasn't hurt. I could tell that by the way he gathered two cushions together and lay his head on them. He was always one for comfort and he was also obviously resigned to what the narrow- minded idiots of Calleva might refer to as his "fate.' "Reward' would have been more appropriate. Marcus used exactly the same technique as he'd used with me. They talked! With a complete disregard for my friend's enjoyment and comfort I was inwardly screaming for the action to speed up. From where I was sitting, I had a good view of Marcus' humped rump. His penis appeared to be growing out of Perfidus. I wanted to see it in – all of it.

The disgraceful state of the public baths was the first topic as I recall.

"The drains need something better than that sloo...oo... uice!" and Marcus' backside was slightly lower.

A long pause – and the baths gave way to town planning. "Something needs to be done about the main ro...oh...oh...d!" and still Marcus wasn't entirely into him. They were talking about chariot racing of all things at the time – or, rather, Marcus was doing the talking. The sport hadn't reached Britannia at the time.

"When you're in Rome you'll be able to go every week," said Marcus.

"Not... much ... chance ... of ... that," Perfidus panted.

"Of course you will. Rome needs lads of your ability. I'll write a letter this evening. Hold still now..."

I wonder if you agree that it's the most magical moment in a young man's life. Watching it happen is nearly as good as experiencing it for yourself. The young man's head jerks upwards as the massive buttocks lower. I couldn't see Perfidus' face. I didn't need to. I knew what he was feeling and I knew what he was thinking. It's at that moment that you realize why the gods decree that young men are slender and beautiful. The fat boy becomes a bony, clumsy teenager who lies awake worrying about the spots on his face, frantically making what he thinks is the best use of his cock. Then comes the metamorphosis. The tragedy is that there are not enough men like Marcus (dare I say "of Marcus' caliber?') to help you appreciate that a man's hand feels much better than your own; that a man's mouth is infinitely more satisfying and, when the moment comes, the initial pain is nothing compared to the eventual pleasure. You realize that those lonely, frantic fumblings – even the parental embraces of your early years, were just a foretaste of the delights to come. I used to feel embarrassed if my dad put his arm round me. Being hugged by Marcus was another matter.

But I must stop philosophizing and take you back to that room. Perfidus was the one in Marcus' arms that afternoon and, although I couldn't see them, I knew where Marcus' fingers were. Both of them were grunting noisily and in time with the contractions of Marcus' military-trained gluteal muscles.

By that time, as I knew from experience, both of them were too far gone to notice me. I stood up and slipped off my tunic. That felt better, more "natural' somehow. I went over to stand by them. My cock acted like a teacher's pointer as I looked down on them. But this was nothing like the boring geography lessons I'd had to endure. "Observe, boys, the shape of the country, ".... "Observe, boys, the length of Marcus' legs and the way they encompass the less hairy but delightfully shaped legs of his partner. May I now draw your attention to that gloriously shaped and powerful behind that he is using to such good effect? Those little beads of moisture you see forming on his back are the result of his exertions. You might care to add something of your own..."

Why not? I was pretty near anyway. It would have to be got rid of somehow. I stepped forward.

"Ugh!"

"Ah!"

"Ugh!"

"Ah!"

John Patrick

"Aaah!" I stood with my feet apart and my hand on my cock and joined in. Our grunts and cries echoed back at me from the mosaic floor and stone walls.

All fell silent. One after another. Marcus first, then Perfidus and, finally, it was my turn. Marcus didn't seem to notice the shower of semen that landed on him – which is just as well or he would have laughed at my bad aim. Some went in his hair. There were a couple of spots on the back of his neck and the last few drops mingled with the perspiration on his back. Not my best effort, especially compared with his. I knew – and Perfidus knew – where his was and Perfidus gave every indication of wanting more. He brought his hands back and pressed them on Marcus' asscheeks. I remembered doing the same myself.

Whether he got another injection that afternoon I don't know. I picked up my tunic and my sandals and padded back to the bath-suite. I was in there for ages. They showed no sign of appearing so I dressed and went out into the garden. The new slave was busy making tiles for the floor in the new wing. I stopped and watched him for some time. Finally, Perfidus appeared.

"Have a good time?" I asked.

"Yeah. He's a great guy, isn't he? He's going to try to get me a job as an architect in Rome. The emperor's keen on building."

"Good for you."

I still don't know if he had been aware of my presence. He never mentioned it but then I never told him that the cock he'd enjoyed so much had been in me. He asked me to walk more slowly on our way back to the town. He said his legs ached. I tried not to smile.

The other three were easy. My account of the delights of bathing in a private bath suite and Perfidus' boasting about his new job worked wonders. Marcus soon had five partners – enough when you consider his occasional visits to the North and the preparations for the imperial visit. One by one I watched three asses being expensively and carefully lubricated. One was large and rather hairy, one as soft and malleable as cream cheese, and the other was so compact that it might have belonged to a little boy and not a 19-year-old. From my little seat in the comer or from behind a pillar I watched Marcus savor their cocks. The

161

first was so densely surrounded in hair that he sneezed. I would have described the second as disappointing but Marcus didn't seem to think so. The third, Campester, was so short in stature that Marcus had to get down on his knees. Campester was far from short in another dimension though.

Each had his own distinctive sound. After the Emperor's visit when I was in Marcus' writing room helping with the correspondence I could tell who he was with and how far he'd got by the sound alone. Inevitably, and sometimes far too soon, they all fell silent.

Their silence wasn't confined to the villa. Each one talked about his future prospects but not how he had managed to secure such a good job. Campester knew about the imperial visit. I know that because I was in the room when Marcus told him. Getting eight inches of Legatorial cock into Campester's tight, little-boy ass needed a lot of relaxing conversation. But nobody said a word outside.

We never even saw the Emperor. The procession came in via the little-used east gate. He stayed at the villa but we couldn't get near it because of the Praetorian Guard. Marcus went North with the Imperial party and was away for three weeks. He returned with the scrolls appointing us to our various jobs, each one bearing the imperial seal.

We went to say "goodbye' on the day before we traveled. As I'm sure you will understand, there was a great deal of coming and not much mention of going that day.

In the evening I sat out on the steps overlooking the lawn and took my last, long look at the town I was never to see again. The slave was carrying the last few tiles over to the new wing.

"Give me one," I demanded.

"Why you want?" He had picked up a bit of Latin since Marcus had bought him. He put down the hod and handed me one. I searched around and found an iron nail and wrote in the still damp clay: "Pertacus, Perfidus, Campester, Lucilianus, Campanus. All fell silent..."Make sure that one goes in the middle of the floor," I said.

THE LOVING CUP
James Hosier

It's been a long time since I last wrote. I would have written from England but Sir Thomas didn't think it was a very good idea. So... three years later, here I am back home. The computer still works so if any of you have been wondering what happened to young James Hosier, here we go:

I knew I'd never make it to the Ivy League but I thought I might have a chance somewhere where the ivy grew on the outside walls. Three years of learning Business Administration in a place like that would have suited me fine. Dad's boss, Mr. Valdinger had different ideas. I've told you about him in previous accounts of my secret sideline. He's the guy into Culture with a big "C' and, possibly because he hasn't got a son of his own, he's always taken a lot of interest in me. I don't think there is any other reason. The thought makes me shudder.

It happened that Mr. Valdinger went to some sort of party at the British Embassy in Washington. Why the British should have invited the Chief Executive Officer "Kookalux' is beyond me. Maybe they were after a cheaply fitted kitchen. They didn't get one but Mr. Valdinger came away with an idea. I don't know if you are the same as I but if there's one thing that makes me see red, it's having plans made for me. I endured six weeks of one- sided phone calls. Dad went off to see someone. I knew it was something that concerned me but not one word was said to me. "We didn't want you to be disappointed if it all fell through," Dad said later.

In June of that year we went to England. Dad had some business to do there with a firm that made things for hotel kitchens. That left my mother and me to spend four days alone in a place where they drive on the left, where the guys who designed their cabs have obviously never heard of the principle of streamlining and where nobody knows how to make a good cup of coffee. We went around and we saw things – some of which were quite interesting. Then, on the next to last day, we went to Cambridge – all three of us – and I found myself being interviewed by Professor Sir Thomas Richards, Head of Business

Administration at the university. He was definitely the strangest man I'd ever met. He was very tiny – not much more than five feet and five inches. He had a strange chirping voice and his eyebrows were enormous. I'd never see anything like them. They extended outwards like horns. He looked more like an owl than a man – an impression heightened by the way he perched on the edge of his desk rather than sit on the chair.

"So, you want to come to Cambridge, James?" he said.

The idea had its advantages: An MBA from a university that everybody in the world had heard of, three years of independence from Mom and Dad plus the fact that some of the guys I'd seen strolling about there were real cock-raisers. I'd been fucked twice by Michael on the day before we left the States but they still had an effect on me. I just said that the idea was appealing. I didn't say which idea.

I'd had to write a short essay describing myself. I'd done that, at Dad's instigation, in the hotel in London. Sir Thomas reached behind him and picked up the familiar three sheets of punched paper.

"This is very lucid and rather more interesting than those I normally read," he said. "Have you ever considered writing commercially?"

I thought fast. It was hardly likely that he or anyone else could have read them.... "I have, as a matter of fact," I said.

"Really? How very interesting. What do you write about?"

"Oh ... er.... teenage adventure stories for "STARbooks Press' in Florida," I said. Well, "teenage adventures' was pretty near the truth.

"How fascinating! I don't think we have any other undergraduate authors." After that he asked lots of questions about my school and sports. My swimming record seemed to go down well. The more I thought about it, the more the idea of studying in Britain appealed. When the interview was over he said he would be in touch. We shook hands and that was that. We flew back to the States. Dad phoned Mr. Valdinger but I wasn't at home at the time. I was spread out on Michael's bed happily providing a hundred dollars' worth of All-American teenage ass.

Later, when the rubber was in the trash can and we'd showered and were sitting in his lounge he said the opportunity was too good to miss. He'd miss me but there would be long vacations.

Greg, my other regular client, thought the same. Greg is a very successful businessman so his opinion counted for a lot. All his opinions. After all, you don't ignore the views of a guy who tells you you've got the most beautiful ass in the world and your cock is the most perfect he's ever seen. I left his place considerably richer after satisfying his appetite for spunk – and determined, if I could, to go to Cambridge.

Janet was upset, of course, and so was I, at the thought of leaving her. But she was due to go to college in September too and she was headed for the west coast. We wouldn't have seen much of each other even if I stayed in the States.

There was a long exchange of faxes between Cambridge and my school and Cambridge and "Kookalux.' Unlike my parents, Cambridge sent me copies of everything so I knew what was going on. The letter announcing that I had been awarded the Rutherford Scholarship providing for an American citizen to study there wasn't too great a surprise. The award from "Kookalux' was. I'd still have to go easy on spending but I wouldn't be poor. Besides, one never knew. There were three gay men in our town who parted with cash for my services and Cambridge was quite a big city.

I'll spare you pages and pages of description of Cambridge and its University. If you're that interested you can read about it elsewhere. It's a beautiful city – old, full of ancient traditions. Standing in the chapel of King's College and hearing the choir singing is enough to give even an American teenager a lump in his throat. Business studies, I am pleased to say, were taught in modem buildings by teachers with a modem outlook. The block I lived in was modern too. There were four other Americans on my floor and their presence offset a lot of homesickness. Paul Brosz in the next room was a particularly nice guy. He was there for the rowing. Physics, which he was supposed to be studying, took second place. He was enormous – and I don't mean just his muscular development. I caught one or two glimpses of it. We used communal showers on the ground floor. I went out to the river Cam once or twice to see him in action. Rowing was the only type of action, unfortunately. Paul had a girlfriend back in the States – as I did too of course.

The first three months passed happily enough. It was at the beginning of December that I ran up against Sir Thomas Richards again. He very rarely gave lectures. He was crossing the quad dressed in his full regalia, which made him look even more like a bird – a parrot this time.

"Ah, James Hosier," he said. "Settling down all right, are you?"

I said I was. "And how are Michael and Greg and that other one – the doctor? They must be missing you dreadfully."

I nearly died on the spot! "I've been reading some of your work," he continued. "What a devious young man you are! One would never have guessed."

I stammered something, imploring him, as I recall, to keep quiet.

"My dear boy! You have nothing at all to fear from me. I am far too old and too wise. Between ourselves it's nice to have someone here who is of my line of thinking but so much younger. How many of the undergraduates have fallen for your charms so far?"

"None at all, Sir Thomas."

"Dear me! Dear me! I am surprised. You keep your secret remarkably well which is sensible of you. No doubt it will happen. In the meantime, one could make use of you in another way. Perhaps you would call at my rooms some time when it is convenient."

"I don't really think I have the time," I said, trying not to show the repulsion I felt. He was at least sixty.

"Have no fear, my dear boy. I merely wish to talk business but perhaps if you prefer we could meet in a more public location. How about the "Golden Hind"? I believe they do very good lunches there?"

I said that sounded a much better idea and so, on the following Thursday, if you'd been there (perhaps you were) you might be interested to know that we were the oddly assorted couple in the alcove. Me in jeans and Sir Thomas in a dark suit, stiff collar and tie – every inch the English gentleman.

"I have read all that you have written for "STARbooks' and I've prepared this," he said as we tackled the starters. He reached down to the brief case by his side and brought out a huge sheet of paper covered in figures.

"What is it?" I asked.

"An analysis of your business. For a student of Business Studies, may I say that you seem to have some very hazy ideas."

"It's more of a paying hobby than a business," I said. "I'm not

like that."

"So you repeatedly write. Nonetheless it is a business. Have you considered what we call depreciation?"

"Not really. How?"

"You are eighteen now, going on nineteen, as they say in your country. Correct?"

"Right."

"And you have to face the fact that after reaching the age of thirty, the chances of earning money in the same way as you do now are pretty remote. Correct?"

"Right. I'd say more like twenty-five."

"That's realistic. So I want to make a suggestion...." Naturally enough, I thought the same as you're thinking. I was about to say "Get stuffed' but he carried on. He continued all the way through the main course and the dessert and was still talking when we were sitting in the lounge sipping brandy from huge glasses.

"But why?" I asked when he had finished. "There must be thousands of people you could do this for and get paid for doing it."

"I have spent my entire life, my dear James, sorting out companies of one sort and another. Potteries and plastic factories; foundries and farms. I shall derive enormous pleasure from this – a vicarious pleasure I grant. We shall diversify but not too much. Remember that your body is your greatest asset. As soon as an opportunity presents itself, I'll make sure you meet the right people. People who pay rather more than your friends in America."

For the next six weeks both he and I were busy. My twice- daily walks over to his rooms were noticed of course and for once, I was able to dispel any (possibly jealous) rumors by telling the truth. I became James Hosier, Limited with a bank account in the Channel Islands. I bought twelve rolls of polythene through an agent in the Philippines and sold them in Belgium without even seeing them. I snapped up three similarly unseen ex-army Land Rover trucks in Oman and they went off to Japan. We spent delightful evenings together, poring over the faxes that had come in and planning the next move.

"To the tailor tomorrow, my lad," he said on one evening, when we were wondering about three derelict trucks.

"Tailor? What for?" I asked.

"Reception in London. One or two people there who might be useful clients for your first line of business. Not one of them is over thirty so don't worry."

There are probably more tailors in Cambridge than there are pubs. We went to one Sir Thomas had known since he'd been a junior "don' (the Cambridge word for a university teacher in case you didn't know.) The guy looked it too. I was measured and checked, measured and checked until I began to wonder if I'd have to spend the whole day there. It was worth it though.

Two weeks later, I collected a tuxedo and pants that fitted perfectly. Closely too, as Sir Thomas observed. "Worth paying for the best. It shows off all your attributes and you can charge it against income tax," he said.

The reception was held in the ballroom of one of London's biggest hotels – right in the middle of Mayfair. The guest of honor was some guy who'd gotten a medal of some sort for bringing a new AIDS drug onto the market. I shook his hand and wandered from group to group. Most of them were talking about investments and annual turnovers and possible expansions but there were some that looked a bit more interesting. I was chatting to Peter somebody-or-other when I happened to turn my head in the direction of Sir Thomas who was deep in conversation with the guest of honor. He caught my eye and nodded solemnly.

"Are you married, Peter?" I asked.

"Not actually, no. You're not either I presume."

"Dead right, I'm not. Not yet."

"The unmarried state has certain benefits doesn't it?" he said, looking at me intently.

"It sure does," I said and I would have enjoyed more of that conversation when another guy came up. He was about twenty -three or -four. He had blond hair that flopped over his forehead and must have restricted most of the vision of his left eye.

"Peter! I haven't seen you for absolutely yonks!" he cried. They shook hands. "Well, aren't you going to introduce us?" he asked.

"Sorry. This is James Hosier. He's American. James, this is Barry Ffoulkes-Bennington and he is as British as you can get!"

"Well, English actually. Right back to the sixteenth century and probably well beyond that," said Barry.

I was half expecting a limp hand. In fact he had quite a firm handshake. I soon began to feel quite sorry for him. Peter wandered off leaving us together and it was soon apparent that we had nothing at all in common. I had never shot grouse or anything else. I had never been to Switzerland for the skiing. I had only the vaguest idea where Lake Como (where his family had a villa) was. I was praying for Sir Thomas to come over and rescue me when Barry said, "It's terribly stuffy in here, don't you think? I've got a room upstairs. Why don't we go up there and talk? At least there's a window one can open."

I was surprised because I thought he was anxious to shake me off. I followed him out of the ballroom, weaving round the groups of people and out to the elevator.

His room was on the fifth floor. The view from the window was of Hyde Park and reminded me of my room at Cambridge, save that at Cambridge there are deer roaming in the park, not people.

"I can't wait to get these things off. It's like being in a strait-jacket," he said. He stood in front of the wardrobe mirror and undid his tie. The thought occurred to me then that he might – he just might – be after something more than company and if he did, I should be in trouble. Sir Thomas had tied my tie for me. I hadn't a clue how to do it. He took off his jacket, then waistcoat. He peeled his shirt up over his

169

head, revealing a remarkably strong and very brown torso. I was anxious to sit down lest he spot its effect on my crotch. Unfortunately he sat on the one and only chair and started to take off his shoes and socks. They were followed by his pants and crimson Y – fronts – and, apart from the gold Rolex on his wrist, Barry was naked.

"I'll have a shower when you've gone," he said.

"Oh. Sure. Sorry. I'll go now," I said and turned towards the door.

"Not yet. Not yet," he said, "Stay and talk to me."

I didn't mind staying. He had a really nice looking cock. Naturally I tried not to stare but it was difficult not to. He sat in the armchair with his legs apart. I liked the color of the hair round it too. It was a sort of dark bronze color; the exact shade of the many statues in Cambridge. On the other hand I really didn't feel inclined to listen to more monologues about the sports and pastimes of the upper classes.

"I think we've talked about most everything there is to talk

about," I said.

"Rubbish! Of course we haven't. You haven't told me much about yourself. What are your hobbies? What are American schools like and which one were you at?"

I sat on the bed facing him. I told him about swimming and I told him about my motor bike – not, of course, the hobby that took up most of my time. My description of the school system in the States puzzled him. I began to think of myself as a creature from another planet. He kept saying things like "Good Lord!' and "I'll be damned.' For a start, there was some confusion over the words "public school.' I guess I should have known that a country that drives on the left would call its private schools "public schools.' Barry had been a student at one of the two top notch "public schools' and was amazed that an American could get into Cambridge University after having gone to a mere "state school.' His school had "an arrangement' with both Oxford and Cambridge that sounded to me as if it ought to be looked into by the Monopolies Commission. He had spent two years at Oxford and then, when the University and his parents realized that there wasn't a lot of point in him staying on, he left and had been doing nothing ever since.

"What do you live on?" I asked.

"Oh that's no problem. I don't think it was ever intended that I should work. It's the company that I miss. They say that school days are the happiest days of your life. We used to have some great times. You would have missed out on that, having to go home at the end of every day."

"Missed out on what?" I asked.

"One can't say. Old school traditions and that sort of thing. It was good though. Bloody good."

"A bit of cocksucking when the teacher's not around eh?" I said.

The effect on him was almost electric. He sat bolt upright and his cheeks turned red. "Certainly not!" he said and then, as he sank back in the chair again, he added, "We never went that far. Just a hand if you know what I mean."

"Oh yes?"

"It was frightfully funny, actually," he said. "The school sport was fives. So you could invite a chap for a game of fives in full hearing of everybody else. Five fingers, see? He knew of course. We were a pretty small circle. Actually, I shouldn't be telling

you this but you're an American and that's different."

I couldn't see how, but I could see that the memory was beginning to turn him on. Cocks are a bit like clocks in that respect. Watch one closely and you can't see any movement. Turn away and look again and it's moved. Barry's cock had lifted slightly and was bobbing up and down in time with his pulse. It was worth trying....

"Tell me the full story," I said.

"I don't think I should do that. Why do you want to know?"

"It's interesting. I need to learn as much as I can about British traditions."

"I see. I suppose you would. There wouldn't be anything like it in America."

I tried not to laugh. He started. His "circle' was called "The Loving Cup' because the guy who ran it had a golf trophy in the form of a cup which they used to wank into. All kid stuff but he obviously enjoyed it – and, more to the point, he was enjoying the memories.

"I should stop," he said. "This is getting embarrassing." He pointed down to his cock and his cock was trying to point upwards to the finger.

"I would have said that was something to be proud of," I said. It wasn't bigger than mine but it was a good size. Greg, who is a cock fancier, would have given it pretty good marks. "Was yours the biggest?" I asked.

"No it wasn't, actually. There was a chap called Michael Okinjawa. He was an African Prince and his was enormous."

"A bit difficult to get it all in your mouth at once, you mean?"

"We never did anything like that. I told you, "Just "fives. ".I've heard about it, but I've never done it or had it done to me."

"Sorry. How about the others?"

"Peter, whom you met downstairs has got a good one. At least he had in those days and I don't think they get smaller, do they?"

"I don't think so."

His cock, by this time, was standing to attention. Possibly without thinking what he was doing, he put his fingers round it. "Ah! They were good times. I miss them a lot," he said.

"And so, by the look of it, does your cock," I said. "You can't go downstairs again like that. You're going to have to do something about it. Would you like me to attend to it for you?"

He stared. "But you're an American," he said.

"What difference does that make?"

"Well, you're not one of the circle."

"True but I know how to handle a thing like that. Come over here and lie on the bed."

"Well ... er ... I don't really know. It wouldn't be right...." Nonetheless, he got out of the chair and took a few steps towards me. For a moment I wondered whether to stay where I was and catch it in my mouth but that would have shaken him rigid. (He couldn't be more rigid than he was in one respect.) I stood up and to one side. Still muttering about it not being right, he lay down and stared in the same direction as his cock was pointing – at the cut glass lamp on the ceiling.

He looked much more attractive like that. The lock of hair flopped back. It was somehow better to be working on someone with two eyes. I liked his lips too. They were thick and fleshy but I resisted the temptation to bend over and kiss him. I think he would have run a mile if I had.

"You put your fingers round it and move the skin up and down. I guess you've done it to yourself. Oh, we'd better get a towel or something out of the bathroom to save making a mess. I'll get one," he said, sitting up. Gently, I pushed him back into a supine position. "Just leave everything to me," I said and put a hand on the inside of his thigh. That was enough to stiffen my cock. Fortunately, my new shiny black pants held it down. I sat on the bed next to Barry and slid my hand up and down. His skin was very cool; very smooth and felt slightly damp.

"Put your fingers round.... No don't. That feels good. Oh yes! That's great. How did you learn? Oh yes!"

By that time both hands were working on him. I carried on for a few seconds and then put my right hand under his balls. By the way he jerked around you'd have thought my fingers were electric. He liked it though. So did I for that matter. I like balls, especially when they're as big and as sensitive as his. Unfortunately I didn't have long enough to give him the full Hosier treatment. A drop of pre-cum formed on his cock, ran down the shaft and its place was taken by another. He'd dosed his eyes by that time which was just as well. Barry Ffoulkes - Bennington was going to get quite a shock.

I made myself as comfortable as possible, took a deep breath and lowered my head. It's the odor that gets to you first. Do you find that? Everyone is slightly different and every one seems slightly better than the last guy. The last guy in my case was Michael. Greg's a bit too old to be a real turn on. Michael's still in his twenties.

I took the tip between my lips and just touched the already sticky slit with the tip of my tongue.

"Good God! What are you ... Aaaah!" That was all he said and I couldn't have answered even if I'd wanted to. It slid up into my mouth like it had been yearning to do that for years. Maybe it had. It had been a long time since I'd had anything quite so good too. I could feel the veins against my tongue and it was throbbing like it was about to explode and pushing uncomfortably against the back of my throat. Greg has the ability, when mine gets to that point, of swallowing my cockhead. It's a trick I've never learned so I had to move up a bit. Barry let out a long gasp. I went down again until I almost choked and then up. I don't know how long it lasted. Not long enough – that's for sure. I was just getting accustomed to his taste, savoring it to the full, sucking on it as hard as I could when he arched his back, gave a long gasp and came.

It is just possible that his cockhead was in my gullet at the time. Maybe that upward thrust did it. I don't know. I know that I didn't get as much in my mouth with him as I did with Michael. Not that I was disappointed. With Michael there are always a few drops that get spilt. My mouth filled with Barry's. I had time to swallow that lot and then the last weaker spurt. I took everything he produced. I could have easily coped with more and there wasn't so much as a single stray spot anywhere.

"God almighty, that was amazing! You must have done it before," he gasped.

"Oh, once or twice. Perhaps Americans are not so backward as you think," I said.

"But swallowing it like that! That must be really revolting. I'm sorry. I should have warned you but it happened so quickly. At school there was time to tell the chap to have the cup ready. I really am sorry. If you have to go to a doctor or anything, I'll pay of course."

"There's no need for that. It's all good protein," I said. It was very good, as it happened. I ran my tongue round my teeth to

savor the flavor. Barry got up. "I'd better have a shower I think," he said. Stay around. We can go downstairs together.

I was strongly tempted to offer my services as a shower attendant but thought better of it. At least I had time to relieve my aching balls whilst he was in the bathroom. I threw the sodden handkerchief out of the window. It landed a few feet in front of the top-hatted guy who guarded the front door. He stepped forward, poked at it with his umbrella and then looked up. I made sure he didn't see me.

Barry emerged and dressed. He tied his tie so quickly that I couldn't see his fingers. It had taken Sir Thomas fully five minutes to fix mine. Barry turned from the mirror and faced me. "Look," he said. "I don't want you to take this the wrong way but I'd like to give you some money. I know there are chaps in London who do this sort of thing for money and I've no idea how much they charge. You see, if I don't pay you, I'll feel guilty. I mean ... you might think I love you and I'm not like that. I suppose you've no idea what the going rate is."

Back in the States, I charged Michael a hundred dollars for much more. Thinking about the possibility of having Barry in my ass and slightly confused by this embarrassed little speech I said, "A hundred pounds."

"Of course. No problem. Are you sure that's enough?"

I was about to correct myself and do a bit of currency conversion but he'd opened up his wallet and brought out two fifty pound notes. I said nothing.

When I told Sir Thomas, he fell about laughing. When we left the hotel that evening and the doorman held the door open, Sir Thomas said "Give him a tip, James. He might think you're in love with him if you don't."

That was the beginning of an extremely lucrative college career. Barry called Sir Thomas to get my address. A reunion of the "Loving Cup' was planned at his home. Would I care to- come?" I said I'd be only too delighted to come and I hoped they would come equally happily.

But I'll tell you about that next time.

LOST IN THE WOODS
Keith Pruitt

My previous job required that I work a split shift and it was a wonderful schedule, and especially so after I found the wonderful cruising areas of Austin known as Bull Creek. Since most afternoons were free, I would go to the green belt area northwest of downtown Austin and hike the hillside or walk the trails. It was wonderful exercise, and since I was in the middle of a fitness program and needed to continue to lose body fat, I found it easy to motivate myself to take the short drive to the creek in the afternoons.

Springtime comes early in Austin with great bursts of green leaves and reawakening grass and wild flowers. The season had just begun this Monday afternoon with warmer than normal temperatures, so I decided to go to the creek and walk the trails and hillside. Now when I say the hillside, believe me, the hillside was quite a challenge. Rocky and treacherous terrain was carved out in trails from the bottom rounding the hillside twice to the very pinnacle of the mountain. Walking the middle trail to the top would leave you breathless and exhausted. Generally, I had to rest for about fifteen minutes before descending the rocky climb.

On any given day, one would find sometimes a dozen guys spread out over the hillside or along the trails on the flat side which was across the creek. It took me weeks to learn all the hiding places that were to be had on the hillside. The action ranged from older men out to find some chicken to hot muscular college studs on the hillside. For the most part, most guys were not very careful about what they did or where they . did it. Some would be well hidden, others might walk right up and give blow jobs right along the trails for everyone to see. And there were some mighty hot scenes.

On the occasion of my visit this fine spring day, I pulled into the parking lot to discover about five cars with no guys or girls in sight. The creek area seemed to be vacant alerting me to the fact that everyone was in the woods. So I got out of my car and began walking toward the wooded lot near the entrance to that part of the park.

There were two areas that were cruised on the flat side. The wood lot was out in front near the parking lot and restrooms running back a few hundred feet, and went from a small hillside about 150 yards to the rock bed of the creek. The creek was broad at the highway and then narrowed to a small waterfall digging into the bed-rock into a narrow channel that had been damned by boulders to form a nice swimming hole. Trees stood out in the middle of the water providing a neat area from which a rope could be tied, enabling swimmers to swing and jump into the water. In the hot Texas summers, this hole of water is usually filled if there is water to be found anywhere.

The second cruise area is a vacant field behind the wooded lot. There is a trail leading back to the field and through it along the creek bank and then meandering through the grasses of the field. At the very back of the field, which was dotted with small cedar trees, was a clearing where still existed the foundation of what had been a pioneer house. It was made of stone and was a neat place to sit and meditate.

Generally, the field was recognized as private property, and you had to be careful not to get caught back there by police, but they rarely showed up in those days. Those days were BG – that is, Before George (Bush). The authorities weren't so keen on stomping through brush and hip-high grass trying to catch gay men doing the nasty.

I walked through the path of the woods, but there was no one to be seen. So I decided to go back to the field to see what was going on. I had walked up on very hot scenes before, and I was hoping that today I would be as fortunate. The flowers were beginning to bloom in the field showing an array of color and beauty from poppies and bluebonnets. I decided to walk the path on the creek bank which was lined with large Texas Live Oaks. It was a beautiful walk, and this particular afternoon provided a great deal of soothing tranquility. Only the water of the creek and the birds that were nestled in the trees provided sound in my otherwise remote and quiet world.

That is until I got about halfway to the back. Then I looked through the trees and into the field and spotted three guys standing spread out from each other. Two of the guys I recognized as older chicken hawks from previous encounters. The third was standing behind a tree and almost completely out of my line of sight. It was obvious from viewing the scene that the third guy must have been the most interesting of the three the way the other two kept maneuvering trying to come closer to him. I knew the M.O. of the two I could see: they went for only young, hung, and dumb. If they were blond and blue eyed, so much the better. So I knew immediately that the prize I sought was on the other side of the tree.

You see, the three of us have similar tastes. The major difference: I am twenty years younger, better looking, with a much better build. The only problem: they were much better endowed. About twice my size to be exact. Now mind you, I am considered physiologically average. These guys had monsters in their 501s. I knew I would have a chance if I could only get within view of the younger guy. I can hold my own with the best-looking guys in town. My friends always have kidded me that if I was in a room with a hundred guys, I would always end up with the best-looking one there. It does happen. I'm not sure why, but I'm not complaining.

I walked to the end of the path which extended through a tom-down fence into the pine thicket of the field. The young lad was standing on the other side of the large pine tree, and I could see him now. And he finally noticed me. He was, shall we say, a beautiful young thing. Standing about five-nine, the young lad had light brown hair just turning from the blond of his early adolescence which was trimmed nicely and fell along the tops of his ears. He smiled slightly at me soliciting one in return as well as a slight tug on my crotch to signal my interest. He nodded to acknowledge his interest as well and smiled a bright toothy grin. He wasn't the muscle-bound type that you usually encountered out here, but seemed the boy-next-door type that just seemed to melt my heart. He was definitely the type to steal your heart.

But I had competition for his body today. Slim, the old man who had stolen many a trick from me, was quickly maneuvering his way toward the lad. When the kid saw the guy coming he took off down the path toward the front of the field.

"Shit," I cursed aloud. I figured he had gotten spooked and decided to run, and I was in no mood to give chase today. I decided for once that if I was what he wanted he would just have to find a way to get back here alone. So I waited. Time ticked by slowly, and, at last, I decided that Slim had won again. He had, on several trips to the creek, walked right up and even grabbed a guy's dick right out of my mouth while I was in the heat of passion. I hated the bastard, and now it appeared he had again succeeded in gaining the attention of a young stallion, with that gigantic pole he carried around.

After about ten minutes of standing around, I heard a rustling in the bushes behind me and turned to see the young man returning. He was smiling at me and wiping a bit of perspiration from his brow.

"I thought you were out of here," I stated as he slowly approached.

"No, I had to lose that guy first. He finally got in his car and left. There is no one else back here. Everyone else is gone."

"That's great," I smiled as my heart began to pound.

I reached over and grabbed the crotch of his white cotton Dockers surprised to find a half-hard cock that felt of sizeable proportions. He moaned and threw his head back and I knew I had a live one on my hands. I felt his chest through his pale yellow IZOD and realized he was solid underneath the shirt. I pulled his shirt up to reveal a lean, tanned body with little chest hair and a small happy trail of hair running to his navel – and beyond. I touched the small nipple of his right chest muscle which brought a small moan from the lad. I tongued its soft, sweet tissue. My other hand was still massaging his crotch feeling his cock growing and expanding across his leg. He tasted so sweet, I just knew I would have to devour every inch of his body.

"You keep your eyes peeled while I give you a blowjob you will never forget."

"Hmmm, I don't know man. I have never let anyone do that," he explained even as I was opening his zipper to release his hardening dick.

"It's okay. You just watch. I promise you will enjoy this more than anything that has ever happened in your life."

"You think so?" he asked.

"I know so," I assured him with a smile. He smiled back as I positioned his shirt so that I could continue to see his hot chest and happy trail. (I get really turned on by a great chest and just a small amount of really sexy hair.) I took my now- hard cock out of my pants, knelt on the grass, and began to lick the tip of his seven-inch cock. He began moaning as his cock twitched toward his stomach. It became so hard that I had to pull it down from his stomach, but every time it would slip from my mouth, the cock would plop against his flat abdomen with a loud thud. He wasn't too large, but he was super-hot. Just right for sucking, as I am given to saying.

I sucked on his small, hairy balls taking both of them into my mouth and bouncing them around with my tongue. He tasted so dean and fresh. I loved the taste he was leaving in my mouth, but I could tell he was getting so dose to going over the edge.

"How does that feel to you, lad?" I asked this more to give him a break than any desire to really know. It was all too obvious that he was exceeding cloud nine, and his heart was racing past the speed limit.

"Oh, I've never felt anything like that in my life. I've never been sucked by a guy before."

"Is this your first time to be with a guy?" I asked, doubting that it could possibly be my luck to be with a virgin.

"I've jerked off with a couple of guys in the shower at the college, but I've never even touched a guy before."

"Oh, tell me I've died and gone to heaven! You are so good looking. You know, I am truly honored to be the first."

"Thanks, and I'm sure I'll never forget this. You sure know what you're doing. I like that. You're making me feel so good. I'm so dose to coming. ...I don't want to rush it, but I've got to get back to school. I've got a class in a little over an hour."

"Never fear, I will put it into high gear." And knew just the thing that would send him rocketing off into the third dimension. I gently licked the head of his now-leaking cock. A droplet of pre-cum was dinging to his piss slit, so I licked it off very deliberately teasing this kid. I looked up into his light brown eyes with my baby blues giving him the sexiest look I possessed. He smiled and dosed his eyes. Just as he did, I suddenly swallowed his entire cock, right up to his pubic hairs. The size of the head made it easily slide right down my throat. I manipulated his cock head with my throat, sending his body into shivers.

He began moaning loudly as I began pumping his cock in a piston manner with both my mouth and my hand. My other hand was now jerking my cock trying to get off at the same time that he came. I knew he was dose, but I wasn't. I was so into sucking his delicious piece of manhood that I was even losing my erection.

"Oh God, I'm going to shoot," he warned, but I kept sucking, wanting to taste his savory load. He grabbed my shoulders and began thrusting wildly into my mouth, and then, at last, let out a yell that would have scared even the bravest in a dark room.

I felt the first spurt of hot lava hit the back of my throat almost causing me to gag, but I swallowed instead, something I rarely did any more. It tasted bitter-sweet. He soon was shooting gallons of seed into my mouth filling it to the point that I was forced to open slightly to let it run out of my mouth and onto the ground. He was standing on his tiptoes but had quit thrusting now. I deep-throated his cock one more time causing him to back away.

"It's sensitive," he giggled.

I continued to choke my meat hoping he would stay put while I got off from just looking at his body. When he started to pull up his pants, I stopped him.

"Don't go, please. I'm so close. I just want to look at that beautiful body while I get off."

"Okay, but hurry, please. I really gotta go."

My dick wasn't cooperating this time, and it seemed I would never get off. He started to get dressed, and I jumped to my feet.

"Just leave the shirt up, please. I'm going to shoot pretty soon." I had my hand on his shoulder holding him close to me. I could feel the wonderful warm energy he was emitting, and it seemed to fill my very being. My dick immediately stood rigid in my hands as I pumped furiously standing on tiptoes to give extra power to my orgasm.

He seemed amazed as he watched my dick getting harder. He began to wrap me in his arms, standing behind me, pulling me back into his stomach.

"Come on, baby. Shoot that load."

That was all that was necessary. I felt my balls tighten.

"I'm going to explode, baby."

182

"Do it you hot man. Come on shoot that load for me. I want to see it go flying out of your cock."

"Yeah. Here comes. Yeah ... yeah ... yeah," I screamed as jets of cum now flew across the air and onto the leaf-covered

ground.

"Oh yeah, baby. What a load!" he exclaimed tapping me slightly on the chest with the palm of his hand.

We quickly gathered our clothes about us exchanging pleasant smiles and glances as we tucked everything bade in place. "You are so hot," I exclaimed. "What's your name?" I asked. "Mike," he answered. "And yours?"

"I'm Keith," I replied. "Thanks for making my day."

"Believe me, it was you who made my day. I will never forget this, Keith. That was everything I wanted my first time to be. Thanks for making it so special. So can I ask you a question?"

"Sure."

"How old are you?"

"I'm 33. How about you?"

"I'm ... well, old enough," Mike smiled.

"Wow. You're so hot, Mike. I just want to take you home and chain you to the bed so you can't get away."

Mike started laughing. Then he reached over and gave me a slight peck right on the lips. Electricity again flowed through my body when his soft, warm lips met mine. I felt my nuts chum and my dick jumped as his hand touched my shoulder. And then he turned and walked away. I continued to watch as he walked down the tree-lined path, his ass seeming to beckon me to follow. But I just watched until he was far out of my sight.

I heard a stirring among the trees on the other side of the path to my right. Someone was coming down the other path. He was in sight now. It was Slim. He stood looking toward me. I smiled gently and wiped my mouth on the sleeve on my shirt and walked into the path leading out, which Mike had taken leaving Slim, standing alone, wondering what he had missed. And oh, did he miss out!

THE FIRST TIME I SAW HIM
William Cozad

The first time I saw him was when he whizzed me on his skateboard on the sidewalk near where I lived. He was my age, maybe a little younger. Medium height and slim, with short brown hair and bright brown eyes. He was wearing baggy shorts that hung down so low you could see about two inches of the white briefs he wore underneath. I wanted to yank those shorts down then and there.... "Sorry dude, I didn't mean to scare you," he said, hardly slowing down. "No problem, man," I called after him. I did a double take when I saw him go into the house next door, which had been vacant for months. That night at the dinner table Mom talked about what a nice woman the new neighbor was. Her husband taught English at the community college and they had a son named Andy. "I hope you'll be friends with Andy. It's hard to be uprooted and leave your old school and friends," she said. "Yeah, right," I said. "It wouldn't hurt to show him around a little," Dad said. I thought, I'd like to whack him upside the head with his skateboard for scaring the bejesus out of me.. "Yeah, right," I repeated. Dad gave me a glance that let me know he didn't like my attitude. I dummied up. "Sure, okay. I saw him going into the house earlier," I said. After dinner I went upstairs to my room. I blasted my stereo with the grunge CD I'd just bought at the music store in the mall where I worked that summer. I fantasized about piercing my nose and getting an infinity tattoo and dressing like the lead singer. But I figured my dad might kick me out of the house and not pay for my college. When he yelled up the stairs about the noise, I cut the sound down to a dull roar. When I was ready to crash, I stripped down to my shorts and turned off the ceiling light. That's when I noticed the light on in the upstairs room of the house across the way. There stood Andy getting undressed.

Kneeling down at the windowsill, I watched him tug off his T-shirt. I wanted to lick that chest – smooth and lean. He kicked off his sneakers and pulled off his socks. He slid off his baggy jeans. He stood there in his white cotton briefs and then peeled them off. He had a fat, uncut dick and big balls. Watching him undress gave me a raging boner. I'd been checking out the guys who came into the music store that summer. I was hoping that the new neighbor would exercise naked

185

or maybe jack off. No such luck. He doused the light. The room was black and I couldn't see anything. I hopped into bed. I slept in my shorts. Andy slept in the raw. I wondered if he was horny like me and had to jack off before he could go to sleep. I reached down inside my briefs and jacked my dick. I thought about Andy and whipped off a load, dozing off with sticky shorts. In the morning I was woken up by my mom knocking on the door and calling my name. "This house better be on fire," I growled. It was Sunday morning and my day to sleep in because my folks no longer made me go to church with them. The door opened and there stood Mom all gussied up for church with her hat and gloves on. Andy was with her. I rubbed the sleep out of my eyes. "Willy, meet Andy, your new neighbor," Mom said. "Oh dude, it's you. Hey, whassup?" he said. I sat up and shook the cobwebs out of my head. I bunched the covers around me because I had a boner. "Well, you guys get acquainted. We're off to church," Mom said. "Sorry to wake you up," Andy said. "Oh, I like getting up in the middle of the night."

"I can come back later." I heard my folks' car pulling out of the driveway. "No, that's okay. I always wake up grumpy."

"And horny," he said. He pointed at my crotch-bulge in the covers. "Yeah, well...." My jaw dropped when he walked over and grabbed my dick and squeezed it. "I saw you watchin' me last night," he said.

"What...?"

"You heard me. You were spyin' on me."

"Well, wasn't much to see."

"Why, do you have a bigger dick?" He flung back the covers and exposed my tented briefs. "Want that taken care of, don'tcha?" he said. I couldn't believe this was happening. Sitting on the edge of the bed, he clutched my throbbing dick in my cotton briefs. He bent down and nibbled at my briefs and licked them until the outline of my dick was clearly visible. Hooking his fingers inside the waistband of my briefs, he peeled them down. I was so hot that my big dick just exploded. I splattered pearly white cumdrops all over my belly and bush. The jizz trickled down my dick and balls. Damned if the new neighbor boy didn't dean up my cum with his tongue. He licked my dick and lapped at my balls. My dick stayed stiff. "Got a big fuckin' dick! Shoots a mean load. And your cum tastes sweeter than mine."

"Jesus, did you go to that queer high school I heard about on TV," I said. "Nope. I never did nothing like this before. Honest. That's not to say I didn't want to, ya know? I just never had anybody look at me the way you did." Andy looked down. "Your dick stays hard even after it shoots." Andy stood up and stripped off his clothes. His body was smooth and creamy. His uncut prick looked even bigger up dose. "Whatcha doing?" I asked. "I wanna suck you. When my mom told me the guy next door was my age I never thought it was you. I buzzed you on my skateboard because you looked so macho and I wanted to know you. Then I got scared because you acted pissed off, so I split." I lay back on my pillow and watched Andy get down between my legs. What a way to wake up. He clasped my dick and swabbed the head with his tongue. It was a delirious feeling. Holding my dick, he flicked his tongue over my balls. He stuffed them into his mouth and jacked me off at the same time., "Suck my cock," I said.

He spit out my balls and gobbled up my dick, but he could only take it about halfway down. I watched him tug on his own dick and the rosy crown poked out of the hood. He jacked his dick while he sucked on mine. "Oh yeah," I groaned. Andy tried to take all of me down his throat. He gobbled up even more of my dick, but he choked. He had tears in his eyes. Gaining control, he got back down on my dick and clutched the shaft while he bobbed his head up and down. He continued to beat his meat while he sucked on my cockhead He eventually came up for air. He plopped down on his belly beside me on the bed. "You wanna fuck me, don'tcha?" he said. "That's what queers do. They do it in the ass." He reached back and spread his buttcheeks, exposing his pink crack with light brown fuzz and his tiny puckered hole. I scooted over and rubbed his firm, smooth ass. I straddled his calves. He watched me over his shoulder. "I wanna feel your dick up my ass, dude. I want to know what it feels like." I kneaded his asscheeks and spread them. I rubbed my finger in his steamy crack. "Lick it first," he said. "Whaddaya mean?"

"Like a pussy ... you know, you get it all wet and juicy so I can take your big dick." It never crossed my mind to fuck a guy before, let alone lick his asshole. That seemed so gross and nasty, At the same time, I was willing to do whatever it took to stick my big boner up his butthole; I was so horny that my vision was blurry. Instinct took over. I just dove in and started licking away. It wasn't as bad as I expected. His crack tasted fresh and kind of soapy because he must have just taken a shower. I stuck my tongue up his tiny hole and tongue-fucked it. "Oh yeah, that feels good." I slurped and slobbered in his ass. My face was smeared with spit but I didn't care. I had the biggest hard-on of my life. I could actually feel the cum boiling in my balls. "Okay, stick your dick up my ass. Let me have it. Fuck my ass! Fuck it now!"

Listening to his hot talk just got me homier. He wanted his ass fucked as bad as I wanted to fuck it. I reared up and slapped my hard dick against his buttcheeks. Pre-cum oozed out of my pee-hole. I smeared the sticky stuff all over his buttcheeks and rubbed it into his wet crack. It took a few tries because his hole was so tight even with the spit and pre-cum, but my bloated, purple dickhead soon popped into his ass-ring. "Holy fuck! You're gonna split me in two. Go slow, man." He was delirious with my cockhead in him. I slipped in a few inches of shaft and felt his ass-ring snap around it. I don't know how his tiny hole took my big dick. I was just glad it did. "Stay still a minute ... Whoa, shit ... my god, it feels like a fucking fence post!" I waited but my anxious cock throbbed wildly. My nuts buzzed. Damned if my horny new neighbor boy didn't back up on my big dick all the way because I could feel my pubes scratch against his virgin ass. "Okay, I can take it now, I think. Go for it. Fuck me. Fuck me in my ass." He moved his ass around and ground it against my pubes. This was too good to be true. I had to see my big dick penetrate his virgin hole. I sat back on my heels and watched my engorged prick slide in and out of his wet, hot, tight fuck-hole. "Let me have it. Show me what you got." I sawed my big dick in and out of his clenching ass. I could feel every nook and cranny of his cherry hole. "Fuck me harder. Deeper. Faster." I went for broke. I bored and stroked his asshole. I worked up a full head of steam. I was working up quite a sweat as I relentlessly pumped him. He loved it. He groaned, "God, dude, it feels like a battering ram. Oh shit, I'm gonna shoot! Holy fuckin' shit, I'm gonna blow. Yeah, keep fucking me, though. Make me fuckin' shoot. Oh, Jesus H. Christ!" he yelped as his asshole clenched around my big dick. Feeling his spasming asshole and knowing that he got off from me fucking him, I crammed my exploding dick all the way up his ass and blasted gobs and gobs of cum into him. I collapsed on top of him. I clutched his shoulders and sucked on his neck, giving him a hickey, while his butthole siphoned my balls and my cum filled him. I stayed on top of him until our heavy breathing subsided and my bloated prick deflated and plopped out. I rolled off him and noticed the overflow of my cum trickle down his thigh. He rolled over on top of me and pinned me to the bed. "Okay, now it's my turn."

"What...?"

AN EAGER LOVER
Sonny Torvig

"...Suddenly my virgin ass was invaded, first by one rigid finger sneaked into its hot embrace, then another to join it. They found me near death, collapsed in the meager shadow of a dead camel, my skin blistered and cracked, mouth caked with dry blood and wind-blown sand. I thought it was another dehydrated illusion as hands pressed against me, my limbs being moved to lay me flat. Shadows fell over my sun-blinded eyes, shadows with voices, which would have brought tears of relief, had I any tears to shed.

I had set out from Tarim, well-equipped and with six Bedu as guides and bearers. The camel train had been a dozen animals, their tufted headgear and belled limbs a bright contrast to the bleached bones they would soon become. But then, I was a confident Westerner, unaware of the desert's full malevolence. The Bedu were born for the desert and traveled well prepared, but even they could not have foreseen the meeting with people they counted as foe. The desert was the last place I thought it likely to turn a comer and walk into a vengeful enemy.

Only two of us survived the fray, our beasts scattered, along with their burdens, and of the caravan only two could be found. There we had crouched into the freezing night, a meager fire our sole comfort. We talked only briefly of our limited choices, much less about the meager possibility of survival. Then followed the fiercest battle I had ever encountered. It was we two versus the sun and sand, and as the valuable days crept by, along with the traveled distance, the odds against us steadily increased. Waterskins soon emptied, and food vanished despite our merciless rationing. My companion never uttered a word of complaint, insisting at every dividing of the remaining food that I take first choice. I cringed now that I was too weak to refuse him. We grew weaker with each passing day, the night's cold cutting us to the bone, the day's heat searing every drop of water from our emaciated bodies. Hope faded as fast as the supplies. I lost all track of time and days traveled, only a dogged determination to survive driving me on towards the merciless horizon, permanently teasing us with the knowledge of the Hassi well beyond it. My companion collapsed before me, his life slipping away before my dry and aching eyes. To have come as far as we had was testament to the human spirit; but to have lost him in what must have been just a day or two away from salvation, was indeed a hard blow. My own will suffered badly, and it was with no great surprise that the following lonely day the camel settled itself for the last time. I hunched beside it, too weak to argue, and rested my head against its still-beating flank. I might have managed another mile or two, but suddenly even another step seemed too much. Sleep was all I wanted, to close my gritty eyes and, just for a few moments, lie in slumber. I had a sliver of shadow, a slice of one dried fig, and no strength left for the fight. I dosed my eyes and slid towards my own death.

A voice spoke quietly in my head, warm fluid slipped between my blood caked lips. The dream was a good dream. A dream of sipping water, shadow from the blazing sun, and the comfort of human presence. I slipped deeper into the soothing bed of sleep.

I awoke to the ghastly cold of night, my body shaking under a single blanket, the mirage of a fire dose by. I shuddered and curled tighter, trying to imagine my illusion heating my shaking bones. I slept again in defense, hiding away from the ruthless cold. Dawn returned to lighten my eyelids, and with it came more liquid slipping between my lips. I basked in its cool, drew into my nostrils the scents of a cooking hare. Voices formed a quiet chorus about me, a heavenly band of angels come to accompany me on my day of judgment? I tried to open my eyes, expecting them to resist, and cried out in panic. Liquid dribbled over my blistered eyelids and slipped between to free them. I blinked, and although I could not see clearly I thought I saw men, several men. I thought I saw camels tethered. I thought I saw a pot of stewing food, well-filled water skins.

Much later, I came to realize it was no illusion. The steady nursing of water and shade had given flight to my imaginings, and I had dragged myself to sitting, staring about me like a madman. My movement brought a hawk-faced man to my side, offering me first the waterski, then a small helping of the food I thought I had dreamed. I tasted hare amongst the pottage, and truly gave thanks that hare had been born and raised in heaven! The bearer of my salvation offered me more water. By degrees I recovered over the next full day, and in the following dawn I mounted a willing camel for the beginnings of my true initiation into the nomadic existence.

For the next two years, I lived a life I had never imagined possible. The hardships of desert travel carved me into a survivor, lean and without too many entanglements from my Western upbringing. I grew to love and understand my companions, and in due course I came to be accepted as a temporary member of the small group. We skirted the great wastes of the Empty Quarter on frequent occasions, and in me grew the wish to see its center, to travel its forbidding sea of wind and sand. Restlessness found a place dose to my heart, and there it nestled, sending out its roots and stems.

And as these things will, the day came when I had no option but to go. And with six companions I set out to still my unquiet spirit. We went prepared, we went well armed, we went with my knowledge of the stars to guide us, and their knowledge of the desert to keep us alive. What none of us could have foreseen was our meeting with such an exotic nation, men who would change us all forever. We could not foresee our searching the Empty Quarter to the end of our lives, all in the hope of finding these people just one more time.

The march had taken us over the Uruk al Shaiba, a hard and grueling two days of achingly slow progress. The ground had been rough and we had our bruises to prove it while the camels began to look more gaunt than was advisable. In the desert, the knowledgeable man grazes his beasts where he finds any vegetation whatsoever, for their next meal is never guaranteed. He takes his lead from his surroundings, unlike the westerner who travels for speed and a quick arrival. I had found the lesson bitterly hard to swallow, but in the Empty Quarter I followed my companions' lead. We found sparse grazing after the hardship and for a while at least the beasts ate their fill. We ate well ourselves, the staple of hare stew and unleavened bread, augmented with a little dried fruit cut from wedges of compressed figs and dates. And it was in this replete state that our hosts found us. As those first there I would have thought us the hosts, and it our beholden duty to make the fellow travelers welcome. It came as a surprise to us all to find ourselves treated as the visiting guests.

The sudden arrival of these heavily armed young men was exceedingly unsettling. However, no harm seemed intended, and very soon the usual questions and answers began. Which tribes had we both encountered, where was our intended way forward, and finally, did we intend to move on immediately? All these we answered to their satisfaction, apart from the last. Great agitation resulted from our intention to leave within a day or two. We were suddenly the focus of their most charming persuasions, persistent and unrelenting. I began to grow a little uneasy, especially as they became insistent that we join them in their own camp. The presence of so many weapons persuaded us that to say no was the greater risk, and it was with one hand constantly on the highly ornate pommel of my very practical dagger that I followed our small group into the midst of the other's encampment. We were ushered into the largest of the tents, and in the golden light of the lamps within I made out quite a number of half-naked men sitting around a central feast. I bowed low to the man who sat at the head of the gathering, and made my formal greeting to him, "Salam alaikum."

The big man smiled warmly and indicated that we join the meal. "Alaikum as salam." His voice was deep and resonant, and in the low light of the fire his face shone with good humor and a healthy diet. I found it hard to imagine him traveling great wastes of the desert and still looking as healthy as he did, and tentatively enquired as to how he managed to remain so well- nourished in the desert. I patted my own stomach, solid with muscle, but poorly fed by the standards evident around me. He laughed. "I drink the milk of youth, my friend. You would do well to try its vital powers for yourself. Perhaps then you might add up to more than just skin and bone."

The others in the room laughed quietly and rubbed their own sleek bellies, a sheen of oil on their skins reflecting the light of the crackling fires. The big man indicated that we seat ourselves amongst his companions, and I found myself between two openly affectionate younger men, reading that warmth as brotherly, to begin with. The meal began, and as was the custom it was we the visitors who were pressed to make the first choice of food. These men might have been on the verge of starvation, but still it would have been the same. A younger boy began to sing in his light tone, a song of lost love and longing, and in the desert stillness it filled our hearts with a strange aching.

The brother on my right placed his hand upon mine and asked how long it had been since I had shared my blanket with another, and just being asked the question drew my heart out to him. I shrugged, and made light the absence of intimacy in my life, but still his warm hand remained.

By now the boy had begun an extraordinarily sensual dance about the fire, only a light loincloth to cover him. He was breathtakingly beautiful, and his voice pulled unacknowledged emotions from deep within me. I turned to my companion and complimented the boy. He in turn laughed, "He is a man, Nasrani, but a man who has surrendered his seed for the sake of his voice." He gripped his own loincloth and indicated a cutting movement. "We have several amongst us of the same, men who have followed their songs into limbo; becoming neither men nor women." He looked again at the singer, and I could not help but notice how his full lips silently mimicked the slow song, lips that bore a sheen of oil from the meal and brought forth in me feelings about intimacy previously unrecognized

I shifted a little uncomfortably where I sat, and dragged my attention back to my traveling companions. Mahsin was deep in conversation with his nearest host, and to my surprise I saw how Salih had abandoned all but his own loincloth, and was sitting with his arm over the shoulder of his companion. The atmosphere in the tent was of friendship and welcome, and slowly but surely I let my guard relax. My two brothers tugged at my burnous, and as I had begun to feel the growing warmth of the enclosed space I gladly shrugged it from my naked shoulders.

I looked up from my food as the big man dapped his hands for attention, and I watched as he handed the singer a delicate bracelet of interwoven silver and gold. The young man bowed low before his Amir, and backed away into an adjoining tent. I heard laughter from the gloom there, and noticed how one or two of the men around the periphery of our gathering had slipped away to this other place.

"Nasrani?" I looked up, to see the Amir rising to his feet. "You wish to join us in our sleeping lodge? You must be our guests for the time until you leave!" I glanced at my companions, and all I saw was an eagerness to agree. I bowed acceptance, and felt the heat of my dose companions suddenly closer. A hand stroked across my back, another gripped my right hand. "Come, Nasrani, we will prepare you first."

I looked to the silent brother in question, but he simply smiled, and tugged my hand.

The lower lights in the other tent cast a sheen of health on all present, and it was with confidence that the "brothers' laid me on soft silken rugs. I began to doze as warm hands soothed water, then oils into my desert-dry skin, massaging the journey's tensions into warm pleasure. I rested my chin on my forearms and looked about me. Around the deeply cushioned area small dusters of the tribesmen were occupied in their massage and oiling. One or two of the number padded from one group to another their loincloths abandoned to reveal their hairless bodies. I frowned to myself, but kept the question for an appropriate moment. I was maneuvered onto my back, and with a hot towel over my eyes I reveled in the soft massaging of my body. It did not concern me that my own loincloth was gently removed, but a suppressed giggling prompted me to remove the towel. Falih, as I had now come to accept him, gingerly stroked the matt of hair around my cock. "You are strange, Nasrani, the Amir does not like us to have hair on our bodies and all of us are kept in this manner." He tugged his loincloth away, to reveal a body naked of hair. "This is a strange and ugly sight to us. You must be a lonely man to be so adorned!"

I frowned, unable to make the connection between body hair and loneliness. Al Auf smiled down at my ignorance and tugged at a curl of thick hair. "Amongst our tribe Nasrani, one who is not free of this hair is one sworn to solitude. Is it the same amongst your tribe?"

I had to smile in my dawning comprehension, to be mistaken for a celibate! "No, it is not so amongst my people, and if I offend your eyes please feel free to remove what is unsightly." I replaced the towel with as much insouciance as I could muster, naked amongst strangers who felt free to caress my pubic hair. The application of a warm lather to my entire body was a pleasant enough experience, but the following defoliation was to say the least a worrying time, especially as what I must assume was a form of razor scraped close to my nipples, then groin. I involuntarily held my breath as stroke by stroke my thick mat of hair was removed. I felt the air strike my skin in a way I found exciting in its own right, but even as my cock pulsed and grew with this new stimulus, so too did my embarrassment. I heard no giggling, only the low breathing of the brothers, and the scraping of the lubricated razor.

I was maneuvered onto my face, and again my body was anointed with some warm preparation, once again coming under the intimate attentions of my barbers. I could not help but hold my breath as my buttocks were parted by a warm and slightly slippery pair of hands, and even there the razor removed all evidence of my passage from boy to manhood. I am only glad that no slip or clumsiness removed any more than the hair which bore evidence of that journey.

As naked now as the day I was born, I lay under the more soothing attentions of Falih and al Auf. Heavily scented oil was smoothed into my bared skin, and its healing warmth seemed to penetrate into my very bones. I was feeling more alive and alert than I had felt for many years it seemed, as with a pleasant anticipation I was rolled onto my back, more oil then massaged into my skin. Then I felt a lighter oil being used, one that merely softened my skin. I say merely, but perhaps I use the work unadvisedly.

Falih was humming to himself as he liberally anointed my lower abdomen, and as a drop of oil slowly trickled down over my balls I felt his fingers linger along the soft flesh of my cock. Only it was not soft for very long. Deeper and deeper into the skin he worked, and as a direct consequence my cock snuggled ever tighter between his warm fingers. I sighed in the deepest pleasure now, as he began to draw back my foreskin, my entire body feeling as naked as the tender skin of my glans as air stroked its wetted surface.

I sank deep into a state of semi-trance as this pleasure occupied my whole body – the rhythmic attentions of my gentle masseurs, the warmth of my body, the comfort, the intimate surroundings. I heard a deep sigh of passion dose by, and the rapid quiet slapping of skin on skin somewhere. Now, when I focused on what was beyond my own tingling pleasure, I began to be aware of many noises dose by: Moaning and a low crooning, rapid panting, quick snatches of unsteady breath. My own breath caught in my throat as wet warmth suddenly engulfed my glans. I raised my head and looked from under the towel, to see the tousled head of al Auf lowering over my rigid cock. Deeper and deeper he took me down his throat, and hotter and hotter the flesh of my cock became.

The shock of seeing a younger man sucking my trembling cock deep into his hot throat unleashed all manner of wild sensations, all now rushing through my entire body. I let my head fall back and groaned as again and again his wet and eager mouth sank down over me, the growing pressure towards orgasm setting my hips to spontaneous jerking. Firm fingers dug into my ass cheeks as I lifted dear of the silken carpeting, and oily fingers sought out my tight bud of involuntary defense. My complete attention was fixed on my groin where my cock was being so feverishly devoured by my young lover, when suddenly my virgin ass felt a slithering and parting, as first one rigid finger sneaked into its hot embrace, then another to join it. The slithering invasion of my tightest hole propelled me higher into the air, and with intoxicated vocal surrender I came, sending a huge load down al Auf's tender throat.

He was now panting and moaning in his own intense pleasure, and it was with another shock that I realized that al Auf's rhythm was being dictated by another man knelt behind him, fingers digging into his soft hips as he immersed his own rigid flesh deep in the tight young ass.

I looked over to Falih as I gradually subsided and my softening flesh slipped from his companion's creamy lips. He was lying dose by, his fingers teasing another man to distraction. His eyes dosed in pleasure as I slid my hand over his sweet round belly and took his soft cock into my fingers, feeling the thickening warmth beneath them, the silky skin that felt electric to my touch. He smiled with wetted lips as I began my attentions, his olive skin slipping back to reveal a flushed and sleek cockhead. As my own excitement had gradually subsided I had become more aware of my surroundings, of the tangle of naked flesh that writhed and slithered around the floor of carpet and cushion. I began to feel light-headed and faint as I absorbed the sexual extravagance surrounding me. Here I could lap at the well of youth and virility, drink deep the creams of pleasure and excess.

I lay in warm rapture as others' hands strayed over my body.

Fingers teased my cock, cupped the fiery balls beneath its soft length. I reached up with my left hand and took another's urgent thrusting to my lips. Al Auf giggled in delight as I licked along the base of his desperate cock, sucking first one then another shot of cum into my hungry mouth. The smell of his sex was intoxicating, the sounds of orgasm from all comers inflaming my every desire.

I rolled nearer to Falih and submerged his engorged cock deep down my throat, his groan of delight spurring me to greater efforts. His hips began to pump the hard length of cock flesh harder against me, and to begin with, as I lay over his heat, I wanted to let him slip free, to breathe freely again. What distracted me in that moment was the feeling of hands manhandling my hips higher, strong hands.

As I was maneuvered from behind, Falih's cock slipped more freely down my throat, the angle I was being held at making it easier for me to accept his outpouring when it came. And come it did! With his loud groan and a frantic jerking, I was bounced upward, my nose flattened against this hot oily belly, jets of cum bursting from his cock and filling my mouth and gullet. I drew back to swallow frantically, then bobbed down to suck his very youth from him.

Fingers dug into my scalp as his hips jerked violently, bursts of heat hitting my tonsils, gushing into me. I felt the first touch of hot and firm cock against my ring, and the upsurge of nervous passions ran like electric currents down to my swollen cock. I had a mouth full of slippery hot flesh, and even while I basked in that joy I felt the added arousal of pressure against my last defense. Sliding inevitably deeper inside me was what felt like the biggest cock in the continent. Slowly but unstoppably I was stretched wide as inch after inch of hot flesh filled my surrendering hole. I caught my breath as deeper and deeper it slipped, my hips being dragged backward by the man's strong grip.

I let Falih's softening cock slip from my wet lips as I looked over my shoulder. The man behind me was grinning widely, his oiled body the focus of three others' crazed attention. His eyes almost crossed as his rigid belly muscle pressed hard against my ass, his cock as far inside me as was humanly possible. He began to rock me now, and I dosed my eyes to concentrate on the sensation of huge flesh filling then emptying me. As he impaled my body on his ferociously hot length I ached for release, and when he withdrew from me I instantly ached for his cock to once again push deep inside me. His rhythm was languid, and within minutes I had shifted into a semi-hypnotic state, rocking on my knees and elbows as he grunted in pleasure behind me. Lips touched mine, Salih's sweet young lips. Often we had lain close together for warmth during the desert nights, all of us, and sometimes he and Mahsin had made love. But in all those years I had only been a dilettante when it came to loving men. I had allowed them to please me sometimes, and on one occasion I had awakened to find Salih lapping on my morning's erection, but other than half- hearted inclusion in their intimacy I had abstained. Now, to feel my faithful companion's sweet lips on my own, his tongue tasting another's cum on mine, I was overcome with lust.

I was still being pounded in a quickening rhythm, but Salih too was being fucked to the same beat, each synchronized.

It was with an ache that I had to let Salih slip from me as my man began to reach his trembling ecstasy. His panting had become more vocal, his other suitors more fierce in their attentions. He was the focus of so much lust. His great length pounded into me relentlessly, and I rocked back and forth as his heated strokes grew more jerky and less deep. I knew he was near, feeling his length inside me pulsing and swelling still further. Suddenly, a face grinned up at me from below, it was the singer and he was already closing wet fingers around my own aching length. In moments I felt him suck me deep into him, maneuvering into a position to be ready for my impending delirium.

With a fierce thrust of his hips against my ass my lover unleashed a torrent of cum into my guts. Again and again I felt its gushing heat erupt inside me, and in those roaring moments of outpouring my own balls frothed up and unleashed their abundance deep into the singer's agile throat. For those few moments I was on a plane of physical intensity I had never even dreamed existed.

Very gradually, inch by tingling inch, I felt softening cock sliding from my hot, temporarily satisfied ass, and felt a dribble of warmth as cum trickled down my inner thighs. A hot tongue lapped at the creamy flow, soothed my throbbing hole. I sank down, temporarily sated and with my immediate needs tended. The singer smiled creamily up at me, his soft fingers stroking my slick belly and ass cheeks, licking me dean of cum and sweat. Salih had moved slightly away and was bent low at the hole of the Amir himself, licking deep and hot at the altar of penetration.

I dosed my eyes as unending attention was lavished upon my tingling body, teeth nibbling at my flushed nipples, tongues lapping where only moments before a great cock had gushed forth its libations. I sighed in contentment, alive only to the moment. I heard the cry of Salih again, and opened my eyes to see him rearing up, his thrusting cock now vanishing into the tender ass of the young singer, his back beaded with sweat. I looked about me, and all around there lay my companions with their lovers of the moment, all of them lost in the pleasures of the flesh. The air around us was thick with the scents of cum and sweet oils, my mind raised to a plane of physicality I never wanted to slip away from. I could have stayed there forever, loving and being loved in a constant cyde of slithering flesh and lust-fueled lubricants.

I sank into a deep well of sensation, my entire body alive and awake to each and every brush of a finger, a slither of hungry cock. My face ran with cum, my neck forming a pool of cream where any could lick their fill. My hole burned with fervid wanting, needing filling. My cock ached for the touch of fingers on its slicked skin, or the heated wet vacuum of a hungry throat. I reached out, and within moments I felt the awakening flesh of my next eager lover.

How long we remained so I cannot say, for in that thick tangle of naked men time had no meaning. What I can remember is how we awoke. The rising sun had begun its merciless dominion over the desert sands, and in a stupor we could only link with being drugged, we awoke alone but for our beasts.

I was the last to stagger to my feet, throwing off the night's blanket. My companions were padng around the perimeter of our camp, looking for tracks or signs of the other tribe's passing. None of us found any evidence of even their presence in this lonely wasteland. All of us found ourselves doubting our own minds, but it was Salih who remembered where proof would lie.

With our loincloths abandoned we stood naked in the desert morning, our hairless bodies tingling in the passing air, our bodies still bearing the signature of raking fingernails and biting teeth. What had changed between us was our previous distance. We had become overnight a sapling from the greater tree, and from that day forward our evening camps were what made each hard day's travel worthwhile.

It was time to celebrate..

THE BIRTHDAY BOY
An Erotic Novella by K.I. Bard

"Doing him so he'd do me was easy compared with discovering
how much I liked the feel of a warm, lively penis in my mouth...." • • •
"It xoas as if I'd landed in boy heaven where guilt about the male body
didn't exist."

One The Birthday Boy

It was Walt's idea. "Live a little!" he scolded, as he often does.
"You're the oldest young person I ever met." Walt's finger wagged like
a grade school teacher lecturing a naughty boy. It's really annoying
when he gets on his "Let's improve Harry" kick, but I put up with it
because he means well, and also from appreciation. It was Walt, after
all, who got me out of the closet. I owe him. Oh, sure. I'd have
eventually worked free, but he sped me along.

So when Walt decided I was to see a drag show to celebrate my
twenty-sixth birthday, well, I agreed even though drag held little
personal appeal. Truth is, I cooperated to soothe Walt because now that
he's forty and we're no longer nearly so close, he needs outside
interests. If hauling me to a drag show was what he wanted, so be it. I
knew how to get what I wanted later, my reward for cooperation.

I know people who shed a former lover and then avoid him. After
two years, Walt and I reached a friendly separation with occasional
reunions for either social or carnal purposes. Walt's a dam good fuck,
really, because he gets into it. Fact is, though, I don't believe him when
he moans praise for my "wonderful dick." I think he says it to be sexy
more than from any exceptional skill on my part, though it's nice to
hear. I guess I'm fairly OK when it comes to screwing. I'd like to be an
A+, but it more likely I'm just a little above average, say a C+ or B-.

When Walt bustles back into my life with another of his whims, I
try to be decent even when he gets in my way. On occasion I'd like to
shut him out completely, but I see (or is it feel?) how scared he is of
getting older and being alone. Since I got past twenty-five I've had a

few short periods when I'd wonder about my future, too. Tolerance is best, even if it means doing something I don't entirely want, like spending a night watching queens on stage in prelude to whatever cake-and-candle ceremony Walt planned for later. Chances were excellent something would get blown, and I don't mean candles.

Actually, once I was inside and the show started, well, I was glad. It's still not my thing, but it takes a lot of talent and the individual performances were much better than I expected. Walt was bubbling with commentary, supposedly delivered for my benefit, though his attention to me had other benefits, if you know what I mean. Walt could look worldly and wise while I played along letting him fill me with his flow of witty observation.

The star of the show was a truly formidable black queen who was saved for last. Until she came on the audience was warmed up by a progression of performers, one of whom was a tall, elegant number using the stage name Phyllis. She had a breathy voice that sounds like it's licking the side of your neck with a tongue you know is going to dart into your ear any second. Phyllis was a beauty, too, who strutted with style and wit. By then I had a fresh respect for the stripping skill a queen hones so well. Phyllis made an impression even before she made a foray into the audience where she brilliantly insulted a series of appreciative victims until she got to me.

The closer she got the more nervous I grew, which included sinking lower in my chair. I wanted to be invisible and in that fashion stupidly gave exactly the signal that brought the queen to stand before me to ask, intimidatingly, "What do we have here?"

Walt poked me with an elbow.

"Damn you, Walt!" I thought to myself while trying to win the war by giving the questioning queen my steadiest gaze. I should have known my chances were nil.

"This one looks about my speed," Phyllis announced to the amused gathering who expected her to pluck me to pieces for their enjoyment. "The staff puts these out whenever we have a birthday boy out front. So cute." She held up the cheap, plastic table decoration of a diapered baby swathed in a HAPPY BIRTHDAY banner. Then, letting the decoration fall with dramatic disregard the queen swooped in. "The real thing: SO much nicer!" She announced having pushed onto my lap where she wiggled seductively. "Got a live one here, boys!" She purred to the approving onlookers. "Something hairy this way comes." Phyllis delivered more exaggerated grinds while abusing Shakespeare along with me. "It is hairy, isn't it Harry?"

My mind went blank. How did she know my name? Or was I hearing wrong? Had she meant, "It is hairy. Isn't it hairy?"

At my side, Walt was having the time of his life.

That explains it, I told myself. He conspired to cause this, the bastard. I'd get even later. In the meantime there was a queen on my lap and a hard, throbbing cock in my pants, intent on making a breakout from its fabric prison. It was an impudent, insistent erection of the type deserving a good beating, but there being a time and place for everything. Walt's going to pay for this! I assured myself with anticipated satisfaction.

"That's just for starters, Harry, to warm you up." Phyllis lifted my chin with a finger to turn my head before she rose to deliver more banter to "her" audience.

Is it over? I asked myself through a glaze of sweat while Walt wiggled in his chair, slapped my back, and leaned to deliver a giddy whisper. "You were quite a hit. Someone you know, you devil?". "You bastard."

"She knew your name."

"Thanks to you," I hissed. Walt blinked. Know how it is when a reaction is real? Either Walt wasn't part of what happened or he was a better bluff than I remembered. It had to be bluff, though, didn't it? Phyllis drifted away, destroying one admirer after another. I was the only one given so much special treatment, so it had to be planned. The show continued, and before long it was time for the main act consisting of powerful singing and good impersonations, not that I give more than a few diddles for either Streisand or Garland, thanks all the same. Then, the big ending and much applause as all the queens shared the stage. I clapped along with the rest, but more from respect than doting appreciation. Finally, the commotion faded and the club settled to a more familiar world of smoky haze and boozy conversation when half-drunk men eye the competition while looking hungrily for prospects.

Walt sat back with a satisfied look. "Now was that so bad?" he chided with a smug air. "Bad enough." I played my part. "'Scuse me." An immense hulk addressed me. I recognized the body from out front. He worked at the club, probably a bouncer. "Yes?" He offered a piece of paper. "One of the acts sent this."

"Thank you." I took the paper while Walt smirked. "More of your work?" I eyed my companion. "Me?" He aped innocence. "Yes you! I know damn well it's you, so don't try to deny it." Walt's face fell. "It's not me. I know how sensitive you are. You think I'd put you on the spot, other than taking advantage of the club's 'birthday rate'?" Walt was frugal. He could be telling the truth. "It has to be you." I decided not to be fooled. "It wasn't me." Walt was convincing. "What does the note say?" He added, returning my attention to the unopened paper. "It says," I read aloud in cryptic tones, "'Please come backstage so we can talk. Please. Phyllis.'" I frowned at Walt. "I had nothing to do with it."

"You even look innocent." I spewed sarcasm like air spray. "Let's find the back stage, then." Walt stood. "Unless you'd rather go alone."

"And disappoint you?" I countered. "I'm in the dark as much as you." Walt stuck to his innocence. I'd know soon enough and would make him pay for this little episode. It wouldn't take much to reawaken my erection. We'd see who was full of tricks then! Going backstage wasn't encouraged. Even the note from Phyllis didn't make entrance easy, but eventually we were let in amid stares of surprise and annoyance from the tangle of backstage helpers sharing the cramped costume and prop area. "The Diva is in back." One of the crew wanted us out of his way. "Not her. Phyllis."

"Phyllis? Oh. Straight through this pack then first left."

"Thanks." Walt and I made a speedy trip, given the fact we seemed to be in everyone's way no matter how we tried to avoid them. You should try picking your way through a crowd of unhappy wannabe queens. It's an experience. After that trial the task of knocking on the door I faced was a relief. "Who?" A voice boomed. "I have a note from Phyllis." I answered, feeling like a fool. "Phyllis? You expecting anyone?"

"Yes, yes, let him in, will you?" We entered a room shared by performers, each of whom appeared in some halfway condition between male and female. One with make-up removed bore a man's face atop feminine attire. Phyllis, who stepped forward, still wore make-up along with most of her costume. "I'm so glad. It's been such a long time." I was suddenly the recipient of an unusually masculine hug coming from an unexpected source. When Phyllis let go and stepped back I had only one thing to say. "Who are you?" I gulped in embarrassed confusion. "You don't recognize me, do you?" Phyllis looked amused, and, being in queen mode, would make the most of my predicament. "Look, girls," she announced to three mostly disinterested performers. "An old, old friend of mine was in the audience tonight. We were kids together." That got some response. I needn't detail exactly what, either. After the snide comments stopped Phyllis looked at me. "Have you figured it out yet?" I shook my head. "Think back," Phyllis encouraged. "Before I was Phyllis I was someone you knew very well." It hit like a cannon ball. "Phillip!" I gasped. "Phillip Tower!"

"That's right, Harry. You didn't forget!" Any reasonable person would be bored silly with details of the reunion that followed. I'd last seen Phillip when he was just a boy, and though we'd known one another well there'd been a dozen years of separation. I was stunned he recognized me, despite his assurance I hadn't changed all that much since we were boys. Maybe I only felt a lot different than I did back then. In any case, meeting Phillip again was a lot to deal with. More than I was ready for at the moment, which is part of the reason why I was so relieved when he suggested we get together in a few days' time. I agreed and was given an address and phone number. After that, Walt simply led me away, my head buzzing with aftershocks and recollections. Back at his place, Walt could not contain his curiosity. "You little devil, you." He teased. "Imagine knowing a drag queen as a child."

"He wasn't a drag queen then." I answered. "Not even a little?" Walt dug for details as people like him are prone to do. "Well...." I smiled, beginning to remember my very first sight of Phillip Tower, though it wasn't Phillip who interested me then. It was... Walt broke my budding recollection. "The look on your face is killing me with curiosity, you know, and I hope you're not in a hurry, Harry." I shook my head trying to focus on now while then kept flickering at the edges. "No rush." I exhaled. "You'll stay," Walt paused expectantly, "a while?" I nodded. Walt showed a relieved grin. "I got you a birthday cake. Want some?"

"On top of booze?" I shuddered. "Well, how "bout a birthday fuck, then?" Walt got around to that sooner than I expected. "Can't put a candle on that." I decided to keep him in suspense, "I'll say! With you it's more a string of firecrackers. Poor frigging cake gets annihilated."

"Going to try flattery?" I kept him hanging. "I'll try whatever it takes." I stood up. "Silly old man." I teased, starting to unbutton my shirt. "You know why I'm here well as I do."

"Can't always be sure with you, though." Walt bore a serious look. "Sometimes you're difficult to understand."

"Years of practice." I turned his dilemma into my accomplishment. It was time, though, to get things moving. "Do I get my birthday fuck out here in the living room?" I stripped my shirt."

"His bedroom's nicer." Walt stepped closer to speak softly while reaching to gently stroke the back of my neck.

"Mmm." I slipped into a familiar embrace.

"I want to hear..." Walt spoke in breathy bursts between flashes of kisses we shared lavishly on lips, neck, nose, "all about," lips again followed by licking under the chin, "you and Phyllis."

"You mean," I broke free long enough to speak that much before sucking on his tongue for a moment before finishing, "Phillip."

Walt exhaled a gasp.

"It'll take a while."

"Let's hope." Walt slid a hand past my belt to massage my rear as we executed an entwined shuffle toward the bedroom.

"I mean it, Walt." I sought a moment of refuge. "It's complicated."

"You can talk while we play, can't you?" Walt squeezed my cheeks.

"Just so you know. It's not a short story."

"You talk and I'll see what I can do to amuse your wonderful dick in the meantime."

"You asked for it." It's hard to sound original while someone is removing your pants. "It started..." I had a realization. "It started because I wanted to be a Boy Scout."

Two The Birthday Suit

There were parts of my past I didn't consider very often and which I'd seen no reason to reveal to Walt. As an adult, I felt there was little cause to dwell on one's early youth. I routinely glossed over the years spent at a religious private school. Yet it was precisely that experience that shaped so much of what followed later. In fact, the story meshes perfectly, starting when I was eight and saw my first group of Boy Scouts. I wanted to join on the spot and was terribly disappointed to learn I had to be at least eleven to do so. Three whole years of waiting was an immense time span to me then, and to make matters worse my church school disapproved of Boy Scouts. No amount of pleading on my part would sway my parents once they knew the church alternative to Scouts was a group called Catholic Squires.

Indeed, I was told I should be happy because I could become a Squire immediately. I hoped for the best, but I was suspicious (and rightly so) g how much "fun" would be possible from a church-dominated youth program. Instead of attractive Scout uniforms, Squires wore white dress shirts with special Squire ties. In place of camping and hiking, we had visitations to neighboring parishes topped with occasional processional pilgrimages.

I consoled myself that it was better than nothing, though in my heart I knew Squires was very close to nothing, while the Boy Scout program of my dreams bore an astronomical score.

I'd have remained doomed as a Squire throughout adolescence had my father not lost his job. The jolt of unemployment shocked him into action.

We left Illinois, where my father built coal-mining gear for Coppertone, a city in northern Michigan where my dad landed a suitable position maintaining copper-mining machinery. For me, this meant separation from parochial education in synch with something I didn't understand at the time, namely the onset of puberty.

I arrived in Michigan a naive, studious boy who, in consequence of continual parental pressure, had been pushed ahead a year in school. To further complicate matters we moved into Michigan more than a week before their school let out for summer vacation. I was the only boy around while everyone else was in school. Having nothing to do I was simply tagging along with mother when I saw a poster advertising a Boy Scout event, a fund-raiser for summer camp.

That's all it took to reignite my desire to be a Scout. In fact, I was so intent on becoming a Boy Scout I struggled beyond the usual rule in which I was to be seen and not heard to begin asking questions of various clerks and store owners. "Excuse me, sir, but could you please tell me where the Boy Scouts meet?" I was awfully formal as a child, but it was a habit that sometimes elicited sympathy, as it did then when one of the clerks took pity, made a call to a friend with a son in the Troop, and then told me what I sought. The boys met Monday night at seven in the elementary school activity room.

"That was it," I explained to Walt, "and I felt as if my time had finally arrived because it was Monday and I only had to wait until after supper before my dream could come true."

"You know," Walt sighed, "it's not that I don't find this terribly interesting (Walt loves being a sarcastic bastard), but so far the only interesting thing has been playing with your cock while you talk. Anything interesting going to happen soon, hopefully before the grim reaper comes my way?"

"Ha-ha." I frowned before adding, "What you're doing is interesting."

"I discovered this a few years ago, or don't you remember? It seems sometimes you go out of your way to ignore my embellishments."

"It's not possible to ignore that one." I tensed and jittered in synch with his handiwork. "When you're sufficiently turned on, all I have to do is touch this part of your cock a certain way with a fingertip and it wags like a puppy tail, and just like a dog the little fellow drools." Walt demonstrated the trick yet again. "It's not so little." I protested after the jolt passed. "And I'm not so old, either." Walt evened the score for my earlier tease about his age. "Okay, okay, I get it."

"And just when am I going to get it?" Walt shook my dick by its base. "You've been blabbering along for minutes and not yet a hint of Phillip."

"That's because," I had to suck in a quick breath, "Oh that feels good. That's because the start doesn't involve Phillip. It was his older brother, Peter, who attracted me."

"Why you young scamp." Walt vibrated my member again. "Played the field like a budding queen, did you?"

"Didn't know what to do or how to do it." I smiled at the memories of my naive past. "But in my first glimpse of Peter, Phillip's brother, I knew I wanted to be his friend."

"A dishy number?" Walt asked before quickly swooping down to gently suck my crown between slick lips. "That's a little too distracting." I sighed with pleasure. "That's better. Peter wasn't gorgeous. He was more the pure boy type, a leader who stood out in the crowd of Scouts assembled that evening. He was just tall enough to matter, and he had a way of taking charge. When I spoke to the adult leader, he told me I had to join a Patrol in order to be in the Troop, and there was no hesitation on my part when he asked which Patrol. "That one." I pointed to the tangle of boys with Peter at its core. "Good enough." The adult nodded before calling out, "Peter! Get over here!"

"You're determined to drive me insane, aren't you?" Walt objected. "Are you ever going to get to anything good?"

"If you give me a chance." I protested, adding, "Used to be you were after me to slow down." I aped Walt's tone. "Well, there were times you fucked like a deranged weasel." Walt chuckled. "You seemed to enjoy it," I said in ten-percent pout. "I did, but you were rather frenzied. If you could have seen your little ass humping away." Walt enjoyed some amused recollection. "As if you could." I rose to twenty-five-percent pout.

"In the mirror, dearest, your rump was the blurred object that in winter looked like a pale fish belly."

"Sounds ugly." I made a race.

"Will you get to Phillip now?" Walt bent to apply another kiss where it mattered.

"OK. But once I get to Phillip I'm going to stop."

"That a threat?"

"Only if you don't want my version of a deranged whatever fucking you silly."

"I'm all ears."

"Promise?"

"Scout's honor." Walt joked, saluting me with my own erection.

I returned to storytelling; complete with how thrilled I was at Peter's happy acceptance of me into his Patrol, even though I soon learned my addition simply meant his patrol was now the largest with eight boys. While that fact registered, it didn't get in the way of wanting Peter to like me nor of exerting myself to become a full participant as soon as possible. My enthusiasm hit an obstacle, though, in the form of having to pass the requirements for Tenderfoot before I'd be allowed to go camping. Until I made my first rank I'd only be eligible to attend meetings, which meant I'd miss my chance to go to summer camp in a month's time.

Once I realized what was at stake, I grew desperate and begged Peter for help. Not having school to attend, I had time to work on becoming a Tenderfoot. Peter loaned me his Scout book so I could begin, and he agreed to meet me right after school the following day. As it turned out, he lived a short distance from me, just up the block at the next corner. Even at such a young age I had a distinct feeling of destiny at work over the way things were falling so neatly into place. I felt both challenged and excited, but most of all I was determined to become a true-blue Scout.

The next afternoon, I paced nervously while waiting for the school bus to deposit the bigger kids, like Peter, who got out of school a half hour after the first grade-school kids streamed home from the nearby elementary building. I all but ran to Peter when I saw him fly off the bus and in the process embarrassed both him and myself, but I couldn't help it. I found him immensely appealing plus I had a raft of Harry The Woodsman fantasies about my brave new life in Northern Michigan. My over-eager gaff was soon out of the way as Peter conducted me to his house. With much more commotion than I was allowed at home,

Peter led me in where I had to shed my shoes at the door before following him upstairs to his room.

His room was to become an important space in my life, and it was different enough in layout to warrant description. At the top of the stairs, in what would properly be called a story-and- a-half house, there was a fairly large open area. I've been in many homes and can't recall ever having seen such a layout before or since. That space was Peter's room, but it wasn't his alone, I learned on my very first visit because, as we crested the top of the stairs, there was no way not to be confronted by the room's other occupant who was posed in a squat with his back toward us. That, as it turned out, was Philip, and that first time is especially memorable because he was naked as a jaybird.

"Naked?" Walt broke in.

I nodded. "Except for one thing. He had Peter's Scout neckerchief around his neck."

"Oh, cute."

"Want me to continue?"

Walt made a pondering face. "Well, just a little more, I suppose. In fact, this does sound rather interesting."

"Well, it was all I could do to keep from staring at what I assumed was a very young boy I guessed to be little more than a toddler."

"But he wasn't, was he?"

I shook my head, remembering how Peter ignored the naked presence at the top of the stairs. I tried to do the same, except for fleeting glances I stole whenever the figure wiggled or made some noise with a toy car on the tile floor. My attentions were, in fact, evenly split between two competing attractions. First there was the nude boy Peter ignored, and then there was Peter, who began changing out of school clothes. My own habits were to do such things behind closed doors. Peter's casual manner stirred something new in me, and I envied his composure as he talked while stripping to briefs and he tugged at the pouch with no hint of shame. It was as if I'd landed in boy heaven where guilt about the male body didn't exist.

With too much efficiency and speed, Peter was soon wiggling into his after- school clothes, which he collected from the floor. The area around his bed was also his closet. That's where his school attire went. The bed on the opposite side of the open area was, in contrast, quite neat, the naked boy having apparently hung things up as he removed them. With Peter dressed again, the primary object of interest in the room was the nude we pretended to ignore until the figure stood.

You'll have to take my word for it that I wasn't terribly familiar with male bodies, aside from my own which remained in many ways a mystery. So, when the "little" boy suddenly stood I was surprised at his height while feeling much more than surprise by the fact that his penis, visible in profile, stuck out like the handle of a fry pan.

"Well now," Walt purred, "that's some beginning. Not only is our young drag queen naked, but he's erected, too. I bet that got you going."

"I sure noticed, but it was Peter, remember, who interested me."

"He was that special?"

"Decent good looks, a broad smile, an athletic body; what wasn't there to like? He was the friend I imagined when I closed my eyes and wished for some hand other than my own to touch me."

"Like I'm doin'?" Walt petted and squeezed at the same time.

I gave a nod while realizing it was time. "You know, Walt, I can't hold off forever."

"You do marvelously well, though."

"Had a good teacher, but it's time for the fucking to begin, isn't it?"

"If you insist." Walt grinned while quickly preparing himself and getting into position. Doing so he teased, "You going to fuck me till my nose bleeds?"

"Wish you'd stop making an issue of my having said that once. It's just a line I heard in a movie. I thought it was funny at the time."

"With you, dear Harry, it's almost true, though. I don't know how you restrain yourself to last so long."

I wasn't entirely clear how I did it, either, except for realizing I distracted myself instead of focusing on my penis. If I didn't think about what my dick was doing or feeling I could last longer. Once I paid attention to my cock, though, I caught up in a hurry.

"You're the one who coached me." I reminded my friend. "You made me aware of habits that got in the way of better sex."

"Yes, but you exceeded my instruction."

"And that's a problem?" I teased, keeping my mind detached as I prepared entry. "Ready?"

Walt nodded rapidly.

After five years of association I knew what worked with Walt, which included mounting him at a slight angle. Experimenting, I'd tried screwing him while rotating slowly like a drawing compass making an arc. Straight face-to-face or the stacked position was OK, but it was better if I got off- center to do what I called an interlock. Walt's position had to be just right and I had to manage an extension straddle, but the result was a prolonged fuck that I enjoyed and he loved. I could almost put him into a trance.

Walt exhaled a breath of accommodating pleasure. "I don't know how you do it, but you feel perfect once you're in."

"We're a good match." I smiled while making the first slow moves and trying not to focus too much on what I was doing.

I took my mind back to where I left off telling about Phillip the first time. His nudity made a big impression for lots of reasons. How I envied his bare freedom while dismissing that very attraction by associating it as something only a very young child could get away with. Anyone much beyond kindergarten should "know better." My mind worked to fit the bare boy in Peter's room into an acceptable category, and at first that tactic worked. It was successful precisely because Phillip was so physically unlike his brother. Where Peter was dark-haired and robust, Phillip was death-camp thin and ghostly pale as if made of plaster and white paper. When he stood and I saw his penis jutting, I had to revise my conception of him because he was obviously beyond kindergarten age. Even so I made him only a few years older, perhaps seven.

My conclusion about Peter's little brother was promptly aided by Peter who, like me, seemed to ignore his brother until the younger boy placed a three-finger hold on the tip of his penis. His doing so aided my view that he had to be a little kid, because I'd only seen toddlers do things like that, small boys hanging onto themselves through bathing trunks. Peter's reaction fit my own rather nicely when he complained, "Philly. Leave it alone."

Warned, the boy quickly let go of himself and shook the offending hand as if it had acted of its own accord without his will or knowledge.

"You're not supposed to be wearing my stuff, either." Peter added, referring to his Scout neckerchief.

The nude boy did a bodily shake at being reprimanded and promptly reached to remove the neckerchief. No sooner had he obeyed by lifting off the neckerchief than he showed a flash of defiance by dropping the cloth to use his erection as a hanger.

His was a bold yet familiar act because I'd done the same thing many times, except I did it in private to test how much my penis could support when rigid. Small items of clothing or wash cloths were no problem. Big bath towels were too much. It both shocked and intrigued me that Peter's brother would do it publicly, because he plainly meant to be seen and to annoy his brother.

In response Peter emitted a low growl of disapproval which said, "Let's go."

I nodded and followed, daring no more than a brief final glimpse of the young boy looking down at the suspended neckerchief.

Downstairs, Peter took me to meet his mother, who looked up from reading to say hello and smile for a moment before returning to her book.

"Harry's a new Scout."

His mother didn't look up. "That's nice."

"I'm helping him."

"That's good."

"Mother," Peter paused, "Phillip's playing with himself again."

Peter's snitching almost rendered me senseless because I didn't expect it. Instead, I expected a megaton explosion of female outrage.

Fact is, I was reminded of an incident when I was seven or eight and my mother found me and a neighbor boy examining ourselves.

He was sent home with a rebuke, and I expected similar treatment until my mother turned to show her face. Then I knew, and terror hit as she began shaking and stripping me, between times reaching around to swat my rear hard enough to cause pain and copious tears. I bawled like an infant as she removed every bit of my clothing while screaming she would show me what would happen if I ever did such a thing again. She dragged my wailing form to our front door and forced me outside with the admonition that if I wanted to expose myself I should do so where I'd be seen.

To make matters worse she called for an audience of whatever children were within the vicinity. By then I was reduced to a cowering ball of sobs and tears, clinging to her legs, but she undid my hold and left me out there. I heard whispers and giggles. I didn't dare face anyone. I hugged myself tighter and have no concept of how long I was there, but when I finally heard the door behind me open, I looked and saw the kids were gone. Mother grabbed me roughly and took me right into the tub, where I was roughly scrubbed before being put to bed in the middle of the day. I lived in a torment of shame for days or even weeks, plus being forbidden to ever again see the boy I'd been caught with.

Mine was, indeed, a sobering memory, one made all the more curious by what often occurred during baths those years. As best I recall, my bathing involved a meticulous washing of my penis. It felt nice when I was six and even nicer a year or two later. I'd erect nearly every time and my mother always said the same thing after her well-soaped washcloth had done its work. "I wish you wouldn't do that," she'd frown before swatting my rear and causing yet another tingle to course through me.

I was eleven before I was finally allowed to bathe myself, and then only because father intervened. Even that wasn't a sure thing because mother waited to inspect me after each bath and if she wasn't satisfied, for example, with how scrubbed my head looked she'd take charge.

Utterly humiliated. I'd have to stand in the tub as she shampooed my hair while I kept my genitals (shrunk by fear) covered by my hands until she'd rap my knuckles with a brush and demand I stand up straight. Of course, she wanted to prove who was boss, but there was something creepy about the way she looked between my legs. After the third or fourth such showdown in six months father again stepped to my aid by insisting that from then on any re-washing of my head be done at the bathroom sink instead of with me standing naked and tearful in the tub.

When I met Peter I was still a very timid and naive boy who brought considerable anxiety to the otherwise exciting development of his body. So uninformed was I that I viewed the dramatic increase in erections as a sign of some dire malady I was far too ashamed to mention, especially since the affliction brought with it an oddly appealing set of new feelings. The stiffness that frightened me also conveyed a pleasurable tingle I thought was better for me to suffer in silence.

With youthful experience such as mine it's no wonder I learned to detach myself from sex. I had to in order to survive, and I'm not in the least lying when I confide the fact the only sex play I knew was mild indeed, and included no active masturbation. I studied, admired, hefted and squeezed with no concept that more systematic exploration could yield increased pleasure. I was too young for a wet dream to trigger orgasm. The only known purpose for a pee-pee was to pee. Growing stiff and tingly between the legs was a puzzle, though by this time I'd begun to realize I wasn't the only boy so afflicted. Even in the rigidly religious school I left behind, whispers spread that certain things happened to boys. The word boner was hissed and there was a rumor that a few fellows met some secret place to do more than talk. I tried to imagine what they might do, but despite burning curiosity I risked nothing more.

Knowing what I did then, was it any wonder I stood back anticipating a fearful display of feminine wrath when Peter complained of his brother's behavior? Can you imagine my profound confusion when Peter's mother merely looked up for a moment before saying calmly, "Well, I hope you didn't bother him."

My stupefied shock wasn't helped when Peter moaned, "Mother!" in a tone that would have earned me a swift slap to the face for showing disrespect. "He's too old for stuff like that."

In a completely unperturbed voice Peter was told. "He'll get over it, just like you did."

Peter answered with a disgusted moan that would have earned me another act of corporal discipline before saying to me, "Let's go."

Shocked, yet deeply intrigued, I followed meekly as Peter led to the kitchen where he rifled handfuls of cookies without first asking permission. "Take some." Peter instructed through a cookie crumb accent. When I took a single cookie he looked amused and then dumped a few more into my shirt pocket before leading outdoors.

"My brother's a pain." He complained.

"Little kids," I said by way of adding what I believed to be sympathetic understanding,

"It was funny when he was little. We lived in Indiana then. He was always sneaking out of the house, or he'd come back not wearing anything. We'd find his clothes all over. We had a swimming pool there. Why bother with trunks? Philly'd say he forgot to put something on after a skinny-dip."

Peter's words were more revelation than he could have guessed.

"He likes it or something." Peter kicked the ground. "I bet there's none of the neighbors didn't see him bare in our yard a dozen times last summer and bunches more the year before."

"Little kids do that." I tried to be helpful.

"Phillip's ten." Peter grumbled, "Too old for stuff like that."

"Oh." I had nothing more to offer.

With mixed memories where shame and confusion joined erotic highs it's not all that difficult to understand the tempering of my erotic pattern. Muscle control and the special breathing Walt taught me helped a lot, but there comes a time when the pleasure of dangling near the edge of orgasm is less enjoyable. The need for a guy's internal pump to kick in gets too big.

"I'm getting there." I broke a long silence.

"Jesus, Harry," Walt exhaled, "You're close to another record. Were you this damn good with Phillip?"

I shook my head. "I wanna cum, Walt."

"Can't you hold off a little longer? Try for your old record again?"

219

I nodded after a moment of thought. By then the orgasm pulse dropped enough for me to relax and allow it to fade instead of peaking. The inner sensations can be confusing because they're somewhat similar, but if you practice holding off ejaculation for an hour at a time on a daily basis... well, you figure it out.

My mind went back to earlier days instead of focusing on the way Walt's ass felt, like the perfect slicked hand ideal for cuddling a penis. If I stayed in and synchronized my thrusts I could keep going unless I goofed and my cock crown got too close to Walt's grabby ring of muscle, capable of yanking the juice right out of me if I let it. Of course, I never thought about such things when I was a kid. In fact, when I met Peter and fell for him I had no experience with orgasm. I was a truly a virgin in body and mind.

Having no idea why my urges attracted me toward Peter, I nonetheless gave myself to them, doing so the way a boy of my devout religious background would, which means I actually felt I was giving myself to him. For years I'd been told how fortunate were those who happily gave themselves to God, and finally I had a feeling of willingness to give my all in the service of Peter and my Scout patrol. It was pretty heady stuff, and I was really into it. I think I needed something like that to make up for the sudden lack of church/school dictatorship dominating my life.

I spent nearly every spare minute studying the Scout book Peter loaned me, and with few other distractions to get in my way was soon ready to start passing Tenderfoot tests, which weren't difficult. It couldn't have been more than a day or two before I again met Peter after school at his house. That time, I'm sure, Phillip was nowhere to be seen and on the following occasion he watched TV. Without Phillip in his birthday suit, the upstairs bedroom the boys shared was nothing more than a big room which on one side held Peter's untidy world while the other was Phillip's organized universe. I could almost have convinced myself that what I'd seen on my first visit had been imagined, except for the fact it was literally burned into memory and I acted it out on a daily basis taking Phillip's role in the privacy of the bathroom.

By the end of the week I'd done all I needed to become a Tenderfoot Scout. All that remained was Peter's approval by signing his name to what was called my Boy Scout Scorecard. After Peter signed, all that remained, according to Peter, was a brief examination by our Scoutmaster who'd confirm Peter's decision. After that I'd be a full-fledged Scout and could wear the uniform. More importantly to me, I could attend my first camp out.

Maybe you can imagine my enthused excitement the day I was to again meet Peter after school to receive his final approval. It was, I am certain, a Friday, which meant there was only the weekend between me and the coming Monday night meeting when I'd hand over my scorecard. I was pleased with myself, and even Peter seemed impressed by how quickly I accomplished everything. When he suggested, because my new bike wasn't yet a reality, we hike so he could show me around, I trooped along with a feeling of newly gained importance. The prospect of being a Scout was enough to make me strut, not to mention secretly imagining myself on the way to becoming a leader equal to Peter.

Peter's tour was the sort of thing one boy would do for another, which means he didn't take me to see the barbershop, gas station, or grocery store. He headed to the fringes where the houses thinned and streets led nowhere because at one time they thought the mine would be bigger and Coppertone would be two or three times its eventual size. Along the edge of town was half-wild country where kids could scrape out a ball diamond or build forts in the occasional clumps of trees.

Our hike, with Peter narrating various of his escapades in what I learned kids called "the fields," was informative and pleasant, though I found anything with Peter enjoyable. After skirting the more used portions of "the fields" Peter led me toward a brushy area in the process of being slowly reclaimed by forest. It was out there, amid uncounted numbers of young aspen trees sprung up like broom straws, he paused, stopping with hands on hips, to ask, "You gotta take a leak?"

Unthinkable though such an utterance would have been in my former life, I understood it to be an invitation. I also knew I had to adjust to a much different way of life than the one I knew, which included some nuns scrupulously supervising boys' use of the bathroom where we peed in relative privacy with eye-proof partitions separating us. I nodded and followed Peter's lead. I remember the instance very clearly because it was the first time I urinated outdoors.

Being accustomed to indoor privacy, I nervously made water, doing so as if there was, indeed, a physical partition separating me from Peter. I kept that stance until he tore down the imaginary wall.

"These things don't get much sun, do they?" He asked, automatically drawing my attention where he wished, which was to observe him wag the last dribble from his penis while he unashamedly observed mine.

"No." I agreed in a dry breath.

"C'mon." He zipped up and led me toward a dark green hump which, I discovered, was a car driven into the brush and then junked. The wheels and tires, of course, were long gone and all the glass was shattered to popcorn bits, but the vehicle's back seat was relatively intact. Peter plunged inside to occupy one side of the seat while motioning for me to follow.

"What's here?" I asked stupidly, while actually feeling uneasy about entering a car that didn't belong to me to sit on a dirty seat.

Peter ignored my fussy display. "There's another test you gotta pass." He informed me using a tone that said "I'm boss."

"What?" I protested, feeling disappointed and doubtful of his assertion I'd missed something on the Tenderfoot Scorecard.

Peter leaned toward me. "Gotta show yer a real guy."

"How?" I half whined.

"You gotta show the guys you get a good bone."

"Bone?" I was honestly confused.

"Yer boner. Yer dick." Peter explained, looking at me like I was from Mars for not knowing.

"Who says? That's not on the Scorecard." I objected in principled fashion.

"Everyone has to. Even me. I had to do it. There can't be no limp dicks in our Patrol." Peter laid down the law and then obligingly led the way. "See, this is all ya gotta do." He demonstrated by swiftly undoing belt and zipper to shove pants and underwear to just above his knees while he scooted forward. With one hand Peter patted his tummy just

222

above a dark flash of hair while the other hand provided three-finger support to a rapidly erecting penis. "See? Just gotta show you get a good bone. Let's see." Peter wagged his penis, the most beautiful thing I'd ever seen, and so persuaded me to do in an instant what I never dared before.

"Like this?" I asked in a dry hiss after copying him move for move. I lacked Peter's luxurious show of hair, but otherwise I didn't do too badly, and I was sure I'd never been any harder than that moment.

"Like that." Peter nodded. "Let's feel."

Before I could believe he meant it, he was doing it, squeezing my penis in a way that felt better than anything I ever managed alone. There had to be magic in his hand.

"You got a good one." Peter decided aloud. "The guys will let you in, no sweat."

The news was great. The fact he then removed his hand from me wasn't so good. My penis felt suddenly deprived, but I didn't know of what or why. All I could do was watch Peter grip himself and tug the skin down tight. Out of pleasant desperation I did the same.

Peter nodded. "The best thing," he began an urgent whisper.

I leaned closer to get a better look at the glowing member he displayed in its fullest, crowning majesty, and then I let out a choked gasp, but not because of anything we did. A foreign movement startled me and I panicked at the sight of a head that had suddenly popped up to spy on us. "Get out!" Peter snarled at the head, which he recognized while fear got in my way. It was Phillip, who poked his head down and then back into view, but at a slight distance that time. By then my penis was back where it belonged and Peter's looked visibly reduced from its glory only moments before. "It's only Phillip." Peter frowned while fingering himself. I shook my head. "Get outta here, Philly!" Peter yelled at his brother, who stepped back another foot or two but kept watching. Peter looked at me. "He won't tell." I wasn't persuaded. My head shook. Peter's penis wilted into decline and he gave up, quickly yanking his pants up and saying, "Let's go." As we left the car, Phillip ran off. "It's not like any girls saw us." Peter started throwing rocks at nothing. "Just Phillip." He threw again. "Wanna come here tomorrow?" I shook my head. I'd been told I'd be spending the day with my parents and was expected to obey. Besides, I had good reason to do so. "I get my bike tomorrow." Peter nodded. "Sunday?"

"Can't." On Sunday I was forbidden to stray from home. "Monday after school?" I offered. It was Peter's turn to shake his head. "Come get me before the meeting Monday night, OK?" I agreed. Walt's voice broke through. "You're at your old record. See? Aren't you glad?" I nodded. "But things are getting blurred. Sometimes I can't tell if I'm going to pop or not."

"Another five minutes?" Walt took a much greater interest in records than I did. "OK." I exhaled and let myself return to suspension. "It'll be great when we can do it with girls, won't it?" Peter's voice was different. "You have a girlfriend where you came from?"

"No." I had nothing to contribute. It was better to let Peter do the talking, which he did with little encouragement. Peter's enthusiasm for girls was foreign to me, like listening to Mandarin Chinese. Remembering that early experience of feeling removed from Peter's excitement helped calm my rise toward orgasm with Walt.

After that oh-so-intriguing incident with Peter, I thought about its every aspect over and over.

In private, I tried squeezing myself to elicit the same thrill he'd given me, but although it felt nice it wasn't the same. No matter what I tried I couldn't duplicate Peter's effect, and 1 attempted many methods, activity prompted by the fact I got hard more often than ever before. It was as if I'd been activated, my boner machine set on high speed.

Even the new bicycle didn't relieve me and I got familiar with my new two-wheeler while coping with a nearly continuous erection. Talk about double duty.

When Monday evening arrived and it was time to meet Peter, I was all but desperate with some form of wordless need that left me aching and confused. I didn't know what to do other than hope Peter would show the way.

I arrived early and Peter led me upstairs while he changed into uniform, an act he accomplished by again stripping to shorts and tugging at the pouch of his briefs while I observed with obvious envy.

My mind was unable to avoid its one-track focus. "When do I... you know?"

"You mean?"

I nodded, hoping like crazy each of us understood coded talk.

"We got a weekend campout, so we get ready for a week of summer camp. Probably then. All the guys gotta be there. I'll tell you what to do. One of the older guys told me when I did it. It's no big deal."

"Oh." I'd have to wait longer than I wanted to.

What's worse when you're a kid than having to wait for things to happen? If there is a perfect torture to inflict upon the young, it's that. Make them wait in limbo. If they survive that, they'll withstand anything. Of course, when you're actually young your sense of timing is hardly reliable because a long time really isn't a few weeks. My expectations aside, Peter didn't intend to leave me in the dark for too long.

It was after the meeting and we were on the way home. "C'mon." He led us between houses to an area where two close-together garages plus a tall picket fence formed a dark pocket. "In here." Peter plunged into the gloom where all I could make out was his face. There was no missing other clues, however, because his back thumped against a garage wall while out of the shadows came the distinctive sounds of a Scout brass buckle being undone followed by a zipper yanked down. "Yours out?" Peter's question kicked me into motion.

"Yeah." I hissed extricating my erection from confinement.

"Let's feel."

Again, he grabbed me in a way so sudden and unexpected I nearly buckled at the knees. "Feel mine." He husked to me with sufficient fervor to overcome my weakness. "The tip's the best part." He exhaled, circling around mine while I copied his actions. "Okay." Peter's hand left me and without warning pushed my hand from him. "After you show yer bone then let "em see ya got plenty of what the girls need, right?"

"Right?" I agreed in total ignorance, my stupidity made all the more acute by the fact Peter was doing something that made an odd, not-quite-raspy noise at an escalating tempo.

"Go-od, hu-h?" Peter's voice came in breathy spurts I couldn't fully read beyond their surface.

"Yeah." I agreed while my body shook with nerves going crazy from unfocused arousal.

"Almost." Peter hissed an intense whisper.

"Almost what?" I asked myself in desperate dialog.

"There." His voice seemed to stagger, or maybe it was his feet or his back thumping the wall. "There." He repeated a whisper-moan before releasing a long exhale of relief.

"Yeah." My voice echoed his, but for a different reason, mine rising from despair rather than resolution.

Peter was silent for what seemed a long time. "A guy shouldn't do it too much." He sounded spent. "Takes everything out of ya."

I nodded to the dark.

"Sure feels good." Peter emitted a giggle of relief. "Ever wonder if you do it too much?" Peter sounded suddenly on a giddy high.

"Sure." I agreed because it was the thing to do.

"Better go."

I heard Peter begin fumbling, followed by a careful zip up and buckling. "We better." I followed suit struggling to jammy penis inside without hurting it. I remember how my erection ached in one way while the rest of me was pained in another because I had no idea what I'd just witnessed. It was something, but what?

"I think," I gasped to Walt. "Oh shit!" It was starting, one of those strange orgasms that happen when you've held off too long.

On some of those the peak is gone and all you get is a feeling of draining away, like dumping a basin of water or the way you felt as a little kid waking up to find you've wet the bed.

"Jesus!" Walt slammed his fists against the mattress because I was fucking hard into him as I tried to salvage more of a climax. "Jesus!" Walt repeated."

"Fuck." I began folding atop him. "Oh, fuck!" I came to a halt. My heart began slowing. "Beat your old time by nearly a quarter hour."

"Yer killin' me, Walt." I exhaled onto his chest. "Nice way to go, isn't it?" I managed a half chuckle in response. "If you say so." There's more to sex than a particular-size penis, a certain number of thrusts, or an average series of spurts. Your emotions are part of it. What I like is different from what a guy feels unloading his rocks thinking he wants to start a baby. Sex with yourself differs because it meets other emotions. With Walt there are other elements because he's done so much for me and I've got many feelings for him. He can annoy the hell out of me, but he knows when and how to push me, too. We've shared a lot. I try to give him the benefit of the doubt. "You're one of the best parts of my life, know that?" Walt gave my exhausted rear a friendly squeeze. "Thanks." I cuddled into him. "You're pretty good yourself," I paused to effect, "for an old guy."

"Rat." Walt pinched my butt. "OK. I had it coming, but you're a good target because it bugs you when I tease."

"Were you always so mean? Were you unkind to Phillip, or should I say his brother?"

"If I was, I usually didn't mean it, and when I tease you it's only to make you squirm."

"I suppose it's worth putting up with a few of your flaws." Walt snuggled me to him. "Careful." I teased playfully. "You got some, too."

"Don't remind me." Walt hugged. "Some days it feels like they are all I have." I raised my head. "They're not." I put my face against his chest. "Let's sleep." Walt agreed by shifting with me, settling down, letting go. "You'll tell me more about you and Phillip tomorrow, won't you?" I nodded.

Three Frosting the Cake

It's a funny thing remembering how infatuated I was with Peter, and the way I viewed Phillip with such disdain. In my mind he was a little kid who was, even worse, a sneak and a spy. I convinced myself I didn't like him, but a few days later we had an encounter, one prompted by the fact I kept pedaling my new bike past his house in the hope I'd spot Peter, who wasn't home. Midway through one of my round- the-block circuits a bike flew up from behind and made a grit- skidding stop in front of me. Phillip looked over his shoulder to ask, "You lookin' for Peter?"

"No." I denied what was true. "Just riding around." I tried to sound haughtily superior.

"C'mon." Phillip offered to lead.

I've no idea why I agreed. "OK."

He led, it came as no surprise, toward the abandoned car where he'd spied on us, but my suspicions were defused when he kept pedaling, taking us deeper into the scrub brush that fringed the town site. Finally, he got off his bike and walked it into a screening tangle. "Leave our bikes here."

"It safe?" I asked, city suspicions getting in the way of country realities.

"Sure." Phillip shrugged. "I'll show ya a good fort."

"OK."

What Phillip led to wasn't what I'd have called a fort, but it was clearly the domain of kids who dragged assorted cast-offs to the spot to employ them in mixed domestic roles. A huge truck tire rim served as a fireplace ring. Facing it was a car seat I wouldn't have sat on for anything. Instead, I sat on a large log that faced the fire on the opposite side. Once I settled down Phillip joined me by sitting astride the log instead of parallel as I did. In Boy Scout mode I took a skeptical view of the surroundings, but before I could offer a professional opinion a hand suddenly tickling my crotch startled me.

"Hey!" Reflexively, I banged my knees shut.

Phillip giggled. "Now you got me. Like it?" He wiggled fingers inside the trap.

The question facing me was, "Should I like it?" I knew I'd approve if Peter did it, but what of Phillip? His hand worked deeper. It felt good. "OK." I parted my knees.

Instead of following up immediately, Phillip said, "Over here." He led me to a rickety roofed shelter where a combination of cardboard and carpet pieces formed a pad. "Down here." Phillip patted.

I lowered myself to sit, rather primly, until he pushed me to lie flat with one hand while the other toyed along the border of tummy and trousers. During this, I used a trick I put to good use in later life; I separated myself from the experience while allowing things to go forward by reminding myself I'd seen Phillip naked and hard, just as he'd seen me. Somehow there was less anxiety in a forbidden activity being repeated than existed in its initial occurrence. In that mode I acted as observer while he uncovered me.

"It's nice." Phillip leaned back to view my erection.

"You, too." I mouthed, knowing this was a transgression that had to be shared.

Phillip did so quickly, his smooth-skinned rod a near perfect miniature of my pubescent boner. His, however, was ticking up-down more rapidly than mine. "Almost big as Peter's." Phillip revealed perhaps more than he realized.

"He's got more hair." I commented on what I envied.

Phillip explained why this was so while beginning a delicate series of examining motions, squeezing me, then himself, bending me one way, then following on himself. Phillip's handling of me didn't impart the same excruciating thrill his brother had, but it was very nice and grew better as he began to jiggle me in an unaccustomed way that turned suddenly uncomfortable.

"Oww...." I complained.

"Sorry." Phillip adjusted his grip. "This is what Peter likes."

His new treatment was better on several counts, not the least of which had to do with his mention of Peter plus the fact Phillip revealed a level of familiarity with his brother of which I was enormously envious. "Uhh ... Ohh." I was unable to form words for the firecracker feeling Phillip's hand ignited in my penis. The sensation frightened me as much from its uncommon strength as from fear he might stop. My head began rocking side to side and I thought of wriggling away as if survival depended on not being overcome by whatever it was threatened to engulf me. "Stop! Please ... stop!" I tried sitting up, only to discover doing so only added to the growing enormity that boiled into reality as globs and splatters fell onto my tensed tummy.

"Gosh." I heard Phillip say in awe.

I couldn't make sense of what happened. The closest thing being that I'd peed on myself, except pee wasn't cloudy white goo. It felt as if something inside had ruptured. There was relief, but worry, too, boiling up quickly to fill the newborn void.

"That's more's Peter's been able to do."

My addled brain grabbed at the offered straw. If it happened to Peter more than once, then the event wasn't fatal and I wasn't doomed to premature death during which my ruptured innards would slowly ooze out, like pus – the other thing my pre-teen mind offered in association with something strange that might come out of a penis. I'd been present when a neighbor's dog burst a skin infection.

Fortunately, my nose detected no stench similar to that awful mess. "Peter?" Into that single utterance I crammed a ton of questions.

"Peter does it all the time."

"Oh," I sighed, with immense relief.

"Wanna do me?" Phillip asked, but apparently one look was all he needed. "Never mind." He commenced rapid rubbing himself until he tensed, rising onto his knees. He shuddered visibly. I realized his hand slowed. Phillip caught his breath before sighing, "Wish mine did it, too."

I remained stunned but began to realize, this was what Peter was going to show me in the car and what he'd done to himself in the dark after Scouts. At that point I had yet to know its name, much less its future role in my life. 1 looted at Phillip's penis, visibly unchanged, whereas mine lay like a plump, semi-hard night crawler above a sparse grass of pubic hair.

"Know what Peter really likes?" Phillip gave himself a comforting squeeze before focusing on conspiracy.

I shook my head. "What?" I spoke with almost no breath.

"I'll show ya." Phillip moved closer and picked up my penis, which nearly stood unaided. A few tickles finished the job. Phillip grinned as he brought his face nearer. "You can't tell anyone, even Peter." His breath fanned my tip.

And then, my penis realizing what was going to happen before I did, my erection strained upward to greet the mouth that swallowed it and made me gasp so hard I feared spinal injury from the jolt.

It wasn't until the following forenoon that I got around to telling Walt the part of my story where Phillip opens the door into my sexual seclusion. His reaction is of interest.

"I never thought to do much digging," Walt added during a reflective pause, "into your early sex, Harry. I assumed you added erotic experience in easy stages. I had no idea you went from drought to deluge in one day."

"In around ten minutes." I corrected.

"First hand job, first orgasm, and first time being blown all in one package. Remarkable I hope you showed your appreciation." Walt adopted one of his favorite wiser-than- thou tones.

I shook my head.

"You didn't?" he gasped, several octaves higher.

I shook again. "I wasn't interested in Phillip, remember, and I had it in my head that a younger boy was obliged to do things for older ones who didn't have to do anything in return."

"What rigid little attitudes you had." Walt frowned. "Sexual selfishness is not a good habit. It's one I'm glad you're over."

"It took a while."

"How long?" Walt relaxed into listening mode.

Actually, I couldn't have said at that moment how much time it took. I may have halfheartedly petted Phillip's penis that first time, but my focus remained over ninety percent focused on Peter, who remained my ideal. In contrast to his robust elder brother, Phillip was painfully skinny and incomplete. It was all but impossible for me to idealize such a pathetic character as Phillip despite how grateful I was he'd shared the big secret with me. Once I was, so to speak, on the inside there was no further need to bother with Phillip, was there?

Walt asked if I hadn't at least jerked the boy off by way of thanking him for doing so to me. I had to admit I hadn't. "I didn't know how. Hadn't even done it to myself, yet. You think I'd have displayed my ignorance to him?" I shut down Walt's inquiry with countering questions.

"I'll give you that," Walt surrendered, though not without adding, "But I don't like the image of you as such a one-way character."

He wasn't about to give up entirely, though. "So, did you go from there to have a successful union (his disdain was obvious) with the hunky, older brother?"

"Sort of." I blushed.

Walt rolled his eyes. "Well, let's hear it."

Funny thing is, important as these events were, I have trouble being precise. I think a day or two passed during which I did little other than watch for signs of trouble. If sex was the biggest sin, after all, I didn't want to bring myself to ruin so soon. I waited to see if my penis would erect of its own and whether or not I could pee. I'm sure I needed at least twenty-four hours to observe before I began to feel safe. With that out of the way, I began to experiment. My first self- administered orgasm waited more than a day, but within forty- eight hours I had the bugs worked out and was, so I thought, ready for Peter. By then Coppertone's school was out for the summer and I had visions of months-long wonders with my idol.

This dream plan I tried putting into action on a midmorning some days after Phillip jerked me into paradise. I knocked at Peter's door and stood waiting, only to be greeted by Phillip wearing a bathrobe. He grinned and stepped backward. His robe parted. Under it he wore pajama bottoms from which his erection protruded like a naughty reminder.

"Peter home?" I asked while trying to keep my eyes from Phillip's member.

"Watchin' TV. C'mon." Robe restored, Phillip led me toward the noise of morning cartoons, a diversion forbidden me at home, where I was expected to observe constructive entertainments.

No matter how distracting I'd found Phillip's display, what I found in front of the TV proved more so. Peter was sprawled on his tummy, chin propped on folded arms, before the TV. For attire he had a single garment, undershorts so worn as to seem gauzy. The material highlighted the globes of his ass. I could have spent the day looking at his long lean body, but Peter rolled onto an elbow, saw it was me, rose, and said, "Let's go up."

I followed, half my mind absorbing every move of muscle while the other half cringed at the treatment I'd get at home were I to loll before the TV in nothing but briefs.

Too soon we were in his room, where Peter sat cross-legged on his bed. I joined him, though with both my feet on the floor. We jabbered, probably about Scout things, while I stole looks at his crotch, an area of fascination for multiple reasons. First, Peter appeared perfectly at ease in underwear he'd worn for more than a day – guessing by the discoloration of the pouch they may have been into the third or fourth day. My mother would strangle me if I didn't wear clean underwear every day, but that wasn't what fixed my attention. Peter's briefs were more than dingy. They were threadbare to the point his left leg-hole was stretched out of shape. A gray noodle of elastic dangled sickly from a ragged tear. More importantly, a half-dollar-sized area of scrotum gained exit into the open at the stretched leg hole, and that tantalizing area of flesh was all I could look at, despite repeated attempts to control myself and look Peter in the eye.

Under those conditions I no longer had a concept of time, so I can't say how long I struggled before being overcome by desire so strong it demanded I act. Trying to make my action appear one of light entertainment, I grinned while pointing at the area of exposed scrotum as if noticing it for the first time. "Look what I see." I gaped while letting my finger draw closer and closer, that being the best way I knew to judge his reaction. Peter never said, "Go ahead. Touch it." He didn't need to because he made his permission perfectly clear by leaning back, which caused his groin to elevate. The trail was clear and I brought my fingertip to tickle his ballsac while we each grinned and giggled as combined nerves and arousal kicked in simultaneously.

What a pleasure it was to nuzzle that warm, delicate flesh with my finger, and if that wasn't reward enough, it was soon multiplied a thousand times when I observed definite motion from the opposite quarter of Peter's briefs. I was giving my friend a boner. The shape of his penis filled in detail as I watched, smiling in synch with him. With an easy laugh, Peter tugged at the pouch fabric to allow more room, and after no more than a few seconds of that lifted his waistband fully to allow the trapped erection to clear. Then, with care, he lowered the elastic waist until it snugged his penis, leaving only the tip exposed, pressed firmly against his tummy.

Peter's head nodded. I hadn't learned semaphore as a Scout, but I read that signal well enough. My finger had permission to tickle two areas. The exposed scrotum and revealed glans were both fair territory and I roamed from one to the other while he leaned further back in obvious enjoyment. I hadn't completed too many revolutions before Peter increased the scope of our play by pulling the elastic down to the base of his penis, which then stood throbbing at attention above the carpet of dark curls I so envied.

I wanted a good long feel of Peter's member, somewhat darker and fatter than mine, and I especially wanted to explore its sensitive tip. But when I saw a dewy bead of moisture at the outlet I had reservations because I mistook the fluid for pee, which was "dirty". So unimportant an issue got in the way, and I avoided pee contact by petting and squeezing the lower area of shaft until, after only the briefest of contact, Peter pushed my hand aside so he could further lower the elastic to a snug juncture under his balls. That accomplished, he swiftly uncrossed his legs before leaning back all the way. He was giving complete and full go-ahead to do whatever I wanted. I couldn't have been happier or more flattered. Even my fear of his pee was vanquished and 1 began to move up and down with most delicate friction while the bead on his tip tripled in size. I knew I was well on the way to making his penis erupt in the unspeakable pleasure I'd so lately come to know. Peter's body craved my touch and he moved, like the tide, in rhythm with the moon-force of my transiting hand.

I was in paradise, but not for long. The combined feel and appearance of Peter's erection held ninety percent of my attention. The other ten percent, however, grew suddenly aware when the cartoon noise from below suddenly quit. A bleat of complaint rose from Phillip's voice, followed by a motherly tone, "You know the rule. Up in your room if you're going to do that."

Peter realized what was about to happen before I did, because he tossed my hand aside, sat up, and restored his briefs as Phillip made a bee-angry flight up the stairs. Storming angrily into the room, Phillip acted as if we didn't exist. In full pout he stomped to his bed and shrugged off his robe before flinging face down onto the mattress, which he then humped a few times in none-too-subtle fashion before lying still.

"Let's go." Peter was up and flying into clothes while I sat in muddled confusion, my face burning from shame plus frustration. The prospect of possibly getting caught with Peter's penis in my hand was frightening, even if it was only Phillip who'd have seen us. And yet, I wished to continue. I wanted to do much, much more. "Your house?" Peter broke through my agony with a question. My mother, who insisted on approving of any friend I wished to have, was impressed by Peter, which meant he was allowed to visit. Peter led the way, and, in pursuit of him, I took one final look back before descent removed the opportunity. Phillip was on his side by then and just in process of sliding his pajama bottoms down. That was the last I saw.

At my house, after suitable formalities to mother, we were hardly in my room before Peter dug into his pants to bring out an erection, something I'd lost upon nearing home. He nodded for me to join him, and I was in the process of digging out my noodle when mother's voice interrupted with a chill. I zipped and dashed to the door in time for it to collide with me causing a commotion that allowed Peter time to restore himself, after which he was every inch the proper Scout. He engaged mother in polite conversation in such a way she'd never have believed that seconds before he'd been wagging an erection at me. Mother was quite taken with Peter and was happy to serve him lunch along with me, while for his part he seemed quite eager to again sample her cooking (cooking was something I gathered his mother didn't spend much time doing). Peter showed no sign of the agonized regret I felt from the interruption.

As for me, I wanted to eat and then get out of there, hopefully to the outskirts of town where abandoned cars and kids' forts called with erotic opportunity. My suggestion to bike into the woods was rejected by Peter, who looked at his wristwatch and said he was expected to help his father at their store, called The Mercantile, that afternoon. "We can go together, before I have to work." Peter suggested. Without much enthusiasm I agreed because being with him was better than separation, even if the prospect of picking up where I left off grew further and further away.

In actual fact, Peter had in mind an attempt at what I believed was no longer in the cards. Being first interrupted by Phillip and then by mother was too much bad-luck omen for this boy. But, outside the rear door of The Mercantile was a man-high pile of cardboard boxes where Peter carefully made his way. "In here," he called, adding the sound of his zipper going down as final inducement. Once again, Peter was full hard while I was barely able to find enough hose to pee,

though sight of Peter made me yearn otherwise.

How fickle fate can be. Nothing of consequence had time to begin when the rear door banged open and another box was added to the pile. The latest disturbance was enough to panic me, which attracted the notice of Peter's father, who wanted to know what I was doing in there. Peter (a master at speedy zipping) spoke up to say we were looking for boxes. At that point the man said he was glad his son was early because he needed help. I'd have to come back some time when Peter didn't have to work. Feeling as if God cursed me for sexual thoughts, I all but ran away.

"Your just reward," Walt observed with smug satisfaction, "for having ignored poor Phillip."

"I told you," I moaned in frustration, "I was keen on Peter. Phillip was just a little kid. Give me a break, will you!"

"For the moment, only. Until I decide your fate." Walt was leading up to something, wasn't he? "You can tell me about your eventual consummation with Peter."

"I wish I could."

"What?" Walt gaped aghast.

"It took a while, that's all. It took lots longer than I wanted it to."

When you're a kid all sorts of things get in the way, and for the next few days either demands on my time or on Peter's denied any opportunity to follow through. In fact, it wasn't until the weekend campout when the chance would return. In the meantime I consoled myself with self-entertainment when possible, which was a LOT less than I wished.

"So you eventually got the boy of your dreams?" Walt teased. "I hope he was worth the wait."

To be mean I did nothing but shrug.

"Well, aren't you going to tell me?"

"You want details, I suppose.".

"You're damn right I want details, and plenty of them, too." Walt put up a good front.

On that weekend campout I'm not sure what made me most excited. I may have been keyed up by getting away from home for my first night in the woods, but a lot of my excitement had to come from the big test when I faced the entire Patrol to show I wasn't, as Peter so precisely put it, a "limp dick". With a feeling of not being prepared for what I'd so long anticipated, Peter signaled the time had come.

"OK, guys," he gathered us with soft spoken orders, "time for Harry's inspection, right?" Peter grinned at the assembled group, which turned suddenly eager in a suspiciously quiet way.

"This is gonna be good." One of the fellows tittered in a tone as if he was rubbing his hands in anticipation. "Rudy." Peter spoke in a commanding whisper. "You stand guard. Tell us if anyone comes."

"Why me?" Rudy wailed. "Shhh!" Peter shushed him before adding, "Cuz I say, that's why."

"No fair! How come it's always me?" Peter ignored that argument. "Your turn is after. You're on guard." Rudy stomped off, obedient but mumbling. "OK, Harry, you first." Peter pointed to a tent. "Go to the back. We line up three on a side." With mixed feelings I crawled inside. I'd have chickened out had Peter not told me what to do. I was ready, but without confidence. The others piled in on either side. The interior felt jam-packed with bodies. "Now?" My voice quavered in falsetto. "Go 'head."

"Let's see yer noodle."

"Think he'll find it?" There was no escaping the wisecracks, but preplanning helped because I decided I'd go for broke. With nervous hands I stripped off my T-shirt. "Here goes." I'm not sure if I spoke aloud or to myself as I undid belt and zipper before doing a slow striptease. I wiggled my clothes down while my penis reacted by going up. Jitters kept me from getting fully hard, but twelve eyes added an unexpected thrill to a respectable boner. "Yeah, it's okay."

237

"It get any bigger?" I knew I had to endure some teasing, which I hoped to curtail by following Peter's suggestion that I insist the others join me. "You gotta do it too,' I croaked. "Noway."

"Who says?"

"I'm not." Peter put a stop to that. "We gotta, guys. Nobody gets to be a lily-liver." Peter led the way. My sole erection was joined by six others, each with a personality of its own. Peter's was (for me anyway) the leader because he had the best total package of penis, pubic hair, and nice balls. A couple of erections matched his, but they fell short on hair or balls. Peter had it all. "Now this." I began stroking myself. "We never done this before." One of the guys giggled. "Liar."

"Cuz you couldn't do nothin'."

The wisecracks were no longer aimed at me alone. "Holy shit." Someone hissed. "Man, this is..." A statement went unfinished. "I'm gettin' there."

"Me too." So was I. Boys achieve orgasm with little difficulty and less time. It could have been the group sex atmosphere that brought me along so quickly, but I'm certain it was Peter who finished the job. At the first sign of his sperm I gushed, my eyes riveted on his fist, which squeezed hard, trapping most of his juice, as it turned out, until he slowed and relaxed. As his grip released, a gush of goo burbled up and over his upraised tip while around me my own heavy breath echoed that of others. If you want the truth, I don't think we were in the tent for more than five minutes, but I finally saw Peter in action. Once I had, I wanted more. "That's it?" Walt was incredulous. "All that build-up and you didn't even touch Peter? The whole thing over in a few minutes?" I made a version of "That's show biz!" with my face. "You deserve," Walt began with a nasty grin, "a good beating for being a story-telling tease, or at least part of you deserves to be beat within an inch of its six-inch life."

"Will you spare my life," I played along, "kind sir, if I tell the shameful tale of my seduction of Peter?"

"I'm holding this Peter hostage until you do."

"You're too kind." Walt applied a too-firm grip. "Get talking." He demanded. I didn't have to be told again. Leaving the tent, we were in a good mood. You know the way guys act after something "good". After that I felt more accepted. I was part of the big-boy secret, and I hung near Peter's elbow to be available at first opportunity. At that point I'd have done anything. ("Want me to hold your penis while you pee, Peter?") But while I looked for openings in one direction some unfinished business popped up. "Hey! What "bout me?" Rudy complained, jogging to intercept. "Now you gotta show Rudy." Peter used my proximity to advantage, although not the one I wished. My jaw dropped. "My tent," Rudy ordered. "Me, too," Rudy's tent mate, Richard, offered. I nodded agreement, thinking I'd get it over with while being somewhat intrigued with another chance to observe Richard's penis, one of the largest. "Get crackin'," Rudy ordered when we were inside. It's funny (without being amusing) how small boys can be such a pain. Rudy sounded like a cranky little old man.

"We make a circle first." I insisted on some control. After we formed a tight-facing group, I undid my buckle with a flourish before lowering pants and underwear so Rudy could examine my rubbery dick.

"That ain't a boner." Rudy fussed. "Let's see yours." I countered. "No how," Rudy shrilled.

"Peter said we had to. We all did, even Peter." Richard demonstrated he was on my side verbally and then physically by exposing himself. The sight of his semi-erection assisted my recovery In high-pitched complaint, Rudy grumbled,

"I gotta?" His penis, when it was finally produced, proved a pipsqueak like its owner.

"You gotta jerk it too, right Harry?" Richard prompted.

"Yeah," I agreed, suddenly fascinated by the way Richard's arousal transferred to me. I was totally turned on again.

"I ain't gonna do nothin'," Rudy whined while making wrist motions at supersonic speed. In any case, Rudy's combination of gnat organ and excessive haste were of little interest compared to Richard's luxurious member, manipulated at a tempo that reverberated in me with increasing success. Richard smiled at me. "You gonna?" I nodded, "Yeah."

"I'm getting outta here." Rudy zipped and scooted in the amount of time needed to crook a little finger. Richard and I barely registered his departure, or at least I hardly noticed because my gaze was fixed on Richard's hand and the attractive cylinder it worked with loving enthusiasm.

"Man ... Ohh!" Richard gulped, rising onto his knees as a fresh delivery of semen made a watery escape.

"Mmm... mmmnnn," I responded to the sight with a burning orgasm of my own, two mini-spurts followed by a succession of timid drools. I sat back on my heels when it was over and looked as my penis toppled from rock to rubber. "You quittin'?" Richard's voice broke the calm I expected to fade into comfortable nothing. I looked up in blinking puzzlement.

"Keep doin' it. You'll get another one." Richard's voice was a perfect emulation of the process of inducing orgasm, which at that age was part contest, part struggle, and all thrill. A squishy noise rose from his groin as fingers and fresh sperm became applied erotic ointment. "I like doin' it at least twice."

"Twice?" The idea had immense appeal. "Lots of times three." Richard's voice wheezed exquisite tension.

"Uhh." I worked at myself and was surprised by a sudden return of stiffness coupled to a now-familiar ringing at the tip of my penis. "Man!" I panted as a new level of excitement built.

"Tol' ya." Richard's tone mirrored mine with enjoyment. "This is gonna be good." Richard's voice trembled as he bent, focusing ever more intently on the cascade of sensations that all but defies description.

"Good," I echoed, and it was. For a minute or two I was immersed in the feeling until a tremendous inner heave sent a few pearls of moisture down the core of my penis to leave me spent but smiling. The feeling was so satisfying I continued milking myself for echoes of pleasure after all the sharper highs drained away. It still felt good, though different.

"Last one's always best." Richard's voice reminded me of his presence. I looked up to see he was doing the same as I, his fist performing a wet glide of slow-motion enjoyment.

"How many times you do it?" I was more than curious.

"Till it stops, I guess," he said, his grin filled with meanings that I recognized.

I nodded.

"Let's change hands." Richard whispered, but he really meant something else, as I discovered when his hand replaced mine. "Do what I do, okay?"

I nodded.

After very little of that Richard added another modification, "Get our pants off."

That made it even better. We knelt face-to-face with twin cylinders in every combination possible that way before lying down hip-to-hip. The more bare body on view the nicer it was, and once a guy lets you handle his dick you can assume permission to touch other places, which gave access to Richard's balls, so fascinating to me. He introduced me to the unsuspected thrills of having my neck stroked and nipples fingered.

I was in sex heaven, and Richard intended penis paradise by kneeling astraddle me so our nuts rubbed, his light fur tickling my tight covering. It was all I could do to keep from jerking him wildly to climax because I wanted to shoot so bad I felt insanity threatened if I didn't have relief soon. But instead of bringing matters to a head, I followed Richard's lead drawing the skin of his penis tight and shaking it lightly, just as he did to me, or delicately tickling the nervy spot under the tip when he did mine. Richard proved an education, and when we finally quit I think it was the first time I ever felt, for lack of a better expression, deep sexual satisfaction.

I was shot, or at least my dick was. Even so, when I left Richard I went in immediate search of Peter. "You were a perfect little tramp, weren't you, bad boy?" Walt administered a flogging to suit the offense. "I suppose you were a perfect kid." I spoke and acted in kind. "Oh, that's nice! Keep up at that pace and you'll need some tissue."

"Well, behave yourself or I'll make your bald guy puke." I teased. "I haven't heard that one in a long while." Walt gave a theatrical giggle. "First time I heard it was with Richard, and I tried using it first chance with Peter."

"Back to him, are we?" My story continued. Four Blowing Out the Candles Now that I was one of the guys, I wanted more, and having set my goal on Peter I realized the obstacles in my way included Ray, Peter's assistant. Ray was the tallest boy in the Patrol plus he had impressive balls, real danglers. Having red hair meant his pubic hair lacked visibility. He may have packed a better total package than Peter, but his groin appeared bare and his huge nuts were almost freakish. Of course, I had to dislike him, so I found fault wherever I could. Ray made it easy for me by being what is sometimes called a pill. If he didn't get his way, he'd get in a huff. In that sense he was easy competition. On the other hand, he was a year older than I and was already a First Class Scout with plenty of experience while I was a novice Tenderfoot. I faced an uphill trek, but I was going to succeed with Peter, and if Ray had to be vanquished in the process, well too bad. A boy may very well know what he wants while lacking any tact when it comes to getting it. I was no exception there. To get my way I employed nothing subtler than a whine. I found Peter and complained. I didn't like my tent. I didn't want to sleep there. Why couldn't I sleep in his tent? My shrill made Ray frown. "You can't sleep with us. You're just a Tenderfoot."

"I can if Peter says so. He's boss." I insisted. "If you move in I'm movin' out."

"See if I care." I taunted while thrilled that success came so easily.

Through all this Peter's leadership skills were either lacking or went unused. "It's up to you guys." He contributed nothing to help either Ray or myself, which in a way cleared my way to continued assault. The fact that Peter stepped back removed support from Ray, who gathered his gear to replace me in the tent I'd abandoned.

"It'll be just us." I thrilled at the prospect of finally having Peter to myself.

"Our boy finally has his heart's desire," Walt purred, giving my boy a long, familiar stroke.

"You trying to start something, old man?" I teased without being nasty.

"Continue." Walt gave boy a shake as if waving a pointer at a blackboard.

I don't know how typical my memories are, but I remain amazed at how fresh some aspects of the experience are. Maybe erotic anticipation or first love supercharges one's memory, but it's odd how some (quite minor?) things stand out. My entire body felt different once I was assured of having Peter alone for an entire night. A form of trembling made it impossible for me to be still. It wasn't a bad feeling, mind you, but it grew and in doing so had an increasing impact on my behavior. I was eager plus edgy with what I now realize were unvoiced desires.

Crawling after Peter into "our" tent after Taps faded (the bugle echo leaving sharp tingles along my spine) I was giddy . in a jabbering way. I couldn't shut up, plus I faced an intense virginal desire to engage in what I now know is nest building. I wanted our nest to be just right, so I promptly busied myself putting things in what my young mind conceived as order within the impossible-to-organize confines of a tent occupied by naturally untidy Peter.

I tried to decide things such as where to put my shoes while Peter continued. My babble of observations, suggestions and questions was ignored except for reminders to "keep quiet after Taps." Fact is, even simple things that first camping trip were a struggle. Whereas Peter's pack was comfortably Spartan, mine was overfilled, requiring brute force to remove its tight-packed contents, which defied re-packing when our outing concluded.

My first night, of course, I was on the steep end of a learning curve, so I was utterly innocent when I suspended homemaking to pay attention to Peter who, by then, was undressed. He was busy picking at a toe while sitting on his sleeping bag in undershorts. I didn't know whether to be charmed by his casual demeanor or repelled by the possibility of foot odor.

But as Peter was, after all, the person I idealized above all others, I took what I thought the brightest tack by asking, "Where's your pajamas?"

243

"Pajamas?" Peter looked up from his toe work to stare. If his look wasn't sufficient, the tone of voice used was.

"Just kidding'," I hissed, not knowing whether to be relieved at the prospect of pajama-freedom or disgusted at the thought of sleeping in dirty underwear. The only antidote to internal tension was action, so while Peter returned to worrying his feet I peeled off my clothes to match his state of undress atop my sleeping bag. "There." I announced in a whisper.

Peter glanced, making a face. "Gonna sleep in grubby undies?"

Now I was lost. Would I ever know what to do?

"Here's the best way." Peter informed in an active whisper while scooting into a tucked position on his back. "I read about camping, books say to sleep bare ass." Peter skinned off his briefs and gave them a casual fling.

The sight of his naked body provided yet more charge to my system, causing the persistent stiffness between my legs to surge to a yet higher level. In fact, I'd been turned on for so long, I might have begun to think the natural state of my penis was hard. But, as Peter didn't have a boner and I did, I decided to be coy and tried to hide it.

"Thinkin' "bout yer girlfriend?" Peter teased, which meant he'd been watching.

"Maybe." I was unable to say more.

"What's her name?"

If Peter kept up this line of questioning I was doomed. "Mary." I took the first name that came to mind and hoped the mother of God would forgive me.

"She nice?"

I nodded. I'd never met the Blessed Virgin, but her reputation was good, though not beneficial to my penis, which went from scale ten to nine. I needed things to go where I wanted them. I had to do something. "Are you going to make your bald guy puke?" I asked, my glance going back and forth from my middle to Peter's. Making use of Richard's joke was all I could think of.

"Bald guy?" Peter frowned.

244

I regretted my jest. Maybe it wasn't so funny after all. "You know." I opened my legs and gripped myself to emphasize the bald head in question.

Peter stared a moment before going, "Oh, that's really funny."

"You going to?" I had my hopes up along with my penis.

"Already did." Peter answered, making himself comfortable in his bag.

"Uh?" I was totally mystified. I'd been in the tent with him the entire time and had seen nothing.

My confusion must have been more than abundant enough because Peter explained. "You were there."

He meant hours ago when we all did it. "I thought," I said, weakly, unsure how to explain.

"Well." Peter turned part way on his side and allowed a bare knee to protrude from his unzipped bag. "Maybe if you tell about your girl. She got nice tits?"

Holy Mary forgive my sin. I'd talk about tits until hell froze if it would encourage Peter, whose free hand I watched make a ripple inside his bag as it slid along his hip before plunging down.

Love of breasts was a foreign tongue, but from overhearing I gathered enough to know bigger was better. I had precious little to go on beyond that, until Peter provided a prompt about nipples. This set me upon a glowing and utterly fictitious tit fantasy guided by subtle motions I watched take place as movement in Peter's sleeping bag until, finally, I could take no more. "Let me see?" My voice begged.

Peter threw his bag aside. "Sure." He said as if it made no difference either way.

But it mattered to me, again in reverent awe of his splendid endowment. "Can I?" I whispered.

"If ya want." Peter removed his hand and settled back so I could explore until, far sooner than I wished, he put his hand over mine to guide me through the grip and tempo he preferred. "I'm gettin' there," he panted, rolling quickly onto his back, upsetting my rhythm in the process. "Fas'er. Fas'er." He urged, head rocking side-to-side.

245

I was aroused by the musky odor rising from his groin and I was envious of his substantial penis, especially when it filled dramatically right before he clamped his hand like a vise atop mine to apply death-grip pressure intended to turn free ejaculation into a strangulated release that oozed over my knuckles and added a mushy sound to his wheezing. I was along for the ride, my hand a surrogate in partial control of an experience at which I was still a novice. I could only wonder what it felt like having so much stuff pour out your penis. It had to be, well, it had to be tremendous, the best thing ever.

My glorious fantasy didn't last long.

"Mess." Peter exhaled and destroyed my image of bliss. "Got something to wipe?" The reality was a wet plop that grew progressively colder.

"This." I dug my brand new Scout handkerchief from a pocket. "Anything." Peter paid attention only to swabbing himself, after which he tossed, almost rudely, the cloth for me to catch. Using two fingers, I put it aside. "Want me to do ya?" Peter yawned, none too inviting. "Will you?"

"Just let me catch my breath. You start, okay?" His head rolled toward me. "I'll watch. Say when you're ready."

"Okay." Of course, keyed up as I was, soon as the word was out I was ready, and in two shakes I was more than ready. "Hey!" Peter giggled as the first of my slime appeared. He pushed my hand aside and took hold to add rough, firm strokes that conveyed the combined feel of torture plus exquisite pleasure. "Wait till yet dick's a year older an' you can really come." He tossed my penis aside before casually wiping his hand on the inside of my bag. "I'm shot." Peter rolled away. "Put the flashlight out when yer done."

"That's it?" Walt chuckled. "So much build-up for that?"

"I wonder why I kept liking Peter so much."

"Thought you said he was cute."

"He was, but he wasn't gorgeous."

"All-American Boy?" I nodded. "It wasn't him, then, so much as what he represented to you, right?"

"Probably so."

"Was Peter more of a lover after that?"

"I wish." How best to untangle so many things wound together? I continued idealizing Peter while getting to know the rest of the guys, who mostly accepted me. But such comfort as I found never lasted long. I'd about learn how to feed a fire during breakfast only to discover I knew nothing about constructing a latrine. And unlike Richard, Peter was not eager for sex play at the drop of a hat. After lunch, we were supposed to clean our tents, and while doing that I tried engaging Peter in roughhouse wrestling I hoped would lead to something else. He promptly pinned me and then went on with the assigned task. It wasn't until that night I managed, with some coaxing, to interest him in sex. Peter was frequently critical of my stalls, and I let him criticize me freely because I was infatuated with him. I'd put up with almost anything in the hope he'd like me and I'd become his second-in-command. I often heard Walt say he was stupid when in love, and I resented the comment as implied criticism. But when I recall how I was about Peter, I see too well what he meant.

I was a fool for Peter, and a few days after the weekend camp-out I was at his house making yet another of my kowtow visits when his mother added herself to the mix.

"I'd like to talk to you, Harry." Mrs. Tower called me aside.

Peter, suddenly curious, stuck at my elbow for a change.

"Not you, Peter, just Harry. This is between him and me. Why don't you wait outside?"

This was serious and I shook with nerves turned terrorized when left alone with Peter's mother.

She didn't waste any time. "I want to talk to you because Phillip told me what you and he did together."

My life was over. I wanted to bawl but was too shocked to do even that. I fully expected to be denounced before being turned over to my mother for execution. "I'm...." I began with a lower lip that refused to go further.

"I'm so pleased, if it's true." Her voice was earnest.

I was sure she couldn't possibly mean it. This was either a trap or I had yet to discover what she was talking about.

"Phillip told me how you said you wanted to be his friend, and I want to make sure you meant it."

"Wait a minute." Walt broke in. "When the hell did that happen?"

"Give me a chance, will you?" I complained.

I had to recall the incident myself. Which I didn't until I remembered what happened a few days after Phillip took me to first orgasm. I was on my new bike, the other love of my life, when Phillip appeared and offered a ride. I almost said no, but didn't, either out of respect for his brother or because part of me hoped for a replay. In any case, we pedaled off, Phillip leading in the same direction as last time.

"Let's go someplace different." I called.

Without hesitation he agreed. "Okay." Phillip set about to show me places I'd yet to discover.

He made a good tour guide and I was glad of his company, even when he stopped and suggested we hike along a creek bed. I had a good idea why Phillip wanted privacy, and I wasn't wrong. He stopped, supposedly to pee, which was also a way to start things, which he did by showing a boner after urinating. There was no missing his intention nor is there adequate way to explain my reaction. I wouldn't have minded the sex, but I was struggling with things, such as pride, self-image, worry (about doing it too much or with the "wrong" people), and, most of all, my infatuation with Peter. I saw sex- play with Phillip as disloyal to my ideal.

I looked at Phillip's erection while trying to decide. "Let's be friends first." I finally said, because that got me off the hook without being hard on my ideal's little brother. Phillip looked at me for a long second before bending at the waist so he could stuff his bone away. "Sure. C'mon." He led me along a rough path that followed the creek as a progressively fainter track that eventually faded to nothing at the margins of a marshy beaver pond. We explored for several hours of innocent association. "That's it?" Walt chimed in. "That's what his mother meant? You must have been one relieved kid."

"Better believe it." I exhaled relief at the memory of my long- gone fright. "Phillip's not like his brother." Peter's mother talked while my emotions stabilized. "Peter makes friends and gets along well with other boys. Phillip's shy in comparison. It's unusual for him to show an interest in someone. I'm so glad if you want to be his friend. Is that what you want?" I nodded. "You're sure?"

"Phillip's nice. He knows a lot." I gave my youthful opinion. "Well, he's talked to me about you almost constantly, and I know he was looking forward to your return after the camping trip." I nodded again. "You don't have to mention to Phillip that I talked to you, or tell Peter what I said, either. Peter can be very defensive about his friends." I glowed at being placed in that category. "I won't say anything."

"Peter's got a ball game this afternoon. Phillip will be back from fishing by then. That would be a good time for you to come by."

"Okay."

"Thank you," Mrs. Tower said, smiling before turning away. "Maybe when you're here you'll help Phillip mow the lawn. It takes him forever otherwise." Cutting grass was a death sentence to me, but I agreed already, hadn't I? "Yes, Ma'am." I sealed my fate. Outside, Peter got on me right away, so I told him his mother just wanted me to help Phillip with the lawn while Peter played ball. "Why don't you get on the team, too?" Peter suddenly wanted to pull me in his direction. There was no reason to tell him the truth, that I was useless at sports. "I don't mind helping." I sounded the brave martyr. "It's your funeral." Peter shrugged off my mood in a dismissive way that hurt, not that I'd show it.

"If you ask me," Walt offered out of the blue, "the woman conned you. Damned creatures can't be trusted, can they?" Not infrequently I listened to Walt's views of womankind, and I continued to wonder at his animosity toward them. I suspected a story lay behind the attitude, but I'd never been able to dig it out. "Well, it worked out okay."

"For her," Walt scoffed. "She got a free babysitter plus yard boy."

"It was more than that." I spoke softly while trying to remember all that happened in consequence. First, it didn't take long for Peter to learn I was spending more time with Phillip. It became a contentious issue. Peter resented "losing' me to his brother. With no subtlety whatever, Peter warned, "You can't trust him. He makes things up, lies all the time."

"What about?" I knew better than argue when Peter was upset. "'Bout everything. Bet he makes things up "bout me." Peter's voice rose to a shrill level of invective. I knew what he was trying to cover up. "We don't talk about you. Phillip doesn't say things like that. We just play cards."

"Old Maid!" Peter broke with scorn. "It's a dumb game, but it's fun!" I burst, because with Phillip it was fun. "He's hopeless, an' if yer not careful it'll rub off on you." Peter's warning dropped to a level of less personal threat. Telling Peter he wasn't being discussed was a very smart thing. It was also true, because we were busy having fun. "I bet you were." Walt cackled. I frowned at his interruption. "This'll take forever if you keep butting in."

"Get on with it, then." He shook his head. Sitting cross-legged on Phillip's decently made bed we played many games of cards while I made occasional glances at Peter's unmade bed to imagine him lying there. Fortunately for my love-sick heart, Phillip introduced me to another of his passions, model rockets, and we dove into that pursuit with all the frenzy boys that young always seem to bring to an activity. "Did you have sex with him or not?" Walt demanded, fingering my glans with dexterity. "Yes." I squirmed. "But not right away."

"Only you," Walt performed a swirling motion around my crown, "could have had so complicated a boyhood."

"I wasn't the only one." Reminded of those days, I felt a belated, tinged-in-sadness smile invade as I realized how my association with Phillip, despite having got off to a bang, turned so readily into something Platonic. Trite and old fashioned as it will appear, I established limits with Phillip that provided what amounted to buddy-dates. There were games and activities done when Peter, to whom I remained loyal, was absent. After his second or third erect-penis display, Phillip realized that potent blandishment was insufficient to sway my stated goal of "friendship first."

Not that I was equally committed to purity in all comers of my cramped little life. I still wished to get close (and if possible naked) with Peter. Simply being within a few feet of him caused me to want to undress and in so doing "give" myself to him. I didn't fully understand either the impulse or the image, one in which I pictured myself as the "fair creature" crouched in a seductive sprawl, an image I found immensely appealing by the way, at the feet of an armor-clad knight holding the reins of his war mount. In no small way was my dotage on Peter so great that it caused me to forego the ready opportunity for erotic play with Phillip. I hoped to win Peter by delivering to him, as another gift to lay beside my prostrate form at his feet, a reformed brother. Boys can take idealism to devastating extremes.

Having made a case for my purity of deed and motive, I must confess an equal amount of activity in the opposite direction. I don't simply mean playing with myself either, something I did with as much regularity as could be achieved. When a "suitable' opportunity presented itself, I was disloyal to my ideal with no hesitation. Indeed, I justified myself by saying I was gaining experience.

Richard, who a few days before the Troop was to leave for summer camp, asked me to be his tent mate because Rudy was a last-minute cancellation. I grabbed the chance with neither guilt nor pause. I knew Richard would be far more fun than Peter, plus I didn't have enough balls or energy to stand between Peter and Ray. Ray was a better, more experienced Scout than I. The wise thing was to step aside until Peter tired of him and saw my worth. In the meantime I'd make progress as best I could, which might as well include the advantage of Richard's offer to bunk together.

My week of Scout camp was memorable indeed. Aside from all the official activity – cooking over open fires, swimming twice a day, canoes to paddle, nature trails to follow, an archery range to use, and so on – there was a private life suddenly thrown into sound-barrier-shattering speed. The first day or so Richard and I rubbed ourselves sore before easing off a day or two to recover. Recovery, which was a normal part of sexual release for our ages, was pushed aside when we realized easy opportunity would vanish at the end of camp, so we returned to Mach-scale activity, a pair of totally demented erections who lived to puke.

Aside from the devil-may-care freedom of having sex whenever a swimsuit was doffed or a toe wiggled seductively, there were other advantages to having contact with Richard, who was more experienced than I. He hinted at, and revealed what lay on the road ahead for me. His passion for keeping records (which became goals to exceed) wasn't something I shared, but I learned from him that I couldn't harm myself by having orgasms, despite how deathly potent they sometimes felt. Indeed, Richard and I could pump each other dry and still continue at high erotic key. I began, however, to see myself in a place between the two extremes. There was Peter, who saved his juices for a small number of big releases, versus Richard, who ran with his reserve on empty. I was interested in the middle ground, where I could enjoy occasional forays into Richard-inspired highs, or save up to relish Peter-inspired heights of another sort.

With directness and relish, Richard amended and expanded my erotic education, an activity he enjoyed much as I. One question lingered, however, and after a few days I had to probe into why Richard stayed friends with Rudy. At first, Richard skillfully evaded my questioning until persistence on my part finally paid off, after I promised not to tell. The big secret was that when they were alone Rudy enjoyed extensive play sessions with Richard's "big one". Rudy, who could be such a mouthy twerp, found surrogate satisfaction through Richard. When Richard confessed that, I knew it was true. No other explanation could account for the Rudy/Richard connection.

At the conclusion of camp I returned home looking (much to my father's pleased relief, I'm sure) like a 100% boy quite unaware he was wearing socks capable of standing by themselves. I was ordered to take a bath before doing anything else lest I pollute the entire house.

Following that, I ate home-cooked food while falling asleep at the table. Being indoors was remarkably sleep-inducing, as had been the ride home, where all eleven boys packed into a station wagon were soon zonked out with mouths open in the colloquial fly-trap position. I didn't need to play with myself for a day or two after returning. That provided a nice reward because when I broke the fast I enjoyed a richly Peter-like spew of accumulated juice.

Having repeatedly made mention of Father, I should follow with a bit more because at that time his influence made itself felt. Father was so happy with my advancement as a "regular boy' that he readily obliged when I wanted something to augment my masculine development. My goal was a tent. Within a week that wish was granted, father imagining me using it to further myself in a healthy outdoors life. You can imagine why I wanted a tent, a safe place to indulge in extended self-exam.

Of course, I was aware my backyard bedroom – the back yard being the tent's immediate location – had multiple possibilities, and the first person I brought there was Peter. He was returning after a ball game when I spotted him and dragged him, somewhat unwillingly, to view my prize and, from the look on his face, the team hadn't played its best. With pride, I pointed out its best features while Peter slowly relaxed, his ball and bat gleaming in the sun outside while he sprawled with head on arms in the shadowed interior.

My glowing tour completed, I took note of Peter, a feast of male charms spread within reach. His baseball shirt accented his forearms while the pants fit snugly at the crotch. "I like your outfit." I commented like a fashion expert.

Peter looked down toward his toes. "Bunch of nice girls watched, but we lost."

"It wasn't your fault." I consoled my hero.

"Couple of "em were real nice." Peter's eyes half closed.

"Good tits?" I followed an instinct otherwise foreign to me.

It was Richard who'd informed me of the need to first "warm up" a girl, intelligence provided him by a cousin. All I did was apply the principle to Peter. I warmed him up with talk which led to the conclusion I wanted, that required closing the tent flaps before gaining access to Peter's remarkable penis. He was the tent's first visitor. Success with him a good omen, indeed. Of course, I hunted up Richard, who seized the opportunity in a twinkling. Of the various boys lured into my tent, about half were game, not that I invited dozens. The number was more like six or seven.

"And Phillip?" Walt wanted to know.

"I was getting to him."

Phillip was the third boy in my tent, where he listened sitting cross-legged in polite curiosity. "It's nice." He observed, looking at the overhead roof as if it was actually interesting.

"I already showed Peter."

Phillip looked disappointed.

"And Richard," I added swiftly, "because they're Scouts."

Phillip nodded, accepting my explanation.

"You can come here whenever you want." I offered, hoping I sounded genuine.

"Can I sleep over?" Phillip asked, leaning forward from the waist.

"I can't. You see, my mom won't let me have anyone out here." I covered with a lie. The truth was my mother didn't approve of my association with Phillip. Peter, she continued to warmly approve of, but Phillip was a different matter. "I don't trust that kid." My mother voiced her prejudice that way, and I knew what she meant. Phillip was "different.' Mother didn't want me too near a source of possible contagion. Phillip's posture slumped as he twiddled idly with a kneecap outside his summer shorts. "Harry?" He began. "Do you like me?"

"Sure." I answered right away, because I did. "You're not just saying it?"

"You can be here when I am. I just can't have anyone sleep over, yet." I had hopes, however. "I like your tent." Phillip looked up. "What if you put it somewhere else?" I realized Phillip's angle. "They won't let me. Mom says I have to be older before I can camp on my own."

"Because I like you." Phillip shifted to his real concern. "We're friends," I stated, thinking I said so mostly because it was what Phillip wanted and not yet realizing it was true for me. "Can I ask something?" My guest fidgeted. I shrugged. "What's it like being older?"

"Older?"

"Your age, or like Peter?"

"Why not ask him?"

"He won't tell me. He says not to bother him, or if I have to ask then I'm too little to know." It hurt me to realize Phillip was accurate in characterizing his brother. "Ask me, then." Phillip sat to hug his knees. "I thought sometimes you were mad at me."

"Heck no." I gave a friendly smile, followed by laying on my side to look at him. "Peter said...." Phillip needed a gulp of air to steady his voice, "you were only being nice to me because he asked you to." I frowned. "He's...." I couldn't bring myself to call him a liar. "It's not true." Phillip exhaled. "How come you don't....?" He began but stopped. "What?" I had to be sure. "You know," Phillip answered, suddenly bringing a knee to nudge my middle.

"Let's dose the flaps."

In the shadowy interior Phillip came alive, uncovering my groin, then his, while I lay back, satisfied for the time to give him the access he wanted. Phillip gave my penis a thorough investigation which ended with the conclusion he thought it was bigger and there was more hair than before. Then he commented, "Peter's does that, too." He meant the pearl that sometimes oozed from my erections. The presence of that bead in some instances and its absence at others, notably when alone, remained a mystery. As Phillip explored the pearl grew.

I knew what he was going to do, encouraging him by petting his inner thigh and reaching for his erection as his lips dropped to caress my crown. The sensation, as before, was exquisite. My throat gasped an intense sigh while my butt thumped. Getting sucked was really, really good, and I lay there wondering why for weeks I kept from doing this with Phillip or why I avoided it with Richard.

Phillip knelt at a right angle to my side where he paused to ask, "Like it?"

His lips were just a fraction removed from my saliva-wet tip, which wanted to tear loose in order to again be in his mouth. I nodded with bug-eyed enthusiasm.

Phillip smiled before resuming.

I stretched further to improve my grip on his member.

Much as I might wish to claim (or you may want to read) an extended session of oral sex, the combination of Phillip's experience plus my excitement-shortened fuse provided a too- quick end. Though achieved too soon, my orgasm was great, a definite WOW!, compared to the usual wow! or occasional Wow! For the moment sexual release left me too vague for concern with Phillip. I lay back with contentment, not even realizing I was merely holding Philip's organ with no attempt at pleasuring it.

Phillip made no complaint, however. Instead, he seemed pleased at having brought me to a dramatic conclusion. After watching me until some degree of visible alertness returned, Phillip grinned. "You like it more than Peter."

My rally continued. "Does he," I began as curiosity burned sharper, "do it to you, too?"

With a half frown Phillip shook his head. "No."

"I will." Saying it was obvious.

"At last!" Walt shouted. "You've redeemed yourself!"

"Thanks. But I did it for a selfish reason," I confessed.

"So he'd do it to you, I know; that would be standard."

"At the time it didn't feel that way. I felt guilty more for "using' Phillip than about the sex."

Five A Warm, Lively Penis

Something I didn't get into with Walt was how sucking Phillip for the first time proved so profound an experience. Doing it so he'd do me was easy compared with discovering how much I liked the feel of a warm, lively penis in my mouth. It wasn't dirty at all, and I got enormously heated at feeling his excitement build into the tick-tock clicks that represented Phillip's dry orgasm. The fact I liked it so much was scary, as was the way I wanted to do it more often. It worried me how much I felt drawn to that form of sex instead of being attracted to breasts and girls the way Peter was.

Walt didn't hear about my cocksucking fascination because he was more interested in general things, like whether or not Phillip and I paired off. I'm not sure about that, but for the next two years, Phillip was, except for myself, of course, my primary erotic outlet. There were a few more – rare and then rarer – contacts with Peter. Richard was good for sleep-over invitations for a year, until he gave them up. About then I made friends with a new boy named Paul. We were both young and different and we knew it. He even wrote poetry! I'd sit on his bed reading it aloud. Paul claimed I read his poems better than he could, and after declaiming myself through one of his huskier efforts he was so moved he gave me a spontaneous kiss on the cheek.

The kiss mortified me (Walt said he expected it of me at that age) but it also inflamed me with a desire to do something to Paul. I honest-to-goodness think it was an urge to fuck him, but I hadn't yet learned boys could do that to one another. Between aroused passion and embarrassment, I glowed so red- hot it's fortunate I didn't ignite his bed sheets. Instead of that I took what was for me a rare and unexpected gamble.

Hands shaking as I set aside Paul's poem, I said, "If you want to kiss something." I unzipped to expose a quite- respectable hard-on.

Paul was red, too. "It's huge!" He gaped.

"Well, let's see yours." I took another wild leap.

He obliged.

"Looks the same to me." At least his erection didn't appear tiny. "Well?" I finally asked to break the impasse. "I thought you wanted to kiss something."

He gave my dick a quick peck.

"Not like that." I took charge. Pulling him close, I popped the head of his penis into my mouth for a warm, wet tongue bath. Paul shook, trembled and moaned. I stopped long enough to get his pants shoved down so I could fondle his nuts while I played his flute. It didn't take much for him to pop. Paul was not an especially good sex partner. I don't know why. His efforts with me felt more like fumbling while what I did to him was too advanced or something. He acted afraid of what I did, whereas I was barely satisfied by his attempts. The other problem was Paul's sporadic sexuality, a rarity of response occurring after six weeks or so. It just didn't work and before the year was out he was hanging with a more artsy group of kids while I continued a slow drift with scouting types plus a few individual sport players – runners and swimmers. The steady fixture in my erotic world was Phillip, as I explained to Walt in a synopsis covering two years of sex play that ended when his father sold The Mercantile and they moved. The summer before I turned fifteen was the last I'd see Phillip. "What are you going to do about him now?" Walt pressed on. "I should call, of course. He gave a number and invitation. I'll follow up."

"What if it's not the same?"

"I don't expect it to be. We're not kids anymore."

"He's probably got a lover." I shrugged. "Knowing you, you'll procrastinate until it's too late."

"This time you're wrong."

"You're going to sleep with him, aren't you?" Walt stated, his closing query a mere formality. "Are you jealous?" I wagged. "It's obvious you will."

"You're clearly stressed or something. I haven't seen him in a dozen years. What makes you think either of us intends to jump in the sack?"

"Care to wager?" Walt pushed. "This time you're going to lose, old man." I had to get in a dig. "If I chicken out..." I finished with a promise of what I'd do if events proved him correct. Walt smiled. "It'll be worth seeing." He sounded confident. "You won't be smiling when you lose, because then it'll be you in the limelight."

"Not a chance." Walt slapped my thigh. "Not so much as the remotest possibility, my little sex pot. You'll be ready to mount him before you've finished coffee." God, but it's annoying when Walt's smug. All that remained was to show him he was wrong, an easy supposition on my part as a reunion with Phillip remained days away. Phillip's apartment was in one of those more-or-less gay sections of the city. Every urban area has similar neighborhoods where assorted rainbow couples feel a degree of acceptance usually denied, for example, in the suburbs where conventional families view same-sex or inter-race pairings as threatening. Otherwise, Phillip's building made little impression. He answered the door quickly enough and then came the first hurdle. I'd thought about this instant more than anything else, and I'd decided on my move regardless of his appearance. Whether he answered as male or female I'd do the same thing. Stepping inside while he held the door open I leaned to give him a friendly but not too familiar kiss. Shutting the door, Phillip blushed. "I'm glad you did that." He spoke, though looking none too glad. "Why?" I smiled. "I was so afraid," he took a breath, "you'd be difficult, hard to reach. You weren't always easy to figure out when I knew you."

"So I've been told." Walt had been saying much the same for years. "I always thought I was transparent as glass." I added what I honestly felt was true. "In some ways," Phillip smiled, "but you were also mysterious and very, very private at times. It drove me crazy."

"Sorry." I blushed. "Nothing to be sorry about. And now that I'm recovered let me give you a kiss before I drag you to the kitchen while I finish cooking."

"Nice." I spoke after more solid lip-to-lip than I began with. We topped it off with a warm best-buddies hug. "You look good this way, too." I commented on Phillip's appearance as a man. "Thanks." He flushed slightly. "Now if you'll follow me." Not everything needs be repeated here, but some things are worth the effort. "Would you believe," Phillip spoke over his shoulder from the stove, "I remember the very first time I saw you?"

"I remember it, too." I responded before asking, "Are you sure I can't do anything to help?"

"Keep me company is all. Tell me what you remember." I gave a condensed version in diplomatic fashion. "It must have been strange seeing a naked kid crouched in the middle of the floor. I wasn't very attractive at that age either."

"You weren't too ugly." I teased. "Know why I wasn't wearing anything that afternoon?" I shrugged. "Peter said you liked running around bare."

"I was waiting for Peter, but I was expecting him to be alone. When you appeared, I was interested."

"You're making that up." I made my skepticism sound like a tease. "No. It's true. I thought you were the most appealing person Peter ever brought home. I had feelings for you from the start, and I was very aware how you watched my every move."

"I was shocked, but intensely curious, too. Yours was the first erection, other than my own, I ever saw. It fascinated me. "Peter gave me shit about it later."

"How is your brother?" I finally had to ask. Phillip gave a succinct review. He rarely saw Peter, who disapproved of Phillip's life. Peter was father to a family of six, though there could be more. "You had a thing for him, didn't you?" Phillip's voice teased without insult. "More than I realized."

"He was a charmer, and you were just one more of his conquests."

"Ouch!"

"It was easy to fall for Peter. It's what he wanted from people. He was a terribly confident kid, wasn't he?" Phillip turned, looking for me to respond. "More than me." I agreed. "You'd stand back and scope things out. That's what I remember."

"That's me."

"We'll be eating soon. Want to set the table?" While I did that I had time to think, especially about Phillip waiting for Peter that first time. His statement was more than suggestive, and I wanted more details. Less than halfway into the appetizer I forged ahead. "What did you mean when you said you were "waiting' for Peter that afternoon?"

"You mean, why was I waiting for Peter?" I nodded. We had begun to eat. "Peter was the one," Phillip began in an even voice, "who taught me about sex. When we were little we did the usual toddler stuff. Mother never interfered. Her attitude came from free love, flower-child days. But after Peter turned ten his interest in sex, and in me, changed. For three years he treated me like a sex slave, really. My goody-goody brother who could do no wrong was a complete sex pig in private. But after he turned thirteen he changed again. He began looking down on me for having done what he wanted. He also did much less with me."

"I don't get why you were waiting for him, then."

Phillip nodded. "Actually, I liked the sex and missed it. I knew when he'd come home from school sometimes I could get him interested."

I brightened. "The schoolboy's proverbial 3:30 wank."

"That's the idea."

"But I was with him …"

260

"...Which was very sexy for me, you realize, because you showed an interest in me when Peter didn't."

I nodded, a fuller picture forming in my mind. "He never...." I hesitated, then finally finished asking, "abused you, did he?"

"No. Not physically. Never. What hurt was the way he thought about me."

"He could be stem."

"He could be a friggin' prick, if you'll excuse me being blunt. There's no reason to deny it. Peter was a bossy, self-centered kid."

I nodded, remembering some of the attacks he directed at me in later years.

Phillip sat back after swallowing a last bit of food and asked, "Remember the time I hid Peter's rubber?"

I took the moment to assess my rediscovered friend. At twenty-four, Phillip was both boyish and carved adult. He combined the masculine with the feminine. It was difficult to associate him with the close-to-ugly gawky boy of ten I'd first seen so long ago. His laugh was good-natured and free, not as it had been when outside forces (often Peter) clouded Phillip's everyday moods. Even when I had little contact with Peter, I still wanted him to like me and, of course, Phillip grew up dominated by an athletic Alpha male. But, awash as I was in memories, there was no struggle finding the one Phillip sat grinning about as if it were fresh within the hour.

How easily returned the recollection of that earlier summer returned when Philip told me his father was trying to sell The Mercantile. It was news I didn't want to know, so I went forward as if no such possibility existed. I simply was not able to accept a future with my ideal (Peter) and its corresponding reality (Phillip) absent. At fourteen, I convinced myself I could make things go away by ignoring them. I wanted no disturbing ripples.

One day that summer, in exactly such a make-believe mood, I strode, dressed in dazzle-white tennis togs, out of the house to consider my next move. One thing is certain. I was no whiz at tennis. The main appeal of the sport was the way it suited some personal needs at the time. Though I knew I wasn't like other foxys and didn't crave what they mooned over, I still had to fit in somehow. Tennis was a way of doing so. In some respects the game itself mattered little. What counted was that, so far as I was concerned, I believed I looked good in my tennis outfit. I kept my tennis shoes close to pristine while my mother ensured my socks, shorts and delicately decorated T- shirt were perfect. With a can of balls (there's some raw symbolism) in one hand, and my racket tossed visibly (more symbolism) over my shoulder, I believed I presented an utterly convincing and appealing picture of a successful young male.

Mediocre players, however, have trouble finding tennis mates. We're too good for beginner matches and far too poor to satisfy the hunger of serious opponents. If I phoned around looking for a mate I'd usually harvest an amazing bundle of evasions. The other tactic was to stroll to the courts and hang around in hopes of snagging a game or two. That approach was good because it allowed me to be seen going to and from the courts plus providing time in a supposedly masculinizing atmosphere of competition.

On the day in question, Phillip's hurried appearance was no help because he usually sniggered at my tennis fantasy. The mere sight of him reminded me of the possibility I might, indeed, look silly instead of masculine. My first thought was to get rid of him.

"I'm just leaving," I announced.

Phillip paid no attention to my attire, which he usually mocked. "You gotta come quick." He sucked deep breaths after running. "You can't miss this for anything."

"What?" I had to be skeptical.

After first looking around to see no one was too close, Phillip dug in his pocket to produce what looked like a pale party balloon.

"What? I repeated, as yet unable to make a connection.

"It's Peter's rubber," Phillip hissed, quickly putting the object away.

"Rubber?" I gulped aghast at such an invasion of privacy. I thought a boy's rubber should be private.

"He's got Kathy at the house right now," Phillip whispered in giddy excitement that rose to a shrill peak as he continued, "but I've got this!" He patted the rubber's hiding place.

"That's mean." I had to defend my idol, distant though he'd become.

"C'mon." Phillip tugged. "I got the intercom on in the basement so we can listen. This won't last forever. You gotta come now."

"Okay." I was pulled by Phillip's demand more than my interest.

I knew full well of the Tower family attitude about sex. The second year I knew him Peter was proud to show off his very own rubber, a condom provided by his mother, who also provided him with information of the type that bewilders the conservatively moralistic while titillating the average kid with abundant possibilities. Peter's mother was supposed to have said, "I don't want you to have sex at your age, but if you do then use this." More amazingly yet, she added a graphic description of how he was to wear it, talking about his erection and semen as if his cock were a nose and the condom a tissue.

It took me a long time to convince myself that Peter's account was true because in contrast my mother would have castrated me if she thought I bore any intention of using my penis for anything but urinating. I'm sure I wasn't the only boy who had doubts, either, as the majority of us assumed the real truth was he'd pinched the rubber from his parents' bedroom or bought it from an older kid.

Within a few months of showing off his prize possession, Peter claimed a successful use. Considering the name of the girl he said cooperated, his claim stood an eighty percent chance of being true.

As for the intercom, I'd not paid much attention to it except as yet another of Phillip's fascinations. His latest kick was electronics. He'd mentioned the intercom and wiring various rooms. Now, suddenly, it all made sense. A new area of possibility opened as Phillip quietly led me into his basement workshop where we leaned over his bench to listen, heads bumping together, through the frail speakers of crude headphones.

It took a minute to adjust to the hiss and background noise which resulted from Phillip's having to crank the volume up in order to capture sound from the hidden microphone. The goal of spying on Peter must have been on Phillip's mind from the start. He provided, however, no explanation beyond a hissed, "I knew he'd bring her over when my mom said she'd be gone."

The facts were still sorting themselves as I listened, gradually beginning to form a picture of what took place upstairs.

"I can't find it." Peter's voice rose in a bemoaning wail.

A softer voice mumbled a response I was unable to grasp.

"Please. Just this once!" Peter begged after the other voice fell silent.

"No." That came through loud and clear.

"Please." Peter persisted. "Look how hard you make me!"

Like Phillip at my elbow, I couldn't help chuckle about that.

"It's like this for you." Peter pled his cause.

The girls voice was clearer. "I don't care." She sniffed as if turning down the offer of a sandwich. "It's ugly." She added, causing me to think she was defective for not recognizing a handsome penis when she saw one. "Please." Peter kept up his tactic in pleading tones. "I won't even touch it." Came the reply. "But I can't find my rubber." Peter repeated before switching tracks. "We got our clothes off, why not try it, just a little." He offered in appealing steps. "No!" Giggling, Phillip whispered in my free ear. "He rinses his rubber to use again. That way mom can't tell how often he does it." I nodded while trying to follow incomprehensible noise from above. "He's in the closet," Phillip giggled again, "looking, because that's where he hides it, shoved over a broom handle to dry."

"Maybe I should go." The girl's voice registered. "Don't." Peter sounded alarmed. "We can kiss an' make-out, can't we?"

"You have to put something on that first. It drips." Her tone sounded revulsion. "It won't hurt you." Peter explained where reason made no difference. At my side, Phillip demanded attention. "I'm going up." He whispered. "You keep listening. If I yell loud for help say you came over looking for someone to play tennis."

"Wait." I mumbled, none too pleased at getting an unwanted role. But, Phillip didn't wait. I returned to listening, at the same time telling myself I could slip away if I had to. After a few seconds I again caught the gist of the situation overhead just in time to hear Phillip make a noisy arrival at the front door. "Who is it?" Peter's voice rose in panic.

"Just me!" Phillip answered, in bright-sounding innocence. "You go away! I'm busy."

"Jus' got to get something." During these brief exchanges, there was a sound of rapid movement followed by an unnatural silence. My bet was the girl hid in the closet or powder room. "Well, hurry up so you can leave." Peter sounded rattled. "It's my room, too. How come you're naked?" he asked innocently. "Because it's hot up here."

"That why you got a boner?"

"Don't either." Peter made a firm denial. "When are you leavin'?"

"So you can finish playin' with yourself?" Phillip teased mockingly. "Just get out!"

"Geez!" Phillip whined. "Let me get what I came for, and I gotta take a leak."

"Go downstairs." Peter unintentionally revealed where his "date" hid. "Why?" Phillip's voice sounded further. "Get away from there." Peter shrilled, his voice moving toward Phillip. "Door's locked." There was a scuffling sound and heavy breathing. "Tol' you to get outta here," Peter insisted while struggling. "You got someone up here? Why didn't you say?" Phillip sounded innocently cooperative. "Because it's none of your business, that's why!"

"Who is it?" Phillip played dumb. "Just get out already, will you?"

"So you can finish?" Phillip teased in an agreeable way. "Look, nothin's gonna happen. My rubber's gone." Peter put two and two together, "u you took it "

"Why didn't you take mine?" Phillip breezed. "Yours?" Peter sounded as surprised as I was. "You got one?"

"I asked Mom for one," Phillip paused, "in case." Once again, the Tower family attitude toward sex bowled me over. I was fourteen going on fifteen. Phillip was two years my junior. But if I was round with a rubber I could count on my mother seeing that my penis was surgically removed. The contrast was stunning, but I had to keep following events upstairs. "See? Brand new." Phillip apparently displayed his virgin condom. "Gimme!" Peter demanded. "Hey! Give it back!"

"I need it. Now get out."

"I'm tellin'. I am. Really." Phillip employed a standard threat. "Know what'll happen if you do." Peter used his "I'll kill ya" voice before using a friendly "it's me" tone outside the bathroom door. "I got one." He sing-songed intelligence the girl already knew unless she was deaf. "You can come out, anyway. It's only Phillip." There was a dead silence, then the sound of movement as a door cracked open. "I better go," a timid female voice announced. "He's goin'." Peter offered assurance. "An' I got one now, so it's OK." From a different part of the room Phillip's voice broke in, "Will you do it with me, too? Or take your top off an' show yer tits?"

"Shut up, Phillip!" Peter snapped. "He's just talkin'. He don't mean nothing."

"Why can't I do it after you?" Phillip sounded convincingly innocent. "This is sick. You're both sick. I'm getting out of here."

"No! Wait!" Peter begged. "I'm nicer than Peter." Phillip's voice announced. "Shut up, you!" Peter snarled as opportunity fell to tatters. "I'll get you for this. I will!" Peter's frustration had a focus named Phillip. There were sounds of a scuffle followed by a solid thud. A set of feet, the girl's, made a hurried flight down the stairs, adding rhythm to the onset of Phillip's painful wails and whimpers followed by theatrical yells for "Help!" Thinking shit, I remembered my cue. I'd better do something to get Phillip out of his jam. The door of the house slammed, signaling the girl's departure. It was clear for me to exit my hiding place while Phillip's yelps grew louder. "Anyone home?" I yelled up the stairs.

"Who the ... go away!" Peter blustered. "Come up," Phillip wheezed.

"I'm being killed ... Ohhh!" I made cautious progress until my head poked into view and I saw Peter's naked body crouched atop Phillip.

"What do you want?" Peter sneered while trying to silence Philip with a hand over his mouth. "Looking for a tennis partner. A girl ran out, then I heard Phillip. What the heck are you guys doin', anyway? Looks weird. Really weird." My assessment of "weird' behavior caused Peter to back off. If I thought it odd to find Peter in a bare ass crouch over his brother, surely any other observer would think the scene positively perverted. It was more than enough to stop Peter from hammering Phillip. He switched focus.

"She look mad? Was she goin' home?" He rose swiftly, giving me a good view of a penis I'd not seen for months.

"Where's your clothes?" I asked. "Where's the rubber?" Peter fussed, scrabbling on all fours to provide alternating views of charm followed by ugly. Not moving, Phillip lay on the floor and moaned. "Maybe I can catch her." Peter drew my attention, grabbing cut-offs he jumped into without underwear to save time. A loose shirt followed. Then sockless feet were jammed into battered sneakers before he made a leaping descent down the stairs followed by a loud passage through the door. The house was suddenly calm.

"He's gone." Phillip sighed with great relief while rising from his dead-man feint.

"Lucky he didn't kill you." I felt shaky after the strain.

"Worth it, wasn't it?" Phillip chuckled while weakly rising.

"You're crazy. You're both crazy," I concluded, steadying myself by sitting on Phillip's bed.

He shambled over and flung down alongside me. "You shoulda seen him when I came up." Phillip giggled. "Were you listenin'?"

I nodded. "You were good." I smiled.

"Too bad you missed seein' his face when I showed him my rubber." Phillip rolled slightly while one hand patted my thigh.

I looked down at his fingers which played 1-2-3-4, 1-2-3-4, 1-2-3-4 in rapid sequence without moving either up or down from their midway position on my upper thigh. Inside my tennis shorts, however, there was activity. Phillip sensed it. I watched as his finger-drumming turned into a slow invasion up the inviting leg hole of my shorts. First needing to wet my lips. I asked, "What if he comes back?"

More intent on fingering me than answering, Phillip ensured my condition before shrugging. "He knows we goof around." His tone said, "So what?"

The confusion of my life at that time revolved heavily around exactly such attitudes. On the one hand a "So what?" attitude toward sex was a handy relief, but if truth were admitted I'd have had to say sex with Phillip mattered. It was not a "So what?" issue no matter how convenient that sounded. What I did with Phillip was important to me, but why couldn't either of us say so?

"We don't get a bed too often." I provided necessary justification while fingering Phillip's front.

"Want me to suck you?"

"Let's do it together." I suggested a mote elaborate approach.

Phillip stood quickly. "Take my pants down. I like when you do."

I slid off the bed and knelt. I liked doing that, too. It was a treat to be close as his penis sprang into view. I'd learned to top the treat, like adding chocolate syrup to ice cream, by mouthing the tip of Phillip's eager erection for a minute before shifting positions so he could uncover me. "Mmmm." I sighed atop his penis, sliding it fully into my warm, welcoming mouth.

"Ahh." Phillip gulped in appreciation. "Still wanna play

tennis?" Phillip asked in passion-tinged tones. I shook my head side to side. "Ohh." He exhaled. "That's nice. Now your turn...." In a matter of weeks, the Tower family moved away. There was no way to know that afternoon would be our last. Twelve years later, the shock of Phillip's departure felt fresh. "There was hardly any time after the prank on Peter before you moved." Phillip nodded. "I know." He looked as if he was going to say something, then his eyes darted aside. "More coffee?" He asked. "Maybe a half." Phillip poured. "One thing I have to ask," I began, not entirely sure how far to go. "How did you recognize me? It's been so long." He smiled. "Well, you've changed, that's true enough. You're not a boy any more, but I always look at the audience before each show, and there was something familiar about your face."

"That's it?" I couldn't believe it. "No. That started it."

"How then?" Phillip stood before stepping closer. "Right there." He pointed to an area where my neck and collarbone joined. "Right there." He repeated, touching the spot. "I forget it's there," I said of a distinctively shaped nickel- sized birthmark. "I spent lots of time looking at it, remember?" I nodded, recalling times when Phillip's head lay against my chest and we talked. "The man you were with?" Phillip's voice disconnected my recollections. "Is he your boyfriend?" I shook my head. "My ex." Phillip exhaled, shedding an expectant tension I hadn't recognized until he released it and set it free. "I made dessert."

"Does it have a name?" I smiled, feeling the mood shift. "Triple-layer madness." Phillip answered with a nervous smile. "Is it served between sheets?" I reached for his hand and felt him tremble. Many enjoyable minutes later I was happily implanted in Phillip's ass where the familiar feel of Durex met the unfamiliar sensation of Phillip's access point. "Why didn't we do this back then?" I asked, being in no hurry. "You were older. Why didn't you?"

"Never thought of it."

"We were moving toward it, though, remember?" Phillip hunched toward me, his heels taking turns digging at the small of my back. "A little."

"I never learned this," Phillip exhaled, "until we left Coppertone."

"Oh?"

"After we moved ... well, things got rough. We were in farm country. Peter wasn't popular or important anymore because we didn't own a big farm, only the smallest general store. Peter needed someone to fuck. I didn't dare let him know I liked it."

"I was ... lots older before I tried it, you know."

"I used to think about you – how nice it would be with you instead of Peter. I knew it would be like this." Phillip sighed. "Like this?" I slow-rocked my question into him. "Easy and nice, not a mechanical screwing from Peter."

"God, I had such a crush on him," I confessed. "But, I really liked you more than I realized, too."

"And I liked you." We locked eye-to-eye. "But, I didn't know it until after we moved away. When you weren't there any more ... well, that's when I knew."

"God," I whispered at remembering the pain of past loneliness and the near impossible hope for eventual reunion. "Twelve years." Phillip summed up our collective mood. "I'll never last that long," I joked. "Peter never lasted twelve minutes. He was strictly a two- minute man." We chuckled in unison. "I was thinking," I smiled at a face that meant so much to me. "Walt said we'd end up in bed. Now I owe him."

"You remember Ricky backstage?" Phillip stroked my upper chest while I moved inside him with slowly increasing heat. I shook my head. "A young kid. Just turned nineteen. His act's a mess, kind of a demented cross between Lucille Ball and Ricky Ricardo."

"That one."

"He sure noticed your friend. Ricky likes "em older." I smiled. "It'll take more than that to pay off Walt."

"Oh?" I told Phillip the bet I had. Hearing, Phillip sat up to hug me in a "don't move" embrace. "That," he whispered in my ear, "will be worth seeing."

"All or nothing." I kissed Phillip. "Not nothing." He lay back, opening himself more and more

as our connection grew and years of separation were pushed aside.

A week later, I paid my debt to Walt, who had to bail me out afterward. It was just my luck there was an undercover cop in the audience. When I paid up by doing a striptease atop our table I was arrested soon as my briefs fell. The owner of Phillip's club was spared a fine because I wasn't part of an act. I was a customer who got "carried away.' Walt's face wore an uncharacteristic smirk the entire time it took to get me free.

As we left, a cop going off duty couldn't resist sneering, "Fuckin' fags."

"That's the plan." I retorted loudly, while grabbing Walt's arm in girlfriend fashion before allowing myself to be steered away without further confrontation

Outside, Phillip and Ricky waited in the car.

Walt delivered me to Phillip's apartment, then left with Ricky. The perpetual smile on Walt's face made me glad. Walt's private summation: "The kid's got energy."

It was nice seeing Walt happy again. Come to think of it, I was happy myself. The look on Phillip's face had a story, too. For that matter, either of us could pass as the poster boy for satisfaction. And, having found one another again, we had to see if things between us would complete the cycle that goes from good to getting better. Phillip, who returned to my life as memories of a distinctive, darned good kid, grew into a fine and loving man. I'm lucky being with someone who does drag without being a drag

.

About the Editor

JOHN PATRICK was a prolific, prize-winning author of fiction and non-fiction. One of his short stories, "The Well," was honored by PEN American Center as one of the best of 1987. His novels and anthologies, as well as his non-fiction works, including Legends and The Best of the Superstars series, continue to gain him new fans every day. One of his most famous short stories appears in the Badboy collection Southern Comfort and another appears in the collection The Mammoth Book of Gay Short Stories.

A divorced father of two, the author was a longtime member of the American Booksellers Association, the Publishing Triangle, the Florida Publishers' Association, American Civil Liberties Union, and the Adult Video Association. He lived in Florida, where he passed away on October 31, 2001.

...aring any underwear. "Excuse me," I said, having a hard time look...

...inded by that bulge in his crotch. "but don't I know you?" "Maybe

...ind of t... ...bout a

...with Ray... ...God, y

...t loser?... ...in?" h...

...id. "Lik... ...s stron...

...ce body... ...e on G

...lly, he l... ...I ever

...up to t... ...any ide...

...staking... ...ie sam...

..., I coul... ...ery lor...

...ood raci... ...ie swe...

...ng with... ...e in st...

...we go c... ...behin...

...ill see u... ...in pul...

...ed?" he... ...vent to...

...rivacy. ...grabbe...

...hard. I...

...k, tracir... ...t, so f...

...ed it, ha...

...with m... ...bing d...

...obing, I... ...n cock...

...ie sound of unzipping filled the small space. I don't know who's h...

...but before I knew it, I had his rod in my hand, and mine was in his...

...t to do?" he asked, his tone challenging. I knew exactly, and sank t...

www.ingramcontent.com/pod-product-compliance
Lightning Source LLC
Chambersburg PA
CBHW052018020726
47501CB00004B/1127